THE ASCENSION

MICHAEL
CARROLL

THE ASCENSION

a SUPER HUMAN Clash

PHILOMEL BOOKS
AN IMPRINT OF PENGUIN GROUP (USA) INC.

PHILOMEL BOOKS
A division of Penguin Young Readers Group.
Published by The Penguin Group.
Penguin Group (USA) Inc., 375 Hudson Street, New York, NY 10014, U.S.A.
Penguin Group (Canada), 90 Eglinton Avenue East, Suite 700, Toronto, Ontario M4P 2Y3,
Canada (a division of Pearson Penguin Canada Inc.).
Penguin Books Ltd, 80 Strand, London WC2R 0RL, England.
Penguin Ireland, 25 St. Stephen's Green, Dublin 2, Ireland
(a division of Penguin Books Ltd).
Penguin Group (Australia), 250 Camberwell Road, Camberwell, Victoria 3124, Australia
(a division of Pearson Australia Group Pty Ltd).
Penguin Books India Pvt Ltd, 11 Community Centre, Panchsheel Park,
New Delhi—110 017, India.
Penguin Group (NZ), 67 Apollo Drive, Rosedale, North Shore 0632, New Zealand
(a division of Pearson New Zealand Ltd).
Penguin Books (South Africa) (Pty) Ltd, 24 Sturdee Avenue, Rosebank,
Johannesburg 2196, South Africa.
Penguin Books Ltd, Registered Offices: 80 Strand, London WC2R 0RL, England.

Library of Congress Cataloging-in-Publication Data
Carroll, Michael Owen, 1966–
The ascension : a Super human clash / Michael Carroll.—1st ed.
p. cm.—(Super human ; bk. 2)
Summary: Teenagers with superpowers must try to stop a villain who has traveled from
the past in order to irreversibly alter reality.
[1. Superheroes—Fiction.] I. Title. PZ7.C23497As 2011
[Fic]—dc22 2010029600
ISBN 978-0-399-25624-0
1 3 5 7 9 10 8 6 4 2

For Leonia
Forever

PROLOGUE

SHORTLY BEFORE MIDNIGHT, eleven miles from Fairview, South Dakota, the armored superhero Paragon muttered, "Uh-oh."

Lance McKendrick forced open exhausted eyes and looked up to see his reflection distorted in Paragon's dark visor. "Uh-oh? We're a thousand feet up and flying at two hundred miles an hour. I don't want to hear 'Uh-oh'!"

"Fuel's getting a little low," Paragon said.

Lance knew that Paragon had a very dry sense of humor, but was sure that the hero wouldn't joke about something like this.

They had been flying for what felt like forever, but Lance knew it couldn't have been more than two hours. It wasn't the most dignified way to travel, nor the most comfortable: Lance was hanging below Paragon in a modified parachute harness that was fixed to the hero's armored chest-plate, and at first Lance had been worried that the harness's clips might not hold.

Paragon had reassured him that wouldn't happen: He had carried heavier people than Lance many times before, and often for much longer distances.

But the idea that they might run out of fuel had never crossed Lance's mind, until now.

"So," Lance began, "just out of curiosity . . . When your jetpack runs out of fuel, does it happen suddenly or sort of gradually?"

"Suddenly. But I've got a small reserve tank that'll keep us going long enough to touch down. Depending on how high up we are. Don't worry, we'll make it."

"Anything on the radio yet?"

"Nothing. That flash must have carried some sort of localized EMP."

Lance nodded. "Yep, that's exactly what I was thinking."

"You don't know what an EMP is, do you?"

"Not a clue."

"Electromagnetic pulse," Paragon explained. "A burst of electromagnetic radiation that can short out electronics. Which is why *everyone's* radios stopped working."

"But your armor's got electronics, right?"

"Most of my circuitry is shielded. The radio can't be, because if I shield it against EMPs, then—"

"Then it would also be shielded against ordinary radio signals?" Lance interrupted.

"That's right."

Lance raised a weary arm and pointed straight ahead. "Those lights over there . . . That's my school. Drop me there and I can walk the rest of the way."

"No, I'm taking you straight home. You've already been gone for more than a day."

"Yeah, but my folks were sick. They won't have noticed."

A minute later they passed over the Fairview Mall. "Doesn't seem like it was just yesterday," Lance said.

"You're giving up the life of crime, right?"

"After the way you embarrassed me in front of all those people? Absolutely." Lance had been spotted by the mall's security guards as he attempted to scam a group of shoppers with his three-card-monte trick. He'd managed to evade them, but was then caught by Paragon as he left the mall. "It's the quiet life for me from now on. No more superheroes, no more saving the world."

"Quiet life? I don't think so," Paragon said, a touch of amusement in his voice. "Look straight ahead. That's your street, isn't it? I count eight police cars, at least."

"Oh *man* . . . My folks must have reported me missing! I'm going to be grounded forever."

"I'll talk to them, if it'll help."

"Yeah, just say you found me or something. Wait . . . Do they know about the bike?" The previous day Lance had found himself traveling at more than a hundred miles an hour on his bicycle, propelled by a stolen jetpack he'd been unable to deactivate. Paragon had swooped down and pulled him out of danger at the last second, but the bike was totalled.

Paragon slowed and began to descend as they approached the street, then swerved to the left to avoid an ambulance that suddenly screeched around the corner, heading for Lance's house.

Lance dry-swallowed. He took a deep breath to steady his nerves. "Paragon?"

"I know. . . . Just stay calm. No sense worrying until we know what's going on."

From the tone of Paragon's voice Lance knew that the news wasn't going to be good.

Outside the McKendrick home, two dozen police officers

pushed the crowds back as the paramedics ran from the ambulance.

This close, Lance could see that every window in the front of his house had been shattered. The front door was in splinters, and much of the brickwork lay scattered across the lawn.

Lance's feet had barely touched the ground when he unclipped the parachute harness and darted across the street, skirted around the back of a second ambulance, and ran toward the house.

A young police officer shouted, "Hey!" and tried to grab him. Lance dodged around her, vaulted the low wall, and was only feet away from the porch when something strong and heavy slammed into him, holding him fast.

As he struggled to get free of the police sergeant's grip, he was only dimly aware of the man's voice. "Ya can't go in there! Lance, listen ta me—there's nothin' ya can do!"

"Let go of me!" Lance screamed. "Mom! Dad!" He planted an elbow in the policeman's stomach. The man flinched, but his grip held. Lance's kicking heels left rough gouges and furrows in the lawn as he was dragged away from the door.

Then one of the paramedics came out, walking slowly backward, checking over his shoulder as he carefully stepped over the debris-strewn porch.

Oh please God, no! I know what that means—when they come out backward, it's because they're . . . Lance's mind shut down then, refused to allow him to finish the thought.

The paramedic was carrying the end of a stretcher. Moments later his colleague emerged, holding the other end.

There was someone on the stretcher. Lance couldn't see who it was: The person's face was covered.

The sergeant was still talking, meaningless words of comfort that Lance couldn't take in. Then once again he heard Paragon's voice, soft but strong, saying his name.

He felt a metal-gloved hand rest on his shoulder, gently pulling him away from the police sergeant, and found his face pressed up against the cool steel of Paragon's chest-plate.

". . . just came outta nowhere," the police sergeant was saying. "Neighbors say that it was over in seconds. . . . I mean, they prob'ly wouldn'ta felt any pain, y'know? That's gotta be somethin', right?"

Paragon said, "Sergeant? Please, that's enough."

"I just . . . Sorry."

Lance stared at the stretcher as the paramedics carefully loaded it into the back of their ambulance, and then there was more movement at the ruined porch, and another covered stretcher was carried out.

Then a third.

He felt his knees weaken, and he dropped to the ground, unable to watch any longer. "Maybe it wasn't them," Lance found himself saying. "Maybe there was someone else. . . ."

Paragon crouched down next to him. "I'm sorry, Lance. They're gone."

They brought him to the Fairview police station, wrapped him in a thick blanket that smelled of cheap detergent, sat him in the sergeant's office with a mug of something hot that he didn't drink, then closed the door on him while they talked about him outside, occasionally glancing in at him through the door's glass pane.

Lance's mind kept wandering, drifting back and forth.

Crazy, unconnected thoughts and ideas filled his head, and part of him knew it was just the brain's way of dealing with such a horrific event. The process reminded him of a cat stalking a mouse: The cat would look away, pretending to be interested in something else, but every couple of seconds it would look back at its prey to make sure it was still there.

His mother, father, and brother were dead.

Yesterday, they'd been alive and well. OK, perhaps his folks hadn't actually been *well*—like almost every other adult on the planet they'd been infected with The Helotry's plague. But they'd been alive, that was certain.

Ever since the battle at Windfield had ended, Lance had been bursting with the need to tell someone the truth about the plague, even though deep down he'd known that wasn't an option. *Can't ever tell them what really happened, 'cos they'd never believe me.*

But still, it was an incredible feeling, knowing that he was the one who'd got the cure to the superfast hero Quantum, who had then carried it to the rest of the world. *I saved everyone,* Lance thought. *Billions of people would be dying now— maybe they'd even be already dead—if it hadn't been for me.*

Sure, I'm not a superhuman like Roz or Brawn or Thunder or Abby, but I'm still the one who saved the world. That was all me. My idea and everything.

But I can't tell anyone because they'd never believe me and because . . . because . . .

Then Lance looked around the sergeant's office and realized where he was, and why he was there, and the tears came again.

Because Mom and Dad and Cody are dead.

A few minutes later—or it could have been an hour, Lance had no way of knowing—the door opened and Paragon walked in. He pushed the door closed behind him, dragged a chair over next to Lance, and sat down. "You OK?"

Lance stared into his now-cold mug and shook his head.

"There'll be a full inquest. But . . . Lance, it was over in seconds. It looks like they were all in bed when it happened."

"How were they killed?"

"You don't need to hear the details. Not now."

"Tell me."

"You sure you want to hear this?"

Lance raised his head, saw his reflection in Paragon's opaque visor. "Tell me."

"Their necks were snapped. Your folks were asleep. They wouldn't have felt anything. But Cody . . . He has marks on his arms, cuts on his knuckles. He put up a fight. It didn't do much good, but—" Paragon stopped abruptly, then reached out toward the door and closed the blinds. "Lance, look at me." He raised a hand to each side of his helmet. There was a soft *click*, and the visor swung open.

Lance stared. "You . . . You're younger than I thought."

"I just turned twenty-two." He smiled. "If you look carefully, you'll notice that I'm black too. Didn't expect that, did you?"

"Never crossed my mind one way or the other." Lance returned the smile. It was easier to do than he'd expected. "So why are you showing me this now?"

"Because I'm trusting you with my most valued secret. No one has ever seen Paragon's face before. I'm trusting you because . . . Lance, you're a thief and a burglar and a con man, and in theory you're the *last* person I should be able to trust.

7

But you saved the world. You had no powers, no weapons, but you still put yourself in harm's way many times over the past couple of days. You're the bravest person I've ever met. And you need to be brave for a little while longer. You get me?"

Lance started to nod, then shook his head. "Not really."

"It's not over, Lance. There's a reason your house was targeted. We're going to take you away from here, put you somewhere no one will ever find you. The police want you to stay with your aunt and uncle in Wisconsin, but I've told them that's not safe enough. I've talked to Max Dalton, told him everything. . . . He'll take care of things. And if you want, he'll help you to forget, or at least ease the pain. He can do that, block parts of your memory. Said he had to do the same to Roz and Josh after their parents were killed."

"I don't want to forget them!"

"I know. . . . But it could make things easier."

"No. Dalton's a jerk. I'll get through this without his help."

Paragon stood up. "I understand. But he can be a useful guy to have on your side."

"Who did this? Who killed my family?"

"The police didn't want me to tell you, but you'll find out eventually. . . . Lance, in a situation like this we have a tendency to blame ourselves, but you have to understand that this is not your fault, got that? It's all too easy to look back and say, 'If I hadn't done this, then she'd never have come after my family,' but that's just not the case."

Lance shuddered, and drew the blanket tighter around his shoulders. "You said 'she.' . . . Oh no. . . . Please don't let it be true!"

"I'm sorry, Lance. It was Slaughter."

CHAPTER 1

THREE WEEKS later . . .

In the bathroom of her apartment in Manhattan, Roz Dalton winced as she slowly unwrapped the bandage covering her left hand. Dr. Holzhauer had told her that everything was fine: The artificial skin was beginning to knit well with her real skin. "You're lucky you're fifteen," Holzhauer had said. "That's about the perfect age for this. Any younger and you'd outgrow the skin, much older and it'd take longer to heal. It should settle down in a year, two at the most, but soon all you'll have is a few faint scars."

Roz piled the strip of bandage on the edge of the sink and then held her hand up to the light. The new skin had been closely matched in color to her own skin, but Doctor Holzhauer had warned her that it would always be that color: It would never tan.

Roz's older brother, Max, had paid for the operation. He

hadn't told her how much it cost, but he'd made it pretty clear that it hadn't been cheap. "Holzhauer's a genius," Max had said. "If I didn't know better, I'd swear he was one of *us*."

As with almost everything else he did, Max had an agenda: "Artificial skin is going to be a huge market in the next few years. The right investments now will pay off a hundred times over."

Like he needs the money, Roz thought. She wasn't sure whether Max was a billionaire yet, but she knew he had to be close. His superhuman ability to read—and sometimes control—other people's minds made him an incredibly astute businessman. Max always got what he wanted in a negotiation, and sometimes Roz wondered whether he was controlling the other people. Or, worse, reading their darkest secrets from their memories and blackmailing them.

She'd always meant to ask him about that, but somehow she never thought of it at the right time. That made her wonder whether he was able to control *her* mind too. If he was, there was no way to tell.

Roz left the bathroom and walked through the apartment to the south-facing drawing room, where the light was much better.

Doesn't look too bad, she thought as she examined the new skin. She carefully flexed her wrist—the graft covered the back of her hand from her knuckles halfway to her elbow, and aside from the slight color difference and the scars around the edges, it looked just like real skin. She poked the skin just below the wrist. *Doesn't feel real, though.*

On the coffee table behind her, the cordless phone beeped.

Roz picked it up. "Yeah?" She slid open the glass doors and stepped out onto the balcony. The apartment was on the Upper West Side of Manhattan, overlooking Columbus Avenue. From this high up Roz couldn't actually see the street without leaning way over the wall and peering straight down, but to the left she did have a good view across Central Park.

"Roz, don't answer the phone like that," Max's voice said. "It could have been a business call."

Roz raised her eyes. "OK, whatever. What's up?"

"Still stuck in this meeting. Looks like we'll be here for the rest of the day. You OK to pick up Josh from school?"

"You can't send a car for him like usual?"

"It's his last day before the break, Roz. I promised him I'd be there—all of his friends have been begging him to meet me."

"Right, because you're a big-time superhero."

"Exactly," Max replied, ignoring her sarcasm. "Won't be the same if it's just you there, but you can show off a bit. Use your telekinesis to levitate Josh or something like that. That'll keep them happy. And promise them that we'll arrange a party sometime over the next couple of weeks. They can meet me then."

"OK. You could ask Quantum to show up too. The kids would love that."

"Yeah, sure," Max said, in that too-casual voice he used when he really meant "I don't think so." That didn't surprise her: Max didn't like to share the spotlight. He continued: "Listen, that's not the only reason I called. . . . Do you remember Lance McKendrick?"

11

"What sort of question is that? Of course I remember him—he saved my life more than once!"

"Right. Well, if you hear from him, let me know. He's disappeared."

"From where? What happened to him after his family were killed?"

"We had him holed up in a former prison called Hawksley. It's been decommissioned, currently undergoing major structural renovations. We had Lance secured in one of the cell blocks that's not scheduled for work for another three months. None of the workers on the site had even the slightest clue that he was there."

"You were keeping him in a *prison*?"

"We had to make sure he couldn't be found. We're setting him up with a new identity, a whole new past. But last night he went on the run. We still don't know how he got out without anyone seeing him. It's possible he'll try to contact you or one of the others. If he does, you tell me immediately."

"Of course. Let me know when you find him." Roz said good-bye and disconnected the call. She put the phone on top of the wall beside her, then closed her eyes and basked for a moment in the warm sunlight. *Poor Lance. He talks too much and he's a bit of an idiot, but he's not a bad guy. No one deserves to have their whole family taken away from them like that.*

There was a light, warm breeze coming from the west, but aside from that it was an almost perfect summer day. The constant rumble of the Manhattan traffic swamped all other sounds, but Roz always liked to imagine that she could hear children playing in the park.

She loved the park, but hadn't visited it in more than a year. *Have to get out there soon*, she thought. *Just me and Josh. We'll bring a Frisbee and a picnic basket and just spend the afternoon having fun.*

But she knew that Max wouldn't approve. The Daltons were too well known to go out in public without a team of bodyguards. Max had even installed some of his people in Josh's school to make sure he was protected at all times.

As she looked east over the park, she saw that the sky was darkening—thick clouds were rolling in, fast and low and heavy. *Rats. And it started out such a nice day.* But something about the darkening sky felt wrong, out of place.

It took her a moment to realize what it was: The breeze was coming from the west, but the clouds were approaching from the east.

In the cluttered and dusty workshop tucked into the corner of the old barn beside his father's farmhouse, James Klaus sat back and looked with some pride at his creation.

He'd risen just before dawn, when he heard his dad and Faith—his father's second wife—getting up, but they'd told him there was no work for him today. "First day here," his dad had said. "Take it easy. Do what you want. Explore or something."

James had wavered between going back to bed and heading out to the workshop, but it was a short-lived battle. He'd spent the morning working with scraps of metal and discarded strips of leather and tough plastic, and now, on the bench before him, was a pair of heavily modified builder's gloves.

He pulled them on and formed his hands into fists. The gloves were heavy and tight, but felt good. *All right! I'll have to show Dad later—tell him they're for skateboarding or something.*

James was sixteen years old, tall and thin, with deep brown skin and close-cropped hair, and he was happy because he wouldn't have to go back home for another six weeks. *Forty-two days without Rufus getting on my case about every little thing.*

Over the past eight years, James had become an expert at avoiding his stepfather. He'd learned when it was safe to speak and what not to say, learned to never bring friends home or to touch any of Rufus's things without permission.

After his parents divorced, James's mother had received full custody. James still didn't understand how that had happened. His father, Darrien, was a gentle, good-natured, hardworking man who never hurt anyone. Darrien Klaus had adored his wife, given her everything, but somehow that hadn't been enough for her. After a string of affairs she left Darrien for Rufus, who couldn't be more opposite.

As far as James was concerned, the only good thing to come out of their relationship was his half sister, Shiho. She was seven years old, small for her age, and as close to a tomboy as their mother and Rufus would allow.

For the past two weeks James had begged his mother to allow Shiho to come with him to the farm for summer break, but his mother had refused: "I spent far too many years in that cesspit! You go if you want, but I'm not letting my only daughter anywhere near the place."

James tidied away his dad's tools, left the barn, and made his way around to the front of the house.

A voice from inside called, "That you, James?"

"Yep. Getting dark again. Looks like there's more rain on the way." James pulled off his boots and left them on the porch, then stepped into the kitchen.

Faith was sitting at the desk in the corner, typing on the old Macintosh computer. She looked up as James filled a glass of water at the sink. "Hey. Your dad's out in the north forty. Should be back soon—we can eat then."

James drained the glass in one go and wiped the back of his hand across his mouth. "Cool. What are we having?"

"What do you want?"

"Well, what have we got?"

Faith smiled. "Oh, if only the fridge had some sort of doorlike mechanism that allowed people to open it up and have a look. You could . . . James, what on earth are you wearing?"

He spread his hands to show her his gloves. "Made them myself. Y'know, for skateboarding. To protect my hands. What do you think?"

A frown line creased Faith's forehead. "Hmm . . . You'd have more protection with a helmet and kneepads. And speaking of your board," she added, pointing to where it rested inside the door, "put that thing away. I nearly tripped over it twice."

James picked up the board and was about to reply when something caught his attention. He looked out the window at the darkening sky and concentrated, focused his hearing. Until a few moments ago he'd been able to hear his father humming to himself as he steered the rattling and rusty tractor across the fields toward the house. Now there was nothing. Not even his father's heartbeat.

He darted out of the house and skidded to a stop. He could hear his dad's life signs again, but now they were coming from half a mile south of where they had been, and he was on foot.

This is not possible, James thought. Then he glanced up. The sky was blue and cloudless. A perfect summer day.

In Midway, Abigail de Luyando looked on eagerly as Solomon Cord—Paragon—popped the trunk of his car. He'd parked in the alleyway behind Abby's apartment block, and now that they were sure no one could see them, Cord said it was safe to show Abby what he'd brought for her.

He lifted the large, cloth-covered object out of the trunk and began to unwrap it.

"So this is my new armor?"

"Armor's not ready yet, but this is way cooler!"

To Abby it looked like a jumble of odd-shaped chrome bars and steel cables. The main part was hinged in two places, each section almost two feet in length, folded back on itself like the stems on a giant pair of spectacles. A thick cable was loosely strung between the opposite ends. Cord passed the device to her. "Not too heavy?"

"No. But what is it?"

"You'll see." He pointed to the middle section. "Keep that part vertical, and hold the grip here, in your left hand. That's it. Arm straight out by your side. OK . . . Now, see that switch next to your thumb? Well, hit that."

Abby flipped the switch, and the whole device seemed to jump in her hand. It happened faster than she could see: The upper and lower sections had snapped into place, and the cable between the opposite ends was now taut.

"This is a custom-built recurve bow," Cord said. "A compound bow would be smaller, but this is a simpler mechanism. Less to go wrong. It's got a draw strength of about four hundred pounds, so it should be well within your range. Since your enhanced strength seems to be more effective with metals than anything else—I wish I knew why that was—that's what the whole bow is made from. The limbs and the riser are Alloy 1090. That's a really strong high-carbon steel, practically unbreakable—well, *you* could probably break it, but I don't think many other people could—and the cable is woven strands of osmium, one of the toughest metals there is."

Abby gave the cable an experimental tug. "Wow . . . And you're just *giving* me this?"

"I figured you need a long-distance weapon. Your sword is fine, but you haven't had enough practice with it yet. With the bow you'll be able to stop an opponent long before he can reach you." Cord reached into the car trunk and—with some effort—lifted out a large quiver packed with arrows. "The arrows are carbon steel shafts and fletching, fitted with osmium tips. All this osmium cost Dalton about thirty thousand dollars, so keep track of your arrows."

"I've never shot a bow before. How do I . . . ?"

Cord passed her an arrow. "This end is called the nock. It fits onto the cable just here, between the two markers. The pointy end of the arrow rests here, on the bit cleverly called the arrow rest. I've modified it so that once the arrow is in place, it'll stay put—just in case you need to use the bow while running or jumping or whatever. So . . . you hold the cable with your index finger above the arrow, the middle and ring fingers below. Keep the pinkie out of the way. And you just pull back." Cord quickly looked around. "OK, it's safe. Give it a go."

"What will I aim at?"

Cord pointed to the far end of the alley. "That crate is about a hundred yards away. See if you can hit it from here. Aim for the very center. If you don't hit it the first time, we can adjust the sights."

He instructed Abby on how to aim the bow, then stepped back. "Take your time. . . . Fix the sight where you want to hit the crate, draw back the string . . . Right back . . . Tuck your right hand under your chin. The string should be just touching the tip of your nose. OK. How's that feel?"

Abby grunted. "It's not easy, but I can do it."

"That's good. It means the draw is about right for you. Now, don't just open your hand when you let go—pull back a little at the same time."

There was a loud *whip* as Abby released the cable, followed immediately by an even louder *thunk* from the far end of the alley. The wooden crate didn't even move. "I missed."

"OK, let's find the arrow and see how much you missed by." He passed Abby the quiver and she hoisted it onto her shoulder. "You've got forty-three arrows there. You could maybe use ordinary arrows, but they mightn't survive being launched from the bow."

They walked side by side along the alleyway. "Thanks for this, Mr. Cord. I can't believe that you spent all this money on me."

"First, it's not Mr. Cord. It's Solomon, or Sol. But never call me that when I'm wearing the armor, OK? Second, it's not *my* money, it's Max's. I just designed and built it. You're going to have to practice, Abby. A lot. An arrow from an ordinary bow could easily kill someone. An arrow from *this* bow could kill an elephant."

"How do I fold it back up again?"

"Give it here and I'll show you," Cord said. He took the bow from Abby's hands and pointed out the levers set into the riser, one above the grip, one below. "You pull these out and the cable will go slack enough for the limbs to collapse. I had to build a machine to do it—I don't have the strength to do it myself."

They reached the end of the alley. "I can't see the arrow," Abby said. "It's too dark."

Cord looked up. "Could be a storm coming."

"Hold on a second. . . ." Abby crouched down in front of the crate. There was a nickel-sized hole in the front. "Hey, maybe I *did* hit it." She moved around to the back of the crate. There was a matching hole—its edges splintered a little—on the other side. "Yeah, I think I did! That means the arrow went right through, so it should be . . ." She peered along the arrow's path. "Wow!"

"Wow is right," Cord said.

The arrow was embedded in the brick wall at the end of the alley—only the last eight inches of the shaft were protruding.

Cord took hold of the arrow's shaft and pulled—it didn't move. "I think *you'd* better do it."

Abby slid the arrow out of the wall and examined the tip. "The pointy bit is still pointy." She grinned. "I like my new toy!"

"Glad to hear it," Cord said. They began to walk back

toward his car. "Don't shoot it at people unless you absolutely have no choice, because in *your* hands this is more dangerous than a gun."

"Can you get more of this cable? Because I was thinking that I could use it like you use your grappling-hook gun. Like, I could be on the top of a building and shoot the cable across to the next building, and then climb across."

"I'll definitely look into that. But with your strength you could probably just jump from one building to another."

"*Or . . . ,*" Abby said, grinning, "you could build me a jetpack like yours."

But Cord didn't respond. He was staring along the alley. "Where's my car?"

"You didn't leave the keys in the ignition, did you? Around here we call that 'public transport.' "

"No one can start my car but me. I built the transmission myself."

Abby looked down at the alley floor. . . . "Wasn't there a pile of garbage bags just here?" She turned around. "And the crate is gone. Something weird is going on. . . ."

Lance McKendrick felt something cold and hard and metallic press against the back of his neck.

There was a sharp click—the sound of a gun being cocked—and a woman's voice said, "You have three seconds to give me a reason not to shoot you, kid."

CHAPTER 2

LANCE SLOWLY RAISED his hands. "It's not what you think."

"Sure it's not," the woman said. "You're telling me you didn't see the tape outside? The bright yellow tape with the words 'Police Line—Do Not Cross' all over it? Or maybe you can't read, is that it?"

"I can read. And I saw the tape. But I'm not trespassing."

"I saw you picking the lock. Quite expertly, I should add."

"I lost my key. This is *my* house."

A pause. "Name?"

"Lance McKendrick."

"Age? Date of birth?"

"I'm fourteen. My birthday's September the second."

"What year?"

"Duh! *Every* year."

Lance felt the pressure of the gun's muzzle ease, then the woman said, "From what Max Dalton told me, only *you* could make such a lame joke with a gun at the back of your head. You can lower your arms, Lance."

He relaxed and turned to look at her. She was in her mid-twenties, he guessed. Tall, with lightly tanned skin, blue eyes, and brown hair. She was wearing a long black duster over a skintight blue-and-silver costume.

"Who are you?" Lance asked.

"A friend of Max. He sent me to look for you when you disappeared from Hawksley last night."

"You're another superhuman, obviously."

"Yes. I suppose you could think of me as Max's secret weapon. I have certain skills that make me ideally suited to be your bodyguard—though you're clearly not without skills yourself. You got out of the cell block, stole a car belonging to one of the builders, and drove it—very badly—halfway across the state before they even noticed you were gone. How exactly *did* you get out of Hawksley?"

Lance grinned. "You think I'm dumb enough to tell you that? I might need to escape again one day. Anyway, I've already figured out six other ways out of that place."

"Then you won't be going back there." The woman looked around the sitting room of the McKendrick house. It had been almost demolished in Slaughter's rampage. "I'm sorry about what happened to your family."

"Yeah. Me too. I had to come back. They wouldn't let me see the place after . . ." He looked down at his hands and realized they were clenched into fists. "What makes someone *do* something like that?"

"I wish I knew. I've encountered Slaughter a couple of times. She's . . . insane. That's the only way I can get any sort of handle on her. As for why she came here . . . From what Max learned from the minds of The Helotry's leaders, they were after you ever since you broke into their warehouse and stole their prototype jetpack. They had you down for execution."

Lance brushed the splintered remains of a wooden lamp off the arm of the sofa and sat down. "But they caught me when we were in Oak Grove. They brought me to their HQ. They could have killed me then."

"They needed to know what you knew. Plus you managed to talk your way out of being killed. More than once, I'm told. Why did you come back here, Lance?"

"I wanted to collect some stuff. And . . . I had to see where it happened."

"You put yourself at risk, leaving the prison. For all we know Slaughter could be watching you right now."

"I couldn't stay there any longer. I mean, apart from the boredom, the security was a joke. No disrespect to you and the rest of Dalton's hired help, but I'm fourteen and I don't have any superpowers, and I still managed to break out and find my way home."

"Go and get what you came for. You've got five minutes, and then I'm taking you to our backup location. You cannot come back here. Ever. Do you understand that? If you value your life at all, you'll never even set foot in Fairview again."

Lance nodded, and stood up. "Who are you, anyway?"

"Amandine Paquette. Call me Mandy. But if anyone else is around, use my code name: Impervia."

He walked over to the ruined bookcase and rummaged

through the books on the floor. "I've heard rumors about you. You're supposed to be super-strong or something like that, right?"

"Close enough."

Lance picked up two heavy volumes of his mother's prized *Encyclopedia Britannica* and handed them to Mandy. She had to put her gun back into its holster to take them.

He pointed to the wall behind her. "I was going to take that too. . . . But I don't suppose you'll let me."

Mandy turned to look at the large photo. It showed Lance and his brother in their best clothes, sitting on the floor in front of their parents.

"No, it's too big."

"I wasn't going to take the frame and the glass. Just the picture."

"Probably not a good idea. You're supposed to have a new identity. That wouldn't really work if you're carrying around a huge photo of yourself with your family." Then she turned back to face him. "And don't think I didn't notice what you were doing, Lance."

Lance did his best to look surprised and a little hurt. "What?"

"You lifted my gun from the holster and tucked it into the back of your jeans." She let the books drop to the floor. "Hand it over."

He took a step backward. "I'm not going with you."

"Slaughter will find you."

"Don't you get it? I *want* her to find me! And when she does, I'm going to kill her!"

"Her skin is bulletproof, Lance. You know that—you were right there in Midway when that soldier shot her in the head."

"Right. And later when she was unconscious, he put his gun in her mouth and wanted to blow the back of her head off. Well, I'm liking that plan more and more. She murdered my family!"

"And you want to make her pay for that by letting her murder you too? Get real, kid. You have less chance of hurting her than you'd have of knocking the moon out of its orbit by throwing stones at it. I've read your profile, Lance. I know you. Even if by some miracle you managed to get Slaughter into a position where you *could* kill her, you wouldn't do it."

Lance pulled the gun out of the back of his jeans and handed it to Mandy. "She took everything from me."

"I know."

"My mom and dad worked for *years* to buy this house. It was way out of their price range, but they wanted the best for me and Cody. They both had to take second jobs." He suddenly laughed. "Dad took guitar lessons. I was about four, I think, when he started. He borrowed a guitar from a friend, and every Tuesday night he took lessons at the community college. On Thursday nights he had a bunch of people here teaching them what he'd just learned. He was always just one step ahead of the people he was teaching, but he had them believing he was an expert."

Mandy smiled. "Now, who does that remind me of? Come on. We've been here too long already. You'd better just get your things."

Roz watched as the heavy gray clouds rolled in from the east. They were coming in fast and low, obscuring the buildings on the far side of Central Park, then over the park itself, until all she could see was a thick mist.

It lasted only a moment, and then the sky was clear again.

The ever-present hum of Manhattan's traffic was gone.

And in the middle of Central Park, where there once had been grass and trees and people, there was now a one-hundred-and-fifty-story glass-and-steel building.

James Klaus suddenly realized that there were voices coming from the north forty acres. Thousands of voices, mixed with the hum of hundreds of electronic machines, the roar of dozens of powerful engines.

Behind him, Faith came running from the kitchen. "*James?* Is that you?"

He turned around, confused. "Of course it's me. I . . ." He stopped. Faith had been wearing a loose sweatshirt and faded jeans. She was now wearing a long off-white dress belted around the waist.

"What are you even *doing* here?" Faith asked. "Is this some sort of trick or something? How did you do that?"

"What do you mean? I've been here since yesterday! And when did you get time to change your clothes?"

They stared at each other, then Faith said, "How did you get here without the Praetorians seeing you? I know your dad's made friends with some of them, but they wouldn't allow this."

"Praetorians?"

"Over in the north forty. The training camp. The soldiers, remember?"

"What? This isn't making any sense," James said, looking around. He walked over to the half-closed barn door. "Look, the tractor is in there—there's no way Dad could have gotten back and parked it without me hearing him!"

"Your father hasn't used that old thing in years. I doubt it still even runs."

"No, I saw him driving off in it this morning—and I could *hear* him driving it just a few minutes ago!" He walked into the barn and placed his hand on the tractor's engine casing. It was cold.

Lance slung his brother's backpack onto his shoulder and held up the yellow tape outside his house as Mandy ducked under it.

"I'm parked on the next street," she said. "Then we have a three-hour drive to the rendezvous point, another two to the backup hideout."

"Do you have anything to eat in the car?"

"No, but we can stop on the way."

Lance ducked back under the tape. "No need. I'll get something from inside. Otherwise it'll all go to waste. Got the keys?"

Mandy tossed the keys to him, then he ran back up the drive and unlocked the door, trying to remember whether he'd eaten the last of the chocolate-chip cookies he had stashed in his room. *Need my toothbrush,* he remembered. *And a towel.* The towels in his cell in Hawksley had been paper-thin and fraying along the edges.

He pushed the door open. The hallway was clean, and completely free of debris.

Lance stopped. *What the . . . ?*

He looked back toward Impervia, but she was gone.

Then, from the kitchen, a familiar voice: "Lance? Is that you? What are you doing back so early?"

Lance dry-swallowed. "Mom?"

CHAPTER 3

SOLOMON CORD COULD feel the skin on his arms begin to tighten into gooseflesh as he approached the entrance to the alley.

"I do *not* like this," Cord muttered. "Abby, stay put. I want to take a look first." A line of cold sweat ran down between his shoulder blades, but he suppressed the shudder. Abby was unsettled enough already; he didn't want to make her any more nervous.

With his back pressed against the alley's brick wall, Cord slowly peered around the corner.

The street was empty, and almost spotlessly clean. No cars, no pedestrians, not even the gang of teenagers loitering at the intersection who earlier had stopped whatever they were doing to watch his car as it passed them.

We're not where we should be.

He moved a little farther out, and a shadow momentarily

fell across his face. Cord shielded his eyes against the sun and looked up. There was a tall metal lamppost almost directly in front of him. *OK. I know* that *wasn't there before.* If the post had been there when he'd driven into the alley, he'd have had to come from the other direction to make the turn.

Then he noticed the thick cables radiating from the top of the post. Each of the six cables led to other posts. Each post had a cluster of at least three security cameras.

Cord ducked back into the alley. "We're in trouble."

Abby walked up to him. "What is it?"

Cord absently chewed on his lower lip for a moment. "Not *exactly* sure."

She leaned past him and looked out at the street. "It looks different. All the lampposts . . ."

"That's just it—they're not all lampposts. Look up."

"Cameras. Those things *definitely* weren't there before. And the billboard . . ." She pointed to the side of a building on the far side of the street, close to the intersection. "That was an ad for Uncle Harry's Ice Cream. They just put it up the other day." The billboard had been replaced with a large array of black panels. "What do you suppose that's for?" Abby asked.

"Could be solar cells," Cord said, peering around the corner again. "I can see four more of them from here."

Abby bit her lip. "Mr. Cord . . . Where *are* we?"

James walked across the farmyard. "Faith, what's going on here?"

His father's wife shrugged. "You tell me. How did you get here from Midway?"

30

"Look, I've been here since yesterday afternoon. You don't remember that? Dad made us eggs on toast this morning."

"He makes eggs on toast nearly every morning." Faith looked James up and down. "You're seriously telling me that you got here *yesterday*?" She reached out and placed the palm of her right hand on his forehead. "Are you feeling all right? Why aren't you in school?"

"But it's summer break."

"Don't play games with me, James! Schools haven't had summer breaks in *years*."

To himself, James said, *Either I've gone mad, or everything has changed without me knowing about it. Or maybe I was* already *mad and this is the way things have always been. No, that can't be right! Everything's changed, and the only way that could happen is . . . if this isn't my version of reality. This is a parallel world.*

He knew that some scientists believed that, in theory, time wasn't just a straight line flowing from the past to the future: It branched constantly, like an infinite number of forks in the road. Every decision—no matter how small—gave birth to a whole new universe for each possible outcome. Some physicists even theorized that it might be possible to jump from one universe to another.

But it was all theoretical—there was no way to prove that there was anything more than one universe.

If it is *true*, James thought, *and somehow I've been pulled into a parallel universe, then . . . Then there could be another* me *here.* "Call my mom," he said to Faith. "See what she has to say."

"What?"

"Just do it, please. Ask to speak to me."

She nodded, and he followed her back into the house. Her hand was trembling a little as she picked up the phone and dialed the number. James's mother, Shawna, answered on the third ring. "Shawna? It's Faith."

James listened in: One advantage of having superhuman hearing was that other people's phone calls were no longer private.

"*You* again. What do you want now?" James always felt a little embarrassed at how rude his mother was to Faith. It wasn't as though his father had run away with her—Shawna had thrown him out after she met Rufus.

"Is James there?"

"Of course not. He's in school."

"Are you sure?"

"Yes I'm sure! He wouldn't cut classes."

"Just check, will you?"

There was the sound of the handset being dropped, and then Shawna called out, "James!"

There was no response: James could hear his mother's soft breathing on the other end of the line as she waited. She called again, and a third time, then, "Told you he wasn't here. What's this about? If he *did* cut classes, his teacher would phone here first."

"OK, never mind. I just—" The line went dead.

Faith hung up the phone and started to tell James what had happened.

"I heard. Look, I've got something important to tell you. . . . Don't tell Dad, OK?"

"What is it?" The familiar frown line creased her forehead. "Are you in some sort of trouble?"

"I don't know." He took a deep breath while he mulled over the best way to tell her. "I'm a superhuman."

She smiled. "Uh-huh."

"No, seriously. I can control sound waves. I can hear things happening miles away, and I can even create sounds."

"Can you fly?"

"Well, no."

"Pity. What's your superhero name, then? Are you famous?"

"I'm not famous. I call myself Thunder."

Faith laughed. "You're joking!"

"I'm *not* joking. Listen." The room was suddenly filled with music, as though a full orchestra was playing invisibly in the room.

Faith jumped back, looking around wildly for the source of the music.

After a few seconds James allowed the music to fade away. "That was Edvard Grieg's Piano Concerto in A Minor, *allegro moderato molto e marcato*. All the right notes, *and* in the right order."

Faith had been staring openmouthed at him. "How did you *do* that?"

"I can re-create any sound I hear. I can invert it, modify it, do anything I like to it. I can nullify sounds too. Pretty handy for sneaking into and out of the house at night."

"OK. You're a superhuman."

She still doesn't believe me, James thought. "I am. Maybe that's got something to do with what's happening here, maybe not.

The reason I'm telling you is that either I'm not where I should be, or the whole world has changed. Things are suddenly very different. Like the soldiers camped in the north-forty fields. How long have they been there? What are they there *for*?"

"It's a training camp. Back when things got bad, the army told your father that everyone had to do their part. He had to give up the forty acres, and provide the soldiers with milk and cheese and vegetables."

James bit his lip. "How do you mean, 'back when things got bad'?"

"How could you not remember this? The terrorist attacks, the bombs, closing the borders? Anchorage?" Faith ran her hands over her face. "You're scaring me. You really don't remember any of this? You don't remember Anchorage?"

"I don't remember it because it never happened!"

"How can you say that? A hundred thousand Americans *died* in Anchorage!"

"You're talking about Anchorage, Alaska? What happened there?"

"There was a bomb. Daedalus planted it. He tried to hold the city to ransom, I think. . . . No one knows for sure what happened, but the bomb detonated. Anchorage is gone. James, the whole of the United States of America has been under martial law for the past three years."

The building in Central Park dwarfed everything around it. It was rectangular at the base and tapered slightly until a quarter of the way up—about forty floors—where it broke into a series of tall, thin towers, some of which were still under construction.

I'm dreaming, Roz thought. *That has to be it. This is a dream.*

The lack of noise was almost as disturbing. Instead of the constant rumbling of countless engines all she could hear was wind rustling through the trees and a faint, but continuous, ringing from somewhere nearby.

As she watched, a pair of large, flat, roughly rectangular craft detached themselves from one of the towers, their battered yellow paintwork giving them the look of construction vehicles. They drifted smoothly away from the tower, one descending toward the northern end of the park, the other passing almost directly overhead.

It moved steadily, unwavering, following the course of the street below, and in complete silence. Its undercarriage featured a series of eight circular blue-white lights, but she could see no other source of propulsion.

At the end of the block the craft banked to the left, heading south, and Roz looked back toward the towering building.

A third flying craft appeared, coming in over the east side of the city. At first Roz thought it had to be some sort of misshapen zeppelin, but as it slowed to a stop alongside the tallest tower, she could clearly see that it was no helium-filled airship; it was hundreds of yards long and four or five stories tall. Its sides were punctuated with windows, and its hull glinted like polished steel.

Roz shook her head. *No way. No way can something that big move so silently!*

Another, smaller vehicle detached itself from the giant craft and gracefully drifted upward; it resembled one of the flying construction vehicles, but was painted a dark green. *Military colors*, Roz realized. *The big one is the equivalent of an aircraft carrier!*

She reached out for the phone she'd left resting on the wall; it was gone. *What? I'm sure I—*

Movement to her right caught her eye, and she turned to see—through the now-closed glass doors—a terrified-looking young couple staring out at her. The man was brandishing a large ornamental poker.

The poker wavered in his grip. His voice muffled by the glass, he shouted, "Who are you? How did you get up here?"

Roz shook her head. *No, this can't be happening.* The apartment's décor was all wrong, as though she'd somehow ended up on the wrong floor, but this was the only apartment in the building that had a balcony.

With her hands raised in the hope that the people inside would understand she meant no harm, Roz stepped up to the door. "Please, don't panic." She very carefully slid open the door.

"Who are you?" the man asked, almost shouting to make himself heard over a constant ringing noise. "What do you want from us?"

"I don't know. . . . What's going on here?"

The woman said, "She must have climbed up the outside! Henry, she climbed up the outside!"

"I . . . I fell, I think." Roz raised her right hand to her head. "The last thing I remember, I was with the construction crew and we were coming from the park." She pointed in the direction of the new building in Central Park. "The hatch was open. We were joking about. I must have slipped."

"No," the man said. "No way. You're only a kid. They'd never let you on one of the flyers."

"My dad is the overseer. I must have hit my head. Is there any blood?" While the couple peered at her, Roz desperately tried to think of a way out. The ringing noise was still reverberating through the building, and she suddenly realized what it was: an alarm. "I should go. I'm sorry I frightened you."

The woman said, "You *can't* go. You know the rules. Once the alarm goes, everyone has to stay where they are until the Praetorians get here." She frowned. "What's *wrong* with you that you don't know that?"

"I told you. I must have fallen." *Who are the Praetorians?* Roz wondered. She decided that she didn't want to wait around to find out.

She concentrated on the poker in the man's hand, used her telekinesis to pluck it from his grip and pull it across the room toward her. She snatched it out of the air and tossed it to the floor behind her. To the woman, she said, "You. Cancel the alarm."

The woman was staring at her in complete shock. "It . . . It can't be canceled. Only the Praetorians can do that."

"How long will it take for them to get here?"

"Not long."

"*How* long?"

"Ten minutes, maybe fifteen."

"Good. OK, I want you to—"

Then the apartment door was smashed open, and within seconds Roz was looking down the barrels of six high-powered assault weapons.

• • •

Lance slowly walked into the kitchen. His mother was carefully pouring something from a saucepan into a dish. The air was heavy with the peppery tang of her homemade tomato soup—an odor that Lance had never expected to experience again.

The TV was chatting to itself in the corner, and Lance's father was sitting at a small desk in the corner wearing headphones and typing at a computer terminal Lance had never seen before. His father saw him, hit a few keys on the keyboard to clear the screen, then removed the headphones. "What happened now? How come you're not in school?"

His mother stopped what she was doing. "You didn't get suspended again, did you?"

"Mom?"

"What was it *this* time? Stealing test papers? Selling forged hall passes? Honestly, Lance, you're going to have to learn to toe the line. If you don't, they will expel you. You know what that means—an automatic draft into the Youth Corps. I know they keep saying they won't be sending the Youth Corps overseas, but I don't believe that for a second. Is that what you want? To end up riddled with bullets and dying on a field somewhere in France or Spain? Why can't you be more like your brother? You don't see *him* getting into trouble every second day."

His father said, "You answer your mother, Lance."

Lance felt like he was going to faint. "I'm sorry. . . ." *How can they be alive? I saw their bodies!* Then he shook himself. *No,*

38

I didn't. I saw three covered stretchers. The cops wouldn't allow me to identify the bodies—they said there was no need.

His whole body trembling, Lance stepped up to his mother and wrapped his arms around her. "You're alive!" The tears came then, and he didn't care. "I thought . . . They told me you were dead." He turned to his father. "Both of you, and Cody. They said Slaughter smashed her way into the house and killed all of you!"

Mr. McKendrick shook his head. "I knew it. It's drugs, isn't it? You've taken something. What was it, Lance?"

"What? No!" He let go of his mother. "Dad, haven't you wondered where I've been for the past three weeks?"

"Why would I wonder that? You've been here or in school." His eyes narrowed. "Why? Where have you *really* been?"

They really don't know what I'm talking about! But . . . He looked around the room. *I was in here a few minutes ago—the place was wrecked.* He looked back out into the hallway—the front door was intact, and there was no sign of any damage.

"I'm just kidding," Lance said. "No, there was a fire drill and we were all sent home. Something went wrong with the alarm and they couldn't shut it off."

It's not them. It's me. Something happened to me . . . made me imagine *that they were dead.*

Then he looked past his father, at a photograph on the front page of the newspaper resting on the desk. For a second, he could only stare at the photo of the large, well-dressed man. *No . . . Please, no!*

The room seemed to sway, Lance's knees weakened, and

he had to put his hands on the desk to stop himself from toppling forward.

The newspaper was only inches away from his face now, and he couldn't help but read the article accompanying the photo.

CHANCELLOR CONDEMNS LATEST UNITY EXPANSION

A further fourteen nations yesterday signed trade and defense treaties with Unity, bringing the number of countries falling under the Unity umbrella to one hundred and twenty.

Unity President Lianne Chojnowski hailed the expansion as "a major step forward in uniting the nations of Earth against possible hostile actions by the United States. The American people did not ask for martial law and they certainly did not ask to have their freedom so completely eroded. Almost a quarter of the U.S. adult population works for the state, the vast majority employed to spy on their neighbors; every piece of mail is opened and read, every phone call is monitored and logged."

President Chojnowski's statement concluded with "We stand firm against the actions of the U.S. Chancellor and warn him that any act of aggression against a Unity member state will be met with the appropriate response." It is estimated that almost two million Unity military personnel are currently stationed in the Pacific and North Atlantic. Chojnowski continued: "We again urge the people of the United States to resist the brutal and unconscionable martial law illegally imposed on them by the Chancellor."

Reacting to this, the Chancellor yesterday said, "Unity underestimates the strength of will of the American people. We have never bowed under pressure, and we never will. If they believe that they can threaten us into submission, then they are very much mistaken."

However, on the subject of when he might see an end to the current emergency situation, now in its third year, Chancellor Krodin declined to comment.

CHAPTER 4

THREE WEEKS earlier . . .

From Krodin's perspective the hairless blue giant was moving so slowly that he might as well be wading through a lake of honey. Krodin stepped to the side, easily avoiding the giant's clumsy attack, then lashed out with his right fist, a blow that would have crushed an ordinary man's skull.

The giant staggered, briskly shook his head, and resumed his attack. Curious to see what he would do next, Krodin allowed the monster to grab hold of his arm.

The giant pulled Krodin toward him, at the same time striking at Krodin's chest with his other hand.

Krodin weathered the punch, allowed the giant to strike again. The monster's clenched fist was as big as Krodin's head, the muscles in his arm as powerful as a rampaging elephant's legs. Krodin felt the force of the blows, but no pain.

Then Krodin twisted free of the giant's grip, slammed his

own fist into the blue giant's jaw, immediately kicked upward with his bare right foot, and hit the giant in the throat.

The giant reeled backward, stumbled, landed facedown, and Krodin pressed home his attack. He balled his fists together over his head and brought them crashing down onto the giant's back, over and over.

The giant collapsed, his pain-filled, breathless groans attracting the attention of his terrified companions.

Krodin stepped back, looked toward the giant's friends. The pale-skinned young woman—the witch who appeared to be able to move objects without touching them—was crouched over the boy called Pyrokine.

Not long ago Pyrokine had been fighting alongside Krodin, but he had foolishly chosen to join the enemy. The boy's chest rose and fell in ragged gasps.

Impressive, Krodin thought. In the strange language of this new land—this *America*—he called out, "The flame-boy still lives? He is stronger than I thought. Step aside, girl. I will finish him. He was a powerful opponent and deserves a quick death."

The girl got to her feet, stood over Pyrokine. "No."

The dark-skinned girl shouted, "Roz! Get back!"

Then Krodin was hit by something powerful, something invisible, like a sudden, ferocious gust of wind. *The girl's power*, he realized. "Still you resist me? You are a fool, girl. You will die next."

As he forced himself to remain upright against the onslaught, Krodin saw two of the girl's companions try to pull her away.

Then he felt his body—his very being—shift, adapt to the

invisible force, and he was free. He leaped at the trio, knocked the others aside, and locked his left fist over the girl's face. He lifted her off the ground, pulled back his right fist, ready to strike. "Little witch . . . You. Are. Next!"

Then something crackled and sparked on the ground at his feet: The boy called Pyrokine screamed, "No!" He floated up from the ground, multicolored fire crackling over his broken body. "Let her go!"

Krodin forced his eyes shut against the glare, but he could sense that Pyrokine was approaching.

He started to back away—but he was too late. The burning boy crashed into his arm—a searing, impossible agony stronger than anything the Fifth King had experienced in his long life—forcing him to let go of the girl.

The boy somehow wrapped himself around Krodin's arm, and the fire began to spread. Krodin could feel his skin scorching, melting. *Resist this! I can resist anything!* He opened his eyes and saw the unearthly fire consuming his flesh faster than it could heal. The stench of his own burning tissue reached his nostrils and Krodin screamed, "No! Enough!"

Then, with the last of his strength, Pyrokine said, "No. You don't get to decide when you've had enough. *We* have had enough!"

The flame raced along Krodin's arms, enveloped his chest, his neck.

But it was more than just fire. The Fifth King felt something pulling at him from all directions. He had experienced this before, a few hours ago—and several thousand years ago—when he had been dragged through time.

For a brief moment, despite the pain of the fire, Krodin felt relief. *The boy's power brought me here. Now it is sending me back!*

Then he heard the metal-clad man yelling, "Shield your eyes! Everyone get back!"

In an instant, Pyrokine's body was gone, consumed by its own fire, and Krodin knew that he would be next. In moments, he would be dead.

Krodin collapsed to the ground, his muscles spasming and twitching. He was certain that he was screaming, but he could hear nothing. Then a final, searing flash . . .

And the pain was fading. In moments he could feel cool, damp grass on his back.

Krodin opened his eyes, put his scorched hand up in front of his face, and watched as his wounds began to heal, the charred skin flaking away like fragments of sun-dried clay.

And he knew—in the same way that he always knew such things—that his attackers were no longer present. He was in the same place as before, but it was somehow different.

Krodin pushed himself to his feet and looked around. The large building from which he had come—the "power plant," as the woman Slaughter had called it—was gone, and there was no indication that it had ever been there.

The Fifth King arched his back, stretched his newly healed muscles, and smiled.

He didn't know where he was, or what had happened. All he knew was that, for the first time, he had come within a hairbreadth of death. And he had survived.

CHAPTER 5

"WE HAVE TO LOOK as though we belong here," Solomon Cord told Abby as they walked along West Franklin Street back toward Abby's apartment building. "So stop staring at everything like you're a tourist."

Abby had collapsed the bow and was now carrying it and the arrow-filled quiver under her arm, wrapped in her jacket. "Sorry, can't help it." Everything around was familiar, but just a little different, as though the street had been built from the same plans but by a different designer. The buildings were cleaner, and there was less litter. At this time of the day there would normally be more people about, but now, there was almost no one, not even the usual gang of young men hanging around the corner of West Franklin and Jarvis. "What do you think is going on?"

"I wish I knew," Cord replied. "I've never experienced anything like this before."

"Those cameras look high-tech, so why do they have cables? Why aren't they wireless?"

"Wireless communications are much easier to block or scramble."

"Yeah, but someone could just cut the cables."

"Then whoever's watching would know exactly where the saboteurs are."

They stopped outside Abby's apartment building.

"If everything's changed out here . . . ," Cord began.

"I was thinking the same thing. But we have to check, don't we?" Abby walked up the steps and examined the faded list next to the line of buzzers. "There are some names here I don't recognize, but there's de Luyando. At least it means I still live here."

With Cord following, Abby pushed open the outside door and stepped into the lobby. Contrary to the appearance of the street, the lobby was less clean than it should have been. Two weeks ago—after an encounter between Cord and the daughter of the building's owner—a team of decorators had spruced up the public areas. Now, although the building didn't look anywhere near as bad as it had been before that, it clearly hadn't been renovated in several years. "Oh man, this is freaky. Could we have gone back in time or something?"

"That wouldn't explain the surveillance cameras."

"The future, then?"

"Maybe. We need to find a newspaper or something that'll tell us the date."

Abby considered that for a moment, then went over to the rack of mailboxes, fished her keys out of her pocket, and opened the one marked "de Luyando." There were three envelopes inside. "All postmarked yesterday or the day before. So we're not in the future." She stuffed the envelopes into her back pocket, then looked over at the stairs. "I guess we should . . ."

Cord nodded. "Stay behind me."

She followed Cord up the three flights of stairs, but the closer they came to Abby's apartment, the more nervous she felt. *How could everything have just changed like that? And what else has changed? Did it just happen here in Midway, or is it everywhere?*

"Prepare yourself," Cord said. "There could be a lot of differences. Whatever you see, try to take it in your stride, OK?" He stopped outside the apartment. "Ready?"

"No. But we don't have any other choice, do we?" Abby turned her key in the lock and pushed the door open.

Mrs. de Luyando's voice called out, "Who's there?" and Abby let out a deep breath she hadn't realized she'd been holding.

"That's my mom," Abby said quietly. She stepped into the short hallway with Cord close behind her.

As they entered the sitting room, Alison de Luyando wheeled her chair over to them. "Abby! Why aren't you in school? What were you thinking, leaving school before five? You know better than to be out on your own. You're lucky you weren't stopped and arrested." Then she saw Cord. "Oh. I see. What has she done *now*?"

Abby did her best to remain calm. "Mom, I'm not in trouble."

Cord said, "Everything is fine, Mrs. de Luyando. I just have a few questions to ask you."

Mrs. de Luyando rolled back from the door. "Better come in, then."

They followed Abby's mother into the sitting room. When her back was turned, Abby allowed the bow and quiver to drop to the floor, then nudged them behind the sofa.

When she looked up, Cord was staring at a photo on the mantelpiece.

"Oh, that's my eldest, Vienna," Abby's mother said, beaming with pride. "She's the one on the left."

Softly, Cord said, "Yes, I, uh, I see the resemblance." He glanced at Abby, then stepped aside so that she could see the picture.

"He'd turned up to inspect the troops and one of the girls asked him if they could get a picture with him," Mrs. de Luyando said. She laughed. "They honestly didn't expect him to say yes!"

It was a recent color photo of Vienna standing with another woman and smiling for the camera, both wearing combat fatigues and helmets.

On Vienna's upper arm was a cloth patch showing a blue eye inside a yellow sun.

Standing between Vienna and her friend, smiling and with his arms around their shoulders, was a man Abby instantly recognized, even with his hair and beard cut short. It was Krodin.

When the black-uniformed officers stormed into the apartment, the young couple immediately dropped to their knees with their hands behind their heads.

One of the soldiers shouted at Roz: "Assume the position! Now!" The man's voice wavered a little.

Roz had been trained by her brother's team, three highly skilled former U.S. Rangers. She took a moment to study the situation: The six men were still clustered in front of the door. They looked pale and nervous. That told her they were not experienced at something like this. They should have kept two men on her while the rest spread out to search the apartment for any other intruders.

Each man was holding a large assault weapon of a type she didn't recognize. The weapons were clearly heavy: The soldiers were using both hands to hold them. And behind them, they had left the apartment door open and unguarded, another rookie mistake.

The fact that they hadn't yet opened fire suggested to Roz that either they were extremely nervous or they had not been authorized to shoot. She might just have a chance.

She dropped to the floor, facedown, with her palms flat under her. The soldiers had to readjust their weapons to keep focused on her.

"All right. Cuff her and—"

Roz pushed herself up and forward, aiming between the two nearest soldiers. At the same time she reached out with her telekinesis toward the man on her left and knocked aside his weapon just as he pulled the trigger. The gun coughed a muffled *ptoof* and something rattled off the wall behind her.

Roz was now crouched in the center of the group: She slammed her left elbow into the side of one man's thigh. As he staggered aside, she hooked her right arm around another's legs and pulled hard. The man's knees buckled and he toppled back into one of his colleagues.

Now only two soldiers were aiming at her, one on each side—and she was sure they wouldn't fire in case they hit their own men. She launched herself at the man on her right while using her telekinetic shield to strike the other in the face.

The soldier she hit stumbled backward as the last man ducked aside to avoid her.

Roz dashed out through the door and telekinetically slammed it behind her as she raced down the corridor. She'd lived in this building for years and knew it well. She turned left at the end of the corridor and pushed open the fire door leading to the stairwell. Down the stairs three at a time—she was already two floors down before she heard the soldiers rushing back out of the apartment.

On every floor there was a similar fire door leading from the stairwell. As Roz passed each door, she used her telekinesis to pull it open. The doors' hinges were fitted with slow-closing springs; she hoped that as the soldiers followed her down, they would have to investigate each closing door just in case she had stopped on that floor.

On the twelfth floor Roz had gained enough of a lead to allow her to create another diversion: She ducked into one hallway and hit the call button for the elevator, then returned to the stairwell and continued her descent.

Moments later she heard one of the soldiers shouting, "Elevator's moving! You two, check it out!"

Four left, Roz thought. *But what am I going to do when I get to the ground floor? They could have more men stationed there.*

Roz was on the eighth floor when she realized she had overlooked something important: *How did they get to the apartment so quickly? There couldn't have been more than two minutes between the alarm going off and the soldiers bursting in through the door. Even if they'd been right outside on the street, they couldn't have gotten up to the apartment that quickly.*

Either they were already on their way here for some other reason, or they're stationed in this building.

She was halfway between the seventh and sixth floors when two more soldiers appeared on the stairs below her. Roz almost stumbled and had to grab on to the rail to steady herself.

The stairwell below had been empty: The men had materialized out of thin air.

Roz barely had time to say, "How did—?" before the two men fired. A long red-tipped dart slammed into her neck, another hit her stomach, and her whole body was wracked with pain. She lost control of her limbs and toppled forward. The last thing she saw was one of the men reaching out to catch her.

James Klaus knew that Faith didn't believe anything was wrong with the world, aside from his sudden—from her point of view—appearance at the farm.

Everything he'd brought with him—including his costume—was gone. His room looked as though it hadn't been used in months. All he had left were the clothes he was wearing, his skateboard, and the gloves he'd made.

He'd spent an hour flicking through the old newspapers in the recycling bin, and was now certain that he had somehow been pulled into a parallel world. He made Faith promise not to say anything to his father. "Just pretend I wasn't even here," he'd told her. "It's better for everyone, OK?"

Now he was skating along the winding country roads, almost forty miles from his hometown of Midway, but determined to get there as quickly as possible.

He had considered asking Faith if he could borrow her car, but his father would have noticed it was missing. He'd told Faith he'd walk to Smithfield and take the bus from there to Midway, but she'd told him there were no more buses. "Midway's in a different Habzone. You can't travel from one Habitation Zone to another without a valid permit."

"Then I'll hitch a lift or something."

"You can't. I just told you—travel is restricted. For everyone."

The information James had gathered from the newspapers and from Faith was more than a little disturbing.

Krodin was alive and well.

The Fifth King had appeared seemingly out of nowhere about five years earlier and—somehow—had worked his way into a position of power. He was now the Chancellor of the United States of America, in charge of the nation's security.

Five years, James thought, *and he's already changed the whole country.*

One of Krodin's earliest acts had been to divert huge amounts of money into renewable energy resources, drastically reduce America's dependency on gasoline, and allow the nation to cut ties with other oil-producing nations.

And then Anchorage was destroyed. Almost the entire state of Alaska was now a radioactive wasteland.

According to the newspaper reports, the elusive super-villain Daedalus had been tracked to Alaska by Krodin and almost every other known superhuman. But Daedalus had triggered a nuclear weapon—only he and Krodin had survived the blast. Many people believed that Daedalus had been working for a terrorist organization, or a foreign power, but no one knew for sure.

With no specific group or country to blame, the president announced that they had no choice but to close the country's borders. International travel was forbidden. The land borders with Mexico and Canada were reinforced by a series of forty-foot-high walls, patrolled at all times by armed guards. Automated monitoring stations scanned the beaches and alerted the coast guard if anything suspicious tried to make land.

Krodin had been given the new position of Chancellor, charged with protecting the nation against any and all threats, foreign and domestic.

Three miles from the farmhouse James crested Ridley's Hill and took a moment to look back over the fields. From here he could see the forty acres north of the farm. This season the fields were supposed to be fallow—and yesterday they had been. Now they were the site of a huge military camp. Between hundreds of rows of identical tents countless soldiers marched in formation.

James focused his hearing, sampling sounds from all areas of the camp. He could hear orders being barked back and forth, soldiers on downtime chatting nervously about the coming campaign in Europe, the constant hum of electric motors.

Everything in the camp—the soldiers' uniforms, the tents, the vehicles, and the flags—all bore the same symbol: a blue eye inside a yellow sun.

Krodin, James thought. *We thought he died. . . . We were sure that not even he could have survived Pyrokine's final blast. We barely survived it ourselves.*

The Helotry used Pyrokine's power to open a wormhole in space and time—a tachyon well, they called it—and pulled Krodin out of his own time, more than four thousand years ago. So Pyrokine's final blast didn't kill Krodin—it somehow sent him back in time about five years. Then he did what he does best: He set out to conquer the world.

And he's succeeding.

CHAPTER 6

ROZ WOKE UP IN DARKNESS, to a gentle rocking sensation. Her body was completely numb and she couldn't speak.

Then a woman's voice said, "Hold still, Rosalyn. . . . This will help you to recover." There was a brief, sharp hiss, and almost instantly she could feel sensation returning to her limbs.

"I can't see," Roz said. She tried to raise her hands toward her head, but something was holding them down.

"Sorry, I had to restrain you so you wouldn't remove the blindfold. One of the side effects of Cataxia is extreme light sensitivity. It'll pass in a few moments, but if direct light were to hit your eyes now, you'd have a splitting headache for the next week."

Roz felt a gloved hand gently patting hers. "I know you feel wretched now, but you'll be OK soon enough. You gave us quite a scare, you know, disappearing like that. We didn't know you could *do* that. I hope you understand that my men were very disoriented after their trip. They wouldn't have fired at you if they'd recognized you."

There was the sound of Velcro straps being opened, then Roz could move her arms and legs. "Who are *you*?"

"Agent Amandine Paquette," the woman said, "chief of the Manhattan Praetorian Division. We've met before, at one of Max's social gatherings. We spoke for only a couple of minutes."

"I need to see him!"

"We're taking you to him now." Agent Paquette paused. "I have to ask . . . Your teleportation . . . Was it deliberate?"

"Uh, no. I don't know how it happened. Never happened before."

"That's what we thought. Max said the same thing. He was with the development team in Louisiana when he suddenly just disappeared and reappeared here in Manhattan. Either it's an incredible coincidence or the machine itself triggered a latent ability in both of you. Close your eyes. I'm going to remove the blindfold."

Roz felt the thick cloth being removed from her face, then the woman said, "All right, you should be fine now. You can open your eyes."

Roz winced at the sudden burst of light, and it took her a couple of seconds before the jumble of blurry images coalesced into one. She was inside some sort of gently swaying vehicle, lying on her back, and a young woman in a black uniform was standing over her.

"Now do you recognize me?" Agent Paquette asked.

Roz wanted to tell the agent that they'd met dozens of times. Paquette was practically her brother's girlfriend. *Can't say that*, Roz thought. *Whatever's going on here, I can't let her know how much things have changed.* Roz nodded. "Yes, of course. Mandy, isn't it?"

The agent smiled. "No one's called me that in *years*. How are you feeling? Any nausea? Dizziness? Do you think you might need to throw up?"

"No, I'm OK, I think." Roz sat up, stretched to pull the stiffness out of her limbs. "Max is all right?"

"So I'm told. Teleported all the way from Louisiana to Manhattan. That I can understand, sort of. But you . . . That's a complete mystery, Rosalyn. There's no reason it should have happened to you too. We'll need to run an investigation into this." She inhaled deeply and let it out slowly. "The Chancellor's going to want a *full* report."

"The Chancellor?"

Agent Paquette nodded. "He was very concerned, but I can understand his reaction—I know how close he is to your family."

"I'm sorry, maybe it's a side effect of the knockout drug, but I don't know what you mean."

"He's your brother's best friend, Rosalyn." She reached out and placed her hand on Roz's forehead. "Your temperature seems normal. . . . You're sure you're not feeling sick?"

Roz gently pushed the agent's hand away. "I'm OK. Just tell me about the Chancellor."

"He and Max worked together. . . . You *know* this, Rosalyn! They reconstructed the government, set up the country's defenses. If it wasn't for them, America would have fallen to its enemies a long time ago. But we're prospering now, we're stronger than we've been in a hundred years. And it's all thanks to your brother and Chancellor Krodin."

The name struck Roz like an electric shock. She collapsed to the floor, her stomach heaving. Clear bile spilled from her mouth. Then she felt Agent Paquette's hand patting her gently on the shoulder, heard the woman's voice say, "You're OK, Rosalyn. You'll be fine. It's just the Cataxia. The Chancellor's going to want to see you himself, I think. You know how fond he is of you and your brothers. You're practically the only family he has."

Lance spent the next hour wandering through the house, looking at things, picking them up and putting them down again. He knew that his parents thought there was something wrong with him, but he didn't care. Somehow they were alive again.

And so was Krodin.

The past has been changed. At first, he thought that perhaps Pyrokine's blast had sent Krodin back to his own time, but he quickly realized that couldn't be the case: If Krodin had ruled for a further four-and-a-half-thousand years, the world would be a lot different. As it was, the differences—so far— were relatively small.

On the sitting-room shelves he found a few books and movies he'd never seen before, none of which were more than five years old.

In his bedroom, Lance flicked through his schoolbooks. It appeared that in this world he was a more conscientious student than he had been back home: His notebooks showed that he had made considerable effort to complete the work. They also showed a reasonably high level of concentration—for the most part his notes were neat and concise. Lance was more used to seeing his notebooks filled with barely coherent notes and hundreds of half-finished doodles.

His social studies textbook was the most unsettling. There was a whole chapter on Krodin's rise to power, and it was heavily biased toward presenting the Chancellor as a loyal citizen who wanted nothing more than to see his country "reclaim its rightful place in the world."

The photos of Krodin showed a tall, well-built man wearing an ordinary black suit. His hair had been cut short, and his beard neatly trimmed. But his eyes were the same: they had a look of dark animal cunning and strength.

So Krodin was sent back in time five or six years. Without anyone to stand against him, he worked his way into a position of power. Or maybe he just fought *his way to the top.*

Lance realized that his mother was calling him. "Coming!"

He went down to the kitchen, where he found his parents giving him the "now you're in trouble" look.

"So you lied to us," his father said. "Again. There was no fire drill. Your principal just phoned. You didn't show up for chemistry. And they found your backpack just lying in the middle of the corridor. So what happened?"

"I think I have that bug that's been going around." Lance felt that he was probably on safe ground with that excuse: There was *always* a bug going around. "I didn't want to say anything because I *knew* you wouldn't believe me."

"You don't look sick," his mother said, her eyes narrow with suspicion. "What are your symptoms?"

"I feel a bit queasy. Kinda dizzy too. I didn't mean to leave school—I just wanted to get some fresh air. Then I couldn't face going back in so I came home."

His father said, "So you just *walked* home? How'd you get out of the school? No, don't tell me—I don't think I want to know. Look, you can't do things like that, Lance." He held up his hand with his thumb and index finger about an inch apart. "As it is you're *this* close to getting conscripted! Or don't you remember what happened last month? They would have taken you right then if you hadn't promised to keep your head down and really put the work in."

Lance didn't like the sound of that. "OK. I'll go back. I do feel a little better now anyway."

His mother removed a small booklet from the cupboard next to the fridge, flipped open the cover, and began to fill in a form. "You have to go straight to the principal's office," she said. "Apologize for walking out and tell them whatever they need to hear to make sure they don't report you." She tore off the top sheet and handed it to him.

Lance took a quick look at the form before he folded it and stuffed it into his pocket. It was titled "Emergency Curfew Violation." His mother had signed and dated it, and in the section marked "Reason for Violation" she had written "Unexpected illness (temporary)."

What is going on in this place? Lance wondered. *Conscription, curfews, America on the edge of war? What mad universe is this?*

As he turned to leave, something on the television caught his attention. He walked over to it and turned up the sound.

"Lance!" his mother warned.

"Yeah, hold on a second. . . . I have to see this."

On the screen was a grainy photograph of a blue-skinned man who was more than twice the height of an ordinary human. The newscaster's voice was saying, ". . . reports that the creature somehow appeared in the middle of the prison's main building. The Oak Grove prison is not equipped to deal with superhuman prisoners, and the guards were unable to prevent the creature from smashing its way through the walls and escaping into the countryside."

So it's not just me, Lance thought. *The same thing happened to Brawn. And we're both connected to Krodin. Maybe it happened to all of us.*

He turned to face his parents. "Sorry. We're doing a report on the superhumans in school. Anyway. I'd better get going."

When he reached the kitchen door, he turned back. "Dad? How far is Oak Grove from here?"

Abby had spent the past hour listening to Solomon Cord spinning lies to her mother about who he was and what he was doing in Midway. Cord had told her he was Jason Myers, an inspector for the school board. "If you are talking to anyone from Abigail's school," he'd told her, "please don't mention I was here. Fact is I'm also checking up on them. If you don't mind, I'd like to ask *you* some questions."

At first Mrs. de Luyando had been only too happy to answer anything Cord asked, and by careful manipulation he was able to build a better picture of how the world had changed. But now she was becoming suspicious. "Are you investigating me too, is that it, Mr. Myers?"

"Not at all. No, I just have a few questions, nothing too personal. So, Vienna is the eldest, then Abigail, then . . . ?"

"Tyler and James, they're eight. Twins. And then Stefan and Elvis. They're seven. Also twins."

Cord smiled. "Two sets of twins? Must be quite a handful!"

"At times, yes." Mrs. de Luyando didn't return the smile.

She's not buying this, Abby thought.

"And their father . . . ?" Cord asked.

"He's gone, Mr. Myers. I'm sure that's all in your files. He had an affair and I threw him out. Does that answer your question?"

Whoa . . . Abby sat back. *Dad had an affair? She never told me that!*

"Has he been providing any form of regular child supp—"

The phone rang and Abby jumped up. "I'll get it!" She raced out to the hall and picked up the handset. "Hello?"

A man's voice said, "Abigail de Luyando?"

"Who's calling?"

"Just tell me—are you Abigail de Luyando?"

"Who wants to know?"

"This is Max. The real Max. Do you understand what I mean?"

"Yeah, I think I do. So it happened to you too?"

There was a sigh of relief. "The whole world has changed, and from what I can tell, the only ones who know about it are you, me, Roz, Paragon, and Brawn. Roz is being brought to me now. It's likely that the same thing has happened to Thunder and Lance McKendrick. Thunder lives near you, right?"

"A couple of miles away. But I don't know the exact address, or his real name."

"That doesn't matter. If you get close enough to him, he'll

hear you calling him. Take Paragon and go find him, then the three of you find somewhere safe and keep out of sight. Roz and I will figure out a way to get to you."

"What about Brawn and Lance?"

"Brawn could be a problem. He's gone to ground, but it won't be long before they catch him. As for Lance . . . Last I heard he'd also gone on the run. We've no way of knowing where he was when the change happened. And he's not a superhuman, Abby. We don't have the time to go hunting for him."

"But he—"

Dalton interrupted her. "Cord was supposed to be meeting you today. Is he still there?"

"Yeah, he's here."

"Get him."

"OK, but—"

"Just do what you're told, Abby!" Max roared. "Get him on the phone right *now*!"

James Klaus was still more than thirty miles from Midway when he was spotted by an army patrol.

As he traveled, he'd been using his powers to listen to the patrols. So far, he'd managed to avoid being seen by taking detours and hiding when necessary, but this time he was out of luck.

From what he had overheard, in this world traffic control was stricter than he'd ever imagined. Unless it was absolutely unavoidable, almost no one was allowed to use the highways or other national roads at night or between nine in the morning and five in the evening. This was supposed to be a security measure: The entire country was permanently in a state of high alert.

He was on a long straight stretch of road—a road he didn't remember ever seeing before on his many trips to the farm—when he heard a vehicle coming up from behind. It was still two miles behind him, but the new road offered no cover on either side, and its slight downward slope didn't give him much of a boost on the skateboard.

As the vehicle neared, he could hear the voices of the men inside:

"Satellites spotted him six minutes ago, heading south. Scanned and transmitted the biometrics back to Central. They're backed up right now, but ten'll get you one that the kid doesn't have authorization to be out."

"Farmhand, maybe?" another voice asked.

"On a *skateboard*? Unlikely. You want to apprehend him?"

A third voice, deeper and older: "What do we have him on?"

"We've definitely got him on Habzone breach and unauthorized mode of transport, Captain. If he's been within six miles of the base, we might be able to get him on attempted infiltration of a military installation."

The captain said, "Hmm. Identity?"

"It's just coming through. . . . OK, biometrics give a ninety-six percent probability that he's James Percival Klaus, age sixteen. Listed residence is eighty-seven Maple Towers, Midway. No known dissident connections. Son of Shawna Quillan Klaus, adopted son of Rufus Kenneth Halliburton. One half sister, Shiho, age seven."

"What's he doing out here on a school day?"

"According to school records he was logged in this morning along with the rest of the students. No idea how he ended up this far away. . . . *Here's* something. His birth father is Darrien Tobias Klaus. Original owner of the land now occupied by the base."

There was a pause, and then the captain said, "All right. I'm thinking we haven't seen a Habzone breach like this in a long time. . . . Could be a diversion—I wouldn't put it past Daedalus to use a kid. Contact Central. Tell them we need flyers—Skimmers and Jetmen should do it. Full-blanket coverage, twenty-mile radius of the base. They spot anything else unusual, they're to go in with all guns blazing. We've had enough weird stuff happening already today. Maximum speed. Let's see whether Klaus runs or surrenders."

James cursed himself for not sticking to the back roads. *All right, then. They know who I am, but they don't know what I can do. There's no way I can outrun them. And I'm sure not going to surrender.*

He concentrated on the sound generated by the patrol vehicle's engine, modified it, and sent it back with an underlying grinding noise.

"What the heck is *that*?" the captain asked.

"Uh, sounds like we've stripped a bearing, Captain."

"Any change in our speed?"

"No, sir."

"Keep on him."

Rats! James thought. *I was sure that would work. OK, try this for size.*

He generated a sphere of silence around the vehicle: Now, no matter how much noise they made, they wouldn't be able to hear each other. One disadvantage was that James could no longer hear the vehicle's engines—he could only hope that the disorientation was slowing them down.

There's no way I can outrun them—nowhere to hide.

What I wouldn't give for a jetpack like Paragon's right now, James thought. *Dumb sound-control powers! Why couldn't I have gotten flight or super-speed or something more useful?*

I could blast their truck with sound waves—that might work.

Then he grinned. *Or I could just generate shock waves right behind me, use them to push me along.*

He crouched low on the skateboard, then concentrated, triggered a powerful shock wave in the air right behind him.

The force hit him like a sudden gust of wind, so strong it almost knocked him off the board. He crouched lower and gripped the edges, and tried again. There was another brief surge of speed. He followed it with two shock waves in quick succession.

Yes! Who needs a jetpack when you've got superpowers?

He let loose a steady burst of shock waves, and within seconds the skateboard was hurtling along the road at a speed far greater than its manufacturers had ever anticipated.

This must be what it feels like for Paragon, James thought.

For a moment he considered dropping the cocoon of silence from the pursuing vehicle, just to hear what they were saying about him, but realized that it was better to leave them confused and panicking.

So who's this Daedalus guy they mentioned? A superhuman?

And if Krodin only reappeared a few years ago, what happened to all the other superhumans?

CHAPTER 7

SIX YEARS ago . . .

Krodin watched from the shelter of an abandoned store doorway as a terrified woman darted across the rain-slicked street followed by two cruel-looking young men. The sobbing woman passed Krodin without noticing him, heading for the entrance of the nearby dark alley, reaching it only a few seconds before her pursuers.

A few minutes later Krodin heard her screams. Then—less than a minute after that—the two men emerged from the alley, one of them tossing the woman's now-empty pocketbook into the gutter as he handed his companion a share of the takings.

Krodin had arrived in Detroit a week ago. This was the tenth major city he had visited in the four months since his arrival in America, and he was quickly reaching the conclusion that the people of this era were considerably less sophisticated than those of his own time, forty-five centuries in the past.

They are reckless, lawless. . . . They lack guidance and discipline. Above all, they lack control.

The gleeful men boldly strode past the doorway, and one of them noticed Krodin. He flipped his long, rain-drenched hair away from his face. "Wotchoo lookin' at, freak?"

Krodin ignored him. *Their concept of democracy is flawed. Their leaders spend all their time in office either trying not to offend anyone or working only to secure their next term. And all the while the nation is stumbling along behind them. If the humans cannot understand that, then their race is doomed.*

The young man's friend stopped, came back to stand behind him.

"I aksed you, freak, wotchoo lookin' at?"

Krodin tilted his head to the side as he examined the young man. He was thin, shorter than Krodin, but had a wild look in his eyes. *He cannot honestly want to fight me*, Krodin thought. *He has no reason to believe I'm a threat to him.*

The young man's friend said, "Ferget 'im, Gino. Lookit this guy—he smells like he lives in a Dumpster."

Gino's eyes narrowed as a sly grin spread across his face. "Nah, I don't like the way he's eyeballin' me. He thinks I'm scum. You think I'm scum, doncha, freakoid?"

Krodin considered this. "Yes."

Gino faltered, and Krodin knew that the man had been expecting fear, or passionate denial. Anything but agreement.

"What?"

"I think you and your friends are scum. In a world of greedy, small-minded, cruel humans, you are surely among the lowest. You are utterly worthless. You bring nothing of value to this world. When you are dead, the quality of the human race will rise by a considerable amount."

Gino's left arm flashed out, as Krodin knew it would. But the four-inch blade in his hand didn't reach its target.

Krodin locked his right hand around the man's wrist, planted his left against his chest, and pulled.

As Gino lay screaming on the ground and his friend raced away into the night, Krodin thought, *I have seen enough. If the human race is incapable of saving itself, then it falls to me to take control.*

After the attack by Pyrokine, when his enemies seemed to disappear, Krodin had simply walked away from the suddenly empty field and located the nearest settlement, a town called Windfield. Despite his being unclothed from the waist up, and barefoot, few of the town's inhabitants had given him more than a cursory glance as he strolled its streets listening to their conversations and learning more of their language.

For weeks, he had no idea what had happened to him, until he found a local newspaper that featured a drawing of a nuclear power plant that was scheduled to begin construction: It was the same building in which he had materialized after Slaughter and Pyrokine took him from his own time. Then, construction on the power plant had almost been complete. But according to the newspaper's accompanying article, it was expected to be completed in six years.

Krodin knew then that he had traveled to the past—to a time when most of his attackers were only young children.

He didn't know their names, or how to find them, but he remembered their faces.

But there was one he did know, a young man he would never forget. The man had somehow linked his mind with Krodin's, tried to control him. For a while it had worked, but Krodin's defenses had adapted to the attack.

In this time he doesn't know who I am. But if he truly does *possess the power to control men's minds, then I can use him.*

Krodin tossed Gino's severed left arm into the gutter as casually as Gino had thrown away the woman's pocketbook, then stepped out of the doorway and into the rain.

As he passed the mouth of the alley, he saw the woman lying on the ground. Her face and hands were cut and bruised, her clothing torn to shreds.

She opened one bloodshot eye, stared at him. "Help . . ." Her voice was coarse, barely a whisper. "Please, help me!"

Krodin puzzled over this for a moment. "Why?" He turned away and resumed walking.

CHAPTER 8

WHEN ROZ HAD RECOVERED from the effects of Cataxia—the knockout drug contained in the darts—she was able to get her first good look at the vehicle in which she was being carried.

She had already guessed from the gentle swaying and dipping and the constant speed that it was flying. It seemed to be a larger version of the construction craft she'd seen working on the strange towering building in Central Park.

At the front of the craft two men were clearly pilots; the remaining four soldiers—three men and Agent Paquette—didn't seem to have any part in controlling the vehicle.

"Feeling any better?" Agent Paquette asked.

"A bit. You said something about Max?"

The woman nodded. "He disappeared from the facility in Louisiana at the same time you materialized in that couple's apartment. And you weren't the only ones. The project's controller disappeared along with your brother—we still haven't found him. And one of the monsters . . . Well, I know it sounds crazy because they should all be dead, but one of them suddenly appeared in the middle of a prison."

Roz was finding it tough to take all this in at once. *One of the monsters? She said that as though I'm supposed to know what it means.* "Is Max OK?"

"I believe so. Rosalyn, the Chancellor's taking a direct interest in this phenomenon. He was with the team in Louisiana. The system seems to have worked perfectly— more than once, obviously—but if what happened to you and your brother is connected, then clearly *something* went wrong. Max was right there when it happened, so maybe that could be explained away as some sort of fluctuation in the energy field, but why would it affect you?"

None of this makes sense! "And the, uh, the monster?"

"Well, obviously *he's* superhuman."

"I know, but who is he? Is there any connection between him and the rest of us?"

Agent Paquette shrugged. "It doesn't seem likely. Almost all of the creatures died in Anchorage with the rest of them. Or that's what we believed until today, when this one suddenly showed up. He's about thirteen feet tall, hairless, blue skin. Immensely strong and very fast."

"Brawn!" Roz said.

"He certainly has that, and more. The guards shot at him a dozen times—didn't even slow him down. None of the other monsters have reappeared, as far as we know. A blessing, really. You've heard about the one who dripped acid?" She shuddered. "I saw him once—he was ugly as sin and vicious with it."

So that's what she means by monsters—superhumans whose powers have brought on a physical change. "The man who runs the project . . . I don't think I've met him either."

"No, you wouldn't have. They keep him locked away. For his own safety more than anything else. He's not quite one of us, but he's got a remarkable brain." Agent Paquette swept her arm in a gesture to take in the craft in which they were flying. "We wouldn't have any of this if it hadn't been for him. There has to be *some* connection between him and the rest of you."

One of the pilots called, "Thirty seconds, ma'am."

"Good. One more question before we land, Rosalyn. . . . At the apartment the Praetorians didn't recognize you, which is understandable given what they went through. But why did you attack them? Why did you run? Surely you knew you weren't in any danger."

Uh-oh, Roz thought. "I wasn't thinking clearly. I hope I didn't hurt any of them."

"No, but they're being shipped back to boot camp for retraining. They made some dumb mistakes. Obviously they were rookies—we weren't about to risk sending experienced troops through." She smiled. "But the important thing is that it worked, right?"

Roz returned the smile. "Absolutely. Today's a good day."

The hum from the flying craft's engines began to increase in volume. Then there was a slight bump and Agent Paquette opened a hatch in the side.

As Roz followed Agent Paquette out of the craft, a voice inside her head said, "Roz, say nothing. Just act like you've seen it all before."

Max?

"Just keep calm, Roz. We've got to get away from here as soon as possible, but we won't be able to do that if they suspect we're not who they think we are."

They had landed on a flat concrete expanse ringed by a large structure that was in the process of being constructed—or demolished. Hundred-foot-high metal beams protruded from the ground, many connected to each other by heavy crossbeams. To Roz it had the appearance of an enormous steel Stonehenge.

The agent led Roz—trailed by the three other soldiers—toward a low black-painted building at the north end. She glanced back at the craft: It was roughly rectangular, perhaps fifteen feet high, twice as wide, three times as long, painted a dark military green.

Beyond the craft were three others, identical except for the numbers stenciled on the sides.

"They're called Raptors," Max's voice said. "I have no idea how they work—it's a propulsion system like nothing we've ever seen. I think it might be something to do with the white lights on the underside, but I won't be able to tell for sure until I can pick the brains of someone who knows more about them."

Roz thought, *Max, where's Josh?*

"He's safe, back home in Manhattan. We have to find a way to get him out of the city without drawing too much attention. I've been in touch with Paragon and Abby—they were dragged over to this world too. They're in Midway right now."

Roz hurried to catch up with Agent Paquette, and Max's voice said, "So Impervia's still around. . . . Aside from those of us who crossed over, she and Brawn are the only other superhumans I'm sure are still here."

Yeah, but what happened to the others? And there's something familiar about this place. Where are we?

"East Rutherford, New Jersey," Max's voice replied. "This used to be a stadium, the home of the New York Giants. Apparently football has been outlawed in this world—along with every other form of mass gathering. So many people in one location is considered a major security risk. Roz, I'm going to tell you something and I want you to remain calm, got it?"

OK. Ahead, Roz could see a door opening in the black building. Her brother walked out, flanked by two soldiers.

"On the way here I was contacted by a man with the code name Daedalus. A superhuman, I think. He's working with the resistance and they've got spies everywhere. He says that almost every other country in the world is terrified that Krodin is going to start expanding his empire. They've banded together and formed what they call Unity."

So they can help defend each other? Roz asked.

"No. So they can perform a preemptive strike. They're planning to attack America before Krodin attacks them."

Roz felt the bile rush to her throat again, and had to clap her hands over her mouth so she wouldn't throw up. *No . . . That's crazy! Millions of people would be killed!*

They had almost reached Max now. Inside Roz's head, his

voice said, "That's why we've got to get to safety. We'll talk more later. Just remember what I said, OK? Stay calm. You don't know anything about this."

Agent Paquette stopped in front of Max and saluted.

Max nodded. "Agent Paquette."

She arched an eyebrow. "So formal, Vice-Chancellor Dalton?"

"We *are* on duty," Max said, smiling. He nodded toward Roz. "See you found my sister. Walk with me, Amanda. We need to start putting this together. Figure out what happened."

How can he be so casual about everything? Roz wondered. She followed Max and Agent Paquette into the black building—this close, she could see that it wasn't painted at all: Its entire surface seemed to be covered in three-inch-square black panels.

"Some type of photovoltaic cells," Max's voice said. "Supposed to be close to one hundred percent efficient—that's way better than anything we have back in our world. If we ever get back, I'm taking all this technology with us."

Max, we have to do something! We can't just—

Max looked at her, and thought, "Roz. Let it go."

She took a deep breath, held it for a second, then let it out slowly. *OK,* she said to herself. *We're not in any immediate danger. We play this game until we see a chance to get away.*

Inside the black building was a wide stairwell leading down. Max chatted to Agent Paquette as they descended, and Roz knew from experience that Max was probing the agent's mind, asking key questions to bring specific memories to the surface.

The steps led down to what appeared to be a long, wide

corridor—but as they reached the bottom, Roz realized it was a single large room.

Roz swallowed. *Oh wow . . .*

The room was almost the size of the disused football field above. Hundreds of technicians were working at large benches, assembling countless suits of polished steel armor. The suits were bristling with powerful-looking weapons, and many of them were being fitted with large jetpacks on the back.

Agent Paquette noticed Roz's reaction. "You haven't been here before, have you? This is the first proper phase of the Jetman project. The prototypes have been a tremendous success. If we're going to have any chance of stopping Daedalus, this is it. The factory in Minnesota has just shipped the rest of the pieces. There are still a few bugs to iron out of the system, but we already have Jetmen accompanying patrols in sensitive areas."

Max exchanged a quick glance with Roz, then, to Agent Paquette, said, "This is how we're going to win the war against Unity."

"We have eight hundred here, another ten thousand ready to go into production for phase three."

"Very impressive to see them all in one go," Max said. "What do you think, Roz?"

"I, uh . . ." She forced a smile and walked over to the closest bench. "Any chance of getting one of these jetpacks for myself?"

Inside Roz's head, Max said, "Now we know how this universe's version of Paragon has been keeping himself busy."

Lance McKendrick didn't know what else to do: He went to school.

It's not fair—it's summer break! I shouldn't have to go to school. And what's with the note? A permission slip to be allowed out on the street . . . How could the world have turned into this?

When he'd left the house, he had been surprised by how quiet everything was. There were no pedestrians and there was almost no traffic. Cameras were everywhere, on lampposts, attached to the eaves of houses and stores, strung on thick cables across the streets. *You wouldn't want to scratch your butt in public,* Lance thought.

On the next block he passed the small drugstore where he bought his comics on Wednesday evenings—it was closed. Even the twenty-four-hour laundry next door had its shutters down.

A humming noise approached Lance from behind, and he turned to see a black-uniformed man heading toward him on what he first took to be a motorbike. But as the man reached him, Lance saw that the vehicle didn't have wheels. Instead, it hovered over the ground at a height of about four inches.

Oh man, I want one of those!

The officer was wearing thick black leathers, a helmet that would have looked more at home on a fighter pilot, and slim dark glasses.

"Papers," the man said, his voice laced with boredom.

Lance handed over the permission slip.

The officer glanced at it, handed it back. "Unexpected illness?"

"Felt a bit sick," Lance said. "I'm over it now, though." He slapped his hands together and in a cheery voice said, "Eager to get back to school and hit the books."

The officer stared at him, unmoving.

Not exactly a world-class party animal, are you? Lance thought. "Uh . . . Is that it?"

"Name?"

"Lance McKendrick. Like it says on the permission slip."

"School?"

"Martin Van Buren High."

Another long pause, then the officer beckoned Lance forward with his black-gloved hand. "Get on the back. I'll take you there."

Lance pointed in the direction he'd been walking. "Thanks, but I'm OK. It's not too far, and I could do with the fresh air. You know—blow away the cobwebs."

Through gritted teeth, the man said, "Get on. That was not a request."

Lance walked around to the back of the flying bike—there was just enough room behind the officer for him to sit. He swung one leg over the seat. "What do I hold on to?"

"Grips under your thighs."

Lance looked down—metal rods had sprung from the sides of the craft. He grabbed hold of them.

The bike surged away from the sidewalk, then cut straight across the street and through a junction without slowing. With so little traffic on the road there didn't seem to be much need for the officer to follow the traffic rules.

Lance felt that he should say something. It didn't always work, but sometimes cops went easy on you if you pretended to be interested in police work. "So, how long have you been—"

The officer interrupted him. "Do not speak to the driver."

"Gotcha. Sorry."

Two minutes later the officer steered the bike through the gateway of Martin Van Buren High School. Lance was intrigued that security was much heavier than back in his own world. There, the school had gates that were locked during the school day to prevent any undesirables from getting in— or getting out—but in this world there was a manned gatepost that reminded Lance of something out of a war movie.

The three guards at the gate nodded to the officer and allowed him to pass through. The officer rode the bike straight up the steps and stopped outside the door. "Get off."

Lance climbed down and was a little surprised to see that the officer did the same. *Aw no . . . He's going to walk me right to the classroom!* "Thanks for the lift."

"Stop. Where do you think you're going?"

"To class?"

The officer pulled off his shades as he entered the lobby. He looked at Lance as though he'd never met anyone so dumb. "You have to be signed back in."

Lance made a big show of slapping his forehead with his palm. "Right, right. Of course."

He followed the officer along the corridor. *So what do I do if there's another me here? The news said that Brawn suddenly appeared in Oak Grove Prison—but that's where he was back in the real world. If this is a parallel world, then what happened to the other Brawn, and the other me?*

The officer pushed open the door to the principal's office and walked in without knocking.

Mrs. Mailer was sitting behind her desk. She was in her sixties, a good-natured woman who had always been far too lenient toward Lance's occasional habit of skipping classes or completely forgetting to come to school.

"Truant student. Lance McKendrick. Claims illness. Has permission slip signed by parents. On his way here when I picked him up."

Mrs. Mailer frowned at Lance, then turned back to the officer. "Hmm."

"Problem?" the officer asked.

The principal tutted. "Well, first of all the school day is almost over. You might as well have just taken him home. But more important than that: I *know* you, Eugene Ashton. Don't think I don't remember you coming to me in tears when you were thirteen because you had a crush on Sherrie Stanneck and she called you zit-face in front of your friends. You might be an officer of the law now, but that does *not* give you the right to be rude to me."

Lance hid his grin by pretending to scratch his nose. *You tell him, Mrs. Mailer!*

"And furthermore, you do *not* walk into my school and barge into my office without knocking. Do you understand me?"

The officer swallowed. "Ma'am, I have a task to perform and—"

"Do you think I don't know that? It wasn't so long ago that we had *real* police officers in this city. Men and women who were interested in helping people, not keeping them down. They weren't power-mad little upstarts like you, Mr. Ashton." She sighed. "And you showed so much promise."

"Criticism of an officer of the law is tantamount to—"

Again, she interrupted him. "Are those jackboots you're wearing, Ashton? Because the way you people push everyone around seems an awful lot like fascism to me. The state should work for the benefit of the people, not the other way around. Or is *that* sedition too, hmm? Are you going to report me as a possible dissident and have me dragged away to one of your death camps? Now you can just turn around and frog-march your way back out of here, young man. And next time show a little common courtesy. I know for a fact that your parents taught you basic manners, so use them."

Well said, Lance thought. *Always knew the old bat had guts.*

As Officer Ashton turned to leave, Mrs. Mailer said, "Oh, and you can take this boy with you. He's not one of ours."

"Ma'am?"

"I don't know what he told you, but he doesn't go to school here."

At five in the evening, Mrs. de Luyando left the apartment to meet Abby's brothers off the school bus.

As soon as she was gone, Solomon Cord said, "All right. Let's go."

"We should have left ages ago," Abby said. "Max Dalton told us to go find Thunder."

Cord tossed her the morning newspaper as he moved toward the door. "Top of page one, above the masthead. Today's curfew times are listed. Civilians are allowed out on the street between five and seven."

"The people in this world are insane! How can they just sit back and take all this?"

Cord stopped with his hand on the doorknob. "It doesn't happen overnight. At first the changes are presented as being for the greater good. What's a little restriction in freedom compared with better security? This is how all the best dictatorships happen. It starts out with stricter border controls, then security cameras in all major population centers. Mandatory ID cards, then DNA logging, restricted areas, food rationing . . . And piece by piece everyone's freedom is eroded. By the time the average person realizes that the whole country has been turned into a prison, it's too late to do anything about it."

Abby pursed her lips. "Sol . . . How are we going to get back to *our* world?"

"I don't know. If this is a parallel universe, then maybe we can use whatever brought us over to send us back. But if it's not . . . If the past has been changed and for whatever reason we're still aware of how things should be . . . then maybe there is no going back. This *is* the real world."

"I don't know if I can live in a place like this."

"Then we have to change things. Max said he's heard that Unity are planning a major strike against Krodin. He doesn't know many of the details yet, but it's going to be big, and it'll happen soon."

Abby grabbed her bow and quiver from behind the sofa. "How soon?"

"Within the next couple of days. Krodin's armies are almost ready, and he's apparently got something in Louisiana that'll guarantee his success. Unity wants to hit him before he hits them. So we don't have a lot of time. Max is going to do whatever he can to get us all to safety before it happens." Cord opened the door. "So where does Thunder live?"

"Maple Towers. A couple of miles outside town."

Even before they reached the street, Abby knew it was going to look a lot different now that the curfew had been temporarily lifted, but the scene was far from anything she could have expected.

They stopped in the doorway. "This is unbelievable," Cord muttered.

The people on the street—hundreds, perhaps thousands of them—were all moving at the same brisk pace, almost in single file. Those walking north kept to the outside of the pavement, and those heading south stayed on the inside.

Standing on almost every corner was at least one armed guard, constantly watching the people. Each one wore The Helotry's insignia on the shoulders of their uniforms: a blue eye inside a yellow sun.

Occasionally someone would break out of the line to enter an apartment building, or to join another line. A bus stopped three doors away, and children and teenagers in identical school uniforms filed out. As soon as the last one dismounted, the people at the bus stop climbed on, one by one. It was all done in complete silence, the only sound being the tramp of footsteps and the low hum from the bus's electric engine.

"Let's go," Cord whispered. "You lead. Keep your head down and look like you belong here."

Abby slung the bow and quiver onto her shoulder and stepped into a small gap in the line. Cord followed immediately.

When they reached the junction with Jarvis Avenue, the

line broke up: Some people continued north across the street, others went right or left. Abby joined the line going left.

There were far fewer people going in this direction, so Abby looked back over her shoulder toward Cord. "They're like sheep," she whispered. "Very well-behaved sheep."

She jumped when a voice boomed out from above. "No talking!"

She risked a quick glance upward, and saw that there were now at least half a dozen of the surveillance cameras aimed at her, slowly moving to track her path.

Ahead, a small, squat, army-green vehicle glided silently around the corner, heading toward her. The craft was floating a yard above the ground.

It came alongside Abby and slowed to a stop.

Behind her Cord whispered, "Don't look at it. We're not doing anything wrong."

The hovering vehicle reversed its direction, keeping pace with them.

Oh man . . .

There was a sharp hiss as a hatch opened in the side. A black-clad man climbed out and walked straight over to Abby.

"You. Step out of the line. Now." His voice was stern and gruff.

"I'm just . . ."

He grabbed Abby's arm and pulled her onto the street. "Disobedience. Potential civil unrest." He peered at the bow and quiver on her shoulder. "Unauthorized equipment. Let's see your ID."

"I don't have it with me," Abby said. She glanced back at Solomon Cord—he was continuing on his way.

"That so? That's four demerits right there. I'm taking you in." He tugged at her arm again.

This time, Abby didn't allow herself to be moved. "You're not taking me anywhere."

The man stepped back, his hand lightly resting on the grip of a sidearm holstered on his hip. "By order of directive 8772 I'm instructed to allow you five seconds to comply. One."

Abby shrugged. The bow and quiver slid from her right shoulder and landed in the crook of her elbow.

The man frowned at this. "Two."

Abby unclipped the bow from the quiver, took hold of the grip in her left hand. At the same time she straightened her right arm and allowed the quiver to slide the rest of the way— as it passed her hand, she snagged one of the arrows with her fingers.

"Three."

Abby hit the release switch on the bow's riser and the limbs snapped into place. In one swift moment she nocked the arrow to the string and drew back.

The soldier whipped out his gun and yelled, "Weapon!"

Abby grinned. "Well spotted." The arrow was aimed at the soldier's chest. "Drop your gun."

CHAPTER 9

SOLOMON CORD INWARDLY CURSED as he saw, on the edge of his vision, what was happening with Abby. *Dumb kid's going to get herself killed!*

He followed the line of people around the next corner, then entered the first tenement building. He took the stairs three at a time, stopped on the fourth floor, and looked around. *Need some kind of weapon.*

He knocked on the door of the apartment overlooking the street where he'd left Abby.

It was opened by a young woman in her twenties. "Yes?"

"Random inspection. Need to check your home for violations." He pushed past her and into the apartment. It was almost devoid of furniture. A threadbare carpet, stained and peeling wallpaper, a strong smell of mold and soap.

She followed him. "Wait, who *are* you? You can't just barge in here—"

"Plainclothes division. You think we *all* wear uniforms so you can see us coming? I'll need to see your papers and permits. Now."

The woman hesitated for a moment, then hurried over to a side cabinet and began rummaging through one of the drawers. "I have everything here. I'm not doing anything wrong, I swear. I don't know what you've heard, but it's not true!"

He moved to the window. On the street below, Abby was aiming her bow at the guard. *OK, think! Have to get out there and defuse the situation.*

He turned around and the woman was standing next to him, a large bundle of papers in her hands. "It's all here."

"Sorted by date?"

"Um, no. I didn't know I needed to . . ."

"Do it. Kitchen?"

She nodded toward a closed door. "Through there. Am I in trouble?"

"I think you know the answer to that, don't you?" Cord felt more than a little guilty about treating the woman like this, but he knew he couldn't let his façade slip. If she suspected he wasn't an authority figure, she'd scream for help.

He pushed open the kitchen door and looked around. There was an assortment of mismatched knives tucked into a small, badly made spice rack. He selected the largest knife—it seemed sharp and strong—then returned to the main room.

The woman saw him holding the knife and started trembling, the papers spilling from her hands.

"Are you aware that knives over a certain length are considered deadly weapons and are therefore prohibited?"

"No, I . . . It was a present."

"Indeed. This is confiscated." He moved back to the window again. *Still there.* "If you want to avoid prosecution, ma'am, you have one chance. Tell me the names and apartment numbers of any people in this building whom you know or suspect to be in possession of illegal firearms or other weapons that could be used against officers of the state."

"I don't . . ."

"Very well." He tucked the knife into the back of his belt. "I'm arresting you on the charge of—"

"Apartment 2C! I mean, I don't know for certain, but I overheard them once when I was going past their door. Someone inside was talking about getting hold of some ammunition."

Cord was already moving for the door. "Thank you. Your cooperation will be noted."

He felt like a complete louse as he raced back down the stairs. *If we get through this OK, I'll come back and . . . I don't know. Build her a new spice rack or something.*

The soldier's gun hand was trembling a little, and a film of sweat had appeared on his upper lip. Beyond him Abby could see that there was another soldier inside the flying craft: The muzzle of his gun was protruding from the doorway, aiming at her.

This is probably not the best *idea I've ever had,* Abby thought.

On the sidewalks on either side of the street, the drone-like pedestrians had all stopped moving, but few of them were looking in Abby's direction. She had the distinct feeling that they were all too scared to run for cover.

"Neither of us has to get hurt," Abby said. "Put your gun down. Right now." She shifted her aim to his arm. "If I let this arrow fly, you'll never be able to use that arm again."

From above she heard the faint whine of electric motors as more of the surveillance cameras turned toward her. Then a voice burst forth from the nearest camera: "Unidentified dissident—terminate."

Abby saw the soldier's arm tense—she ducked just as he fired, then released the arrow.

For a moment the man stood there staring at her, a baffled look on his face.

I missed him!

Then his face paled, a thin line of blood ran down his shoulder, and his gun clattered to the ground.

Still crouched, Abby threw herself forward, rolled past him, and snatched up the gun. The second man in the craft jumped out—Abby threw the handgun at him: It slammed into his forehead and knocked him back into the vehicle.

Then she spotted her arrow, buried a foot deep into the side of the vehicle.

She pulled out the arrow—it had passed through the soldier so quickly that it hadn't even picked up any blood— then turned around, grabbed her quiver, and ran.

Cord pounded on the door of apartment 2C. A man's voice from inside called out, "Who is it?"

"There's been an accident—I need your help! Quick!"

The door opened and Cord grabbed hold of the man and shoved him inside the dark apartment, kicking the door closed behind him. "Where's the gun?"

"What?"

Cord spun him around and slammed him against the door. "You heard."

"I don't *have* a gun!"

"You have five seconds. Four. Three. Two. One."

"I swear I don't have a gun! I'm scared of guns—I wouldn't go near one!"

"We have it on good authority that you are in possession of an illegal—"

There was a sharp click from behind him.

The man said, "Oh, you mean *that* gun?"

Agent Paquette accompanied Max and Roz Dalton on the craft back to Manhattan. Roz had said almost nothing since her first look at the Jetman project, but now, as the Raptor flew over North Hudson Park heading for Manhattan, the agent seemed to remember that Roz was there.

"So, Rosalyn, how are you finding the training?"

Training? Roz wondered. Aloud, she said, "It's fine. No real problems so far, I think."

"Good. And the other recruits? Showing any potential?"

Not knowing how else to respond—Max wasn't very forthcoming with his telepathic hints—Roz made a "so-so" gesture with her hand. "You know how it is."

"Of course. But we'll get them up to speed soon enough." She turned to Max. "And the monster hunt?"

Max gave her a slight smile. "I'm sure you can guess my feelings on that particular project."

"You still think some of them could be useful assets?"

"They're not much different from us, Amanda. Physically,

yes, but most of them are smart enough to learn, and I'm sure they'd be only too happy to follow orders in exchange for greater privileges and the illusion of freedom. A sense of purpose is all many of them need."

Inside Roz's head, Max's voice said, "Ask her about the Jetman project—I'm supposed to know everything about it, and I can't keep bluffing. If we can get our hands on some jetpacks, it'll really help us to get away."

Aloud, Roz said, "Agent Paquette? I've been wondering about the Jetmen. . . . What are the criteria for selection?"

"No chance, Rosalyn. They're reconnaissance and front-line troops only. They go in, take out the enemy's major defenses, and we mop up afterward. Projections indicate they'll have a high casualty rate. But they're expendable—we're not. Only ordinary humans are allowed to become Jetmen."

"That makes sense," Roz said. "But still . . . It looks like good armor, and with the jetpacks they can fly. I'd love that. Well, who wouldn't? Those of us who can't fly on our own should *all* get jetpacks—it would make our jobs a lot simpler."

"And that would make us easier targets for the dissidents. We've already lost enough people to those maniacs. And to Daedalus. Fifteen kills in the past ten days," she added, shaking her head. "And we still don't even know where to begin looking for him."

Max thought to Roz: "We need to find this Daedalus guy and get him on our side. Can't ask her about him directly, though. . . . Everyone I've met so far has been afraid of dissidents. It's pretty clear they're rebels who refuse to accept Krodin's rule." Aloud, he said to Agent Paquette, "Right, the dissidents. What's *wrong* with those people? I mean, what do they think they're going to achieve?"

Agent Paquette looked at Max. "What is this? A test?"

"What do you mean?"

"You're acting like we barely know each other. What's going on?"

"Remind me of the rules regarding dissidents, Agent Paquette. As *you* understand them." To Roz, he thought, "We've got her. . . . She's scared, definitely hiding something."

Paquette began to recite: "Number one, any member of the Praetorian Guard caught giving aid to known dissidents will face immediate termination. Rule two—"

Max interrupted her. "You've never broken the first rule?"

"Of course not! Max, what are you getting at?"

"Never allowed a dissident to get away because he was just a kid?"

Agent Paquette's face paled. "How *dare* you! Stay out of my mind, Max! That was . . ." She looked away from him. "He was ten years old, Max. He'd just seen my men arrest his parents for sedition. What was he going to do—start his own resistance cell?"

"Kids grow up, Agent Paquette. Why did you never report this?"

The agent stiffened, her manner instantly becoming formal. "My loyalty has never before been called into question, Vice-Chancellor Dalton. You know that. You're the one who designed the machines that test us every month."

"Correct. And there are some of us who have the ability to manipulate energy. Someone with that power would have little difficulty forcing the testing machines to give a false negative."

"You know *I* don't have any control over energy! You think I'm lying, is that it? Am I under investigation?"

Max sighed and leaned forward in his seat. "Sorry. I had to ask. You know how it is, Amanda—we're *all* under investigation, all the time. After what happened today in Louisiana . . . we can't rule out sabotage. You're chief of the Manhattan Division. Someone with your skills and experience should have tracked down all the dissident groups by now." He looked up at her. "*I'm* not saying that—I'm just repeating what I've heard."

"Vice-Chancellor, my division has one of the highest success rates in the country. In the past six months we've shut down *eight* dissident cells."

Roz said, "But there are others."

Agent Paquette glared at her. "Yes. There are others. Getting them all out will be next to impossible."

Max asked, "What's the strongest lead on a dissident cell you have right now? Because I'm thinking that between the two of us we stand a pretty good chance of success."

"There are rumors of a small cell in the Flatiron District. Nothing concrete, though."

"Take us there. We'll scout around, see what we can pick up."

Agent Paquette left her seat and moved to the cockpit. As she was giving orders to the pilots, Max thought to Roz: "You're going to have to move fast. First chance we get, you find somewhere to hide. I'll cloud her thoughts, make her and the pilots forget you were with us. Then you run, Roz. Get off the island."

What about you?

"It seems I'm too important. I'll be missed. You need to get to Midway, find Paragon and the others. I'll find someplace safe for us."

There's just five of us, Max! Five against who knows how many of them! The odds of beating them are—

"You don't understand, Roz. We *can't* fight them. Unity's military is already moving into place! They're bringing the war to Krodin before he can bring it to them, and I am not getting stuck in the middle of that! They don't understand— they can't beat Krodin. *We* weren't able to do it and we're superhuman!"

We're just giving up?

"Yes. We're giving up. It's the only intelligent solution. We're giving up because Krodin has already won."

CHAPTER 10

FIVE YEARS ago . . .

It was three thirty in the morning, and the lights in the airport's long-term parking lot illuminated only the roads: The parking spots were in almost complete darkness.

Sixteen-year-old Solomon Cord switched on his penlight as he crouched down next to the driver's-side door of an immaculate 1977 BMW E23. He put the penlight between his teeth, unzipped his jacket, and pulled out the long, slim strip of metal he'd had tucked into his sleeve.

It was a tricky lock—considerably harder than most—but he'd cracked one of these before. Once. On the fifth attempt, the door clicked open. *Finally!* Cord gathered up his tools and climbed into the car, then leaned over to check the ignition slot. *All right, this one I can do in my sleep!*

Once he got the engine started, he reversed out of the spot, then drove quietly and smoothly through the airport's parking lot until he reached the Arrivals terminal. He parked the BMW in the passenger loading zone and honked the horn twice.

Moments later a tall man wearing an expensive-looking three-piece suit and a heavy overcoat strode through the exit, followed by a teenager about Cord's age.

Cord got out as the man approached. "When you want to shut off the engine, just pop it in first, take your foot off the clutch, and hit the brakes. It'll stall and cut out. But whatever you do, don't do that until you get where you're going, because you won't be able to get it started again."

The man nodded and smiled. "Nice work, son. What do I owe you?"

"Two hundred, plus ten bucks for the cab home."

The boy said, "Your ad says it's only a hundred."

"It also says that after midnight's double," Cord replied. "Triple-A would have done it cheaper, but you'd still be waiting for them to show up. And they'd probably just smash the window. Not what you want in this weather."

The older man said, "Pay him, Max."

The boy removed a thick roll of bills from his pocket, peeled some off, and handed them to Cord.

"And ten for the cab?" Cord prompted.

"Yeah, about that . . . ," Max said. "Why don't we just give you a lift? We're going your way."

"I'm OK, thanks."

The man nodded at that, then said, "All right. You provide a very valuable service, Mr. Cord. Thank you." He reached into his overcoat pocket and pulled out a car key.

"So you found the key after all that?" Cord asked.

"Oh, we never lost it. This was a test. You passed."

Before Cord could respond, Max said, "Get in the car."

Cord realized that he actually *did* want to get into the car. It was warm, and it'd be a lot more comfortable than getting a taxi back home. He walked around to the passenger side and climbed in.

A few minutes later, as the car pulled out onto the freeway, Cord suddenly sat upright. "What the heck . . . ? What was I *thinking*?"

The older man smiled at him. "Only an idiot would get into a stranger's car, right? Don't worry, you're safe. But you don't know who we are, or why you're here." The smile grew wider still. "You're about to find out, Solomon."

The young man sitting in the back leaned forward and said, "I'm Max Dalton. I'm a superhuman. I can read minds and sometimes even control them, for a while. That's what I did to you. The man in the suit here is Mr. Krodin."

Cord began, "I don't—"

Krodin said, "Solomon, we've been watching you for the past seven weeks. All those aptitude tests your teachers have been giving you? That was at our request. You have an ordinary background, an ordinary education, and yet your intelligence quotient—especially when it comes to mechanical or electronic devices—puts you a considerable distance above the level of genius."

"You've wondered about that, haven't you?" Max asked. "You're sure you're not a superhuman, but you know you're far from ordinary. Well, we can give you the answer to that. One of our colleagues—Casey—has a complete understanding of the superhuman powers. And that's why we want you."

"A job?" Cord asked. "I'm not interested."

Still keeping his eyes on the road, Krodin said, "Tell him everything, Max."

Max said, "We're offering you the position of head of research and development. You'll be working with Casey. You'll have free rein and unlimited resources. Think about that, Solomon. Anything you want to build, you can do it."

Cord shook his head. "Thanks, but I'm not interested. Pull over and let me out. Right now."

"We can't stop on the freeway," Krodin said. "Just listen to what we have to say, OK?"

"Not a chance." Cord unclipped his seat belt and grabbed the interior door handle.

Krodin said, "Max?"

Cord suddenly realized that, more than anything else, he really did want to stay in the car and hear them out.

"The world is in a mess," Krodin said. "The governments like people to think that they steer their countries, that things happen because they want them to. But that's a delusion, like a kite believing that it controls the wind."

"And you think you can do better?" Cord asked.

"We can."

From the backseat, Max said, "What if there was a world leader who couldn't be assassinated, who was totally incorruptible, and who would never die? Sure, the people would no longer be able to vote for who would lead them, but that wouldn't matter if their leader always put the good of the people ahead of his own needs. What do we have then? We have a world with equality for all, no poverty or war or hunger. Utopia. Peace on Earth, forever."

Cord chewed on his lower lip for a moment. "Every empire falls. Democracy isn't perfect, but by its very nature it permits change. So you're starting from a flawed premise. Nothing good ever comes from that. No thanks."

Krodin sighed. "I said you wouldn't be able to reason with him. Max, do your thing."

Later that morning, as Cord was walking to school, he felt an elation—a sense of pure contentment—that he had never experienced before. He was quitting school today, and by tomorrow morning he'd be part of Krodin's team. Together, they would reshape the world. And that could only be a good thing.

Sure, Max Dalton had the ability to control people's minds, but Dalton had assured Cord that he wasn't doing that to him.

CHAPTER 11

JAMES KLAUS STOOD hidden among the small copse of trees that backed onto his house in Maple Towers, Midway, listening to the leader of the squadron of Praetorian guards that had been interrogating his mother and stepfather, Rufus.

"He was last seen making his way back to Midway. You see him, hear from him . . . you even hear anything about him, you contact us. Immediately. Understood?"

Rufus's voice said, "Of course, officer. Absolutely. But I don't understand how he could have gotten from school all the way to his father's farm."

James heard the soldier's boots crunching down the gravel drive, but his step was awkward, uneven, and James knew that the man was walking backward. "*That* is not your concern, Mr. Halliburton. This is a matter of national security. You will speak of this to no one."

"Sure, no problem," Rufus said, his voice thick with barely masked fear.

James listened to the distinctive hum of the Praetorians' vehicle as it drove away, and then the only heartbeats inside the house were from his mother and Rufus.

He was about to scramble over the fence when he heard his mother say, "I *knew* there was something strange going on, the way Faith phoned out of the blue like that."

James cringed to hear his mother almost spit the name. *What has Mom got against Faith? Dad didn't even meet her until after Mom threw him out.*

"She didn't say what she wanted?" Rufus asked.

"No."

There was a hint of amusement in Rufus's voice as he added, "You notice they wouldn't tell us how he managed to escape from them? I mean, on a *skateboard*? Where did he even get something like that?"

There was a short pause, then his mother said, "There's no way he'd have just left school. He's too scared of getting into trouble." She sighed. "It's my fault. I should never have fought Darrien for custody."

Rufus said, "Honey, the kid's trouble. Always has been, you know that. The way I see it, whatever's going on it's for the best. If he's up to something, the Praetorians will straighten him out. If he's not, well, maybe it's time we enlisted him in the Youth Corps. That'll toughen him up. Either way, he'll be out of our hands before too long."

James decided he'd heard more than enough. He left his skateboard under a bush close to the house and walked away.

So this world's versions of my mom and Rufus are still jerks. What a surprise.

Ever since his powers appeared, James had known what Rufus and his mother really thought of him—what they really thought of everyone. They were a bitter, sullen couple who seemed to be happy only when they were gloating about something bad happening to someone else.

This was why James never brought friends home and did his best to keep out of Rufus and Shawna's way. He'd always known that Rufus didn't like him, but it had been a huge shock to overhear his own mother describing him as a "lanky, spotty waste of space."

James had learned a lot about his neighbors too. He'd learned that Mrs. Gascoyne, who lived two doors down, spent at least an hour each day phoning all the betting shops in town and placing dozens of tiny bets on pretty much every major sporting event in the country. He knew that six-year-old Denny Van Hove across the street—who looked like the sweetest little kid in the world—had to be constantly watched by his parents because his favorite pastime was a game he'd invented called "Let's see how fast this thing catches fire." He knew that Kenneth Leyden and Namita McConnach, who lived next door to each other, had been secretly dating for the past eight years.

James spent a long time listening in on Rufus, hoping to catch him doing something illegal, but Rufus had turned out to be extremely law-abiding. A total jerk and a bully, but not actually a criminal.

James strode through the woods—a cocoon of silence

around him so that he didn't have to worry about stepping on fallen branches and alerting anyone to his presence—and emerged on the tree-lined road that led south into Midway.

Usually at this time of day there would be an almost constant stream of traffic heading into and out of the town. Now there was no sign of human activity.

How does this work? he wondered. *If people aren't allowed out except to travel to and from work or school, then how does anything get done?* On the journey from his father's farm he had seen less than a dozen vehicles—not counting army patrols—and each one had been a delivery truck of some kind.

He'd passed factories where work was clearly in progress, but no open stores. The Schaeffer Mall, one of the largest and busiest in the county, was completely devoid of life, yet it didn't look to have been abandoned.

Maybe there's one day a week when the curfews are lifted and the people are allowed out to buy food and stuff.

By the time James reached the start of Betancourt Avenue, which crossed the top of Main Street, he'd seen only twenty-two people—he'd counted—and they'd all been walking in silence, head down, not taking any notice of anything going on around them. Not that there had been much going on at all.

The only thing out of the ordinary was one of the Praetorians' flying craft that came silently zooming in over the city.

Then a few minutes later James rounded the corner onto Main and realized that he'd inadvertently kept up his cocoon of silence after he left the woods.

• • •

The surveillance cameras tracked Abby as she raced along the centerline of Farnsworth Avenue. The cameras were fitted with powerful spotlights—visible even in daylight—that activated as she passed.

The sidewalks on either side of the road were still lined with pedestrians, most of them not even looking in her direction.

What happened to Cord? How could he just leave me like that?

He's not a coward—either he's planning something or he's got his own problems.

She spotted a gap ahead between two tenement buildings and raced toward it. So far, there hadn't been any sign of pursuit—but with the cameras tracking her and the lights giving away her position, she knew it wouldn't be long before the black-clad men found her.

Abby could see only one camera covering the alley, attached to the wall close to the roof—she quickly nocked an arrow and fired: The arrow shattered the camera and its light, showering the alley floor with fragments of metal and plastic.

She took a moment to rest, leaning her back against the featureless brick wall. Like everywhere else in this bizarre version of Midway, the alley was almost spotlessly clean. There was no litter, and the only sign of graffiti was the faint outline of a band name that had long ago been almost completely scrubbed away.

OK, which way do I go now? If Sol hasn't just run off, then he'll be expecting me to find him. So that means he'll have picked somewhere we both know. . . . And it can't be the apartment, so it has to be the diner. She quickly figured out the quickest route to the diner—and then dismissed it. When she broke cover, the cameras would spot her again.

But the cameras are watching only the streets!

Abby collapsed her bow and clipped it back onto the quiver, then withdrew two arrows.

Holding an arrow in each hand, she leaped at the alley wall. She slammed the right arrow deep into the brickwork, used it to haul herself up, then swung her left hand at the wall. With the second arrow in place, she pulled out the first.

She climbed quickly, hand over hand, leaving behind a staggered trail of holes and shattered bricks. As she passed the broken camera, she retrieved the arrow that had pierced it and slipped it back into the quiver. At the top Abby swung herself onto the building's roof, six stories up.

She didn't waste time sightseeing. Whoever was monitoring her through the cameras would by now have alerted the patrols—and the broken camera was a sure giveaway that this was where she had disappeared. She ran across the rooftop, vaulted a low wall between this building and the next, dropped down onto the lower roof of another building, and kept going.

The rooftops weren't quite as neatly kept as the streets below: They were peppered with ducts and vents, cables and pipes, and on one flat roof she passed a collection of weather-stained lawn furniture that clearly hadn't been used in years.

When she reached Main Street, there was nowhere left to run—Abby knew she could jump much farther than a normal human, but the street was just too wide. Below, dozens of people walked silently, heads down.

It's like all the joy has been ripped out of their lives.

About four hundred yards to her right, on the opposite side of the street, was the diner—or what used to be the diner. Its windows had been neatly boarded up, as were the windows of most of the stores on Main Street.

She walked along the edge of the roof, wondering how to get across the street without being spotted. The cameras were positioned on their posts a few feet lower than the roof, so for now she was safe.

Maybe I can jump right onto one of the posts, land above the cameras . . . And then what? There's no way I'd be able to jump to the next one.

Or I could take them all out with arrows—but then that would just give away my position.

Abby stepped over a bundle of cables as thick as her arm and stopped at the corner of the building. It looked easy enough to climb down. *If I'm fast—really fast—maybe I can get across the street before whoever's watching spots me.*

She sat down on the edge of the roof, swung around so that she could lower herself over the edge before she dropped— and again spotted the bundle of cables.

The bundle emerged from a narrow vent in the building's roof and snaked across the rooftop to the edge, where it split into individual strands, each one leading to the surveillance cameras monitoring the street below.

Abby grinned. *Bingo!*

She hauled herself back up and returned to the cables, grabbed hold of the bundle, and pulled, reeling in the slack until it was taut against the vent. Then she dug in her heels and wrenched as hard as she could.

The bundle snapped a lot more easily than she'd expected, and Abby almost stumbled backward. On the street behind her the cameras powered down.

She leaned over the edge and shouted down: "Hey! You people down there! The cameras are off-line—you're not being watched. You can do whatever you like now!"

Some of the people momentarily glanced up at her, then continued walking as though they'd heard nothing.

Oh man . . . What's wrong with them?

A movement to her left caught Abby's attention. A flying vehicle was approaching from the east, coming in low over the rooftops. At first she thought it was a helicopter, but the craft was the wrong shape—squat and wide—and moving in almost complete silence.

There was nowhere for Abby to hide, and it would take too long to climb down the side of the building.

She unclipped her bow, snapped its limbs into place, and nocked an arrow to the string.

The craft came to a stop and hovered thirty yards away, directly over Main Street and only a few yards above the web of cables. A hatch in the side slid open and an amplified voice called out: "Drop your weapon. Lie flat on the roof with your hands above your head. This is your only warning."

Abby turned and ran back across the rooftops.

Stupid, stupid, stupid! I shouldn't have snapped the cable. Cord was right: That just told them where I was!

A volley of red-tipped darts peppered the rooftop around her. She vaulted over a five-foot-high vent and crouched down on the other side of it.

OK, think! It'll take them a few seconds to get to me. . . .

She quickly looked around for some way to escape. It was only when she looked down that she noticed two of the darts protruding from the heel of her left boot. Over her shoulder she saw that a third dart had struck the strap of her quiver.

Whoa . . . That guy's a good shot!

On the next rooftop she spotted a closed, plastic-covered skylight. *There!*

She broke cover just as the craft came into view, dived over the low wall separating the roofs, and launched an arrow at the skylight as she ran.

The arrow fractured the plastic and Abby jumped again, coming down hard—feetfirst—onto the skylight. It shattered under the force and she dropped through.

She landed heavily on a dining table, her right foot cracking a bowl of chicken soup. A family of five—mother, father, three kids—stared openmouthed at her.

The mother began, "What . . . ?"

"Sorry!" Abby jumped off the table and called back, "Enjoy your meal!" as she ran for the apartment's front door.

The corridor outside was bare, dimly lit—and empty. She raced down the stairs three at a time, jumped the last six steps to the floor below, then vaulted over the rail and landed lightly on the next stairwell down, and kept going.

Can't just go straight out onto the street—they'll be expecting that. Have to find another way out.

But . . . They'll know that I know they're expecting that, so maybe they won't *have the street door covered.*

On the ground floor she burst out through the door with her bow loaded and ready, hit the ground, and rolled, but the narrow side street was empty. She looked up—no sign of the flying craft or the soldiers.

Abby kept close to the wall as she quickly ran toward Main Street. At the corner pedestrians passed her by without paying her much attention, as though they saw a girl with a bow and arrow every day of the week.

Then she saw her chance: Trundling along the street was a large delivery truck—it would pass by very close to her, and it was even heading in the right direction, toward the diner.

OK—as soon as it passes, I run out, drop to the ground, skid underneath it, and hold on to the underside. When I get to the diner, I can just let go and the truck'll pass over me.

The truck approached, Abby tensed herself. It came alongside her and she darted forward—and stopped.

The truck didn't have wheels. It was hovering a few inches above the ground, far too low for her to take cover beneath it.

She shifted direction and ran alongside the truck, keeping as close to it as possible.

The truck blocked her view of the diner, but she knew that Flanagan's Bar was directly opposite it—when she reached the bar, she'd slow a little and dart out from behind the truck.

Then everything grew dark. She looked up to see the flying craft directly overhead, keeping pace with her.

The underside of the craft glowed with a series of two-foot-wide white lights, but there was none of the downdraft she'd expect from a helicopter or hovercraft.

She slowed to a stop, waited for it to descend. *I can't outrun it. No sense in wasting my energy trying. I have to stand and fight.*

But the flying craft remained in place.

Of course! They can't get any closer to the street because of the cameras' cables! They've probably called in more men to come for me on the ground.

Abby drew an arrow, nocked it, aimed for one of the craft's white lights. She drew back the string as far as it would go— and loosed the arrow.

Instantly the light shattered, and the craft dipped and swayed a little.

Two more arrows, and the flying machine began to waver. It dropped a couple of yards, lurched to the side. From within the vehicle there came the scream of grating metal. Blue-white electrical arcs flickered across the hull.

Abby grinned. *Yes! It's falling!* Then her grin faded. *It's falling and I'm standing right under it!*

She ran for the sidewalk as the craft plummeted. It snapped through the cameras' cables like they were thread. The rear right-side corner came down directly onto a camera pole and the craft tipped over. It plowed into the street cockpit-first, surged forward, and ripped a four-yard-wide gouge in the asphalt before it shuddered violently and came crashing down to the ground.

Abby was running for the craft even before it had landed. She leaped onto its roof and saw one of her arrows protruding point-first from the hull. She grabbed hold of it by the shaft and pulled it the rest of the way through.

She dropped to the ground just over the hatch, spun in the air, and landed with an arrow at the ready as the battered-looking sergeant climbed out. He wavered, collapsed to his knees, pitched forward so that his helmet heavily cracked off the ground, then toppled to one side and lay still.

Abby lowered her bow. Through the open hatch she could see the prone body of the remaining soldier—the man was breathing, but unconscious.

She crouched down next to the sergeant, pressed her index and middle fingers into the side of his neck, searching for a pulse. *Please don't let him be—*

The man's body twitched and Abby instinctively jumped back. Her heel struck a loose fragment of asphalt, and it took her a moment to steady herself.

Then she looked back at the sergeant: He was holding his sidearm in both hands, aimed at her. "Drop your weapon."

Abby resisted the urge to leap aside. She still didn't know whether she was bulletproof, but she was sure this wasn't the way she wanted to find out.

The sergeant smoothly got to his feet, still holding the gun on her. "I'm an expert marksman. If I wanted to, I could shoot off your ears in tiny chunks, one at a time. Now drop the bow."

Abby opened her hand, and the bow clattered to the ground.

Then a shadow passed over her, and another, and a third. She glanced up to see that three of the large flying craft were hovering overhead, and from each one half a dozen soldiers were rapidly descending on steel cables. Another two were hovering nearby on jetpacks that were disturbingly similar to Paragon's.

Within seconds Abby was surrounded, the red dots from the soldiers' laser sights settling on her head and torso.

"Hands on your head," the sergeant said. "Get down on your knees. Do it!"

Abby did as she was told. *They won't shoot me until they know who I am*, she hoped.

The sergeant holstered his handgun and strode toward her, stopping ten feet away. In his right hand he held a small communicator. "Control, we got her. We're taking her in. She's strong, fast. Almost certainly superhuman. Contact the inquisition and prepare the vault."

She heard footsteps approaching her from behind. Then strong gloved hands grabbed her arms, pulled them down and behind her back. She felt the cold steel of handcuffs on her wrists, heard the ratcheting clicks as they were locked into place.

To the other soldiers, the sergeant said, "Don't take your aim off her—not for a second. She's not human. She took down my Raptor with a bow and arrow."

Abby watched the man as he began to circle around her. "You raise a lot of questions, kid. . . . Who are you? Who are you working for?"

"No one."

"Don't lie to me, girl. I want to know who you're working for, and how they recruited you. How many others in your cell? Who trained you? Where are they based?"

"I'm not working for anyone," Abby said, trying to keep her voice steady and calm. "I'm an independent operative."

Then a slight grin appeared on the sergeant's face, and he leaned closer still. "I know who you are," he said softly. "Don't know why it never occurred to me before. Everyone assumes he's a man, but there's no reason that underneath all that bulky armor he couldn't be a girl. A perfect disguise. It all makes sense now. It explains why we were never able to find you. But the speed you moved at, your strength, your obvious experience, the custom-built weapon . . ."

Abby frowned. "What?"

"Don't try to deny it. You've been waging your one-man war against the state for years. How many of us have you killed? Got to be more than a thousand by now, right? Not to mention billions of dollars' worth of damage. And look at you now. Without your armor and weapons you're just a scared little girl."

"I have no idea what you're talking about."

"Of course you do. You're the biggest security threat in the entire country. The last surviving superhuman to oppose Krodin's rule. You're the one who killed a hundred thousand people in Anchorage. You're Daedalus."

CHAPTER 12.

IN THE FURNACE ROOM of the tenement building Solomon Cord had been tied facedown to a large, heavy wooden table. Only his head was free to move, and even then he couldn't raise it more than a couple of inches.

The two men in apartment 2C had overpowered him with almost embarrassing ease. With Cord distracted by the man with the gun, the one at the door had grabbed the knife from Cord's belt.

They had beaten him and dragged his semiconscious body down to the basement, strapped him to the table, gagged him with a rag that tasted of oil, and left.

And now the door at the top of the short flight of stairs crashed open. Heavy footsteps descended.

A man said, "Interesting . . . Close the door behind me. Don't want the screams to travel too far."

Cord heard the man walk around the table, saw the toes of dust-covered black work boots. A strong hand pulled the rag from Cord's mouth. Cord coughed and spat to try to clear the bitter taste.

"I'm going to ask you three times," the man said. "Who are you? Praetorian?"

"Definitely not," Cord said. "I'm guessing you're not either—which means we're on the same side. Let me go and I'll explain everything."

"Who are you? Resistance?"

"You could say that. But we're not affiliated with any other groups. I'm sure you know what happened outside—the girl with the bow. She's with me. Did she get away?"

"She shot the Praetorian. She escaped. And we've just heard she managed to take down one of their Raptors—alone. What is she, superhuman?"

"Yes."

The man exhaled an angry grunt. "Unity has four thousand fighters and bombers ready to launch, eighty nuclear subs moving into position around the U.S. We are *this* close to getting rid of Krodin, and now you people show up and put the Praetorians on full alert!" He leaned closer. "Now I'm going to ask you for the last time. Do you understand what that means? If you don't tell me what I want to hear . . . they'll never find your body. Or at least, not all of it."

Cord nodded as well as he was able. "I understand."

"Who are you?"

What do I tell him? That somehow the whole world has changed and only a handful of us know about it? That we come from a reality where Krodin died and most of the world never even heard of him?

"Very well," the man said. "If it's any consolation, I won't enjoy this. I just happen to be very good at it."

Cord winced as something sharp pressed into the flesh of his left arm. "My name is Solomon Cord. I'm not a Praetorian. I've come here to take down Chancellor Krodin. I know how to do it—I've done it before."

The man pulled away, was silent for a moment. Then he crouched down and peered at Cord's face. "I don't believe it. . . ."

The man was in his fifties, strong features, unshaven, a receding hairline. He stank of stale sweat and raw onions. "You *are* Solomon Cord."

"You've heard of me?"

"*Heard* of you? We spent two years trying to figure a way to *get* to you. Krodin had you locked up so securely we thought you'd never see daylight again. How'd you get out?"

"Cut me loose and I'll tell you."

The man frowned. "What? You've just given us a gift, Cord. If the invasion fails, we can use you against Krodin. Why would we cut you loose? You're a hostage."

In a gray concrete prison cell two floors below ground level in Northlands police station, Fairview, Lance McKendrick let the thin mattress drop back onto the uncomfortable wooden bunk fixed to the wall.

Aside from the bunk the cell contained only a sink with one faucet—cold—and a toilet with no lid or seat.

Officer Ashton had handcuffed him in Principal Mailer's office, marched him out to the front of the school, and radioed for backup. Less than two minutes later a blue-and-gold-colored patrol car had pulled up, and Lance was bundled into the back and driven to Northlands precinct. He was immediately brought to the cell, his cuffs were removed, the barred door was slammed shut, and he was left alone.

At first he'd tried calling for attention, loudly protesting his innocence, but no one had come.

Now, after what felt like hours of nothing but silence punctuated by the echoes of his own voice, he heard keys rattling in a lock at the far end of the long corridor, then the loud squeal of the barred door being pushed open.

Lance quickly pulled up his socks, walked up to the bars, and pressed his head against them. To the right he saw two people approaching, alternately lit and in shadow as they passed under the ceiling's bare low-powered bulbs: a sullen gray-haired guard who stopped ten yards from the cell, and a slim woman with thick glasses and long hair in a tight ponytail who stopped on the other side of the bars.

"At last! I thought you were going to keep me here forever!"

The woman peered over her glasses at the copy of the arrest form in her hand. "Lancelot Aaron McKendrick?"

He nodded. "Are you my lawyer?"

"My name is Sheridan Pendlebury. I'm your court-appointed counsel."

"OK. So . . . Is that like a lawyer, then?"

"I'm here to advise you of your rights. Pay attention."

"I'm listening."

She cleared her throat and began to read from the arrest form. "Lancelot Aaron McKendrick, you have been charged with and arrested for the crime of knowingly providing false information to an officer of the law. By willingly committing this act you have chosen to forsake all standard rights and privileges accorded to a citizen."

"*What?* But—"

She cut him off. "You have been granted a period of five minutes of this officer's time to present your plea against automatic conviction. If this officer believes that your conviction should be upheld, you will be taken to a juvenile detention center where you will be incarcerated for a period of two hundred and forty days."

"No, listen . . . !"

Ms. Pendlebury raised her hand. "However, should this officer feel that there are grounds for appeal, you will be appointed an attorney and be granted a trial." She looked at her watch. "You may begin."

"But I didn't do anything wrong!" *I'll find a way out of this,* Lance thought. *They'll have to give me a phone call or something. Mom and Dad can bail me out.*

"As the charge states, you lied to an officer of the law. You informed him that you are a student at Martin Van Buren High School when you knew this not to be the case. You are in fact currently enrolled at Rutherford B. Hayes High School and have been so ever since your expulsion from Martin Van Buren High eighteen months ago."

"No, look . . . I never told the cop that I go to Martin Van Buren! I just said I was going to school. He must have just assumed that's where I go to school because I'm in that district and that's where *he* went. Ask him yourself. Ask the principal. He brought me there and I'm walking along the corridor thinking, 'Why's he bringing me here?' but I didn't ask him because, y'know, I was scared."

"You attest that you did not deliberately mislead the officer and that his arrest was in error?"

"Yes. Absolutely. But I'm not blaming him. Not really. See, from what the principal said I think he had a pretty bad time when he was there, so it was probably on his mind. Not his fault—he's only human, and we're all allowed to make mistakes, right?"

"Wrong. However, as there is no record of your conversation with Officer Ashton, I believe that there are grounds for appeal."

For the first time in hours, Lance relaxed. "Yes!" He sagged against the bars. "So you're going to let me out?"

"Mr. McKendrick, please understand that you have not been found innocent. It is merely that your statements have earned you the opportunity to present your case in a court of law. Until that time you will remain incarcerated."

"Oh man . . . OK, then you need to phone my mom and dad, get them to post bail."

"Bail? I don't . . . Mr. McKendrick, I don't know where you think you're living. This is America, not some backward European state with an outdated judicial system! We do not *have* bail. You have been arrested and are awaiting arraignment. Why would we allow suspects back onto the streets where they could potentially re-offend or even abscond?"

Lance backed away from the cell door, shaking his head. "No. No way! People are supposed to be considered innocent until proven guilty! What kind of insane world are you people running?"

She raised an admonishing finger. "Be warned: Criticism of the law implies criticism of the state. That's sedition, Mr. McKendrick. A mandatory sentence of five years minimum to be appended to any existing or pending sentences."

Lance dry-swallowed. *This can't be happening!* "I want to see my parents."

"That is not permitted at this time. I think we are finished here."

"What . . . What happens now?"

"You will shortly be issued a temporary uniform. Your clothing and other personal effects will be placed into storage. You will be given a blanket, which is to be returned at the end of your stay here. The cost of any damage caused to the blanket or your uniform or any part of your cell—other than standard and acceptable wear and tear—will be deducted from your salary."

"Salary? But I don't have a job."

"Every convict or suspect is expected to work for no less than nine hours per day, tasks to be appointed by the Department of Incarceration. For each hour you work you will earn fifteen cents, minus six cents custody tax. Your work will begin this evening at twenty-hundred hours and terminate at oh-five-hundred hours."

"I have to work through the night? You say all that like it's supposed to make sense."

"I already warned you once about—"

"Sorry. You're right."

"Prisoners working for the state do so outside the hours of curfew so as to minimize the impact on the law-abiding community." The woman signaled to the guard. "Prepare the accused for processing."

The guard flicked through a large bundle of keys as he approached. "Move to the far wall and turn around. Stand feet apart at shoulder width. Place your hands flat on the wall at head height, arms stretched out."

Lance did as he was told and heard the keys turning in the lock. The barred door slid open, and he felt the guard's hands on his shoulders.

He tried not to flinch as the guard quickly and expertly frisked him.

What if they give me some hack lawyer and I lose the trial? He shuddered. *No, that won't happen. It's the cop's word against mine. And I can get Mrs. Mailer to be a witness for me—maybe if she says the same stuff in court that she said to the cop, I can argue that he arrested me only because he was angry with her.*

"He's clean," the guard said.

Lance turned around and shrugged. "I could have told you that."

As the guard left the cell and relocked the door, Ms. Pendlebury said, "Your evening meal will be delivered in approximately one hour. After that, I advise you to get some rest, Mr. McKendrick. You will have a long night ahead of you."

"Aren't I entitled to a phone call or something?"

The woman looked at him as though she had never heard of the concept. "No."

When the door at the end of the corridor squealed shut once more, Lance sat back down on the bunk. He slumped forward, head down and forearms on his knees.

He remained in that position, barely moving, until Pendlebury and the guard returned. The woman told him that his
day in court was scheduled for two days from tomorrow.
Speaking softly, Lance nodded and thanked her for the information. He accepted the thin blanket and orange one-piece
uniform the guard passed to him without looking either of
them in the eye.

She turned her back as he quickly stripped off his outer
clothes and put on the uniform, and then he wordlessly
passed his clothes out through the bars to the guard.

When they left once more, Lance returned to his bunk and
lay down on his side with his back to the door and the blanket
pulled over him.

Lance didn't know whether there were any cameras in
the cells. He hadn't spotted any, but they could be concealed.
So he kept his hands hidden as much as possible. It was
important that, to anyone watching, he looked as though he
had given up, as though he had been beaten by the system.
For that to work he had to shield his hands from view so they
wouldn't see him slip them under the mattress and remove
the slim cloth-wrapped bundle.

Moving very slowly and carefully to avoid drawing any
more attention to himself, Lance removed his right sneaker
and sock and slipped the bundle inside. He was sure that he'd
be frisked again at eight in the evening when they took him
out to begin his night's work, and he hoped that the guard
wouldn't search him too closely.

When the guard had locked the door behind him, Lance
had taken a good look at the lock. He'd already seen the
guard's keys, and seeing the lock itself had confirmed his

guess. The lock was a Model 8 Fordingbridge, considered absolutely unpickable without the right tools.

Tucked inside his right sock were the right tools: Lance's homemade tension wrench and half-diamond pick.

Having lowered his cocoon of silence, James stared open-mouthed at the devastation in front of him. A Praetorian vehicle was in the middle of Main Street, its front end half buried under huge irregular slabs of asphalt and tons of gray bedrock and brown dirt.

Overhead three more craft were hovering, and next to the downed vehicle more than a dozen men were aiming their weapons at a small, dark-skinned teenage girl.

Abby! James began to run. He hadn't seen or even spoken to Abby since they'd returned home from the battle at Windfield, but even without her homemade armor and sword there was no mistaking her.

And now she was in trouble. Big trouble, by the looks of things. She was on her knees, hands cuffed behind her back, facing a soldier wearing sergeant's stripes.

He was only thirty yards away now: He'd blocked the sound of his footsteps from reaching the soldiers, but at any moment one of them would spot him.

James let loose a narrow-band low-frequency sonic blast, directed it at one of the flying soldiers. The man's jetpack suddenly sparked and shuddered. He clutched his helmet and screamed. As his colleagues looked on in bewilderment, the man crashed to the ground and started desperately scrabbling at his helmet.

"Get it off! Get it off! The noise—it's killing me!"

Two of the other soldiers moved to help him, and James hit them both with similar blasts, knocking them off their feet. Then he directed his voice to Abby. "Run. Now!"

He saw Abby look around, confused. "It's me, Abby. Thunder. Coming up on your left. Get out of there—I can't blast them all."

Abby tensed her arms, snapped the cuffs binding her wrists, and threw herself at the sergeant. She slammed her fist into his stomach with enough force to lift him off the ground, then—using him as a shield—rushed at two of the other soldiers, knocking them aside like bowling pins.

"Move!" James shouted.

He saw her throw the sergeant into a cluster of three other soldiers. Then she jumped backward, somersaulted in the air to land next to her bow, snatched it off the ground, and started running.

"Head down Tormey Avenue," James shouted. "Your next left."

He raced across the street and caught up with her as they entered the avenue. "How many more of them are there?"

"You tell me," Abby said. "I was too busy to count them."

Halfway along Tormey Avenue they took a right, then a left into the grounds of a small warehouse. Abby pointed. "Over the wall."

"Abby, it's fifteen feet high!"

Without slowing, Abby leaped for the wall, caught the top, and pulled herself up. She lay flat along the top and stretched her arm down to James. "Grab my hand!"

He jumped, caught her hand, and was hauled straight up and onto the wall, landing in a crouch with Abby still holding on to him. "Whoa!" On the other side the drop was much greater than he'd expected—at least twenty-five feet.

As he tried to steady himself, his hand slipped out of Abby's. He toppled over, headfirst toward solid concrete.

Oh no! Instinctively he generated the same kind of shock wave he'd used to propel himself on his skateboard—and found himself slowing down.

He landed facedown with barely a thump.

Abby dropped down beside him, landing lightly on her feet. "How did you do *that*?"

James rolled onto his back and sat up. "Not sure."

"Are they following us?"

James held his breath while he listened. "No. They're still trying to figure out what happened." He exhaled, took a few more deep breaths. "OK. Give me a minute here."

"What did you do to them?"

"Just a sonic blast—shouldn't be any permanent damage." James shuffled to the side and rested with his back against the wall. "Abby, what's going on here?"

"I'm not sure. I was with Paragon when it happened." She handed him the bow and quiver, and sat down next to him. "He made me this, and we were testing it out in the alley behind my apartment building when . . ." She shrugged. "Everything changed."

"I was at my dad's farm, talking to Faith—my stepmom— and I suddenly noticed that all the ambient sound in the area was different. And she acted like I'd come out of nowhere. Abby, I'd been there since yesterday, but she didn't remember that at all."

"There was a thing on the news—Brawn mysteriously appeared in Oak Grove Prison."

"But that's where *we* left him."

"Right," Abby said. "And then we got a call from Max Dalton. The same thing happened to him and Roz. All of us who were there when Krodin was killed. Or when we *thought* he was killed."

James nodded. "So that means Lance could be affected too. Have you heard from him?"

"No. Well, Sol and Max are the only ones who know how to contact him."

"Sol?"

"Solomon Cord. That's Paragon's real name."

"I see. From what I've learned, it's looking like Pyrokine's blast didn't kill Krodin but sent him back in time instead. How far back I'm not sure, but he resurfaced about five years ago. Since then he's been working his way into power. He's the one who turned the whole population into terrified slaves. People aren't allowed to gather in groups of three or more without a permit—and that includes visiting their friends. All public events are gone—no sports, concerts, movies . . . Basically anything that's hard to police has been banned."

"Sol said it's done through fear. Make the people believe that their lives are in danger and that you're the only one who can protect them, and you can do anything you want." Abby jumped to her feet. "He was with me just before I got caught—but I don't know what happened to him. We need to find him."

"I don't think that's the wisest path right now."

"What? What do you mean?"

"If we're going to have any chance of fighting back, we need to get to Roz and Max. Maybe Brawn too, if we can find him before Krodin's people do. Paragon's not a superhuman, is he? And I'm guessing that he doesn't have his armor with him. An ordinary human is going to slow us down."

"We can't just leave him!"

"We don't know where he *is*, Abby. Where would we even begin to search for him?"

"After we got separated, I was heading for the diner—it was the only place I could think of that we both knew, not counting my apartment."

James stood up and brushed the dust from the backside of his jeans. "He's not there now. I can't hear anyone inside the diner, or even near it. Whatever we do, we can't stay here. . . . There are more of those flying machines coming. Five, no, six of them. And smaller ones—one-man craft. And another four guys wearing jetpacks."

"Max told Paragon that the rest of the world has united against Krodin. They're planning an invasion. Max said we've got to find a place to hide out."

"What sort of invasion?"

"I don't know. Max didn't have many details."

James bit his lip. "If they know anything about Krodin, it's that he's practically invulnerable. They're going to hit him as hard as they can. . . . But they must know he was in Anchorage and survived the nuclear blast." James sagged against the wall. "The invaders won't just be targeting Krodin—they'll go after everyone who works for him, and they're not going to be too concerned with who gets in the way. They'll wipe this country off the face of the Earth. We *can't* go into hiding, Abby. We're going to have to stop Krodin ourselves."

CHAPTER 13

AN HOUR AGO AGENT Paquette had directed the pilots to land the Raptor in Manhattan's Flatiron District.

Roz had followed the others out of the vehicle and, on Max's signal, simply walked away. He had communicated with her telepathically for the first few minutes, but she soon passed out of his range.

Now she stood on the corner of East Eighteenth Street and Fifth Avenue. The city looked much as it always had, but the differences—though small—were striking.

There was very little traffic, no cars parked on the side of the street. There were few billboards left in place: Most of them had been replaced with panels of solar cells. There was no one standing on the sidewalks handing out fliers, no one trying to sell fake Rolex watches or Gucci handbags, no one pan-handling for change. No news vendors, no pretzel carts, no taxis, no tourists. The pedestrians all walked at the same speed, mostly in single file and on the correct side of the sidewalk, and no one spoke to anyone else.

Without all the cars and buses, the city even smelled different: The air was crisp and fresh, and Roz was almost sure she could smell the ocean.

There was something else missing from the city, but she couldn't quite put her finger on it.

What this version of Manhattan did have, in abundance, was surveillance: a dozen or more cameras on each corner, watching everything and everybody. At the center of each junction was a raised concrete platform housing four-man squads of armed Praetorian guards.

Roz became aware that she was the only one standing still, so she slipped into the middle of a line of people crossing Fifth Avenue, heading west. She kept her head down as she passed the Praetorians, all too aware that her face would be recognizable to many of them.

How am I going to get to Midway from here? It's got to be a thousand miles, maybe more. I don't even have any money with me.

Do these people even still use *money?* She hadn't passed any open stores, so there was no way to tell.

Another of the squat Raptors passed overhead, and Roz resisted the temptation to stare at it—no one else paid it any notice.

That's what I need, Roz thought. *Get myself one of those things and just* fly *to Midway.*

It had been an idle thought, but after a moment Roz realized that it might be a viable plan. *If I could* get *to one of the Raptors, there's a chance that no one would stop me. They're so conditioned to obeying orders that they might not expect someone to break the rules.*

A siren blared nearby—two short bursts—and it seemed to Roz that the pedestrians had increased their speed a little. She glanced at her watch: It was five minutes to seven. *Curfew's nearly started. What do I do then?*

A few minutes later she reached Seventh Avenue, and as she passed the entrance to the subway, she realized what else was missing from the city: the ever-present rumbling of the subway trains. At the bottom of the subway steps the heavy gates were padlocked.

A faded poster next to the gate read, "CLOSED—Access to NY Subway System prohibited until current security crisis has passed, by order of Chancellor Krodin."

Roz smiled to herself. *That's how I'm going to get out of the city!* She quickly descended the steps and examined the padlock. Three weeks ago, in a town called Greenwood, Roz had faced a similar situation. She'd tried to use her telekinesis to pick a lock, but failed because she didn't know how they worked. Since then, she'd been reading up on locks.

The padlock was heavy, but it was a fairly standard make. *All right . . .* She reached out telekinetically—at times she thought of her power as an invisible and highly flexible tentacle—and began to probe the inside of the lock. She knew that inside a standard lock was a cylinder containing a sequence of pins, each one cut into two uneven parts. When the correct key was inserted, its teeth pushed up the pins so that the cuts in the pins lined up, allowing the cylinder to be turned—this pulled a lever that then opened the lock.

She could sense the pins inside the lock, and her telekinetic control was now fine enough to allow her to manipulate them. One by one, the pins clicked into place, and she sensed the lock's cylinder turn and heard a soft click as it opened. *Yes!*

On the street above a siren blared, a warning that curfew was about to start.

Roz quickly removed the lock from the gate, pulled the gate open, stepped through, and closed and locked it behind her.

She darted down the remaining steps into complete darkness. *Should have a flashlight. If I ever get out of this, I'm going to bring a flashlight with me everywhere I go.*

Her foot collided with something—a discarded cardboard box, she guessed—and she heard the sound of tiny feet scuttling across the tiled floor.

"Oh good," she said aloud. "Rats."

She reached out with her left hand and found the wall again. It curved slightly to the left, and she followed it. Roz wasn't afraid of the dark, but she knew she had to be careful. She might crash into something and knock herself out—and wake to find rats scurrying all over her body—or she might step off the edge and tumble onto the tracks.

The curve of the wall continued for what felt like far too long, and Roz stopped. *Wait, which way am I facing now?*

She knew she'd been heading west as she came through the gate—and that was the direction she wanted to go—but she'd been following the curve of the wall.

No, keep going. I'll get to the gates that lead onto the tracks and then worry about the direction.

She realized that a slight but constant breeze was coming from her right. *OK, so I know that the tunnel branches that way.*

Is this a crosstown or an uptown station?

To get off the island I need to get to the Lincoln Tunnel. That's like twenty blocks north . . . which is absolutely useless information because down here there aren't any blocks, stupid!

There was another breeze, but this one smelled like month-old socks. "Not going *that* way," she muttered.

She moved on, still following the wall on her left, but the foul smell seemed to stick with her. *What is that? Did something die down here?*

Probably did. I could end up tripping over a body or something!

There was a sound too, she realized. A rhythmic, soft, rasping noise, but she couldn't tell where it was coming from. *Another rat? No, not unless it's got asthma.*

Almost a minute passed, and the sound and the smell were still there.

And she still hadn't reached the ticket booth or the turnstiles.

OK, think! What does the inside of the average subway station look like?

Tiled walls. They've all got tiled walls. There's usually a booth and a few ticket machines and a guy with a guitar playing the same three chords over and over.

She stopped, and muttered, "Oh, I don't believe it!"

Another feature of many subway stations was the huge cylindrical support pillars. "I'm an idiot! I've been walking around in circles!"

And a soft voice right beside her said, "I know. I bin watchin' you."

CHAPTER 14

ABBY HAD SNAPPED the bolts on the shutters of an old, abandoned warehouse, and now she and Thunder were hiding inside.

"What can you hear?" she asked. "Is it safe to leave yet?"

"Not yet. They're not going to give up easily."

"We can't wait here forever. They'll check this place eventually."

"I know, but I'll hear them coming. So . . . this Daedalus guy," Thunder asked. "What do we know about him?"

"Not a lot. That sergeant thought *I* was him—which tells me that they don't know much about him either. He said that Daedalus killed a hundred thousand people in Anchorage. Is that true?"

James told her what he'd learned of the Alaskan tragedy, that Daedalus had been accused of planting the bomb that had almost destroyed the entire state.

By the time he was finished, Abby was shaking her head. "That's insane. . . . No one would do something like that! And for what? What did Daedalus expect to get out of it?"

"I asked Faith about that. She didn't know. She said that after it happened, the whole world went a bit crazy. All the most powerful superheroes—and some of the villains, apparently—were in Anchorage trying to stop Daedalus when the bomb was triggered. Krodin was the only survivor. The problem is, if the Praetorians don't know much about Daedalus, how are *we* going to find him?" He shrugged. "I don't even know how we're going to get out of Midway."

"I've been thinking about that. . . . We could steal one of their hovercraft," Abby suggested.

"Raptors, they're called. Same problem. I can barely drive a car—I don't think I could control one of those things."

"What's your name?" Abby suddenly asked.

"Thunder."

"No, you dope. Your *real* name."

He bit his lip. "Um . . ."

"Back to that again, are we? Look, what's the big deal? We live in the same town, so we're bound to run into each other from time to time. Anyway, you know *my* real name."

"That's because you don't have a superhero name."

"Whatever. So who are you?"

"Look, see, the thing is . . . if you know my real name and say you get captured and tortured, then you might tell them my name, and next thing I know the bad guys are storming into my house while I'm asleep."

"Huh. Listen, pal, if I get captured and tortured and I find out you're asleep and not out there trying to save me, I *will* tell them your name."

He paused for a few seconds. "All right. My name is James Klaus."

Abby smiled. "OK then. That wasn't so hard, was it? Hey, wait a second. . . . You live in Maple Towers. . . . Is your sister called Shiho?"

James's eyes widened. "How do you know that?"

"She goes to school with two of my brothers. And my big sister used to babysit you and your sister. You would have been about ten."

His shoulders sagged. "Vienna, right? I remember her, but I don't think I ever knew her last name. Vienna de Luyando. Wow."

"Good wow or bad wow?"

"Just a surprised wow. How old is your sister now?"

"Too old for *you*, Jimmy. She's nineteen. Besides, you've got competition—I think Paragon likes her."

"I'm not interested in your sister. I was just asking. And my name's not Jimmy. It's James." He suddenly raised his head and looked around. "They're calling off the search, for now." He listened for a moment. "They're setting up a cordon around the whole town—they've blocked off all the roads. And they've got the cameras—they're putting the town on full alert. . . . It's not going to be easy to find a way out with all the cameras."

"We can go across the rooftops," Abby said. "The cameras are only watching the streets."

"Maybe *you* can go across the rooftops, but I can't. I mean,

I think I'm in pretty good condition, but I don't have your enhanced strength and speed."

"Maybe you can use your shock wave trick to float or something like that. It saved you from a pretty nasty fall earlier."

James nodded slowly. "Yeah, maybe. . . ." He walked out into the center of the room, and Abby saw a look of concentration form on his face. "Let's see. . . ."

The warehouse floor suddenly trembled, and Abby jumped up. "What was that?"

"That was me. I'll try again. It could be just a matter of finding the right frequency."

"If you say so."

The floor trembled again, but this time it was much less noticeable.

James laughed. "It's working!"

Abby walked toward him. "I don't see . . ." And then she noticed that his feet were no longer quite touching the ground. "Oh wow!"

"Good wow or bad wow?"

"The best kind. That is way cool. Go higher!"

He rose into the air until Abby was able to walk right under him. "I'm creating a layer of continuous shock waves all over my body. . . ."

"I can't hear anything."

"I know. The frequency is too low for human hearing. Probably scaring the heck out of all the cats and dogs in the area, though."

She walked around him, looking up. "You know what I'm thinking? Maybe it's not so much that you control sound.

Maybe your powers allow you to manipulate the *air*. Without air there's no sound, right?"

"Hey . . ." James drifted back down a little. "You could be on to something there."

Abby grinned. "See? Not just a pretty face!" She retrieved her bow and quiver from the floor. "Ready to go?"

"I'm not sure I'm up to actually flying just yet."

"Only one way to find out." Abby walked back to the shutters.

"All clear?"

"Not yet. . . . Hold on a second."

In the distance she heard a rapid series of gunshots followed by screaming.

James smiled. "That's got their attention. They're moving away to investigate. . . . Good. I reckon we've got a few minutes."

"Nice work." Abby pulled up the shutters to about two feet off the ground, then dropped down and rolled out. James followed a moment later, then pulled the shutters down again.

At the side of the warehouse was an old Dumpster. Holding an arrow in each hand, Abby took a short run, jumped onto the lid of the Dumpster, and leaped as high as she could. Using the arrows as pitons she quickly scrambled up to the edge of the sloping roof, where she found Thunder already waiting for her.

He was floating upright in midair and gently drifting in the slight breeze. "I'm getting the hang of this, I think."

"Can you make yourself go forward as well as up and down?"

James zoomed toward her, a little too quickly. He crashed

into Abby and almost knocked her off the roof. She had to wrap her arms around him to keep from falling. "Whoa, sorry!"

Abby released him and stepped back. "Um . . . if we're all done with our awkward moment?"

He nodded. "Let's go."

She ran along the edge of the roof, jumped down onto the next building, and vaulted over an old chimney stack. All the while, James drifted silently alongside her.

"I've thought of a superhero name for you," he said. "You're pretty fast, so how about calling yourself Lightning?"

"Thunder and Lightning? Oh please!"

"What's wrong with that? It's perfect!"

"It's lame. And it makes me sound like your sidekick. If anything, you're *my* sidekick."

Roz jumped back, away from the sound of the voice.

Her back slammed into the pillar and she jumped again. "Who's there?"

The sound of breathing came again, echoing around the pitch-black station, its source impossible to pinpoint. Then the voice said, "Takes time to get useta th' dark, don't it?"

There was a loud scratching sound, then a match flared and Roz flinched at the sudden brightness.

The match was applied to a candle, then tossed to the ground, and in the flickering light Roz saw that the candle was in the small, grime-covered hand of a girl who couldn't have been more than eight years old. Her hair was long and matted with dirt. She was barefoot, wearing only a stained and frayed summer dress that was clearly too small for her.

"Who are you?" Roz asked.

The girl frowned. "Seein' as you in my place, I th' one askin' th' questions, yeah?"

"You're right, sorry. My name's Roz."

"I dint ask yet."

"OK..."

"Dint say you could talk, neither." The ragged girl stepped closer, holding the candle up to Roz's face. "What you want?"

"I need to get out of the city."

The girl nodded, wet her lips, then ran the back of her free hand over her mouth, wiping away some of the dirt. "You not one a th' bad fellas up there?"

"No. They're the ones I'm trying to escape from."

The girl nodded again, then turned away, walking with a slight limp. Roz watched her flickering silhouette shrink down the litter-strewn tunnel.

The girl reached a branch in the tunnels and stopped. Without looking around, she called, "Well? You comin' or not?"

Roz moved away from the wall and caught up with the girl. "Where are you taking me?"

"First, we go see th' others an' then I'm-a take you to th' link tunnel."

Roz suppressed a shudder. *This is the creepiest thing ever.* "How long have you been down here?"

"Since always."

"What's your name?"

"Victoria."

They passed through a large hole that had been cut into a set of metal railings, and out onto the platform.

"How many people are down here?" Roz asked.

"You stupid or somethin'? *All* of us are down here." The girl turned left, heading toward the end of the platform.

"Yeah, but how *many* is that?"

"Dunno. I only ever see my mom an' my dad an' my brother." Victoria walked to the edge of the platform, set the candle down, then swung over the edge and down onto the tracks. "What you say your name is?"

"Roz." She jumped down next to Victoria and followed her into the tunnel. "How far?"

"How far what?"

"How far to where we're going?" Roz saw a large rat sitting on the track watching them pass, and she suppressed another shudder. She'd always thought she quite liked rats, used to watch them scurry around from the top of the subway platforms. But she'd never been *this* close to one.

"All th' way from here," Victoria said.

Roz raised her eyes. *It's like talking to a five-year-old!*

"I know all th' tunnels an' where all th' food is an' th' water."

"Victoria, where did you live before?"

"Inna house. Came down here with Mom an' Dad an' my brother 'cos Dad got in trouble with th' cops an' we hadda hide. He useta work on th' trains an' he knew about this place an' we live here ever since."

A small doorway had been reset into the sidewall of the tunnel. Victoria pointed to the rusting metal door. "See th' sign? Says 'Bad People Keep Out.' You ain't bad people, are you, Roz?"

"No, I'm one of the good ones." Roz felt an almost

overwhelming urge to wrap her arms around the girl and hug her: The sign on the door read, "Maintenance Area—Authorized Access Only."

Victoria pulled the door open, and Roz winced at the sudden stench that washed over them. It smelled like the inside of a garbage can that had never been cleaned.

She covered her mouth and nose, and ducked her head as she followed Victoria through the door and into a wide, low-ceilinged room. The room wasn't more than fifteen feet square, and was ankle-deep in candy-bar wrappers, empty soda cans, and scraps of paper.

Against one wall, crudely wrapped in old blankets, were three slowly decaying human bodies.

"This is my mom an' my dad, an' that one's my brother," Victoria said. "Ain't you gonna say hello?"

CHAPTER 15

THREE YEARS ago . . .

Ten minutes before noon two EH101 transport copters touched down in the center of Fire Island, Alaska.

Krodin stood watch nearby as the passengers disembarked from the first copter. Leading them was a tall, slim young man wearing a blue costume, mask, and cape, with a large white *T* across his chest. Behind him was a slightly shorter man wearing an all-white costume, then a woman wearing a gray costume with green highlights. None of the three was more than twenty years old.

Following the woman was a large, strongly built man wearing steel mesh armor. His hands were cuffed in front of him and his legs were shackled.

The second copter's hatch opened, and an armed soldier jumped out. He turned back to face the hatch and raised his rifle. "Out. Now!"

A wet-looking, heavily scarred hand grabbed the edge of the hatch and the metal immediately began to smoke. Then the figure moved out of the copter's dark interior into the light and stepped onto the ground.

"Forward," the soldier ordered, shouting to be heard over the roar of the copter's rotors. "Eight steps, then stop."

The man did as he was ordered, and the soldier jumped back into the copter. Both copters' engines began to increase in pitch once more, but before they had even taken off, the dirt around the man's feet was smoldering and blackened.

Krodin walked up to the scarred man and stopped within arm's reach. "Dioxin. Named after a particularly nasty family of poisons. Your skin constantly seeps acidic venom. About the only thing impervious to it is gold."

Dioxin nodded. "Right. Nice touch, lining the copter with gold plating. Must have set you back a few bucks." He looked around. "What is this place?"

The other heroes approached, and the man with the *T* on his chest said, "It's where you're going to spend the rest of your life, Dioxin. An ordinary prison won't hold someone like you, or"—he gestured toward the man in the steel mesh armor—"The Shark."

"Titan, right? I've heard of you. You're supposed to be pretty powerful." He looked past Titan toward the others. "Quantum and Energy. Wow. All the big hitters are here. And this muscle-brained moron has to be the famous Krodin."

"Look behind you," Energy said.

Dioxin turned. There was a large steel bunker a hundred yards away.

"That's just the entrance," Energy said. "The prison is

underground. And you two are the last inmates." She smiled. "We got you. Every single one of you."

His chains clanking, The Shark shuffled forward. "Locking us all up in the one place. That's the dumbest thing I ever heard. Dioxin and I are practically invulnerable. Who else have you got here? The Slayer? Tungsten? Silver Leopard? The Chain Gang?"

"*All* of you," Titan said. "Every known supervillain is now imprisoned on this island. And a few we *didn't* know about. Krodin even managed to find The Red Fury."

Dioxin asked, "And what's to stop us from escaping? This is Fire Island, right?" He pointed to the east. "Anchorage is only three or four miles that way. You're putting some of the most powerful men and women on the planet in the one location. We'll break out."

"No, you won't," Krodin said. "This facility is protected by a small but powerful cobalt bomb. You know what that is?"

"I do," The Shark said. "Cobalt itself is relatively harmless, but its radioactive isotope—cobalt-60—is deadly. You're saying that if we try to escape, you'll detonate the bomb?"

Krodin said, "Exactly."

Under his breath, Titan muttered to Krodin, "Jeez, man, you're not serious, are you? No, you can't be. Where'd you even get the money for all this?"

"The Helotry," Krodin said. "An organization that . . . It's a long story. Let's just say they weren't short of funds."

The Shark said, "You *can't* have a cobalt bomb, Krodin. I just figured it out. A hundred miles in that direction is Mount Redoubt. It's an active volcano. Any significant det-onation here runs the risk of weakening the volcano to the point of eruption. If that happens, it'll spew millions of tons of radioactive dust into the upper atmosphere. Enough to irradiate a quarter of the Northern Hemisphere. That's not just a weapon of mass destruction—it's a weapon of *global* destruction."

Titan took a step back from Krodin. "Whoa . . . What? Is that true?"

Krodin shook his head. "No. It's true that there's a cobalt bomb, but my people have done their homework—Mount Redoubt is safe from the explosion." He beckoned for the other man and woman to come closer. "Titan, Energy, and Quantum. Three of the most powerful superhumans. Except that not one of you has done more than scratch the surface of your potential. Titan, you think you're just a strong guy who can fly." He patted the hero on the shoulder. "If you *knew* what you were capable of doing . . . And Energy? You could extinguish the sun, if only you knew how. As for Quantum . . ." He smiled. "Come here."

With a bemused look on his face, Quantum approached Krodin.

"You're my favorite, did you know that? Seriously. Your power is almost incomprehensible, even to me. But my friend Casey understands it. You think you're a master of speed. But what is speed, except distance over time? Those odd feelings you get, those visions that you haven't told anyone about?" Krodin grinned. "They are echoes from the future. With enough experience you will be able to control time itself." He reached out his right hand and casually placed it on the back of Quantum's neck. "In some ways it's a shame that this is a trap."

Energy frowned. "What?"

"It's a trap. All of your fellow superheroes—except those who are loyal to me—are also imprisoned within this island. You're all going die." Before any of them could react, Krodin squeezed his right hand.

There was a loud *crack*, and Quantum's body dropped to the ground.

"Had to kill him first," Krodin said. "Otherwise he'd be able to outrun the explosion."

They attacked him immediately: Titan landed a powerful punch that knocked Krodin off his feet. Energy blasted him with high-frequency microwaves. Krodin snatched up Quantum's body and threw it at Energy, knocking her to the ground.

The Shark immediately leaped onto Krodin's back and locked his cuffed hands around his neck. "Dioxin—come on! Do your thing!"

Dioxin rushed forward, his acid-dripping hands out-stretched, but Krodin jumped up and back, somersaulting backward over The Shark.

Unable to stop himself in time, Dioxin's hands pressed against The Shark's steel-mesh armor and instantly burned through.

Ignoring the other attacks, Krodin balled his hands into fists and slammed them against the sides of The Shark's head, then kicked the screaming villain's body at Dioxin as easily as if he were kicking a football. "So much for your legendary invulnerability."

Titan crashed into Krodin's chest, grabbed hold of him, and tried to lift him into the air.

"Won't work," Krodin said. "Remember last month when I asked you to fly me to Georgia? Anything you do to me will work only once." He broke Titan's grip and threw him to the ground, then stamped down on his chest hard enough that they could hear the firecracker-like snapping of his ribs.

"You maniac!" Energy screamed. "I knew we couldn't trust you! This whole plan was just to get us in one place?"

Krodin looked at her. "Correct. But you're too late. The bomb is real. I've got plans, and you people are just going to get in the way. So for the greater good of the human race you all have to die."

Titan rolled to the side and used the back of his glove to wipe the blood from his mouth. "We'll stop you, Krodin. Whatever it takes. And we'll find the bomb."

"No, you won't," Krodin said. "You don't have enough time."

Energy stared at him. "How long—"

The sky turned white.

CHAPTER 16

LANCE WAS JERKED awake by an unbelievably loud clanging sound that felt like it rattled through his entire skull.

He looked around to see the prison guard standing on the far side of the barred door, slamming his baton against the bars.

"Up!" the guard shouted. "You got two minutes to get yourself ready!"

Lance pulled the blanket to one side and rolled to his feet. "It's not eight o'clock already, is it?"

"Seven."

"But the woman said work didn't start until—"

"Shut up. Hands behind your back, then walk backward toward the bars."

Lance did as he was told. He felt the handcuffs ratchet into place on his wrists, and four minutes later he was outside the police station being steered toward a waiting blue-and-gold patrol car by another uniformed officer.

"Your first day, right?" the Praetorian officer asked. "Your counsel officer explained everything to you?"

"She explained that I don't have any rights, if that's what you mean," Lance said.

"That's what I mean." The officer opened the car's rear door. "Get in."

Lance climbed into the backseat, not an easy task with his hands cuffed behind his back. "Where are you taking me?"

"No talking."

Lance shrugged. "What difference will it make now? I'm already arrested."

The Praetorian frowned for a moment, then said, "You've got me there." He closed the door and climbed into the driver's seat, tossing the bag containing Lance's clothes onto the passenger seat, then unclipped his radio from his shoulder. "Dispatch, this is O'Meara."

A voice crackled over the car's speakers. "Go ahead, O'Meara."

"About to depart with suspect McKendrick. ETA one hundred minutes."

"Acknowledged, O'Meara. You require support?"

The officer looked at Lance in the rearview mirror. "For *this* guy? No support needed, Dispatch."

"Acknowledged. Dispatch out."

As the officer started up the engine, Lance leaned forward and asked, "So what am I going to be doing?"

"There's a major national beauty competition and they're short one judge."

"Yeah, that's hilarious. Look, can't you just let me go and pretend I escaped or something?"

"What do *you* think?"

The officer was in his late twenties, Lance guessed. He was a head taller than Lance and a little overweight. *Might be able to outrun him*, Lance thought, *if I can get out of the handcuffs. And out of the car.* He sighed. "I *hate* being captured."

O'Meara laughed as he steered the car out of the lot behind the station. "Happens a lot, does it?"

"Feels like it, yeah. Hey, do you remember back a few years when America was a real country and we had real cops instead of you fascists?"

"What? We're not fascists. We're just doing our jobs."

"Right. I was arrested because another officer thought I was lying to him. What sane society puts people in jail for telling a lie?"

"That's always happened, kid. Lies like 'I never murdered that guy' and 'I didn't steal all that money.'"

"Yeah, but they were imprisoned because of the crimes, not the lies."

"McKendrick, you can't talk your way out of this. You did the crime, you do the time. You heard that before, yeah? Sure you did. Well, they don't make up cool phrases like that for no reason, you know."

"Yeah, that's *real* cool," Lance said under his breath. "What about parole?"

O'Meara laughed again. "Parole? There's a word I haven't heard in a few years. There's no such thing as parole anymore. It was a crazy idea anyway. You sentence someone to ten years, then ten years is how long they should serve. Letting them out early just doesn't make any sense."

"I really don't want to go. I want to see my mom and dad again."

"Oh, *here* we go. Try not to cry, kid. It's hard to wipe away tears with your hands cuffed behind your back."

"In my world they were murdered. *And* my brother. Three weeks ago. I came here and suddenly they're alive again. You can't imagine how that feels. And now I'm locked up and it could be months before I even have a trial."

The officer shook his head. "Now the sympathy card. You're really checking all the boxes, aren't you?"

"It's true. My family was killed by a supervillain."

"Is that so? There aren't any supervillains anymore. They're all dead. Except for Daedalus, 'course. And they'll get him soon enough."

Lance was about to ask, "Who the heck is Daedalus?" when O'Meara continued, "But I suppose there's that guy earlier today. The big blue guy. But they'll catch him too."

"He was with me and the others when we fought Krodin. His name is Brawn. I think the same thing happened to him that happened to me. I vanished from where I was in my world and appeared in the same place in this one. In my world, Brawn was in a prison called Oak Grove. That's where he appeared, right?"

"Funny you should say that . . ."

"That's what it said on the news. And the me from this world vanished from school. Same time, same thing. We replaced this twisted reality's versions of ourselves."

"I should let you know . . . Along with the abolition of parole, they did away with the insanity plea. So don't bother trying to pull a Section Eight on me, kid. It won't do you any good."

"I'm not crazy."

"Then you're lying to an officer of the law. Haven't you learned yet how bad that can be? I've heard you can be arrested for that." The officer smirked and let out an annoying laugh.

After a few seconds, Lance asked, "Where are we going, anyway?"

"Emergency repair work. They need all the strong, able-bodied men they can get." O'Meara took another look at Lance in the rearview mirror. "Guess they're *really* desperate."

Lance raised his eyes. "Yeah, you're hilarious. Just drive the car." Then he added, "But, y'know, feel free to take your time. I'm not in a hurry to get there."

Roz sat side by side with the girl, Victoria, on the edge of the subway platform, their legs swinging free.

"They dint wake up," the girl said in a matter-of-fact tone as she picked at a scab on her left knee.

Roz put her hand on the girl's shoulder. "Victoria . . . Please, you have to understand. They're gone."

"No, they're still—"

"They died. Their bodies are left behind but not the . . . not the spark that makes them people. Do you understand what that means?"

Victoria shook her head.

"It's like . . ." Roz tried to think of a way to get the point across to the girl. "See that soda can over there?"

"Yeah."

"It's empty. The can is still there, but the soda is gone. That's what happened to your family."

Victoria sniffed, and dragged her bare forearm beneath her nose. "Daddy found some meat an' he cooked it an' I dint want any 'cos it smelt bad an' then they got sick an' they dint wake up."

Could have been poisoned, Roz thought, *set down for the rats. How long has she been down here? Must be years.* "Victoria, how old are you?"

"I don't know."

"Well . . . Can you remember your last birthday party? How many candles were on the cake?"

"Four."

"And was that in your house, or down here?"

"In th' house, I think."

"And is there anyone else down here? Any other people?"

"I hear their voices, sometimes, but I do hide."

Roz got to her feet, then crouched down and lifted Victoria into her arms. The girl was stiff, awkward, unused to being touched. "You really can't stay here. Do you want to come with me?"

"Mom an' Dad . . ." She sniffed again.

Roz hugged her tightly. "It's OK. You can cry if you want to." This close, the odor from her clothes and body was almost choking, and Roz forced herself to breathe through her mouth. "You come with me. But first we'll go and say good-bye to your family, all right?"

"Will I see them again?"

"No, sweetheart, I'm sorry. You'll see them in your dreams, maybe, but not in the real world."

• • •

James Klaus was freezing by the time he and Abby reached the outskirts of Midway. He'd managed to successfully float—he didn't really consider it flying—over the rooftops without too many problems. Once, an unexpected gust of wind caught him and sent him drifting far from Abby, but he was able to push himself back once he'd stopped spinning and tumbling.

Now they were resting on the roof of a grain silo. James rubbed his arms to keep warm. "It's cold up there. Or maybe using my power so much is just draining my energy."

"Get over it, you big baby. It's going to take a long time to get all the way from here to the East Coast," Abby said. "Unless you can fly me too."

"I'm willing to give it a go if you are," James said. "But it takes a lot of concentration just to keep myself up in the air. Two people could be tricky. It'll work better if you hold on to me as we fly."

"Hmm."

"What's that mean?"

"I'm sure your motives are honorable, James." She stood up. "Want to try?"

"We should try from the ground. First rule of flying: Never jump off something high enough for the impact to drive your skull into your chest."

Abby looked over the edge. "It's about, what, twenty-five yards? I can survive that easy."

"I'm not sure *I* can."

She turned back to him, stepped close, and put her arms around his waist. "Let's go."

James concentrated and built a series of continuous shock waves around his body.

"It's working!" Abby said.

They rose slowly from the top of the silo, drifted over the edge and down toward the ground.

"James, we need to go *up*."

"No, we need to go *forward*. Up is dangerous. And colder. Huh. You all mocked me before because my costume was made from a wet suit. Well, I wouldn't mind having it on right now. Good insulation in a wet suit."

Abby said, "Hold on, this isn't very comfortable." She began to squirm around him.

"What are you doing?"

"You're going to give me a piggyback. And that way I can have my hands free in case I need to shoot at anything."

James shook his head. "This is embarrassing. I hope no one sees us. And I really hope that *Lance* never finds out."

"I think he has enough to worry about," Abby said.

"Could be. I wonder where he is. I'm assuming that the same thing happened to him. But he's probably OK—he can talk his way out of anything. He's probably having the time of his life, wherever he is."

Abby said nothing for a moment, then, "You didn't hear, did you? James . . . Lance's parents and brother were killed."

"Oh jeez . . . When?"

"The night we fought Krodin in Windfield. Slaughter escaped, remember? She went after Lance's family. When

Paragon brought him back home, the house had been half demolished, and Lance's mother and father and brother were dead. Max arranged for Lance to be put in some secure place. I don't know where, but it wasn't with relatives or friends."

"And Max didn't tell *us*?"

"Apparently he didn't consider us at risk. Slaughter didn't know who we were."

"That's not the point! Lance is our friend. Well, kind of. Either way, we owe him our lives. I mean, he could have come and lived with one of us. Not me, though."

"Nor me. We don't have the space."

"We do, but my folks would never go for it."

"Because he's white?"

"No, because they're miserable jerks. Anyway, my stepdad is white. Oh man . . . Slaughter just murdered them?"

"Smashed into their house and broke their necks," Abby said.

"Poor kid. He . . ." James stopped. A thought had occurred to him. "Abby, in this world his family could still be alive. Krodin changed our past, which means that we never fought him and Slaughter at Windfield. She'd know nothing about Lance."

"You could be right. If they *are* still alive, he'll be better off not finding out about it. Think what that would be like—to lose your whole family and then get them back. That could drive someone insane."

The car hit a bump and Lance McKendrick flinched, sat up, and looked around. The car was coming to a stop in front of a set of tall, steel-mesh gates. Behind them, identical gates were slowly swinging closed.

"Where are we?" Lance asked, blinking furiously. With his hands still cuffed behind his back, he was unable to rub his eyes.

"So you're finally awake," Officer O'Meara said.

"Didn't realize I was asleep," Lance replied. "How long have I been out?"

"About thirty minutes. We're here."

"And where's here, exactly?" Through the front windshield Lance saw three men wearing dark-blue uniforms slowly approaching the gates, each with their hands casually resting on their holstered sidearms. Beyond them was what Lance at first took to be nothing more than a large, featureless wall—at least five stories high—but then he shifted his gaze to the right and saw the edge of the wall, and realized that it was the side of a building.

"A prison? Oh *man!*" *So much for my escape plans.* Lance had hoped he'd find an opportunity to pick the locks on his handcuffs—but that wouldn't be much use if he was trapped inside a locked prison.

A door in the inner set of gates opened, and the three uniformed men stepped through. One was carrying a long steel pole with a mirror affixed to the end. The men signaled to Officer O'Meara to pop the trunk and the hood.

"What are they doing?" Lance asked.

"Looking for bombs, contraband, that kind of thing."

Lance watched the men as they quickly and efficiently checked the patrol car.

Lance could feel the panic begin to rise. *If they search me, they'll find the lock picks!* He squirmed about in the seat. "My arms are cramping. Can you unlock the cuffs? It's not like I'm going to be able to escape."

"Just sit still, kid."

"You can lock them again in front of me."

O'Meara looked at Lance over his shoulder. "What are you up to?"

"Nothing. I'm just . . . Look, how am I supposed to do any work if I've got cramps in my arms?"

The officer pointed ahead, toward the far side of the compound. "See those prisoners over there? Repairing the wall? You'll be with them. But you're too small and skinny to be much use. They'll probably just have you sweeping up or something."

Lance stared at the prisoners. There were maybe a dozen of them, all wearing orange one-piece suits much like his own. Three of them were clearing away rubble from the shattered wall, and the rest had formed a chain carrying fresh cinder blocks from the back of a flatbed truck.

In a semicircle around them eight guards stood watch, powerful-looking rifles at the ready.

"What happened here?" Lance asked, though he already knew the answer.

"This is where the blue guy appeared," O'Meara said. "Twelve feet tall, at least. Just appeared out of nowhere in the middle of the prison and smashed his way out."

So this is Oak Grove Prison, Lance thought, *where Max and the others left Brawn after the battle with Krodin.* "They, uh, they catch him yet?"

"Not that I've heard. Only a matter of time, though. Someone that big can't hide for too long."

One of the gate guards slapped his hand down on the hood of the car, stepped aside, and waved the car forward.

O'Meara had driven barely two yards when one of the other guards stopped them. "Prisoner's name?"

"Lance McKendrick."

The guard examined a clipboard, and nodded. "All right. You waiting around to take him back?"

"Nah, boss said to leave him here until the work is done. No sense me driving back and forth every day."

The guard tilted his head to the side and peered in at Lance. "All right."

The inner gates rattled open, and O'Meara drove the patrol car through, then got out and opened the rear door. "Well, this is it, McKendrick. You keep your head down and do what you're told, and the time'll pass before you know it."

"If I have to stay here, they'll kill me," Lance said. "I mean, I know I'm not exactly one of the good guys, but the gangs in here will rip me apart!"

O'Meara frowned. "Gangs? There *are* no gangs, kid. You spent most of the journey criticizing our judicial system, but you didn't take into account that it *works*. You said that everyone on the planet was insane to accept things as they are, but let me tell you, they're still smarter than *you* are." He pointed toward the prisoners working on the wall. "These are the only guys in here."

Abby and James were halfway across Minnesota when he suddenly dropped out of the sky.

Sitting on James's back, with her hands resting lightly on his shoulders, Abby felt a moment of panic. *He's fainted!* "James!"

"We're in trouble. We've been spotted. Two Raptors coming from the south. They've been ordered to capture us if possible. If not, they're to shoot to kill. We're not going to be able to out-fly them."

"Use your power—make them deaf or something."

"I can't, not right now. It's all I can do to get us down in one piece. *Two* pieces. Hold on. I'm heading for that field."

They swooped in low over the land, toward a large copse of fir trees, and then James slowed to a stop a few feet off the ground. Abby jumped down, landing in the long grass. "I think this used to be a golf course. . . . Look, that's a sand trap, right?"

"Could be," James said. "Man, I'm exhausted." He swiveled so that his body was horizontal, then floated down until he was lying flat in the grass.

"How long do we have before they reach us?"

"A couple of minutes."

"We could run," Abby suggested.

"I can't. I'm wiped, and I'm freezing. I feel like I've spent a week lifting weights inside a fridge."

"Oh, thanks a bunch! I'm not *that* heavy!"

He smiled. "I didn't mean that. You think you can take down two Raptors with your bow?"

Abby looked to the south. She couldn't see anything yet. "Maybe, yeah. But I'll have to wait until they get really close—I don't want them to crash and kill the crew. You could blast them with shock waves until they give up."

James raised his head a little. "I'm not sure I'll have the strength. I can hear the crews talking. . . . They know we're the same people they were chasing in Midway." He reached out his hand to Abby. "Help me up. They're almost here."

She grabbed his arm and hauled him to his feet, then unclipped her bow and set it up. "How many arrows do I have left?" she asked as she drew one from the quiver.

"Lots. About thirty-five, forty maybe. So how do we do this? You shoot first and I hit them with shock waves, or the other way around?"

"Let's take one each."

"Here they come."

The Raptors came in much lower and faster than Abby expected, their undersides crashing through the trees' upper branches.

She immediately loosed her arrow—it punctured the first Raptor's fuselage close to the edge without doing any apparent damage.

It shot up and over them while the second Raptor veered to the left, banked full circle as it dropped, then came out of the turn only a few yards above the ground, racing straight toward them.

"Into the trees!" Abby yelled to James. "They won't be able to follow us!"

As she turned to run, James grabbed her arm. "No! That's where the other one is heading. . . . They're going to crash straight down and rip up the forest if they have to. I'll go after it—you stand and fight, Abby."

They looked into each other's eyes for a moment, then James ran for the trees.

Abby whipped out another arrow. The Raptor was almost on her now, and showed no sign of stopping. She loaded the arrow into the bow, aimed it . . .

Under her breath, she muttered, "Please don't make me do this!"

It wasn't going to stop. Abby released the arrow.

It punctured the craft's cockpit glass, passed through the shoulder of one of the pilots.

The Raptor kept coming. Abby ran toward it, jumped up at the last second, landed hard on the top of the hull, rolled, and spilled to the ground on the other side.

The Raptor swerved to the left so sharply that it almost tipped over, then zoomed toward her again.

They are not *trying to capture us!*

Abby ran to the left, but the craft adjusted its course. *Come on, then! A little closer . . .*

She shot another arrow at the cockpit—it clipped the upper arm of the second pilot. For a brief moment she could see the man jerk back in pain, then the Raptor was almost on top of her. Abby dropped flat to the ground.

It passed over her so close that she could feel it brushing the fletching on her arrows. As the rear of the craft approached, she stabbed upward with an arrow and held on.

She was dragged on her back through the grass for a hundred yards and crashed through the damp sand of a long-disused bunker before the Raptor slowed to a stop, hovering almost silently two feet above the grass.

A voice from inside said, "Did we get her? We musta got her."

A second voice said. "Don't see anything back there, Captain."

"We'd better have got her. The little cow coulda *killed* me!"

Well, you were trying to kill me, Abby thought. Quietly, she let go of the arrow and began to climb along the underside of the Raptor. There was no heat or downdraft from the underside's white lights. Whatever it was that allowed the machine to fly, it was far in advance of the technology of her own version of Earth.

"That's one," the captain said. "How's the other ship doing?"

"I can't raise them."

Abby kept clear of the windows as she climbed onto the side of the vehicle, then crawled across the top.

"Got a transponder signal?"

"They're a mile away, on the ground. Not moving."

"Take us there. High arc—give the perps a smaller target. And contact the Alpha team, see if there's any trace of the blue giant yet."

Abby grabbed onto a steel rail that ran across the top of the hull, and the craft surged into the air once more. Then she pulled herself forward, hand over hand, until she reached the cockpit. She held on with one hand and swung herself over the edge.

She stared in at the crew's astonished faces and grinned.

The captain jumped forward, slammed his hand down on the control panel.

Immediately the craft stopped. Abby was flung forward. She lost her grip on the hull. And fell.

James heard the trees crashing and snapping ahead of him as he ran. He had no idea what he was going to do when he saw the Raptor, but he was determined that neither he nor Abby would be captured.

Through a gap in the forest he saw it. It bore down on him like a massive misshapen bulldozer, ripping saplings out of its path, smashing through tree trunks in a shower of splinters, branches, and leaves.

He stood his ground and hit the Raptor with the most powerful shock wave he could muster.

The invisible shock wave struck the Raptor like a tornado: The craft shuddered and bucked, its prow rising several yards into the air before it came crashing down, trembling to a halt in an explosion of shattered glass and jagged fragments of steel paneling.

Oh man . . . Didn't know I could do that. James blocked the sound of his own footsteps from reaching the crew as he slowly approached the Raptor.

The craft's entire hull was dented and warped, as though it had been flown at top speed into some massive, impenetrable wall. *This thing is never going to fly again*, James thought.

There was a groan from inside, and the hatch on the starboard side slid partway open. One of the soldiers tumbled out onto the forest floor and lay still.

James walked up to the soldier and looked at him for a moment before reaching down and pulling the man's gun from its holster. Then he peered in through the hatch.

There were three other soldiers inside. Two—the pilots—

lay slumped across their control panels, their faces, hands, and uniforms covered in small cuts from the shattered cockpit glass. The third soldier was feebly attempting to get up off the floor, but as James watched, the man's arms gave way and he collapsed facedown onto the deck.

No one dead. That's good.

Then he heard a scream from somewhere behind him: "Thunder! I'm falling!"

He stepped back from the downed Raptor and soared into the air, arced toward the source of the sound.

As he cleared the trees, the second flying craft bore down on him, forcing him to rise suddenly to get out of its path.

James spotted Abby a few seconds later, plunging headfirst toward the ground, and knew he wouldn't reach her in time.

He reacted without thinking: He hit Abby with a shock wave that knocked her off course. She tumbled through the air and came crashing down into a large bunker, showering the green with glistening sand.

By the time he reached her, the sand had settled, and Abby lay still and unmoving on the edge of the bunker.

James dropped down next to her, listened for her pulse and breathing. *She's OK, she's OK.* "Abby? Are you hurt?"

Abby groaned and opened her eyes. "Only my pride. And my back and my arms and my legs. What happened?"

"You fell. What, were you on top of that thing?"

She sat up. "Yeah. What about yours?"

"Destroyed." He straightened up, listening. "Your one seems to be leaving."

"They'll come back for us. And there won't be just two of them next time."

"I know." He helped her to her feet. "Let's go."

"Give me a minute to get my breath back." Abby looked around, then shook her head slowly. "This is impossible, you know that? We were barely able to defeat Krodin last time. Now we'll have his whole army against us."

"What else can we do? Sit back and let things go on as they are?"

"No. But it's going to take more than the two of us. How far are we from Oak Grove?"

"A couple of hundred miles at least," James said. "In the wrong direction."

"Because I'm thinking that we need backup. We need to find Brawn."

CHAPTER 17

ROZ DALTON WAS FINDING the going tough. Walking halfway across Manhattan on the surface was one thing, but it was considerably more difficult in the subway tunnels.

After Victoria had said a tear-filled good-bye to her family, the girl collected her few belongings—a man's baseball hat and a stained Cabbage Patch doll with only one arm—and then put her hand in Roz's and led her through the tunnels.

Now Victoria was getting tired, and Roz was carrying her in her arms.

"Don't fall asleep, honey," Roz said. "I don't know the way."

"Jus' keep goin' this way," Victoria said, without looking. Her head was resting on Roz's shoulder.

In her free hand Roz was carrying a flashlight she'd found in another maintenance room, on a shelf that had been too high for Victoria to reach. The beam bobbed and weaved ahead of them, occasionally startling a scrabbling nest of rats.

"I bin all th' way to th' link tunnel, but I never went in it."

"What does it link to?" Roz asked.

Victoria raised her head. "What?"

"Where does the link tunnel go?"

"Dunno."

"But it'll get us off the island, right?"

"We ain't on a *island*, Roz. It's a tunnel."

Roz smiled. "OK." Then the flashlight beam caught something in the distance that she hadn't expected: The tunnel was blocked. It looked as though the roof had collapsed. "Aw *no*."

She set Victoria down while she examined the debris. Tons of bricks, huge slabs of rough concrete, tons of packed dirt, and several foot-thick girders blocked their path.

"We can go through there," Victoria said, pointing to a small gap at the top of the pile.

"You can, maybe, but I think I'm too big," Roz said. She scrambled up the debris and examined the gap. "Yeah, there's no chance I'm fitting through that."

"But you hafta. Th' link tunnel is on th' other side. This is th' only way to get there."

Roz let go of the flashlight and allowed it to float next to her as she pushed against a large slab of concrete wedged close to the roof.

It shifted a little, and Roz heard pebbles spilling down the other side. "It's moving! Victoria, catch the flashlight and keep the beam on me, OK?"

Roz sent the flashlight drifting down to the girl, then pushed again, this time using her telekinetic shield to try to lift the slab at the same time. With a scrape of stone against brick, the slab jerked forward, then collapsed to its side, still at the top of the debris pile but now allowing Roz enough space to get through.

"Yes! Climb up, Victoria—we can get through now!"

But then she noticed her shadow trembling and looked back to see that the girl was staring up at her, shaking.

"How'd you do that to th' flashlight? You made it fly!"

Roz sat down at the top of the rubble. "I'm a superhuman. I have special powers."

"Like a witch?"

"No! Well, maybe. But if I am, then I'm a *good* witch." *I hope*, she added silently.

Lance's arms and back were aching. His hands were covered in small, stinging cuts and bruises, the injuries not helped by the too-big prison-issue gloves; the coarse fake leather had rubbed his skin raw in places.

His only consolation was that the prison guards hadn't searched him well; his lock picks were still tucked into his right sock.

Around him, the other prisoners had worked steadily and constantly, usually breaking silence only when they needed to check something with the guards.

Brawn's escape from Oak Grove Prison had caused a considerable amount of damage. On their first rest break the other prisoners told Lance that the superhuman giant had materialized inside the main prison building. He'd reacted with confusion at first, looking around at everything and wondering how and why everything had suddenly changed.

Two of the guards, believing that they were under attack, had opened fire. Brawn had rushed at the nearest wall, smashed his massive fists straight through the two-foot-thick concrete, and torn a hole big enough to climb through.

"You shoulda *seen* him," one of the prisoners said. "They was shootin' an' the bullets was just, like, bouncin' offa his back an' he didn't even react or nothin', jus' kept pullin' chunks outta the wall, and then he got out here inta the yard and jus' ran at the fence an' jumped clear over it, easy as you or me hoppin' a garden gate. Disappeared across the fields. They're gonna catch him soon enough; fella that big musta left footprints a blind man could follow."

To repair the wall, the prisoners first had to clear away the debris and then pull down the shattered bricks and chunks of mortar that had been left behind. Lance, being by far the smallest of the prisoners, was quickly deemed too weak to shift the rubble or lift the new blocks, so he was put in charge of the cement mixer.

On any other day, Lance would have been delighted. He'd always wanted to operate a cement mixer.

For two solid hours he shoveled sand, cement, and water into the rumbling machine's rusted and battered drum, tipped the mixture into a wheelbarrow when it was ready, and hefted the squeaking barrow back and forth between the mixer and the wall.

When the sun set, the work slowed a little, but didn't stop. A trio of portable spotlights were set up to shed glaring light and confusing multiple shadows on the scene.

At midnight, one of the guards blew a whistle. "Awright. Tools down. Ten-minute break."

One of the prisoners moved toward the guards, his hand raised to his forehead to shield his eyes against the spotlights behind them. "Need the restroom, boss."

The guard named Coleman—Lance assumed he was in charge—jerked his thumb over his shoulder. "Be quick about it. Krejci, go with him."

The prisoner moved to climb through the hole in the wall and into the prison, but Coleman shouted, "Not *that* way, ya numbskull! Mortar's still wet! Go 'round the corner ta the door!"

Another prisoner said, "I gotta go too, boss."

"'Course ya do. Anyone else?"

All the other prisoners raised their hands. Coleman told the rest of his colleagues to accompany them back inside the prison, leaving him alone in the yard with Lance. "What about you, kid?"

Lance leaned back against the cement mixer and shook his head. "I'm OK." He pulled off his oversized gloves and flexed his fists to try to get some feeling back into them.

"So what're ya in for?"

"I'm just awaiting my arraignment. A cop accused me of lying to him."

"They ain't cops, kid."

"Sorry. Police officer."

"They ain't that, either. They're Praetorians. We're about the last bunch they ain't taken over yet. So *did* ya lie ta him?"

"No."

Coleman lowered his rifle to the ground and rested it against his knee, then removed his cap and mopped at his balding head with a stained handkerchief. "Gotta be more to it than that, kid. Lying ta them is bad, but they don't lock ya up for it. Got priors?"

Lance shrugged. "Nothing big. Never been actually arrested before."

"Well, ya picked a good day ta start. So what are ya, some kinda moron?"

Lance started to protest, but caught himself at the last moment. It wouldn't do to have another officer of the law on his bad side. "I was just unlucky."

"I'll say ya were." Coleman looked at his watch. "Ya sure ya don't gotta go use the bathroom? 'Cos we got five more hours a this, an' next break ain't 'til two thirty."

"Maybe I will," Lance said, straightening up. He started to move toward the corner, following the path the other prisoners had taken. "Which way . . . ?"

Coleman snatched up his rifle. "Hold up there, little buddy. Ya don't go inside unaccompanied." He fell into step beside Lance.

They rounded the corner and had almost reached a darkened doorway when Lance stopped and stared at the steel-plated doors. "I . . . I've never been inside a prison before. I was in the cell in Northlands station, but not a *real* prison." *Come on!* he thought. *How long can it take them all to have a pee?*

Coleman raised his eyes. "Fer cryin' out loud, kid, it's just a building! It ain't haunted."

"Yeah, but . . . I shouldn't even *be* here! I didn't do anything wrong!"

The officer reached out with his free hand and grabbed hold of Lance's arm, tugging him toward the doors.

Lance said, "Wait!" and shrugged himself free. "I'll do it myself. My dad always said that a man's got to face his own responsibilities, and he's got to do it on his feet, and do it alone. Otherwise he's got no business calling himself a man."

Coleman considered that. "Yeah, awright. Yer old man was kinda makin' sense there. Pity he didn't think ta teach the diff'rence between right an' wrong, ain't it?"

"He taught me," Lance said. "I . . . I guess I should have paid more attention. You know something? He was never once in trouble with the law. Not even a parking ticket." Lance stopped. He could see from the expression on Coleman's face that he wasn't going to be able to stall the man any further.

Lance took a deep breath, squared his shoulders, and began to stride toward the doors.

Just as they reached the doorway, the doors burst open and the other guards and prisoners began to stream through. Lance saw Coleman step to the left to avoid them—so he stepped to the right.

A group of three prisoners came out in a bunch. Hidden from Coleman's view, Lance ran.

He had just reached the corner when he heard Coleman screaming, "Stop him!"

Lance threw himself at the nearest portable spotlight. It toppled over, crashed into another. Before they had hit the ground, Lance snatched up the shovel and threw it at the third: The head of the shovel struck the spotlight's glass.

Now moving in almost complete darkness, Lance kicked at some of the recently laid cinder blocks, toppling them into the hole.

Then he scrambled toward the cement mixer and hauled himself up and into its massive drum just as the running footsteps rounded the corner.

"Flashlight!" he heard Coleman shout. "Someone gimme a flashlight!"

Making as little noise as possible, Lance began scraping the wet mortar from the inside of the drum and plastering it over his face and body. His hope was that anyone taking a quick glance into the mixer would see nothing but mortar. The drum's opening faced away from the hole in the wall, reducing the chance of someone seeing inside by accident.

"Dumb kid's escaped *inta* the prison!" Coleman said, laughing. "Where's he think he's goin' ta go?"

Another guard said, "So, what, we go after him or leave him? I mean, not much he can do in there. It's all locked up. And he's practically useless out here."

Uh-oh, Lance thought. *If they start loading the mixer . . .*

"Whadaya think we do, Morrison? We put the rest a these guys back inside. Then we go find the little punk! Kid thinks he outsmarted *me*, he's sorely mistaken. And *you*, Morrison, ya can wait out here in case he decides ta come back out this way."

Lance heard their footsteps moving away and slowly exhaled a deep breath he hadn't realized he'd been holding. *OK. One left. How am I going to get past him? Maybe I can reason with him.*

Then he heard Coleman's voice floating back. "Y'all know the drill, men. Escaped prisoner. If ya hafta, shoot ta kill."

CHAPTER 18

I CAN'T STAY HERE much longer, Lance thought. *Either they'll give up the search and come back to work or they'll realize I never went inside the prison at all. Or this mortar is going to harden around me.* The mortar was already starting to sting his skin.

He had no idea how long he'd already spent inside the cement mixer's drum. Twice he had heard another guard come back to Morrison to check in, but for the most part Morrison had remained so silent that Lance had started to wonder whether the man was still there.

I've got to move, find somewhere better to hide.

He reached out and grabbed the lip of the mixer with both hands. The mortar made a quiet, wet slurping sound as he pulled himself forward.

Once his head was free, Lance leaned forward—his stomach now resting uncomfortably on the lip of the drum—

and peered upside down through a gap in the mixer's battered framework. He could see the beam of Morrison's flashlight bobbing about, focused mainly on the hole Brawn had torn through the prison block's wall.

OK, he's not looking over here. . . .

Lance let go of the drum and shifted himself a little farther out; he slid awkwardly forward and down until his hands were resting on the ground, then slowly and silently eased himself out, toppled over onto his back.

He took a few slow, deep breaths as he stared up at the night sky. *All right. I'm out. Now what?*

A quick glance at Morrison told him that the guard was still facing the hole in the wall.

I could run, but where to? He looked toward the high mesh fence cutting the prison off from the outside world. *There's no way I can climb that without being seen.*

Something buzzed behind him, and Lance heard the guard saying, "Morrison. Go ahead, boss."

Coleman's voice crackled over the radio. "Any sign a the kid?"

"No, sir. Nothing at this end. You find him yet?"

A slight pause, then, sarcastically, "Yeah, we found him. That's why I'm askin' you. Just keep yer eyes peeled, Morrison."

Another guard said, "Blasted kid's got to be the world champion at hide-and-seek."

Lance rolled onto his stomach, pushed himself to his feet. The wet mortar clinging to his uniform was much heavier than he'd expected; he felt like he was wearing a suit of armor.

If I run, he thought, *I'm going to leave a trail of this stuff behind me.* Hidden from Morrison's view by the mixer, Lance began to remove as much of the mortar as he could, scooping it off with his hands and dropping it back into the mixer.

As he did so, he looked around the yard. In the almost total darkness it was difficult to see much, but he could just about make out the outline of the now-unladen flatbed truck that had brought the bricks into the prison.

I could hide out in there, Lance thought, and then instantly dismissed the idea. *Pretty soon they're going to start searching everything. I need to get out of the prison.*

He kept a close eye on Morrison as he made his way over to the truck. The guard had the flashlight tucked under his chin like a phone as he scratched his backside with one hand and picked his nose with the other.

Lance tried the truck's passenger-side door. It was locked. He quickly removed the picks from his right sock and began probing the lock. It made no difference to Lance that he couldn't see what he was doing; picking a lock is always done by touch alone.

There was a soft *chunk* as the lock opened. Lance pulled the door open, climbed inside the cab, and slid over to the driver's side.

He reached down to the sides of the truck's steering column, feeling for the ignition slot. With some effort he forced his tension wrench into the slot and gave it a twist.

The dashboard's lights came on.

All right. So I can start this thing. Two important questions: Can I actually drive it, and if I ram the gates at full speed, will I get through?

From what he remembered from his arrival at the prison,

the gates had looked to be very strong. *But then this truck can carry a couple of tons of bricks. . . . It's got to be pretty powerful.*

But which is stronger? The gates or the truck?

He couldn't help grinning to himself. *Well, there's only one way to find out! Drive!*

Lance started the ignition and the truck's engine roared to life.

Abby de Luyando hugged close to James Klaus as they raced through the night air. James had already worked out a way for them to fly separately, but this way was easier, and a little warmer.

But now she could feel his energy flagging. "James? Time to take a break."

"I can keep going."

"No you can't. Set us down."

Far below was a large industrial park containing hundreds of warehouses and factories connected by wide, straight roads.

James drifted down toward the flat roof of one of the warehouses, but Abby nudged his arm. "No, *that* one."

"Why?"

"It's got a chimney. It'll be warmer."

A few minutes later they sat on the roof with their backs to the chimney stack. From deep inside came the repetitive sound of an assembly line. Its faultless rhythm was soothing, and Abby felt her eyes begin to close. "How much farther now, do you think?"

"I couldn't guess. I'm not even certain we're going in the

right direction. If we are, I'll be able to hear Brawn from miles away. He's not exactly stealthy."

"So when we find him . . . what then? There's no way you're going to be able to fly all three of us to New York."

"I haven't thought that far ahead."

Abby got up and stretched. "Man, I'm tired." She walked around in a wide circle, swinging her arms back and forth in unison. "Y'know, for all we know, the soldiers from Unity might already have invaded. With them on our side, we might have a chance against Krodin. But that's no good, because if they *do* invade, then a lot of innocent people will be killed." She laughed at the situation, but it felt hollow. "So we have to stop him *before* the people we need to be able to stop him can get to him."

There was no reply. Abby looked back toward James and saw that he was asleep.

She suddenly felt more alone than ever before. She turned on the spot, looking to the horizon all around, and the enormity of the task ahead made her feel like a single pencil dot on a sheet of paper the size of a football field.

"This is it," Victoria said to Roz. "Th' link tunnel."

After countless twists and turns—Roz knew she'd never be able to retrace her path—through the subway tunnels and maintenance shafts, they had emerged through a side door close to the Manhattan entrance to the Lincoln Tunnel.

Roz smiled and crouched down in front of the girl. "You did good. You got us all the way here!"

"Said I would, dint I?"

"You sure did." She shone the flashlight's beam over the tunnels' asphalt-lined surface. "Finally, we can walk without worrying about tripping on something and breaking our necks."

"I hafta go to sleep now," Victoria said, clutching her Cabbage Patch doll tighter. "An' I'm hungry. We shoulda brung food."

"I told you, honey, you can't eat that stuff anymore. It's all gone stale. It's not good for you." Victoria had survived on candy bars and potato chips scavenged from vending machines throughout the subway system. "When we get to the other side, we'll find something, I'm sure."

Victoria nodded, and Roz could see that her eyes were closing. "Want me to carry you again? You can sleep if you like."

Roz picked her up and carried her out into the tunnel. The air was stale and damp, tinged with the musty odor of fungus and wet clay. Roz's flashlight seemed almost completely ineffective against the darkness, and there was no sound in the tunnel except for the echo of her own footsteps and Victoria's heavy breathing.

Something moved off to her left, and Roz swung the flashlight toward it—twin glints in the darkness flickered for a moment, then vanished. *Just a rat*, she told herself.

She let go of the flashlight and used her telekinesis to raise it up almost to the tunnel's tiled ceiling, angled it so that the beam illuminated the ground ahead of her.

She'd half expected to see stalled cars and trucks, but the tunnel ahead appeared to be completely empty. *What happened to all the cars? Manhattan used to be crazy with traffic.*

There was another noise behind her, and then something brushed against her right foot. Roz yelped and jumped aside, almost dropping Victoria.

Her concentration broken, the flashlight fell, hit the ground with a sharp *crack*, and went out.

"Aw no!" she said aloud, and the soft echo of her voice drifted back to her.

Victoria removed her thumb from her mouth long enough to ask, "What happened?"

"The flashlight fell. Do you still have that candle?"

"I lef' it behind."

"Never mind. We'll be OK." *Now what do I do? Go back? No, better keep walking.*

She reached out to the right with her telekinesis, probing for the sidewall. *Got it.* She walked on, her progress much slower without the light to guide her.

After a few minutes she became aware of a constant dripping sound, growing louder as she walked. *Please don't tell me the tunnel's leaking!*

A hundred steps farther on, she realized that her boots were making light splashing sounds.

A few more steps and she could feel the freezing water lapping over her feet.

A minute later the water was up to her knees.

It was getting harder to walk, harder still to do so quietly. As the water rose to halfway up her thighs, she hoisted Victoria a little higher with the help of her telekinesis, trying to keep the girl's bare feet dry.

We've got to be halfway by now—that has to mean that the water won't get any deeper.

From somewhere ahead Roz heard a brief whisper, followed by someone saying, "Shh!"

She called out, "Anyone there?"

Silence.

"If anyone *is* there, we need your help. The water's getting deeper, and I can't see where we're going!"

Then a voice said, "It'd be a fair bit easier if you walked on the other side. You know. Where the *walkway* is."

A light shone out from the darkness, dazzling her. She blinked rapidly, looked away for a moment. When she looked back, the light was shining off to the side a little, and she could see that it was coming from a flashlight somewhere farther along, on the water.

There was a brief burst of splashing, and then something large and yellow was floating toward her. An inflatable life raft.

Inside, two men were paddling while a third—who seemed to be only a couple of years older than Roz—held the flashlight on her. "So," the young man said. "Who are you, what do you want, and so on. Blah-de-blah-de-blah. I'm sure you know the drill."

"My name is Roz. I'm trying to get to New Jersey."

"And who's this little one?"

"Victoria. She's been living alone in the subway tunnel for years."

"Right. Well, you'd better both come with us, then. My name's Joe Ward. Welcome aboard the good ship *Stolen Life Raft*." The flashlight lowered again, and the young man extended his hand. "Pass her over. Careful now. . . . Don't want to capsize us, do you?"

"It's only a few feet deep."

"And my socks would get just as wet as they would if it was a *hundred* feet deep."

"Don't wake her," Roz said. "She's very weak. Severely malnourished."

"I'll be careful." Joe carefully set Victoria down in the rear of the raft, then pulled off his jacket and draped it over her like a blanket. "Now grab my hand, Roz."

Using the man's arm to steady herself, Roz climbed into the life raft.

"About-face, men," Joe said. "Tonight we set sail for Utopia!"

The men with the paddles grumbled as they awkwardly turned the raft around.

"It'd be easier to just start paddling in the opposite direction," Roz said.

"True," Joe said. "But then maritime custom dictates that ships don't have a reverse gear. Probably. I think it's considered to be bad luck or something. Well, this is Nathan on your left, and on your right is Horace."

The man on the right said, "Bill."

"Yes. Bill, short for Horace. So you're on the run, yeah? Or are you just a couple of weary travelers seeking solace on this bitterly cold winter's evening, except it's the summer and it's quite warm?"

"The first one."

"Good stuff. Now, I have two important questions to ask you, Roz. Ready? First question . . . Who are you running from?"

"That is a long story," Roz said. "I'd tell you, but we'd run out of tunnel before we ran out of story."

"Fair enough. Second question . . . This one is for the

grand prize of eighteen million dollars. . . . Are you sitting comfortably, Roz? Of course you're not. You're in a damp life raft with three strangers quite a long way under the Hudson. Never mind. Here comes the question anyway. . . . What kind of an eejit do you take me for? You think we wouldn't recognize Max Dalton's sister when we see her?"

"Ah," Roz began.

"Ah indeed. Now, I have it on good authority—Nathan here told me—that earlier today one Rosalyn Dalton mysteriously disappeared from where she was supposed to be and reappeared where she wasn't supposed to be. An ability that she has never previously demonstrated. That'd be yourself?"

"Yes."

"So what's going on, Roz? Someone like you could go anywhere she wanted with no questions asked. What's with the tunnels and the hiding and all that malarkey? And picking up this little stray along the way? Not exactly the best way to keep a low profile."

"Like I said, it's a long story."

One of the paddles thumped off solid ground, and Joe said, "Well, you can tell it to the boss. Come on. Up you get."

She followed Joe and the others out of the raft and helped them drag it farther out of the water.

Roz bent over and scooped up Victoria. Still asleep, the girl wrapped her arms around Roz's neck. She moaned a little, and Roz said, "Shh . . . It's OK, honey. We're safe now. Everything's going to be all right." Roz turned to Joe. "Do you have a doctor here? She really needs to be checked out. Poor little thing is freezing."

"No problemo," Joe said, and called out, "Lights!"

The tunnel's overhead lights flickered on, and Roz saw that she was surrounded by dozens of armed men and women.

Joe turned to Roz and rested his hand on her shoulder. "Roz, this is the New Jersey branch of the resistance. As you can see, these lovely ladies and upstanding gentlemen all have guns. So if it turns out you're up to something that we don't like, you'll never leave here in one piece. Well, perhaps you will, but it'll be one big wet, messy piece with an awful lot of bullet holes in it."

Roz shrugged his arm away. "You know, I can't tell whether that was a threat or an audition."

Some of the people in the crowd laughed at that.

Joe grinned. "I like you. You're going to be fun to have around. Follow me—we'll go see the doc."

Joe led her through a crude hole that had been cut into the wall, and through a series of dusty, low-ceilinged corridors. "So what's the deal?" he asked as they walked. "Some people are saying that there's a lot of crazy stuff going on right now. Your pal Krodin is up to something big. You know anything about that?"

"Not really."

"Fair enough." Joe stopped outside a frosted-glass door and rapped on it with his knuckles. "Got a patient for you, Doc."

A shadow moved behind the door, and then it was opened by a gray-haired old woman. "What do we have here?"

"This is Roz, Doc. Just arrived. She picked up the little one back in Manhattan."

The woman ushered Roz into the room. "Poor little mite. Put her on the bed there, Roz, and we'll see what we can do."

Roz laid Victoria down on the bed and stepped back. This

was the first chance she had to see Victoria in proper light. Her arms and legs were filthy and stick-thin, covered in scabs and bruises. Her hands and feet were badly calloused, and her hair was matted with so much dirt that it was impossible to tell what color it was underneath. The only clean part of her body was her left thumb, which she'd been sucking while Roz carried her.

"What's her name?" the doctor asked. She pulled the Cabbage Patch doll from Victoria's arms and passed it to Roz, then leaned closer to examine her.

"Victoria," Roz said. "Her family was living in the subway tunnel. They all died. She's been alone for a long time, maybe a year or more."

"Another of the Praetorian's victims, probably," Joe said. "We've come across them from time to time. In the first couple of months after Krodin took control, a lot of people went on the run, and a fair few ended up in the subway tunnels."

Roz reached out and gently stroked Victoria's hand. "Well, I'm glad I met her. I'd never have found my way through the tunnels without her."

The doctor straightened up and turned to Roz. "Will you have a seat please, Roz?" she asked, pointing to an old wooden chair nearby.

"I'm OK. Hungry and tired, but that's all."

"Sit." It was an order, not a suggestion.

Roz sat. "Look, I'm fine. Just tell me that Victoria's going to be all right."

The doctor exchanged a look with Joe, then crouched down next to Roz. "I'm so sorry."

Roz looked at Joe, then back at the doctor. "For what?"

"She's gone."

"What?" Roz swallowed heavily.

"She died. Only a few minutes ago, I'd say."

"No, she's . . . she's just sleepy, that's all. She's . . . she was just *talking* to me! You heard her, Joe, didn't you?"

He shook his head. "She was asleep the whole time. Roz, she was already very weak when you handed her to me."

The doctor said, "We'll give you a few minutes," then nodded to Joe. They left her alone, closing the door behind them.

Roz's knees felt weak as she stood. She sat on the edge of the bed and placed the doll in Victoria's cold arms. "You go now," she whispered. "You go and be with your mom and your dad and your brother again." She leaned forward and kissed Victoria's forehead, her tears leaving clean tracks in the dirt on her face. "Thank you."

"You were there for her at the end," Joe said as he slowly led Roz back through the corridors. "That's what counts. She didn't die alone."

Roz sniffed, and used the cuff of her sleeve to wipe her eyes.

"Come on, we'll go see the boss, if you feel up to it?"

"OK."

As they approached another door, it opened and a tall, slim woman stepped out.

"Boss, this is—"

"I recognize her, Mr. Ward. It's Rosalyn Dalton."

Roz swallowed. *No . . .*

"I heard about your little friend, Roz. You have my sympathies. It's amazing she lasted as long as she did."

Roz couldn't speak. The shock of Victoria's death was bad enough, but this was more than she could take.

"So what brings you here, Roz?" the woman asked. "Realized that the Praetorians' way of life needs to come to an end? Bear in mind that if your answer is anything other than 'Yes,' you might not like our reaction."

"You . . ." She stopped herself. "Yes. The Praetorians have to be stopped."

"Good. My name is Suzanne Housten. Now, if you have any ideas about assassinating me, look down at my feet. Go on. Look."

Roz looked. The woman was floating two inches off the ground.

"Like you, Roz, I'm a superhuman. One of the very few Krodin hasn't murdered. I'm considerably stronger and faster than you are. I could crush your skull between my hands." Then she smiled again. "But I'm sure it won't come to that, will it?"

Roz shook her head. "No." Her heart was beating like crazy. Every instinct told her to run, to get as far away from this woman as possible.

She doesn't know me! Roz told herself. *As far as she knows she's never met me!*

But Roz *had* met this woman before, back in the real world. Back there, Suzanne Housten went under a different name: Slaughter.

CHAPTER 19

THE TRUCK'S WINDSHIELD was heavily cracked, one of its headlights had shattered, and a large section of the outer gate had snagged on some part of the underside and was slowing the truck down and showering the road with sparks that gave away its position.

Right now, Lance didn't care. He was grinning and feeling very pleased with himself.

He took another glance in the driver's-side mirror; the road behind was dark, but he knew it wouldn't remain so for long.

He had a quick mental debate as to whether it would be best to keep going or stop long enough to free the gate from underneath the truck. *Keep going*, he decided.

According to the truck's odometer he was already three miles away from the prison, much farther than he'd expected to get. *Make the most of it*, he told himself. Another look in the mirror. *Any minute now there'll be headlights and it'll all be over.*

But five minutes later he was still alone on the road, and for the first time he began to feel that he might actually get away. *If there were only those eight guards in the prison, they might* not *come after me. . . . They're going to have their hands full trying to stop the other prisoners from getting through the wrecked gate.*

All right, genius. Think! What do I do? Where can I go?

If Brawn was dragged into this world same as me, then it stands to reason that Roz and Abby and Thunder were too. If I can figure out where they are . . . He frowned. *What's the name of the town where Abby and Thunder live? Midway? Something like that, anyway. . . .*

Last time it took us hours to get from there to Oak Grove, and I was either in the back of the truck or asleep for most of the journey. So there's no way I can retrace the route.

Going home isn't an option. So what do I do?

And then he saw a wavering patch of light on the road ahead. For a moment he thought it was simply a malfunctioning streetlight—the first he'd seen since he left the prison—but then he realized that the light was moving. Heading straight toward him.

Lance hit the brakes and the truck squealed, shuddered to a halt, and its engine cut out. He sat gripping the wheel with both hands as he stared at the approaching light, and it was several seconds before he thought to look for its source.

By the time he climbed out of the cab, the light had reached him. As he shielded his eyes to look up, the light vanished.

Silhouetted against the stars, a small flying craft was silently—but rapidly—descending. The underside of the craft held three circular lights, none of them bright enough to have cast the light on the road.

OK, this isn't good. He knew there was no point in running. *They've caught me, but at least I've caused them some trouble.*

The craft—it was about half the size of the truck—came to a stop a couple of feet above the surface of the road and hovered silently. A door in the side slid open, revealing a faint blue glow from within.

Moments later the profile of a man appeared. Steps extended from inside the craft, and the man strode down them.

He walked toward Lance and into the beam of the truck's remaining headlight.

"Not *you* again," Lance said to Max Dalton.

"I was about to say the same thing." Dalton looked from Lance to the truck, then back. "You just can't stay out of trouble, can you?"

"If we ever get home, I'm going to sleep for a *week*," James said to Abby.

Abby was flying along beside him. They had their arms outstretched and were holding on to each other's forearms. "You OK?"

"Not really. I bet every Praetorian in the state is looking for us. They were at my house earlier, did I tell you that? After I got back from my dad's farm, I went to the house and I could hear Praetorian soldiers talking to my mom and Rufus."

"Rufus is your stepdad?"

"Yeah. My little sister's dad. She's the one I'm worried about—I don't much care what the Praetorians do to Mom and Rufus. They can lock them away forever as far as I'm concerned. But Shiho's only seven. I can't let anything happen to her."

"There's nothing we can do about that now, James."

"We're not great at this superhero stuff, are we? We don't know where Paragon, Roz, or Max are, and Brawn's a supervillain, but we don't actually know where he is."

"He's not a bad guy," Abby said. "He's only your age, did you know that? Imagine being sixteen and blue and thirteen feet tall. No one's ever going to think of him as a hero no matter what he does. Plus he said that he gives off some sort of scent that makes people scared of him. Did you get that when you saw him first?"

James nodded. "Yeah. You look at him and go, 'No way!' and you want to run."

"We're lucky. Whatever it is that makes us superhuman . . . At least *we* look normal. Brawn can't change back. He'll be like that forever. I wonder if it ever goes the other way around. The thing that makes us superhuman gives us these gifts, but could it take away stuff as well? Could there be people who have reduced abilities instead of enhanced ones?"

"I think so," James said. "My cousin was telling me about this guy who lives on his street who's supposed to be a complete genius. He's about my age too, but he's already got four college degrees. He used to be big for his age, a good athlete. People were saying that he was going to be a great linebacker one day. Then when he was thirteen he just started getting smarter, but he was losing all his muscle. They thought he was sick or something, but the doctors couldn't find anything wrong. Now he can barely run a hundred yards without collapsing from exhaustion."

"He sounds like pure bully fodder to me."

James laughed. "He would be, but any bullies who go near him have to answer to their parents—the kid does all their tax returns. For free. He enjoys it, apparently."

"Well, if we ever start our own superhero team, we're recruiting him. Put him in some of Paragon's armor so he doesn't get flattened every time we go up against the baddies, and we're good to go. And we'll need armor for Lance too."

"There is no *way* I'm having Lance on my superhero team!"

"*My* team," Abby said. "It's my idea. And don't pretend you don't like him. I can tell you do."

"When we were in the army truck going to Oak Grove, the guy nearly drove me mad. He just can*not* stop talking."

"Well, he's lonely," Abby said.

"What makes you think that?"

She turned her head to look at him. "Because we *all* are. How many friends do you have?"

"Not that many, but I'm not lonely. There's a bunch of guys at school, and sometimes I hang out with them at the skate park."

"I have some people I see from time to time, but no *close* friends. I haven't had any for years. Neither does Roz. And I'm betting that no other superhuman does. Maybe it's a result of keeping our powers a secret, or maybe it's the powers themselves—they change us physically and mentally, so why not socially too?"

"OK . . . But even if that's true, it doesn't explain Lance, does it? He's not a superhuman."

"Maybe he is. He's pretty smart, and he's good at making up stuff that sounds like it could be true—maybe that's his power. Communication skills. Or some sort of . . . What's that power where you can read people's emotions? Not telepathy, the other one?"

"Empathy. Abby, if Lance had superhuman empathy, everyone would love him. He'd be able to get anyone to do anything he wanted. He could . . . Ah. Yeah, I see what you mean. People don't have to love him—just trust him. It's the perfect power for a con artist." James let go of Abby's arm and flexed his fist for a moment before grabbing her arm again. "Arm's getting tired."

"Want me to switch sides?"

"Not yet." With his other hand he pointed down. "Freeway sign—at last." He slowed their flight and drifted down until they were only a hundred yards above the road. "Can you read what it says?"

"No. Still too far."

The freeway was in complete darkness—since the citizens were not allowed to travel at night, there was little point in lighting the roads.

They drifted closer to the sign stretched across the freeway. "Castleton, seven miles," Abby read. "That's close to Oak Grove, isn't it?"

"I think so. But Brawn wouldn't have *stayed* in Oak Grove—he'd have gone on the run. I'll put you down for a few minutes, OK? I need to divert as much of my energy as I can into my hearing."

James descended quickly, set Abby down next to the road sign, then shot up into the air again. In seconds she was only a tiny dot against the dark road. *OK, concentrate!*

He still wasn't sure how his enhanced sense of hearing

worked—all he knew was that he had to constantly maintain a mental barrier to prevent all the noise around from driving him crazy. Now he relaxed that barrier, allowed the sounds to come flooding in.

There were crickets and other night insects, thousands of them. A steady, unbroken stream of chirps and rattles, hisses and scratching. He filtered out those sounds and tried to make sense of what was left.

Cats howling and purring, dogs barking, humans laughing, talking, snoring. The constant buzz of electricity, the rush of water carried through buried pipelines and flowing over riverbeds. All these he filtered out too.

He stripped out the roar of the wind and the hiss of the leaves it blew, the grass it rustled.

And then there was only silence.

Nothing. If he's around here, he's not on the move. I guess even supervillains have to sleep sometime.

Back in his own reality, James knew he could pinpoint almost any sound up to a distance of about eight miles. Here, the lack of traffic noise meant that his radius could be greater than that. He ran a quick calculation in his head. *Say I can hear up to twelve miles. . . . Twelve squared is one hundred and forty-four, multiplied by pi. . . . That's four hundred and fifty square miles.*

And then he heard a voice saying, "Affirmative. Thermal sensors are showing a definite humanoid signature. And that size . . . It's got to be him."

Another voice, this one female: "Patch the images through to my screen. . . . I see it. That's him. All right, people. This monster is *strong*. I want you all to understand that. He is quite capable of tearing one of our ships apart with his bare hands.

He's also bulletproof, close to invulnerable. But I doubt he's fireproof. I want a tight ring of napalm canisters all around him—don't give him anywhere to run."

Oh no! James flew back down to Abby, swooped in, and grabbed her around the waist.

"What . . . ? James!"

"The Praetorians have found Brawn. They're going to use napalm on him, Abby. They're going to kill him."

Deep under the western banks of the Hudson River, Roz Dalton was trying not to show any emotion as she sat with the leaders of the New Jersey resistance cell.

They were seated around a large table in what had once been a locker room. It was a gray, oppressive room with damp walls and a crude flooring of broken-up wooden pallets.

Aside from Roz, there were four people present. Suzanne Housten—Roz was doing her best not to think of the young woman as Slaughter—sat at the head of the table. On her right was Joe Ward, her ever-cheerful second in command. Next to him was a twenty-five-year-old man called Ted Silvestri, then an older man whom Roz had noticed watching her when Joe gave her a brief tour of the complex. He was gray-haired with a neatly trimmed black beard.

Joe slapped his hands together and rubbed them briskly. "Right, lads. Let's call this meeting to order. We're lucky enough to have with us today the delightful and totally zarjaz Rosalyn Dalton, also known as Roz, who by no coincidence whatsoever is the one and only sister of Maxwell Edwin Dalton. Max is well known to us all as Vice-Chancellor of our fine country and is by all accounts a miserable, humorless excuse for a human being who has a face like a zombie warthog chewing a lemon wrapped in barbed wire."

Housten said, "Yes, thank you for the wonderful image, Joe. That'll stay with us forever." She turned to Roz. "Do you feel up to doing this?"

Roz nodded. "I'll be OK."

"Good. Ted says we can trust you, and I trust him. He has abilities of his own. Ted can always—*always*—tell when someone is lying. You're not the same Roz Dalton we have on file. You're . . . an alternative version."

Roz nodded. "Max too. My brother would never do what your Max has done."

Ted shook his head. "You don't believe that, Roz."

"No, I don't. But . . . I *want* to believe it."

Joe said, "Be that as it may, the fact is your brother is number two on our list of enemies. Right after Krodin himself. If what you say is true, then we should be able to count on Max to work with us instead of against us, right?"

"I think so. But the last time I spoke to him, he was talking about running. He doesn't think we can fight Krodin."

"Because you people fought him before," Joe said, "and only barely won."

"I wouldn't say we won. We survived."

"Because this lad Pyrokine turned on Krodin in the end and destroyed him. Or so you thought."

Housten asked, "Your account of the battle is a little sketchy. You've been holding something back, Roz. What is it?"

Roz quickly glanced at Ted, then looked away. "I'd rather not say."

"I'd rather you did. There's a lot happening in this country right now. If we're going to strike against Krodin, it's got to be soon. The more we know about how you fought him, the better chance we'll have. So what is it? What are you keeping from us?"

Roz wet her lips. "All right, then. You were there."

Housten sat back. "Me?"

"You were there."

"I was there. I see. That explains your reaction when you first saw me. You've met me before."

Joe said, "So the boss here was one of your crew fighting the big fella. So we have you, your brother, the lass with the sword, Paragon, who is apparently not a superhuman but a guy in armor, a kid called Lance who's also not a superhuman and can't do much of anything, Thunder, who can control sound waves, and the big blue guy called Brawn. And now Suzanne, who . . . Hold on a second." He looked at Roz for a long moment. "Ah no. You're kidding."

Suzanne Housten turned to him. "What is it?"

"You were one of the bad guys."

Roz said, "It's true. In my world you call yourself Slaughter."

"Well, that's one we didn't see coming," Joe said. "And what does she do, this Slaughter?"

"She kills people."

No one seemed to know how to respond to that.

Eventually, Ted said, "I'm sorry, Suzanne."

The young woman stood up, walked away. And then came rushing back to the table. "No. It's a lie."

"It's not a lie," Roz said. "You—no, your counterpart in my world—murdered my friend Lance's parents and brother.

And dozens of other people before that. She worked for The Helotry. She was a key part of their plan to bring back the Fifth King."

"That's impossible. I've never killed anyone!"

Joe said, "But you do have a bit of a temper on you." Then he hastily added, "I'm just saying!" when she glared at him.

Roz said, "We had a lot of supervillains, and Slaughter was just about the worst. Fast, strong, incredibly vicious, and cruel."

"Stop it," Housten said. "Please. I'm not like that."

"Maybe not, but *she* was!" Roz snapped.

"You little cow . . . ! You're enjoying this, aren't you? This is how you get your revenge on her, by taking it out on me. Well, I—" Housten stopped, and sat down again. "I'm sorry. You've been through a lot today. But I can understand your anger with Slaughter, as long as *you* understand that she's not me."

"That's true," Joe said. "Roz, if you want us to believe your version of Max as a good guy instead of a bad one, then you have to accept that Suzanne here isn't Slaughter. Are you with me?"

Roz suddenly felt ashamed. *He's right. He's absolutely right.* "I'm sorry. . . . It's just that she . . ."

"You were scared of her," Joe said. "I don't blame you. I never even heard of her before now, and she scares me too. But Suzanne is probably our most powerful weapon against Krodin. If she has the same powers as Slaughter, what do you think? Can she take him?"

"No," Roz said. "Max read Krodin's mind—as much of it as he was able to—and said that Krodin's main strength is his adaptability. If you can find something that'll hurt him, it'll work only once. Maybe twice if you're really lucky. He can adapt to any situation, any danger. He recovers almost instantly from any injury. And he seems to have some sort of clairvoyance. A lot of the time when we fought him, he did it with his eyes closed. Max said he can see a battle as though he's looking down on it from above—able to see all sides at once."

"So who do we know who's a match for him?" Joe asked. "This lad Brawn?"

"Brawn's stronger, I think, but Krodin's much faster and much more cruel. What about this world's versions of the superheroes from my world? Energy, Titan, Quantum, and Heimdall were among the most powerful. And Inferno too. If you want to count the bad guys, there was The Shark, Dioxin, Torture, The Red Fury. . . . Loads of them."

Joe said, "I've heard of the first three. They died in Anchorage. The others aren't familiar. But sure they wouldn't necessarily go by the same code names. You know any of their real names?"

Roz shrugged. "Max might know them."

Suzanne said to Joe, "Daedalus, maybe?"

Joe nodded. "Maybe. Roz, we have connections with Daedalus. I'm sure you've heard the name. He's superhuman. Strong, fast, an incredibly brainy fella. He has some sort of weird intuition about you superfolks. He knows the powers inside out, back to front, and probably upside down as well."

Roz said, "If you've got him on your side, as well as Sl— Suzanne, plus you've clearly got lots of weapons and people, then . . ." She shrugged. "What are you waiting for? Why haven't you attacked Krodin yet?"

Ted simply said, "Anchorage."

Joe said, "Krodin lured all the known superhumans—good guys and bad guys—to Anchorage, and then detonated a cobalt bomb. Blew up the entire city. Everyone thinks Daedalus was behind it, but Ted was able to tell from Krodin's speech at the memorial that he was behind it. If we move against him without a surefire way to stop him, there's every chance he'll do it again. Only next time he might pick an even bigger city. What if he did it in the heart of Manhattan? That's one-and-a-half-million people gone right there."

"But if you don't do anything, then . . . what right have you to call yourself the resistance? You're not resisting. You're hiding. You might as well not be here!"

Suzanne said, "When the time is right—"

"Really? When will *that* be? How long are you planning to sit on your butts and do nothing?"

Joe raised his hands. "Now, hold on there, Roz! You've been here less than a day. You don't know—you *can't* know—what it's been like for us." He ran his hands over his hair and sighed. "The right time to attack Krodin is coming, very soon now. But we have to be certain of winning, because we're only going to get one shot at it. With you and your friends here, and with Unity's forces on the way, we're stronger than we have ever been, but we're still going to need more superhumans. Who else do you know who might have survived Anchorage?"

"Impervia," Roz said. "She's here; I've already met her.

She's very strong, practically invulnerable, and she can fly. Her real name is Amandine Paquette."

"Ah," Joe said. "Yeah, we know her. Number four on our list of enemies. You think we can turn her?"

Roz shrugged. "She seems to be committed to the idea that Krodin's way is the right way. I didn't know her too well back home, but she was a lot more, well, peace loving. But if we *can* persuade her to join us, she'd make a great ally. She . . ." Roz stopped herself. "Number four. Krodin and Max are numbers one and two on your list. Who's number three?"

The others all turned to the older man, who until now had remained silent.

He was absently stroking his dark beard as he stared at Roz. "You are."

CHAPTER 20

THREE YEARS ago . . .

A week after the attack on Anchorage, Krodin stood in the General Assembly Hall of the United Nations Headquarters in New York as he addressed the representatives of all 187 member states.

"Good morning. If I could have your attention, please?" He waited a few moments for the representatives to settle down. "I'll keep this brief. The President of the United States has appointed me to lead the investigation into the recent act of terrorism that caused the deaths of more than one hundred thousand U.S. citizens. I have been granted full permission to use any means necessary to facilitate that investigation." Krodin paused long enough for the translators in the gallery to relay the message to everyone present. "My first act is this: Effective immediately, and for the foreseeable future, the borders of the United States of America are closed."

An angry murmur rippled through the room.

"Until we can determine the nationality of the perpetrators behind the attack on Anchorage, we have no choice but to recall our ambassadors from your countries and remove all non-U.S. citizens from U.S. territory."

The members were on their feet now, turning to each other in confusion, screaming their protests, reaching for their cell phones to contact their governments.

"This is not open for discussion," Krodin said, almost shouting to be heard. "An unfathomable atrocity has been committed against the people of the United States, and we will stop at nothing to see that those responsible are brought to justice."

The Australian representative called out, "This is *madness*, Krodin! What evidence do you have that the attack wasn't carried out by Americans?"

"You want evidence?" Krodin shouted back. "Fine. *Here's* the evidence!" He gestured to the screen behind him.

The uproar was instantly silenced as every representative stared at the screen.

"Most of you won't know what that means. But there's at least one of you who does. We can't prove it. Not yet."

Krodin looked over the sea of guilty faces, then glanced at Max Dalton, who was standing at the back of the room, deep in concentration.

The screen showed a photograph of a fire-blackened human skull. Earlier, Max had scanned the minds of every representative, and now he was coercing their minds into linking the disturbing image with their most guilty secrets. Each representative was now certain that his or her government had some connection with the attack on Anchorage.

In the five thousand years since Krodin was born, one thing had remained constant: Politicians *always* had something to hide.

Two months later, Krodin stood, arms crossed, on the plush carpet of the White House's Oval Office.

He thought that the president was starting to look considerably older than his sixty years. The man's once-dark hair was peppered with gray, the lines on his face were deepening, and there was an edge to his voice that told Krodin all he needed to know: The president was desperate for a solution.

"Krodin, this is not going to end well. Every nation in the world is beefing up its defenses because they're afraid we're going to invade. I can't believe I let you and Dalton persuade me to go along with your plans. And you haven't even found Daedalus yet! So what's the deal there, huh? Is he smarter than you, is that it? More powerful? How is it that you and your think tank of geniuses have made absolutely no progress in finding him? Is this some sort of game to you? More than a few of my advisers are telling me that you're playing us. They think you've been working with Daedalus all along."

"With respect, Mr. President—"

"Shut up, Krodin—I'm talking here!" He sat back in his chair. "I mean, for crying out loud, you're not even a U.S. citizen! You're, what, Egyptian or Persian or something like that? Don't answer. I'm still talking. We've given you everything you've asked for. We declared a state of emergency, closed the borders, quadrupled the armed forces. You've already cost us *trillions* of dollars! Taxes have more than doubled in some states. We've turned America into a fortress. No, worse than that, it's practically a prison. Nothing in or out. You do know that the nation is going to grind to a halt without the oil from the Middle East?"

"We're not going to need oil for much longer," Krodin said. "Solomon Cord's work on photovoltaic cells is—"

"Did I say I was finished? No, I didn't." The president tapped the thick, unopened folder lying on the desk. "And now you want to establish this private security firm of yours as, what, some kind of auxiliary police force? And you expect me to persuade Congress to go along with that?"

Krodin said nothing.

"Well? Answer me!"

Let's make him sweat a little more, Krodin thought, and slowly counted to twenty in his head. "If you'll just *read* the report before you criticize it . . ."

The president narrowed his eyes. "No you don't. You don't get to talk to me like that. Just because you're some kind of immortal superhuman that does *not* give you the right to disrespect me or this office. I could have *you* deported, you know."

Krodin sighed and sat on the edge of the desk. "You couldn't. But I'm not here to make things harder for you. Read the report. It took my people a year to compile it, so the least you could do is . . . Forget that. I'll summarize. The country's law-enforcement structure—everything from the CIA right down to the average cop on the street—is a mess. You've got dozens of departments who barely talk to each other because they're all either afraid of stepping outside their boundaries or they're hoarding their wins like a greedy kid who still has all his candy two weeks after Halloween."

"That's a *gross* oversimplification—"

"Your turn to shut up, Walt," Krodin interrupted. "*I'm* talking now. I'm not proposing a private security firm. What I'm proposing is that all the law-enforcement departments and every branch of the military be replaced with one organization. Not all at once, but certainly over the next five years. They will be the Praetorian Guard. And before you ask, the Praetorian Guard were handpicked bodyguards used by Roman emperors. They were the best of the best. They were utterly dedicated and absolutely incorruptible, just as our Praetorians will be."

"We can't afford that. The training alone . . ." The president shook his head. "No."

"Yes," Krodin said. "I'm not saying we replace the *people*, just the structures under which they work. I give you my guarantee that their efficiency will double every two months for the first year. As for the cost . . . Look at the bottom line." He flipped open the folder and pushed it closer to the president. "This is your combined annual budgets for the police and military. Now look at the next page, the budget for the Praetorians."

The president reached out and turned the page. "It's . . . less than half." He looked up at Krodin. "This is real?"

"Oh, it's even better than you think, Walt. That's just the first year, and it includes the cost of the changeover. The second year will cost you about a third of that. And that's including equipment and training. America can't afford *not* to do this. Think about it. You can divert the savings into education, welfare, whatever you like."

The president's fingers were trembling slightly as he flipped back and forth through the report. "But an organization this size would be almost impossible to manage."

"Not for me and my team," Krodin said. "Superhuman, remember? I'll coordinate everything from the top down. Directly under me will be Max Dalton, Solomon Cord, and Casey Duval working out of my Chicago offices. With their brains and their abilities, we can get this started a lot faster than you might think. A couple of months at most."

"But you're a civilian, Krodin. . . . You don't fit into the political structure. You're not a politician."

"So *make* me into a politician. We're already under martial law. You're the commander in chief. Create this new position and appoint me to run it."

The president pushed the folder away. He sat back, stared up at the ceiling. "I'm going to want to see a much more detailed report, get my own people to check it out, but . . . You could be on to something here. All right, let's suppose we do it." He leaned forward again, and smiled at Krodin. "You'd need a title, of course. Adviser? No, too vague. Overseer wouldn't really work. . . . I know: You can be Chancellor."

CHAPTER 21

ABBY COULD BARELY believe how much control James had over his flight. It had been only a few hours since he first learned to use shock waves to lift himself into the air, and he had found it exhausting. Now he was a master, carrying the two of them over the North Dakota landscape at a speed she couldn't even begin to estimate.

He's a strange guy, she thought. *Carrying a lot of weight on his shoulders.* She guessed that could be because of his supersensitive hearing. *It can't be easy, knowing so many people's secrets.*

She was sure he had a crush on her. *Why else would he have kept coming back to the diner? It certainly couldn't have been for the food. I'll just have to find a way to discourage him somehow,* she thought, *before he completely falls in love with me.*

Still, it was comforting to think that he liked her, even

though he really wasn't her type. Lance, too, had seemed to take an interest in her, but she didn't expect to ever meet him again, so that was less of a problem.

"They're almost there!" James told her. "They're going to reach him before we do!"

"Warn him!" Abby shouted over the roar of the wind. "You can throw your voice, can't you?"

"It's taking all I've got just to keep us moving at this speed."

"Then you need to go on without me—you'll get there quicker!"

"You sure?"

"Do it!"

"All right," James said. "I'll set you down on that hilltop. Don't go anywhere—I'll come back for you." He paused for a moment, then added, "And if I *don't* come back, you get away from here. Find somewhere to hide and lie low for the rest of your life."

Abby saw the small round-topped, grassy hill approaching. "Don't waste time slowing down—just take me in close and let go—I'll be OK."

They swept in so low over the grass that Abby could see it ripple from their wake. "Now!"

James opened his hand and zoomed away.

For a few seconds Abby remained on course, and then she began to drop. *This is a lot faster than it seemed when we were up in the air!*

Twenty yards from the crest of the hill she hit the ground hard and slid across the long damp grass on her side. She tried to dig her hands into the dirt to slow her speed, but instead it caused her to start tumbling and rolling.

She reached the crest of the hill and suddenly there was nothing beneath her but three hundred feet of empty air, and, below that, an abandoned quarry littered with jagged fragments of shattered rock.

"James! Help me!"

But even as she called out, she knew it was too late: James was long gone, his attention focused on reaching Brawn as fast as possible.

The unforgiving ground rushed toward her.

"I was with the patrol searching for Brawn," Max Dalton said, leaning back against the side of the truck with his arms folded, "and then we intercepted a call from the warden at Oak Grove."

"Whose side are you on, Max?" Lance asked.

"Mine, of course. Lucky for you it's also *your* side." He sighed. "I'm not going to turn you in, Lance. Your escape is considered a low priority. They've got Brawn to worry about, there's a huge man hunt out for Roz in Manhattan, plus Abby and Thunder destroyed one Raptor in Midway and another in Minnesota. So what have *you* done today, aside from getting yourself arrested?"

Lance shrugged, and gestured to the truck.

Max gave him a slow hand clap. "Wow. You're a genius."

"Well, what have *you* done?"

Inside Lance's head, Max's voice said, "I'm the Vice-Chancellor, Lance. I can't exactly keep a low profile. Come on. Into the Shrike."

Lance looked over at the flying craft. "So where are we going?"

Inside Lance's head, Max's voice said, "As far as anyone else knows, you're being taken into Praetorian custody for interrogation."

"Where are we really going?"

"Just think the thoughts, Lance. You don't have to say the words. And don't worry about all those memories coming to the surface of the times you called me a jerk. I'm well aware of that. But maybe you'll think differently now that I'm getting you out of here. You owe me."

You still owe me *for saving your life back in Windfield*, Lance thought, but Max didn't respond, so Lance couldn't tell if he was listening.

As Lance climbed the ramp, the pilot turned around and nodded to him. "Good morning, sir."

"Good morning to you too," Lance said.

Max got in beside Lance. "Take us to the Citadel, Brandon."

"Certainly, Vice-Chancellor."

The door beside Max hissed shut and the craft surged into the air, then Max hit a switch on the panel behind the pilot's seat, and a screen rose up separating the cockpit from the rest of the craft. "We can talk safely now," Max said.

"Thanks for picking me up."

"Don't thank me yet. If the Chancellor finds out, he'll come gunning for both of us."

"What's this Citadel we're going to?"

"It's a palace Krodin's having built in Manhattan, in Central Park. But that's not our destination—just somewhere for the pilot to aim at until we can decide what to do next."

"We?" Lance asked. "A few weeks ago you barely acknowledged that I existed."

"I had a lot on my mind back then. Still do, in fact."

"Do you know how to reverse what happened to us?"

"No. I'm not saying it can't be done, but I don't know how to send us back."

"Well, do you know *why* it happened?"

"Not quite," Max said, "but I do have a few ideas. The Praetorians' technology is much more advanced than ours. *Why* that is . . . well, I'll get to that in a minute. In theory they should be on pretty much the same level that we are." He slapped the door of the craft. "Take this Shrike, for example, and the Raptors. They fly through some kind of gravity-nullifying system. We're *decades* away from that. Centuries, possibly. From what I can gather, most of the technology is the brainchild of one man. We need to find him before we can answer all the questions."

"Who is he?"

"Solomon Cord. Otherwise known as Paragon. The trouble is, the Paragon from this reality is gone, replaced by the one from *our* reality. Just like you replaced the Lance McKendrick from here. . . . You don't have any of his memories, do you?"

Lance shook his head. "No. But if we're here, where did *they* go?"

"I don't think it's like that, Lance. It seems to me that there were never actually *two* of each of us. We haven't gone anywhere; the world changed around us."

Lance considered this. "But why didn't *we* change?"

"I'm guessing it's because we were all caught up in the blast when Pyrokine attacked Krodin. That affected us, probably."

"*Probably?* That's not a lot of help! You can read minds, you should—"

"That's useful only if I can access the mind of someone who knows the answers."

"What does any of this have to do with finding Paragon?"

"Everything. That's part of the problem. Even if we can find him, he'll be *our* Paragon, not the one who put all this together. Our Paragon is a mechanical and electronic genius, but he's human, with human limitations. I'm not certain, but I'd lay down good money that the one from this reality was a superhuman."

"Wow . . . Wait, that can't be right," Lance said. "You people get your superhuman powers when you reach puberty, don't you? Well, if the world only changed a few years ago when Krodin appeared, then both Paragons should be the same. They should both be human."

"That's the other part of the problem, and one I haven't been able to figure out. Something—or some*one*—turned this reality's Paragon into a superhuman."

James was able to pinpoint Brawn's location from the sound of the giant's breathing, but he was still thankful for the powerful searchlights beaming down from the Praetorians' flying craft. He counted at least twenty Raptors hovering in place in a wide circle above a shallow valley.

The commanding officer's voice said, "Everyone in position? We don't know what this creature can withstand, so I want everything to hit it at the same time."

James threw his voice into the cockpit of her Raptor and added a background hiss to make it sound like it was coming from the radio: "Just one minute, ma'am. We're reading a minor power imbalance in the engines. Running a check on it now."

Without having to carry Abby he'd been able to increase his speed by half, and was now approaching Brawn's position at what he estimated to be more than a hundred miles an hour.

"Make it fast!" the officer said.

"Roger," James responded. He was closer now, almost there. *Time to add some more confusion to the mix.* He had heard enough of the commanding officer's voice to be able to mimic it. He directed his voice to every Raptor but hers. "All ships, stand down and withdraw. New orders from the Chancellor—the creature is to be left alone. Repeat: You will stand down and withdraw immediately. Return to base and await my instructions. I will follow shortly."

This had better work, James thought. *If it doesn't . . .*

There was a chorus of acknowledgment from the other Raptors' commanders, and the ships began to depart.

He threw a cocoon of silence over the commander's ship to prevent her from countermanding his orders, then darted in directly toward the giant's location. "Brawn, can you hear me?"

He heard a muttered grumble in response.

"Brawn. Wake up!"

"Aw . . . five more minutes, Mom."

He heard the rustling of bushes as the giant rolled over. "Wake up! Now!"

James could see him now, in a small clearing among the trees. He was sitting up, rubbing his eyes, the dew on his blue skin glistening in the starlight.

James came to a stop a few yards from him. For a second James was unsure just how far away Brawn was: His great height made him seem a lot nearer than James's hearing was telling him. Part of James's brain was telling him to run away: Nothing that big could be safe. He took a step closer. "Brawn, you're in danger."

The giant's colorless eyes turned in James's direction. "What? Who are you?"

"Thunder. We met at Windfield, remember?"

"What do *you* want? If you've come to take me back to Oak Grove, then you're going to have a fight on your hands."

"We've already got one. Look up."

Brawn raised his massive head and did a double take when he saw the cluster of Raptors. "UFOs! I *knew* there was life on other planets!"

"They're not UFOs. They're called Raptors. They're crewed by the cops of this world, and they're hunting you."

"Oh. I'm guessing that's not good."

"You need to get out of here, right now. They're planning to use napalm on you. I've distracted them, but there's no guarantee it's going to work for long."

Brawn jumped to his feet. "You strong enough to fly me out of here?"

"Maybe, but not fast enough to escape the Raptors. We might have to fight our way past them."

"That's not going to be a problem. I can take them."

"Let's hope it doesn't come to that. Come on."

Brawn began to stride off through the woods, and James had to run to keep up with him.

"What did you say your name is?" Brawn asked. He

stepped over a meter-thick fallen log that James had to climb over.

"Thunder."

"Oh, right. You were the dude in the wet suit."

James stopped. "Hold it. . . . They're slowing down, turning back."

He lifted the cocoon of silence in the commander's Raptor. There was no one talking, but he could hear the rapid clicking of a keyboard. "She's figured it out already. She's smart. Sending them instructions over the computer."

"Right." Brawn stomped over to the nearest tree. He wrapped his massive arms around its trunk and ripped it out of the ground. He held the trunk over his head and, just as he was about to throw it, stopped and looked at James. "Wait, are we allowed to kill these guys?"

"Uh, no."

"Even though they're trying to kill us?"

"Right."

"No fair." He threw the tree trunk anyway. It sailed into the air and slammed into the side of one of the Raptors in a shower of sparks and splinters, shunting it a good hundred yards back before it steadied itself. "Yeah, they'll probably survive that. C'mon!" He took off again through the trees, his heavy footfalls crashing through the undergrowth.

James rose into the air and followed. He directed his voice toward Brawn. "Where are you running to?"

"Away from those things! I don't know what's going on. One minute I was in my cell in Oak Grove and the next . . . It wasn't a cell, it was a storeroom. With an ordinary door instead of the bank-vault door that used to be there. So I punched my way through it and ran. The prison was . . . different. They all acted like they'd never seen me before. Running and screaming and all going like, 'Aah! It's a monster!' Which is all anyone ever does when they see me coming."

There was a splintering crash as Brawn chose to run through a small oak tree instead of going around it.

James raised himself over the treetops and turned around so that he was flying backward. "They're coming." The remaining Raptors had deactivated their searchlights, but James could tell where they were from the sound of their engines and the faint glow from the circular lights on their undercarriage.

Behind him Brawn's crashing footsteps came to a stop. "I'm gonna sort these guys out!"

"Wait . . ."

But Brawn wasn't listening: In the dim light James saw him leap high into the air to land on the upper branches of a tree—and he was carrying a boulder the size of a car.

James winced as he watched Brawn throw the boulder—it plowed straight through one of the Raptors, clipped a second, and sent it spinning into a third.

"Three in one go! Did you see that? Tell me you saw that!"

"I saw it," James said.

Then something flared on one of the other Raptors, and a bolt of light streaked toward Brawn.

"Missile!" James yelled.

At the last second Brawn jumped, soared over the missile, and came crashing down on top of the attacking Raptor. The craft juddered, tilted to the left, and Brawn punched one massive fist through the hull.

As the Raptor began to fall, he leaped for another one, caught its edge with one hand, swung his left leg back, then kicked out at the hull.

The entire side of the Raptor came away in his hand. "Uh-oh."

Brawn fell, crashing through the branches of a fir tree. The ground trembled when he landed, but he instantly rolled to his feet and jumped again, hauled himself onto a thick branch, then reached up and easily grabbed hold of another that was at least fifteen feet higher.

How can something so big move so fast? James wondered.

Brawn leaped from the tree and snagged another Raptor, but this time he punched his fist through the cockpit glass, grabbed hold of one of the crew, and hauled the man out. "Can you fly, mister?"

James heard the man shriek, "No!"

"Well, let's find out!" Brawn casually tossed the man over his shoulder, then reached into the hull for another one.

He's nuts! James thought. He darted through the air after the thrown man. He snagged the soldier's foot moments before the man slammed facefirst into the ground. James pulled back, slowed the man's descent almost to a stop, then let go.

He returned too late to catch the second soldier: Brawn threw the man straight through the cockpit of an approaching Raptor.

"Brawn, take it easy! You'll kill them!"

"Like I care!"

"Well, which is better? A bunch of dead guys here, or a bunch of wounded, terrified men scaring their colleagues with stories about how powerful you are?"

"They were going to kill *me*. In cold blood. I really don't see the problem here!"

The remaining Raptors began to peel away. *Is it over? Have we . . . ?*

Then James heard the voice of their commanding officer. "All ships—lock on to the monster and fire!"

Another voice said, "Ma'am, our men are still—"

"That's an order!"

"Brawn!" James yelled. "Incoming!"

The giant looked around. "Incoming what?" Then he saw the approaching missiles—twin streaks of fire from each of the remaining twelve Raptors. "Aw, rats on a *raft*!"

Brawn let go of the damaged Raptor and allowed himself to plummet toward the ground.

The missiles altered course to follow him.

James didn't have time to warn Brawn to cover his ears: He blasted the area with a long, sustained shock wave. It ripped out from him at the speed of sound, striking Brawn, the Raptors, and the missiles and knocking them all clear out of the valley.

He felt suddenly drained of energy, barely able to keep his eyes open. *Too much . . . Got to rest, recover, and . . .*

The ground seemed to be moving up to meet him, and he puzzled over this for a second before he realized that he was falling.

Got to wake up . . . Wake up!

A branch struck his right leg; another caught him in the face and scraped a deep cut from his eyebrow to his hairline.

He hit the ground hard.

CHAPTER 22

IN THE NEW JERSEY resistance cell's meeting room, Roz turned to look at the older man. "I'm number three on your hit list?"

He nodded. He was maybe fifty years old, she guessed, of average height and build. Quite handsome in a stern, emotionless way.

"Who are you?"

The man turned to Ted. In a strong, crisp Scottish accent he said, "Thank you, Silvestri. We can carry on without you."

Ted nodded, and as he was leaving the room said to Roz, "I wish you luck."

As soon as he was gone, the older man looked at Roz. "General Christopher Westwood, formerly of Her Majesty's Special Air Service, currently assigned by Unity to assess the situation here."

Joe Ward said, "Krodin's got this country sewn up so tight

that nothing can get in or out. Or so he thinks. He doesn't know about Suzanne—he thinks he has control of every surviving superhuman. Suzanne's been able to fly in a few specialists like the general here."

Westwood continued: "Your arrival has changed everything, Ms. Dalton. We had certain plans in place that must now be abandoned. To get to Krodin we needed leverage. We had teams in place to take out two key people. A man called Solomon Cord—the prime architect of Krodin's latest weapon—and yourself. The only person Krodin really needs is your brother. Without him, Krodin would have to rely on brute strength and fear to hold on to power. But of course your brother's abilities mean that he is almost impossible to reach."

Roz said, "You were going to get to him through me. Kidnap me, threaten to kill me if he didn't do as you asked."

"Correct."

Joe said, "Tell her the rest of it, General."

Suzanne Housten cautioned, "Joe . . ."

"No, she needs to know the whole story. No more secrets. Roz, we were going to go after your little brother too."

"But that's . . . ! You can't *do* something like that—Josh is only ten years old!"

"This is war," the general said. "More than a hundred thousand people have already died at Krodin's hand. He now has the weapons and technology he needs to wage war on every nation on Earth. We will do whatever it takes to prevent that."

Then, cheerfully, Joe said, "But sure that's all in the past now. It's all water that never went under the bridge. Now we have a new plan. We're going to infiltrate the Citadel."

"But even if you can get to Krodin, you're not strong enough to stop him," Roz said.

"It's not him we're after. Krodin's day-to-day operations are run from the Citadel. You think he oversees everything that happens in this country? No, he delegates to a whole bunch of advisers and lieutenants. They're human. With them gone, the whole infrastructure will fall into chaos. And while the rest of them are running around in a panic trying to sort out the mess, our counterparts will strike at the base in Louisiana."

"Louisiana . . . ," Roz said. "That's where Max was—the *other* Max—when he disappeared. What's there?"

Housten said, "Something that we cannot allow them to use. Until you arrived, we didn't know how they got it to work, but now . . . It's already working. You saw the evidence of that yourself."

"What are you talking about?"

Joe said, "That guy from your world, Pyrokine, was a superhuman who had the ability to convert matter into energy. The Helotry hooked him up to the output of a nuclear reactor and used his power to punch a hole through time and take Krodin out of the past."

"Right. Max said it's called Quantum Mechanical Tunneling. I know all this."

"I know you do. But let me finish, 'cos there's a good bit coming up at the end. When Pyrokine tried to kill Krodin, he released enough of that stored-up energy to partly reverse the effects of the time-travel process. So Krodin reappeared just about six years ago. And the reason we figure it didn't send him all the way back to his own time is that Krodin's ability to adapt prevented that from happening. He put the brakes on, so to speak. Are you following me so far?"

Roz nodded.

"Good stuff. So, Krodin twigged what had happened, and he figured that since he was in the past, he was free and clear to do whatever he liked without you and your pals messing it all up again. He recruited your brother, whose mind control and telepathy no longer worked on him. He built his little empire bit by bit, bringing in Solomon Cord and his brainy assistant Casey. And all the while Krodin and Max had a plan. See, at the base in Louisiana they've built the one thing Krodin needs to complete his takeover of the world. They built a teleporter. You know what that is, right? A machine that can instantly transport something from one place to another without having to cover the intervening distance."

There was a sharp knock on the door and a young man rushed in, whispered something to Housten and the general, and then left.

"Where was I?" Joe asked.

"They built a teleporter," Roz said. "And?"

"*And?* Roz, if what we've heard is true, then this thing is capable of sending anyone or anything to wherever Krodin wants. Anywhere at all. Our guess is they nicked the idea from the way your version of Pyrokine took Krodin out of his own time. Nowhere in the world is safe from Krodin. Think about that. Krodin throws a dart at the map and says, 'We're invading *that* country today.' His people in Louisiana gather their soldiers in groups and send them right into the heart of the target country's most sensitive areas. Then he sends another group, and another. And he can keep doing it as long as he has soldiers to send."

Suzanne said, "Roz, their teleporter works. Yesterday morning Krodin's people teleported him from one side of his base to the other, about three hundred yards. Then they teleported a platoon to capture you. They didn't know it was you, they just saw the alert and figured it would be a good test. We are up against a deadline here: We have to find a way to destroy that machine before Krodin can mobilize his men. If we *can* destroy it, it'll set back Krodin's plans for years."

"But he'd just make another one," Roz said.

General Westwood said, "We don't think he can. The Solomon Cord who built it is gone, replaced by yours."

"What about the assistant?"

"Casey's dead. Daedalus killed him almost a year ago." The general looked down at his clasped hands. "Ms. Dalton, Krodin's teleporter was triggered for the first time yesterday at exactly eleven-forty-two Eastern Standard Time. Do you know what else happened at exactly eleven-forty-two Eastern Standard Time?"

She shook her head.

"You and your friends arrived in this reality."

Abby didn't need super-hearing to locate Brawn and James—the sounds of the giant's screams echoed through the entire forest—but as she crashed through the undergrowth and the low branches whipped at her face, she wished she had enhanced vision. *Or a flashlight*, she thought. *Never going anywhere without one again.*

Her neck and her left side were aching from her collision with the ground, and she'd badly wrenched her right foot. She tried to ignore the pain, but that would have been difficult enough over flat ground. The forest floor was uneven, spongy in places, tangled with roots, bushes, and fallen branches.

Worse, she was running in almost complete darkness. The only light came from the Praetorians' Raptors, hovering overhead half a mile away.

The air was thick with the cloying scent of moss and sap, the tang of burning plastic and scorched metal.

She heard Brawn bellowing, the crash of metal on metal, then felt as though she'd slammed into a brick wall—a moving wall that smashed into her, forced her backward.

Abby lost her footing and toppled onto her back as the invisible force washed over her.

A second later, and the forest was still, silent except for the rustling of branches. She glanced up: Most of the lights of the Raptors were gone.

Shock wave, she thought. *Thunder's blasted them all with a shock wave! But if it was powerful enough to take down the Raptors . . .*

She jumped to her feet and ran, no longer caring about the cuts and bruises, the aches and pains.

In moments, she heard a low, constant moan. It was deep, rumbling, so strong that she imagined that even the ground was trembling. And then she saw him. Brawn, lying faceup, sprawled over the crushed trunk of a massive tree.

Abby leaped over the tree's shattered branches and onto the trunk, ran to Brawn, and crouched down next to his oversized head.

"Brawn, it's me, Abby. Are you OK?"

He didn't respond, but in the half-light, she saw his eyelids flickering open. She couldn't tell whether he was looking at her: His eyes were solid white, lacking both iris and pupil.

She patted him on the cheek. "Can you hear me? Brawn, where's James?"

A weak voice right beside her said, "Abby . . ."

She jumped, spun around. There was no one there. "James, where are you? I can't see you."

"Over here. I'm trapped. Follow the sound. And quickly—I can hear them regrouping."

Abby gave Brawn a last look, then scrambled back down to the forest floor. She was about to ask, "What sound?" when she heard it: a soft beep that seemed to be coming from the bushes to her right.

When she reached the bushes, she heard the sound again, a few yards away, leading her deeper into the forest.

She leaped over a recently fallen tree, pushed her way through a thick bush, and saw the front half of a downed Raptor protruding from the ground. Her first impression was that the back half was buried deep in the ground, but then she saw the ragged torn metal along the lower edge and realized that its hull had been split in two.

Something inside the craft was burning, providing enough flickering light for her to see James. He was lying facedown, his legs trapped under the Raptor. The ground in front of him had been swept of debris, and there were deep finger marks in the soil.

"Trying to dig myself out," James said. "Give me a hand, will you?"

"Are you hurt?"

"I'll live. It's not crushing me, but I'm pinned. See if you can find something to use as a shovel. Dig out the ground under me. Quick as you can—they'll be here in a couple of minutes!"

Abby got down on her hands and knees beside James and peered at the torn edge of the Raptor's hull. "You were lucky. Another couple of inches and it'd have cut you in two."

"I know. We're running out of time here, Abby! Just dig!"

Abby smiled back at him. "No need." She shifted forward, reached out to the edge of the hull, and pulled.

There was a *ping* from beneath the hull. Then another, and a third. The Raptor's armor plating shifted in her hands, warped as though it were nothing more substantial than a sheet of copper, and the craft rose by a couple of inches. "That enough?"

"Think so . . ." On the ground next to her, James squirmed free.

She let go and the Raptor crashed back to the ground.

As she reached out her hand to help him up, James's grateful expression collapsed. "Oh no."

Around them the trees' upper branches began to rustle, the sound growing steadily. "It's raining," Abby said.

"That's not rain."

A long red-tipped dart hit the Raptor's hull with a soft clink. Another landed on the ground close to her right foot.

In seconds the darts were coming down all around them. Abby grabbed James's arm and pulled him up. "Come on!"

A dart struck James's back, and he instantly collapsed.

The Raptor! Abby thought. *I'll be safe there!*

She had barely gone two steps when she felt the sting of a dart hitting her arm.

CHAPTER 23

HE'S DOING IT AGAIN, LANCE thought as he watched Max Dalton issuing instructions to the pilot of the Shrike. *Using his mind control. Man, I'd love to be able to do that!*

"As soon as I leave this craft, you will take this boy to my home," Max said. "You may answer any question the boy asks, but do not allow him to countermand my orders. Stay with him at all times, understood? Top speed, Brandon."

Max had departed the craft at a disused airfield somewhere in Minnesota, and as the Shrike ascended, Lance spotted another, much larger craft approaching. The pilot had told Lance that it was the Carrier, Krodin's personal craft and mobile command center.

That had been thirty minutes ago. Now Lance was alone in the back of the Shrike as it zoomed eastward toward New York.

"How fast are we going?" Lance asked.

"Four hundred and four miles per hour," the pilot said.

"Can you go faster?"

"No."

"Oh, right, he told you to go at top speed. So how long have you been working for Max Dalton?"

"About six months."

"Do you like him?"

"No."

Interesting, Lance thought. "Why not?"

"I'm afraid of him. He can read my thoughts, make me follow any orders without question. And he's friends with the Chancellor."

"Tell me Max's darkest secret."

"I can't do that. He's previously ordered me not to reveal anything that could compromise his safety or position."

"Pity. What's your name?"

"Brandon Santamaría."

"OK, Brandon. So where are we now? How long before we get where we're going?"

The partition between the pilot's compartment and the back of the Shrike began to rise.

"Hey, he ordered you to answer my questions!"

"Vice-Chancellor Dalton told me that I *may* answer your questions, not that I must. The dividing partition also acts as a display."

The screen flickered to life and showed Lance a map of the eastern United States. The pilot's voice came over a speaker: "The red dot indicates our position. The green dot is our destination. ETA is displayed at the bottom of the screen. The map is interactive—there's a control panel in the armrest of your seat."

Lance spent the next couple of minutes playing with the controls and watching the map zoom in and out, then he panned it over to his hometown of Fairview, South Dakota, and zoomed in on the places he knew. "This is cool. Brandon, can I use this to find where someone is?"

"Sure. Select the Search option and type the person's name to locate them on the map."

Lance entered "Krodin" and the map pulled back to show the whole of the USA, then zoomed in on the airfield where they had left Max. A series of blue dots appeared, each one labeled with a person's name. "Nice. How do I order your death-ray satellites to zap Krodin with a laser beam or something?"

"We don't have any death-ray satellites."

"Worth asking. Here's a thought, though. . . . What weaknesses does Krodin have?"

"None."

"Yeah, I know he's invulnerable and all that. I mean, is there anything we can do to hurt him? Like take away his favorite toys or something?"

"I believe the Chancellor is completely without sentiment. He doesn't have an emotional attachment to anything or any person."

"So it wouldn't bother him much if we went to his house and keyed his car?"

"The Chancellor doesn't have a house. He lives in the Citadel."

"That's where we're already going, right? Cool. We'll

break in and spray-paint 'Krodin chews his own socks' all over the walls."

"That wouldn't be easy," the pilot said. "It's the strongest, safest structure ever built. It was designed to be completely impregnable."

"Aw, rats."

Then the pilot added, "Or it will be when it's finished."

Abby woke up to muffled voices and blurry images. And pain—her whole body ached, her joints felt stiff and twisted, and when she tried to move, a wave of blinding agony coursed through her skull.

Then the jumble of voices faded to silence, and two dark figures filled her vision.

"She's waking," a voice said.

She tried to sit up, but a firm but gentle hand pressed down on her shoulder, and a second voice—closer than the first—said, "No, you need to rest."

"James?"

"Shh. You should sleep, little warrior. Recover your strength."

"You're not James. . . . Who are you? Where is he?"

"Your friends are alive. Safe and—like you—recovering from the effects of the Cataxia."

Abby blinked rapidly to try to get her eyes to focus, and again asked, "Who are you? Where is this place?"

She was lying on a bed. At its foot, directly in front of her, was Max Dalton. He was holding a small spherical device— not much bigger than a softball—down by his side in his right hand. A thin chain connected the device to a bracelet on his wrist.

Sitting forward in a chair beside Abby was a strong-looking man with bronzed skin and sharp features. He was wearing black jeans and a white shirt open at the collar.

The bronzed man smiled as he spoke: "We've met before, Abigail. My name is Krodin."

She rolled off the other side of the bed and landed on her feet, fists clenched.

He smiled at her. "You're not in any condition to fight, little warrior."

Max said, "Abby, stay calm. Assess the situation before you do anything."

She quickly looked around. They were in a small, sparsely furnished room that contained only a bed and a chair. The walls appeared to be made of metal, and to her left was a closed door that wouldn't have looked out of place in a submarine. She caught the crisp scent of ozone in the air, and could feel a very slight vibration in the cold floor beneath her feet. "Where are we? What have you done with James?"

Krodin said, "Hmm. I can tell by your stance and the pitch of your voice that you're stalling for time while you think of a way out. Don't bother."

Abby glanced at Max; he was shaking his head, wearing an expression that seemed to say, "You don't stand a chance."

"As for your friend," Krodin continued, "his injuries are a little worse than your own. He's being seen to—he should make a full recovery." The Fifth King stood and moved toward the door. It hissed open—sliding into the wall—as he reached it. "Walk with me, Abigail de Luyando. You and I have much to discuss."

Abby's right foot still ached, and she had to almost hop to catch up with Krodin as he strode out of the room.

They were close to the end of a narrow metal-walled corridor. On Abby's left, two Praetorian guards—one male, one female—stood side by side, their powerful rifles cradled in their arms, watching her. To the right was a large picture window. Krodin stood in front of it with his arms crossed, looking out.

"You're terrified of me," Krodin said without looking at her. "I understand that. But for the moment you have nothing to fear."

Abby stopped ten feet away from Krodin. "What do you want from me?"

"You're a warrior, Abigail. Strong, proud, skilled, courageous . . . I need people like you." He beckoned her closer. "Stand by me, Abigail. You asked where we are. See for yourself."

Still keeping her distance from him, Abby moved to the far edge of the window. Several hundred feet below, gnarled tree trunks grew on the banks of a gently rippling lake, their roots visible as though someone had been in the process of pulling them out of the ground. Their long, drooping branches and wide leaves cast intricate patterns of moving shadows on the surface of the water.

Her first thought was that they were on the upper floors of a skyscraper that overlooked the swamp, but then the scenery ahead of her gently banked and shifted to the left and she realized that they were in some kind of aircraft.

"The bayou," Krodin explained. "The swamps of Louisiana. Beautiful, isn't it? I love this place. It's one of the most remote and inaccessible parts of America, not counting the wilds of Alaska, of course—but much of Alaska's not exactly habitable after the destruction of Anchorage."

I should run, Abby told herself. *Jump through the window. It's a long way down, but I can do it. I'm strong enough to survive. He won't follow me—if he wanted me dead, he'd already have killed me.*

Krodin said, "I believe that everyone superhuman has been given specific abilities to perform specific tasks. I'm not a great believer in destiny, but there is surely more to the universe than we can perceive." He shrugged. "I don't know the truth. I don't think we *can* know the truth. But we can still believe." Then he pointed down and off to the side. "There! Can you see that?"

"It's a tree."

"In front of the tree . . . It's gone now. But you couldn't see it. So few of us can. A ball of blue light. They fade in and out of existence. Where they come from and where they go, I have no idea. But I know what they *do*. They make superhumans."

"Superhumans are born, not made," Abby said.

"Superhumans are made, Abigail, by those blue lights. But they affect only certain people. So it would be true to say that we are both born *and* made. There was a young man who once worked for me who had the ability to predict the appearance of the lights. He had an understanding of them that he couldn't express—he just *knew*. Through his knowledge we were able to use the lights to turn an ordinary human—a man called Solomon Cord—into a superhuman. Cord's intelligence and intuition were increased a hundredfold. He invented the gravity-nullifying engine that powers this Carrier and our other flying craft. He did it in a single afternoon. What is odd, though, is that he couldn't always do such things. He often spent a huge amount of time working on a problem—with very little progress—and then all the answers came to him at once." Again, Krodin turned to face her, smiling. "I believe that he had the ability to steal knowledge from the future."

"That's . . ."

"Impossible? Incredible? Perhaps. But it is the only explanation that truly fits. Cord is gone now, replaced by his lesser counterpart from your reality, but much of his work has been completed. We are almost ready."

"Ready for what?"

"War. My enemies are gathering." Krodin stared out at the bayou. "They know about Cord's latest creation, a teleporter. Abigail, in war the single greatest impediment to success is distance. Troops, supplies, and equipment all have to be moved, and that costs money and takes time. With my teleporter, distance is no longer an issue. In an instant, I can send an army to anywhere on Earth. This terrifies the forces of Unity—very soon, they will come here to destroy me. They won't succeed, of course, but better that they try here than in a populated area."

"I don't understand you," Abby said. "You've turned America into a prison and now you don't want people to be killed?"

"I'm not a murderer, Abigail." Krodin sighed. "Think of the world as an apple tree. To get the best apples from it you have to cut away the diseased branches, even if that means such heavy pruning that you're almost starting from scratch." He straightened up and raised his head, searching the sky outside. "With the teleporter under my control I can—and I *will*—seize control of every nation on this planet, and my enemies have done much of my work for me."

"I get it. They form themselves into one huge organization and then you just take it over."

"Yes, it's so much easier and quicker that way. But you and your friends seem honor-bound to try to stop me. I'm asking you now not to do that. If you do, you will all die." Still not looking at her, Krodin said, "You have to accept that this is how things are meant to be. You cannot stop me. Your only options are to join me, or to run and hide. I suggest the former—with you and your friends at my side, the coming war will end considerably sooner. Far fewer innocent people will lose their lives."

Abby shook her head. "No. I will never work alongside you. What you're doing is . . . beyond evil."

He suddenly turned to her, and his expression seemed to suggest that he was impressed. "Exactly. It is beyond evil. I am . . . a force of nature, if you like. You can't blame a hurricane for destroying a village, or a flood for wiping out crops. Yes, people will die in the coming days—but then people die anyway. When I've taken control of Unity, there will be peace. Take the long view, Abigail. I will live forever. This will be the last year a human being need ever fear war, or famine, or plague, or poverty. Think about that for a moment. My conquest of the Earth will be almost bloodless. Almost."

Abby moved away from the window. "You can spin this

around any way you like, but you're still wrong. You don't have the right to decide how any other person should live, let alone the whole world."

"Yes, I do have that right. Every herd, every pack has a leader. I am that leader."

"No! I don't care how strong you are—we'll find a way to stop you!"

Krodin sighed. "You're welcome to try, but all you will achieve is the deaths of innocent people. Do you understand that, Abigail? *Can* you understand it? No matter what you do, I can wait it out."

"You've got the whole world terrified. How can you justify that?"

"Because that's what unites them. The people of the world really should be thanking me for what I've done. Right now, they're too worried about me to fight amongst themselves. Think about that, Abigail. For probably the first time in human history, there are no wars." He leaned back against the glass, looking at her. "You can't escape from this Carrier. Dalton is currently chained to a small device in his right hand. It's only a prototype, constructed a year ago by the same friend who turned Cord into a superhuman. While it's active, the machine saps the energy from any superhuman within an eight-hundred-yard radius. Myself excluded, of course. It worked on me once, so it will never work on me again. Right now, you and your friends are no more powerful than ordinary human beings." He grinned. "And just as fragile. It must be strange for you, Abigail. You no longer feel the coiled strength in your muscles. And for James the silence must be almost deafening. And poor old Max, eh? Without his abilities what is our Vice-Chancellor? A dull, unimaginative shell of a man with all the personality and vitality of a lawn in the winter."

He gestured along the corridor. "We'll be arriving at the base in a little over two hours. In the meantime, you're free to explore the Carrier, but some doors won't open for you, and you will be accompanied at all times by your guards."

Abby turned and walked away down the corridor. She didn't know where she was going, but she wanted to be away from him. The two Praetorian guards fell into step behind her.

He called after her: "You can't win, Abigail. Accept that. You can't beat me."

He is insane! No one has the right to dictate how the rest of the human race should live! There has to be a way to stop him. We'll find a way, some weakness that maybe even he doesn't know about. He's totally wrong—no one is unbeatable.

But she feared, in her heart, that he was right.

In New Jersey, Roz had been sleeping in what Joe called "the guest suite"—a cobweb-filled storeroom with two old packing crates and a musty blanket to serve as a bed—when the door was pushed open.

"Time to go, Roz," Suzanne Housten said. "Your brother and Krodin are both in Louisiana. It's time to move on the Citadel, and you're coming with us."

Roz rolled off the crates and started to pull on her boots. "I have a mission of my own to complete."

"Not anymore. Krodin has found your friends and taken them into custody. They're unharmed, for now. So put them out of your mind, because this is going to be a busy day."

"What about Victoria?" Roz forced herself to remain calm as she said the name. She had spent much of the night trying not to think about how the girl had suffered.

Suzanne said, "When this is finished, we'll send some people to collect the bodies of her family. We'll give them a proper funeral."

Joe Ward entered the room carrying a large carryall. "Morning, Roz. Got some gear for you here. Bulletproof vest, helmet, pants, and gloves. And your very own gun."

"I don't use a gun."

"You do today, kitten."

"Coming into Manhattan now," the Shrike pilot, Brandon Santamaría, told Lance. The partition blocking the rear of the craft from the pilot's area deactivated and slid down.

Lance stared openmouthed at the scene through the Shrike's front windshield. "Oh wow. That's the Citadel?"

Brandon nodded. "Almost complete. One hundred and fifty floors on the highest tower."

The rectangular base of the Citadel took up almost half of Central Park. Its sides tapered in for the first forty floors before it broke into a series of towers of different heights. At the upper levels many of the towers were connected by a complex network of glass walkways.

The Shrike approached the Citadel from the southwest, coming in low over West Fifty-seventh Street and then ascending toward the southern-most tower.

"It's enormous. . . . How long did this take to build?"

"About a year, so far." Brandon pointed to one of the towers on the northern side. "Still some work to be done on the last tower, but the base was completed in two months, and it's been inhabited ever since."

The Shrike circled around the southern tower as it ascended, and slowed as it neared the top. "Floor one-thirty. Mr. Dalton's apartment."

"He gets a whole floor? That's got to be the size of a city block!"

"Almost. The Vice-Chancellor *is* the second most powerful man in the country."

"Where does Krodin live?"

"The center tower. The largest one."

"How many floors does he have?"

"See there, where the central tower extends from the base? From there up. One hundred and ten floors. About three million square feet."

Lance whistled. "Three million square feet in the middle of Manhattan. Sure hope it's rent-controlled."

The Shrike slowed to a stop on the southern side of the tower and a long ramp extended to meet it, closely followed by side rails and a thin, transparent canopy.

Brandon shut down the craft and opened the doors. "You can get out now."

Lance looked down at the ramp for a moment. "*How* high up are we?"

"About a quarter of a mile. I promise you the ramp is perfectly safe."

Lance gingerly put down one foot, then the other. The ramp did seem solid enough.

"If you step to the side and look behind you . . ."

Lance looked. The view over lower Manhattan was staggering. Countless skyscrapers glistened in the dawn light while dozens of Raptors and other flying vehicles drifted silently between them.

"It's so quiet. Peaceful. So . . . what's the word? Serene."

Brandon climbed out and stood behind Lance. "Because curfew is still in effect."

Without looking at him, Lance said, "Way to spoil the mood, dingbat. I was almost getting poetic there for a second. You had to remind me that this is all the work of an insane immortal dictator."

"Please come with me, Mr. McKendrick."

Reluctantly, Lance dragged himself away from the view and turned around to face Brandon, then automatically took a step back. So far, he had only seen the pilot sitting down; he hadn't expected the man to be almost seven feet tall. "Whoa . . ."

Brandon sighed and said, "Yes. I'm very tall."

"I wasn't going to say that," Lance lied.

"Sure you were. Everyone does. We should get inside."

Lance followed the pilot along the ramp to the doorway. As they reached the door, it slid open automatically, and a ten-year-old boy came running out.

The boy stopped when he saw Lance. "Who's this? Where're Max and Roz?"

"Your brother and sister are busy, Joshua. This is Lance, a friend. He might be staying with us for a while."

"All right," Joshua said. "How old are you, Lance?"

"Fourteen."

"OK then." Apparently satisfied with the answer, the boy turned to the pilot. "You're in time for breakfast, Brandon."

They followed Joshua into the apartment. It reminded Lance of the lobby of the most expensive hotel in Fairview. It was enormous, split over two floors with a wide glass staircase leading to the upper floor. The lower floor was dotted with clusters of luxurious leather sofas, large potted ferns, TV screens as big as a classroom blackboard, and, in one corner, a pair of full-sized snooker tables.

Lance whistled. "Man, you'd need a taxi to get from one side of this place to the other. You live here too?"

Brandon nodded. "Staff quarters are downstairs, on the north side."

"I could get used to living somewhere like this," Lance said.

From deep within the apartment Joshua's voice called, "Brandon? Are you coming?"

Lance followed the pilot through the apartment to a set of doors on the eastern side.

"The eating quarters," Brandon said. "The housekeeper is an excellent cook. She'll prepare anything you want."

The doors to the eating quarters silently slid open as they approached. The room was about twice the size of the kitchen in Lance's house and sparsely furnished, containing only a glass-topped table and six chairs.

Joshua was already sitting at the table, and as Lance entered, a pair of saloon-style doors on the far side of the room swung open and a middle-aged woman came through carrying a plate of ham and eggs.

"Two more for breakfast?" she asked as she put the plate in front of Josh.

The pilot said, "Not for me, Maria. But this is Lance

McKendrick, a friend of Mr. Dalton." He patted Lance on the shoulder. "Don't go anywhere until Mr. Dalton returns. Not that you could—the elevators won't operate without the correct codes." He moved toward the door, paused for a moment as though about to add something, then just smiled and left.

What was that *about?* Lance wondered. He suddenly felt a little more awkward, more alone, but wasn't sure why.

"Sit down," the woman said to Lance as she pushed open the doors to the kitchen. "There's more than enough for two."

"If it's no trouble, thanks." Lance sat down at the table next to Josh.

The boy was already wolfing down his breakfast. Around a mouthful of pancakes he asked, "What's your name again?"

"Lance."

"How do you know Max?"

"Oh, me and Max go way back."

"Where?"

"I mean, I've known him for a while. So, do you prefer Josh or Joshua?"

The boy shrugged. "I don't care. Want to watch cartoons?"

"Maybe when I've finished eating."

Josh said, "Cool. Do you want to see my coolest thing?"

"Sure."

"Max gave it to me." Josh reached into the pocket of his jeans and pulled out a round piece of blackened rock no bigger than his thumb. "Isn't that cool? Brandon says it's probably, like, *millions* of years old."

"It's a rock. All rocks are millions of years old."

"It's not just a rock. It's a tektite," Josh said. "Brandon says they're formed when a meteorite hits the ground so hot that it melts on impact. This is one of the drops. Brandon knows all about astronomy and space stuff, and he's teaching me. This one was found in Georgia last year." He held it up to the light. "This actually came from outer space! How cool is that?"

Lance shrugged.

"It's *way* cool," Josh said, sounding a little hurt. "Have *you* ever seen anything that came from outer space?"

"Sunlight?" Lance ventured. "Comes from the sun. That's in outer space."

"That's not the same," Josh said. "Brandon says that lots of asteroids and meteors are made up of iron and stuff and that there could even be gold or diamonds up there."

But Lance had stopped listening. *Brandon's gone*, he realized. *Max ordered him to stay with me at all times. Either Max wasn't using his mind control on him when he gave the order—and it sure* looked *like he was—or Brandon's immune.*

Does Max know about that? No, he can't. There's no way he'd have someone he couldn't control working for him. And he definitely wouldn't employ someone whose mind he couldn't read.

So that has to mean that Brandon is not only immune to Max's power but able to fake his own thoughts so that Max can't tell.

CHAPTER 24

IN ANOTHER CABIN DEEP inside Krodin's enormous flying craft, James Klaus winced as he swung his legs off the bed and sat up. "He's letting us wander free? Seriously?"

"That's what he said," Abby said. She was sitting on the edge of the chair opposite him. "He's *that* confident that we can't stop him."

"As long as we can't use our powers, he's probably right." James raised his hand to his forehead. "How does it look?"

"I can't tell because of the bandage. You were lucky you didn't get your eye poked out." Then she thumped him on the arm. "You idiot—after you let go of me, I fell over the edge of a cliff! If you'd just set me down, I could have gotten to you a lot quicker!"

"How was I to know? It looked like an ordinary hill from the other side. Anyway, you *told* me—" He tried to stand but his knees were too weak.

Abby grabbed his hand and pulled him upright.

"They get Brawn too?" James asked.

"Yeah. Max said they didn't have a room big enough for him, so they have him outside on the landing deck. That's why the Carrier's moving so slowly—they don't want him to fall off."

As he followed her into the corridor, James noticed that Abby was walking with some difficulty. "You're limping."

"Yeah. Hey, remember that time when I told you about how I fell off a cliff?"

He stepped back from her. "Should be me helping you, then." He looked around the corridor. Four Praetorian guards stood watching him.

"These two are mine," Abby said, pointing to the man and woman on the left, "so I guess the others are yours. They don't answer questions, so it's not worth your time speaking to them."

Out of habit more than courtesy, James nodded to the guards, then at the far end of the corridor he spotted Max Dalton talking to a muscular, casually dressed man. "That's him, isn't it?"

"The Fifth King," Abby said. "He's probably right about us not being able to stop him. It'd be like ants attacking an elephant."

"Well, with *enough* ants . . ." James forced a smile—he didn't want Abby to know how he really felt.

Krodin looked toward them and casually raised his hand. It was almost a friendly greeting.

"We've lost," Abby said. "He's so much better than we are that there's no point in even trying. He said . . . He said we should join him. With us on his side the war will be over a lot sooner. Fewer people will die."

"You don't believe that, do you?"

"I don't know. But I'm going to keep fighting anyway. If we can find a way to disable his teleporter, then we have a much greater chance of beating him." She began to move back along the corridor. "We can get access to the hull this way."

Dogged by the guards, James followed Abby through the corridors, up a metal stairwell, along another corridor, and then to a ladder that led up to a closed portal.

Moving with some difficulty, Abby climbed the ladder. As she reached the top, the portal slid open and a blast of cold air rushed in. "There are handrails," she called down to James. "Seems safe enough."

He followed her up and out. The topside of the Carrier's hull was designed to hold half a dozen Raptors at once. Right now, there were three Raptors, eight guards, and one blue giant.

Brawn was lying on his back, his legs crossed at the ankles and his hands behind his head, as though he were simply sunbathing. He looked up as James and Abby approached, and stood up. He glanced at the guards following them, then pointed an accusatory finger at James. "You. You nearly killed me!"

"That wasn't the plan," James said. "But you survived."

Brawn sighed, sat down cross-legged, and looked at James. "So you've got these guys shadowing you as well. Not a lot of fun, are they? Thanks for the save. They were really going to use napalm on me?"

"That's what I heard."

Abby said, "Max told me that they weren't trying to kill you. They were going to drop a ring of napalm around you to stop you from running. Krodin wants you alive—he wants to know why you're here. The Brawn from this reality is, well . . . He's dead."

The giant shook his head. "Man, these are some nasty people. We should have killed that guy back in Windfield. How'd he get here, anyway?" He slapped his hand down on the deck. "And where did this thing come from?"

Brawn listened without comment as Abby told him everything she knew about the situation.

Is he getting this at all? James wondered.

When Abby was finished, Brawn said, "So. Parallel universe. Well, that makes sense."

James couldn't help smiling at that. "Yeah, but it's not that simple. . . . It's not like our universe is still there."

"Then how come we remember the way things should be?"

"Now, that I don't know."

To Abby, the giant said, "So, you again. Abby, right? Have you thought of a good superhero name yet?"

"Not yet," Abby said. "How've you been?"

"In prison. Got a hearing coming up next week. Or I did, before everything went nuts. What about you? And the other girl, Dalton's sister?"

James left Abby telling Brawn about Roz and Lance, and walked back toward the portal. Even without his enhanced hearing he could tell that his two guards were following; their heavy boots pounded on the metal landing deck.

They followed James through the portal and were never more than two yards behind him as he retraced his steps through the Carrier. He found Krodin standing in front of the large picture window, talking to a man who looked vaguely familiar.

The Fifth King turned to face him. "James Percival Klaus, also known as Thunder. That was quite a display of power, James. You took out a dozen Raptors with one sonic blast. Work with me and you'll never have to worry about anything again. Your family will be given whatever they wish. We can send your sister to the best schools. We can even—"

"Shut up. We're going to stop you," James said. "If we have to, we'll kill you. Do you understand me?"

Krodin grinned at him. "I figured you people had an oath never to kill."

"For you I'm willing to make an exception."

"You're welcome to try. But you'll fail, and a lot of innocent people will suffer in the process."

"Better that we die on our feet than live on our knees."

"Tell that to all the people who are going to die because you don't understand how the world works. Grow up, James," Krodin said, and turned back to his colleague.

For a moment, it seemed to James that he wasn't talking to Krodin at all, but to his stepfather. An arrogant, self-assured man, swaggering, indifferent to the feelings of those he felt were beneath him. "Don't dismiss me!" James shouted.

Krodin flicked out his arm and caught James across the chin, sent him spinning to the floor. He skidded to a stop in front of his guards.

"Mr. Klaus, even with your powers you were no more a

danger to me than a light rain. So be a good little boy and walk away while you can still walk."

Facedown on the ground, James coughed blood onto the floor. He felt like he'd been hit by a bus. His jaw ached and his vision was blurred. He rolled over onto his back. *He's making a mistake. We'll find a way. We'll stop him.*

In the tunnels beneath Manhattan, Roz Dalton followed Joe Ward and Suzanne Housten—she still couldn't see the young woman as anyone other than Slaughter—and thirty other members of the resistance as they converged on the Fifty-ninth Street–Columbus Circle subway station.

They were all wearing black jeans, sweaters, and jackets, and most of the time Roz could tell that they were there only because of their footsteps and steady breathing.

It was a long, weary trek, and Roz was exhausted. Her attempts to sleep in the storeroom had given her little rest, and her legs felt as though she had just run a marathon.

"What exactly is the plan?" Roz asked.

Joe said, "You'll see when we get there, Roz. Obviously yesterday's events moved up our schedule and changed a few of the details. And by 'a few' I mean most. But we have you, and we have an extra-special guest we'll be meeting at Columbus. We've also got some people inside the Citadel."

A few minutes later they emerged into the dark and dust-filled main concourse of the Columbus Circle station. Another dozen people were waiting, all strong-looking men and women carrying a variety of weapons.

Joe whispered to Roz, "These are some of the folks Suzanne smuggled in. Lent to us by Unity. Specialists in infiltration."

There was a brief round of nodded greetings, and then everyone gathered around Suzanne.

She turned in a slow circle as she spoke: "You're all expecting a motivational speech. Right. Here it is. Do what you're supposed to do and don't get killed if you can avoid it. Joe will brief you on the details. Where's the prisoner?"

The crowd parted and two men dragged a gagged, blindfolded, and handcuffed man into the clearing and pushed him down onto his knees in front of Suzanne.

Suzanne beckoned Roz closer. "Assuming what you told us is true, you need to see this." She grabbed hold of the man's blindfold and ripped it off.

Staring up at them with wild eyes was an African American man Roz had never seen before. "Who is he?"

Suzanne paused. "You don't know him?"

"No."

"But . . ."

Roz reached out with her telekinesis and gently removed the man's gag. He coughed and spat, then said, "Roz—please try to talk some sense into these people!"

"This is Solomon Cord," Suzanne said. "Krodin's pet superhuman genius. The man who gave him the means to rule the world."

Roz said, "Paragon? I . . . I never saw his face before. Let him up—take off his handcuffs!"

Suzanne began, "That wouldn't be wise. He—"

"Do it!" Roz said.

She moved toward Cord, but Suzanne stepped in front of her. Roz tried to go around her, but the woman grabbed her arms. "Roz, he's Krodin's chief architect. He's the only real leverage we have."

Roz struggled to pull free of Suzanne's grip. "Let him go. You *know* he's not the same Solomon Cord. He's not a superhuman—he's an ordinary human."

Then Joe said, "We know that. But there's a chance that Krodin doesn't. We have to leave a message for him. This is how it works, Roz. You get us in. We take certain key people hostage. And we leave Cord's body for Krodin to find."

"He's an innocent man. He's a hero!"

General Westwood appeared behind Cord, placed his hand on his shoulder. "This is war, Ms. Dalton. Sacrifices have to be made."

"No!" With tears welling up in her eyes Roz lashed out at Suzanne's face with a telekinetic jab. The woman's head snapped back, but she recovered instantly.

"Stop struggling, Roz," Suzanne said. "I mean it. If we have to, we'll find another way into the Citadel and we'll leave *two* bodies for Krodin. Do you understand? This is more important than any of our lives."

Cord shrugged the general's hand away, then awkwardly got to his feet. He turned to Suzanne. "You people are supposed to be experts, but you don't know the first thing about conducting a war of attrition—your plan *stinks*. It's foolhardy and a far greater risk than the benefits warrant. It's suicide. You think Krodin cares enough about any of his people to be upset that they've died? Even if he did care, he's got an eternity to get over it. You might find a way to slow him down, but what about ten years from now? A hundred years? A thousand? He'll still be around. But let me go and I'll show you how to get rid of him forever."

After a long pause, Suzanne let Roz go and stepped away from her. "If you're not on the level, Cord, I'll kill you here and now." She turned to the guards. "Release him."

One of the men stepped forward and unlocked Cord's handcuffs. Cord flexed his arms and arched his back, then turned in a slow circle. "All right. This is the plan. Roz? That telekinetic shield of yours can also be used as a weapon. Do you understand what I mean?"

Roz nodded.

"Now."

Roz closed her eyes and concentrated. She pictured her telekinesis forming a cocoon around herself and Cord, then instantly expanded it. She could feel it ripping out from her body, slamming into the resistance fighters, pressing them against the walls.

"Run!" Cord yelled.

Roz darted for the exit while Cord pulled the gun from the hands of the nearest man.

She raced up the steps and slowed—the subway entrance's gate was locked. *No time to pick it. . . .* She used her telekinesis to smash the gates apart, and stepped over their shattered remains as she continued up the steps with Cord's heavy footfalls right behind her.

They emerged on the west side of Columbus Circle. The area was packed with civilians, some of whom glanced at them before continuing on their way.

"Now what?" Roz asked, looking around for any sign of Praetorians.

"Use your shield to keep the entrance blocked."

She turned back, and saw that Cord was not alone. An unconscious man was slung over his shoulder. Cord turned around and she saw that it was Joe Ward.

"I'm guessing you do have a plan?" Roz asked.

Cord grinned. "Me? I *never* have a plan."

CHAPTER 25

LESS THAN HALF A MILE from Roz Dalton's position, Lance McKendrick was in her apartment stretched out on an enormous leather sofa with his shoes off. He had a large bowl of popcorn resting on his stomach and a brimming glass of fresh grapefruit juice on the glass coffee table beside him.

He kept looking at the phone. He wanted to call his parents, but he knew that would be a bad idea: All phone calls were monitored and logged.

Josh Dalton wandered over to him and asked, "So, who are you exactly?"

"I'm a friend of your sister."

"Are you her boyfriend?"

"Hardly."

"Is that yes or no?"

"It's no."

"And what can you do?"

Lance paused with an overflowing handful of popcorn halfway to his mouth. "Eh?"

"You know. Can you fly, lift heavy weights, see through walls? That kinda thing. What's your power?"

"Well, I seem to be pretty good at getting caught. I think I'll call myself Captain Captured." He laughed, and then stopped when he realized that Josh wasn't joining in. "I guess you've met a lot of people with cool powers."

"A few, yeah."

Josh reached out to the popcorn bowl and Lance automatically snatched it away before he remembered where he was. "Help yourself."

The boy sat down on the edge of the coffee table. "I don't have any friends." He said this in a matter-of-fact way. "Apart from Brandon, and he's too old to really play games. He's, like, twenty-four or something."

"Sorry to hear that," Lance said. "Everyone needs friends."

"Do *you* want to play a game?"

"Sure."

"OK. I'm thinking of a number between one and ten."

Is he kidding? "It's six."

Joshua's eyes widened. "Yes! I thought you said you didn't have any powers."

"I don't. Joshua, when someone picks a number between one and ten, they almost always pick six. I'll give you another one. Think of a vegetable."

"OK."

"A carrot."

The boy sat back. "That is so cool! How did you know?"

"Same thing. People nearly always pick carrots. Don't

know why, though. Tell me something. . . . What exactly does your brother *do*? What's his job, exactly?"

"I dunno." Joshua shrugged. "Works for the Chancellor. Helps him get things done."

"Have you met the Chancellor?"

"Sure, loads of times. He's good fun. He lets me sit on his shoulders, and he carries me around. But Roz says I'm getting too old for that now."

Lance passed him the bowl and stood up, then looked back at the Lance-shaped outline of spilled popcorn on the sofa. "Better clean that up, I suppose." As he was scooping up the popcorn, an idea struck him. "Josh, have you got a deck of cards?"

"No. Gambling is illegal."

"Of course it is. OK, let's have a look at that meteor."

Josh fished around in his pocket and pulled out the black rock. "It's a tektite. And the word you mean is meteor*ite*, not *meteor*."

"What's the difference?"

"A meteorite reaches the ground. A meteor completely burns up in the atmosphere." He handed the rock to Lance. "You're not going to do anything to it, are you?"

Lance held up the small rock between the thumb and index finger of his left hand. "I'll show you how to make it disappear." He closed his right hand over the rock—and at the last moment parted his thumb and index finger so that the tektite dropped into the palm of his left hand. He held his closed right fist in front of Joshua, and frowned as he stared at it. "OK. So I have to concentrate as hard as I can on the meteorite, squeeze *really* hard. . . ." He held out his left fist, now closed over the tektite. "I'm going to teleport it into my other hand." Lance was squeezing both fists so tightly that his arms began to tremble. "Done! And now, I'll teleport it *back*." He frowned in concentration again.

Josh laughed. "That's a terrible trick! You didn't do anything at all!"

Lance sighed. "Ah, you broke my concentration. Now I can't send it back." He uncurled both fists.

Josh stared at the tektite in Lance's left hand. "How did you do that? I was watching the whole time!"

"Misdirection," Lance said. "It was always in my left hand." He tossed the rock back to Josh.

"Show me how to do that."

Standing on the forward edge of the Carrier's landing deck, Abby gripped the handrail and watched the landscape slip by beneath. The wind whipped at her hair and stung her eyes, and if she looked straight ahead, she could almost imagine that she was flying.

James stood on Abby's left, and on her right Brawn was again lying on his back with his hands clasped behind his head, staring up at the clouds.

A few yards away, their guards stood in a wide semicircle around them, constantly on alert.

"So what do we do?" Abby asked. She was sure that the guards weren't close enough to hear them over the constant hiss of the wind.

"We've gotta get off this thing for a start," Brawn said. "But I don't see how. With these guys watching us all the time and no powers we're pretty much useless. He's not going to let us live, you know that? Maybe we *should* sign up with him. I mean, if we assume he's going to win anyway, then we might as well cut our losses."

James said, "Krodin's a tyrant. If we take his side just to make our own lives easier, then we're as bad as he is."

"I understand that—I'm not an idiot. But there's what's right, and there's what's best. I'm just saying that if there's no going back to our world, and there's no way we can stop him, then we'd be nuts to keep fighting. Krodin's right about how the world would be better if there was just one leader. Even if it was a dictatorship, at least everyone would be treated equally. No more poor people, no crime, no discrimination."

"Right. Just a whole planet of slaves instead," James said. "And I know you're blue now, but you weren't always, so don't talk to *us* about discrimination. You haven't been there. You don't know what it's like to always have people judge you by the color of your skin."

"Don't I?" Brawn looked up at him. "What color do you think I was before I turned into a blue giant?" He climbed to his feet. "You guys do what you want. I'm going to talk to Krodin."

Abby reached up and put her hand on his arm. "Stay. Please."

He pulled away from her. "Don't pretend you care what happens to me, Abby."

"We don't want to have to fight you too."

"Fight *me*? You wouldn't stand a chance!"

"We'd prefer not to have to find out," she said. "And I know what you're doing. You think you'll have a better chance of being accepted if you're with Krodin. But he's not going to make you his friend—at best he'll make you his pet."

Brawn stopped. "I just want a normal life. I never asked to

be like this." He slowly turned back to face them. "How am I supposed to ever get a girlfriend? Or even a job? People run screaming when they see me. I just walk down the street and they call the cops on me. I was twelve when it happened, did you know that? No, you don't know anything about me. You see me as a blue giant and you think that's all there is. But I had a life. Not a great one, but at least I had some control over it."

Abby saw that he had tears in his pupil-less eyes.

He sat down again, crossed his arms over his knees, and rested his head on them. "I was twelve," Brawn said. "I was in church. In the choir. I had a solo piece coming up and I was a bit worried about it, and then my hands started shaking. I thought it was just nerves. Then there was pain like you wouldn't believe—felt like my body was on fire. It was over in a few seconds, and all I could hear was screaming as all the people stampeded out of the church. It happened that quick—one minute I was an ordinary kid, next I was thirteen feet tall, blue, and bald."

James said, "You might never become human again."

"That's supposed to make me feel better?"

"No. I'm saying that there aren't just two options—human or monster. You can use your strength to help people. Go back home to your old neighborhood and ignore the screams. Pretty soon they'll get used to having you around. They'll accept you as part of the community. Especially if you stop a few muggings and take down all the pushers. Tell the authorities you want to go back to school. You're still a citizen—you still have rights. I'm not saying it'll be easy, but in the long run it'll be a lot better than living in a cave or whatever."

"He's right," Abby said. "We're all superhuman and we

can't help that, but we do have a choice as to whether we're heroes or villains. People are going to try and make you into a bad guy because of how you look, but just don't let them. It's not like they'd be able to push you around."

"Stick with us," James said. "You know it's the right thing to do."

"Even if we don't have a chance?"

"Especially then," Abby said. "Anyone can be a hero when they know they're going to win."

Brawn lifted his head. "I have an idea."

Roz Dalton and Solomon Cord raced through what remained of the southern end of Central Park—a strip about eight blocks deep—with Joe still slung over Cord's shoulder.

So far, almost no one had paid them any attention, except for the quartet of Praetorian guards who had been stationed on the corner of Central Park and were now lying unconscious and battered on the street.

"That bunch of trees over there," Roz said. "We can rest for a few minutes."

"And decide where we're actually going," Cord said breathlessly. He lowered Joe to the ground at the base of a tree, then dropped down next to him.

Roz looked up through the canopy of leaves to the towers of the Citadel. "I have to get up there. Get my little brother out."

Joe groaned, and she crouched down next to him. "At last. Joe, can you hear me? Mr. Ward?"

"Roz? That you?"

"Yeah, Joe. It's me. I need to get into my apartment. Do you know which one it is?"

His eyes flickered open. "What hit me?"

"I did. Now tell me where I live or I'll do it again."

"South tower, floor one-thirty. The very top." He sat up and clutched his head. "Man, feels like you used me as a bowling ball." He looked at Cord. "Uh-oh."

Cord grabbed hold of Joe's collar and pulled him close. "You morons were going to kill me."

"Uh . . . Does that not fit in with your plans?"

Cord angrily pushed him away and stood up. "How do we get into the Citadel?"

Then a voice from above said, "I'll get you in."

Roz whirled around to see Suzanne Housten descending through the branches.

"You left a real mess back there, Dalton. Broken bones and fractured skulls. You've ruined everything. Those people are some of the most experienced soldiers in Unity. They were the only hope we had to stop Krodin."

Cord said, "Your plan was *insane*, Slaughter. Krodin wouldn't—"

She streaked toward him, and Cord found himself pressed against the trunk of the tree. "Don't call me that! I'm not her!"

Cord didn't flinch. "You're playing the part pretty well."

She let go and stepped back. "Dalton, I'll get your brother out. But you owe me. Big-time. Understood?"

Roz nodded.

"Good. Take my hand."

Roz reached out and suddenly she was being pulled into the air, crashing through the tree's upper branches. They rocketed toward the base of the tower, and then Housten angled straight upward.

Roz thought her arm was going to be wrenched out of its socket. She glanced down and saw the ground shrinking away.

Housten stopped almost as suddenly as she had started. They were outside a ring of windows, looking into the largest apartment Roz had ever seen.

"A good example of Krodin's new world," Housten said. "Your little friend Victoria lived in garbage and died from malnutrition, and look at this place. One rule for the rich, another for the rest."

"I never lived here," Roz said. "And you don't get to talk to me like that! You—"

"Cover your eyes."

Roz threw up the telekinetic shield less than a second before Housten crashed her fist into the nearest window. The two-inch-thick glass shuddered into a spiderweb of cracks. Another blow, and it splintered inward. Housten hauled Roz inside and dropped her to the carpet.

An alarm immediately began to sound, and over the noise Roz shouted, "Josh!"

She saw him, twenty yards away, staring at her with his mouth wide open. Beside him was Lance McKendrick. There was a large glass bowl in Lance's hand with popcorn slowly spilling out of it.

Lance screamed, jumped onto the leather sofa and over it, raced toward Housten, and swung the glass bowl at her face. It shattered instantly, leaving the woman completely unmarked.

Roz grabbed his arm, pulled him away. "Lance, no!"

"She killed them! She murdered my parents and my brother!"

"Lance, it wasn't her—this isn't Slaughter!"

"Let go of me, Roz! I'm going to kill her!"

Housten said, "We don't have time for this. Just take your brother and let's go."

Roz was still struggling to hold Lance back. "No, we're taking Lance with us."

Then something crashed on the far side of the room, Housten staggered and started to twitch, and a tall man in a Praetorian pilot's uniform was rushing toward them.

"Get everyone out of here, Roz!" the pilot yelled. He was holding an oversized black pistol: A thin, loose cable led from the pistol's underside to a pair of silver darts on Housten's shoulder.

"No!" Roz screamed. "Stop—she's with me!"

The silver darts jerked free of Housten's shoulder and dropped to the ground.

"What's going on here, Roz?" the pilot asked, still staring at Housten.

"Who *are* you?"

Joshua said, "Roz, he's Brandon. Max's pilot." He frowned. "You *know* that."

Lance had finally calmed down enough for Roz to risk letting go of him. "And what is *she* doing here?" he asked.

Housten said, "We need to leave right now. The Praetorians will be on their way. I can't carry both of them, Roz. You need to decide which of them is more important to you—your friend or your brother."

Roz turned to Brandon. "You obviously know that something happened to me and Max yesterday."

He nodded. "I've overheard some stuff." He looked from Roz to Lance, then to Housten. "You're going after Krodin, aren't you? Do you think you have a chance?"

"I don't know. But we have to try to stop him before Unity invades. So can we trust you?"

He looked around at them again, chewing absently on his lower lip. "I can see you're going to go anyway, Roz. I'm not the sort of guy who could stay at home while you risked your life. I'm in."

"We need a Raptor," Roz said.

Brandon said, "I'll call one in. And cancel the alarm. Where are we going?"

"Wherever Max is."

"When I left him, he was on his way to Louisiana," Brandon said.

"Suzanne, you said your people have a way to get in touch with Daedalus. We're going to need him."

Housten glared at her. "My people are hardly in a position to contact anyone, thanks to you. Without them I'll never find Daedalus. We're on our own."

On the edge of the Carrier's landing deck, Abby, James, and Brawn watched as Krodin approached.

When Krodin was four yards away, Abby backed up until she bumped into the side rail. "That's close enough!"

Krodin stopped. "What's so important that you couldn't come inside to tell me?"

Brawn and James moved back until they were level with Abby. Brawn said, "All three of us wanted to talk to you together."

Krodin looked from one to the other. "You're going to agree to work with me, but only under certain conditions."

Rats! Abby said to herself. *I was sure we'd be able to string him along for longer than that!*

"More or less," James said. "But—"

Krodin shook his head. "No deals. No conditions."

"But you haven't heard our offer yet," James said.

The Fifth King hesitated for a moment. "I'm listening."

"We'll help you unite the world, to put an end to war, poverty, and injustice, but we won't kill for you," Abby said. "We won't harm innocent people in any way."

James added, "And we won't be working for you. We'll be working *with* you."

Krodin nodded slowly. "I'll take that into consideration."

"And one more thing," Brawn said. "I don't like heights. Either get this thing to fly lower, or find a way to get me inside. We've got to be, like, two miles up!"

"Your concept of distance is pathetic, Brawn," Krodin said. "Our current altitude is only half that. A little more than a mile."

"Promise?" Brawn asked.

"Of course," Krodin said, nodding.

Then James smiled. "That's exactly what we were hoping you'd say."

A frown. "What?"

"Now!" Abby yelled. She grabbed James's hand.

Simultaneously Brawn, James, and Abby threw themselves backward over the side rail.

Oh man, I really hope this works! Abby thought as she tumbled through the air.

CHAPTER 26

TEN MONTHS ago ...

In Chicago, Solomon Cord was so intent on his work that when his computer's screens went blank, it took him a moment to realize that it wasn't a software glitch but a power cut: All the lights in his workshop had also gone out.

Nearby, a flashlight came on, its beam flickering about the room. "Oh great," Casey's voice called. "What did you do this time?"

"Wasn't me," Cord said. He peered around at the darkness, listening. "All the machines are down. We should . . ." His shoulders sagged. "Aw, nuts! The doors seal shut if the power goes. We can't get out."

The flashlight beam bobbed closer. "Remember that time when I said this room should have windows? Remember?

And you told me that every window halves the security of the room?"

Cord ignored him. He swiveled his chair around to the bench behind him, groped about until his fingers touched a rack of glass beakers. "Gotcha!"

"What are you doing?" Casey's voice asked.

Cord counted along the rack and stopped at the fifth beaker. "Our old friend H_2SO_4."

"Sulfuric acid? In the dark? Oh, *that's* clever, Sol. Where do you want me to ship your remains?"

"Casey, this could be an attack. I don't have any weapons in here, do you?"

"No."

"So switch off the flashlight—if this *is* an attack, that'll just tell them where we are."

"No way. The emergency lights will kick in any—"

Something went *klank* in the corridor beyond the heavy steel doors, and Cord felt Casey's hand grip his arm. "Whoa, careful! Sulfuric acid, remember?"

"Sorry. What was that?"

The *klank*ing sound came again, louder this time.

"I do *not* like the sound of that," Casey said. "How solid are those doors, exactly?"

"Solid enough, I hope."

"Man, I *knew* we should have moved to the Louisiana base already. It's a lot safer there. Where's Max?"

"Probably in his office. Try your cell phone."

"I already did. It's not working."

Then Max's voice was screaming in his head: "We're under

attack! Big guy in armor, I . . . No, can't pick up any thoughts from it—has to be some kind of robot. Came out of nowhere. Didn't trigger any of the alarms—took the guards down in seconds! Cord, he's heading right for you guys!"

Cord heard something metallic scraping along the other side of the doors. *Oh man . . . What else can I use as a weapon?*

The whole room seemed to shudder as a powerful steel-covered fist plowed through the reinforced concrete next to the door. Beside Cord, Casey dropped the flashlight, dived to the floor, and began to scramble away.

The room was now in almost total darkness. Cord felt the sweat break out on his back and forehead, and he forced himself to keep calm.

There was the sound of another concrete-shattering punch, then the rattle and hiss of fragments crashing to the floor.

Heavy metallic feet crunched on fragments of brick as the machine—whatever it was—climbed its way through.

Cord hefted the container of acid in his hand as he tried to estimate the distance. Then he pulled his arm back and threw the beaker.

At the same time, he dropped to the floor. He heard the glass breaking, the splash of the acid. *Got it!*

He saw the beam of the nearby flashlight and made a grab for it, but just as his fingers reached it, something slammed into the heavy workbench, shunting it toward Cord and almost crushing him in the process.

Overhead, the fluorescent lights began to flicker. The light was weak, sputtering, but it allowed Cord to see enough to grab the edge of the workbench and pull himself up.

On the far side of the room the flickering light revealed

the black-and-gold-colored attacker striding toward Casey. It was metallic, man-shaped, bigger and bulkier than a human.

Daedalus—has to be him! "Casey! Run!"

Thick with fear, Casey's voice came back: "I can't, I'm trapped. I . . . Cord, I can see his face—I know who he is!" Casey was screaming now. "I know who Daedalus is! You have to tell everyone! He's—"

Cord caught a glimpse of something glowing in the attacker's hand. Then it flared and all Cord knew was light, and silence, and pain.

He woke to see Max Dalton helping him sit up. Max was talking to him, but all Cord could hear was a soft muffle.

Then, inside his head, Max's voice said, "You're OK, Sol. It's gone. What was it? Daedalus?"

Cord nodded, and thought, *I think so. Big, armored . . . Casey said he saw his face. He knows who he is. Ask him. . . .* Then he looked around at the room. It was all but destroyed.

Aloud, he asked, "Casey?"

"He's dead," Max's voice said. "That explosion . . . One of the security cameras came back online long enough to catch it. He was vaporized." He grabbed Cord's arm and pulled him to his feet. "You feeling all right?"

Cord nodded. "Ears are still ringing, but I'll be fine. Max, we have to stop this guy. He could have killed *all* of us. The way Casey reacted—Daedalus is someone we know. Could it be someone who survived Anchorage?"

Max shrugged. "I don't know. . . . A nuclear blast at ground zero? Even Krodin barely survived that. Better start packing up, Sol. We're relocating to the base in Louisiana within the hour."

CHAPTER 27

IN MANHATTAN, BRANDON Santamaría expertly guided the Raptor away from the Citadel and descended toward the park. Suzanne Housten sat in the co-pilot's seat next to him.

Lance sat on one side of the craft, glowering at Housten. Beside him, Roz started to speak, but he cut her off. Out of the side of his mouth, he said, "I know. It's not really her."

"I felt the same when I saw her," Roz said.

"Oh, I doubt that. Slaughter didn't kill *your* parents."

"True. But at least you got yours back. Very few people can say that."

Lance slumped down even farther in the chair. "You're right. Sorry. It's been a tough couple of days. I got arrested, sent to prison, and had to escape."

"I was chased, caught, knocked out, and then I escaped and got trapped in the abandoned subways."

She looked as though she was about to add more—Lance could tell she'd been crying—but he decided not to push it. "OK, you win. Have you had any contact with Abby or Thunder or Brawn?"

"No, but Max talked to Abby yesterday."

The craft touched down, its hatch slid open, and Solomon Cord rushed in, followed by a younger man Lance hadn't seen before.

"No way you're coming with us, Joe," Roz said. "Get out!"

The man spread his arms, pleading. "Aw, c'mon, Roz! I'm a good fighter, and anyway you can't leave me behind because any minute the place will be crawling with Praetorians." He dropped into one of the seats. "Where *are* we going, anyway?"

Suzanne Housten said, "Louisiana."

Joe said, "Oh fantastic. The Deep South. A whole state full of nothing but swamps, screen doors, homemade lemonade, and bare feet."

Lance said, "Hey, my *mother's* from Louisiana, you jerk!"

Roz walked over to Joe. "I said no, and I meant no."

Joe grinned. "Ah, now you're just playing hard to get, Roz. I—"

She grabbed him by the collar and pulled him up out of the seat. "Get out!" She pushed him back toward the still-open hatch.

"No, wait! Seriously, you can't *do* this to me! Suzanne!"

Without looking at him, Suzanne said, "I suggest you find someplace to hide, Joe. She's not going to change her mind, and we sure need her a lot more than we need you."

Then, as though struck by a powerful wind, Joe was

stumbling backward through the hatchway and down the short ramp.

"Brandon, take us up," Roz said.

Cord spotted Lance and sat down next to him as the Raptor surged into the air once more. "Lance. How are you doing?"

"Not so good, Mr. Cord." He nodded toward Suzanne Housten.

"I can understand that."

"How are we going to stop Krodin?"

Cord shook his head. "I wish I knew. But the others are with him in Louisiana, and this time we have Sl"—he stopped himself—"Ms. Housten on our side. Whether that'll be enough, I couldn't say." He leaned back and closed his eyes. "I don't even want to think about it now. Roz, what's our ETA?"

"We've got about eleven hundred miles to cover. About two hours."

"OK. Housten, we need to know what Unity's plans are."

She turned to him. "Yes, we do. And if Roz hadn't crippled General Westwood, we could have asked him."

"Bad news, Roz," Brandon said. "According to the reports Abigail de Luyando, James Klaus, and Brawn are in custody on board Krodin's command ship. Max is with them, but he's . . ."

Roz looked up. "Go on."

"He's not in custody. He seems to have resumed his usual duties."

Cord said, "We have to assume that he's working from the inside."

Lance looked at Cord, who quickly looked away. *He still doesn't trust Max*, Lance thought, *but he doesn't want everyone to know that.*

"What was that thing you hit me with?" Suzanne Housten asked Brandon.

"Stun gun. A prototype. Any normal person would have been out cold instantly."

"Lucky I'm not a normal person, then. You've met Krodin, right? You think we can take him on?"

"Oh, you can take him on all right," Brandon said. "But you won't win." He turned to her. "He could—and probably will—kill you all without a second thought. We're no more important to him than . . . sand or bugs. But Krodin's not evil. Misguided, perhaps, but I've met him many times, and I've never seen anything that makes me think he shouldn't be in power."

What are you up to, Brandon? Lance wondered. *If Max can't control you, then . . . What are you doing here? You can't be working with the resistance because Slaughter doesn't know you.*

Cord said, "Are you kidding me? That was Max messing with your mind, you idiot. He was controlling you like he controls everyone else. For all you know, you've witnessed Krodin butcher hundreds of people and every time Max just wiped your memory."

Josh leaned close to Roz and whispered, "Max wouldn't do something like that, would he?" Louder, he said to Cord, "You're talking like he's one of the bad guys or something."

Lance said, "He controls people's minds and forces them to do whatever he wants. I'm pretty sure that doesn't make him one of the *good* guys."

• • •

The wind ripped at James Klaus's clothing as he fell, catching him and spinning him around so that he could no longer see the Carrier. All he could see was the ground rushing toward him.

Abby's hand was locked around his wrist, as his was around hers. Her eyes were closed and he could feel her nails digging into his arm. He knew exactly how she felt. If Krodin had been lying, they would be dead within seconds.

The figures ran through his head: *Five thousand feet. Accelerating at thirty-two point two feet per second squared . . .* James spread his arms and legs wide to increase his wind resistance and slow his fall. *Oh man, this had better work!*

To his left and a little below him he could see Brawn, falling faceup.

Then the howling wind jumped in volume so suddenly that for a moment James was sure his eardrums had burst.

A shock of pain ran through his arm and he almost screamed. Abby's grip was almost grinding his radius and ulna together. Then he realized what was happening, and he didn't care about the pain.

He glanced over at Brawn again. The giant was laughing.

James heard Abby praying softly to herself.

"Hey," he said. "You can relax your grip."

Abby's eyes snapped open. "We're alive? It worked?"

With his free hand James jerked his thumb over his shoulder. "Take a look."

Brawn seemed to be accelerating away from them,

streaking toward the ground. He was laughing. "Oh, I'm gonna do *this* again!"

Brawn crashed straight through the treetops and hit the swamp hard in an explosion of bark, leaves, and turbid water.

James touched down with Abby on a nearby patch of relatively dry ground. "He's still laughing. I guess that means he's OK."

Abby walked to the edge of the swamp where Brawn was climbing out. She grabbed his hand and pulled. "Ew! You're covered in slime!"

James searched the sky for the Carrier and found it—a dark dot against the clouds. "We can't stay here. They might send someone after us—and if they do, it's my guess they'll have the power-damper with them. Brawn, you're faster than any of us. You think you can run while carrying Abby? I can fly."

The giant nodded, spraying James with drops of muddy water. "Sure. But if they get close enough to us, we're gonna lose our powers again. So better not fly too high. The real question is . . . where are we going to go? We can't go near Krodin as long as he has the power-damper."

Abby said, "We don't have a choice. We'll just have to come up with something. Pity we couldn't take Max with us."

"So what do we do now?" Brawn asked.

James absently chewed on his lower lip as he looked around. "I'll hear them coming, so we have the advantage there. . . . We have to get to Krodin's base."

"Right. Get to Dalton, and get rid of the power-damper."

"No, our first priority is to destroy Krodin's teleporter."

He pointed in the direction the Carrier had gone. "We can't be too far out from the base. Let's go."

Abby and Brawn trudged through the swamp after him.

"It'll be guarded," Brawn said, ducking under an overhanging branch. "We need to find a way to disable the Praetorians first."

"Again, not our first priority."

Abby said, "Yeah, but if they're between us and the teleporting machine, then . . ."

He turned around and stared at her, looked up at Brawn. *How can I ask them to do this? Even Brawn. Back home everyone thought he was a villain, but he's not.*

Abby put her hand on his arm. "What are you saying?"

"If we can't disable Krodin before the attack by Unity, we're looking at all-out war. Millions of people will die. And those men, Krodin's guards . . . I'm saying that we will do whatever is necessary to destroy the teleporter. Do you understand me? If we have no other choice, we will kill those who get in our way."

The Raptor was halfway across New Jersey when Brandon called out, "Incoming! We've got sixteen marks on a pursuit vector, attack formation."

Roz jumped to her feet. "Full speed!"

"Already pushing the red line. They're coming in at almost twice our speed. We've got about three minutes."

"Raptors?" Cord asked.

"No, too small and too fast."

Housten said, "I'm picking up four Jetmen—just launched themselves from the lead Raptor. They're going to try to board us. And there's another eight flying Skimmers—one-man craft. Not a lot of firepower or armor, but they're fast and very maneuverable." She called up a display on the screen: It showed a low, sleek craft not much bigger than a surfboard. The pilot lay horizontally on the inside and controlled the craft with his feet as well as his hands. "Takes a lot of skill to fly one—which means we're up against the best pilots the Praetorians have."

"Getting a transmission," Suzanne said.

A voice crackled over the craft's speaker system: "Unauthorized Raptor, this is Agent Paquette, chief of the Manhattan Praetorian Division. You will disengage your forward thrust and prepare to be boarded. This will be your only warning. Respond."

Roz said, "How do I talk . . . ?"

Brandon hit one of the controls. "Go ahead."

"Agent Paquette, this is Roz Dalton."

A pause. "Roz, what are you doing? You do *not* take a Raptor without filing a flight plan. What's your destination?"

"Louisiana."

"I see. You don't have permission. Bring your craft to a halt and prepare to be boarded."

"Sorry, can't do that."

"That wasn't a suggestion, Roz. If you do not comply, we will consider you a hostile and take appropriate action."

"Max has worked your mind over pretty good, hasn't he? You used to be one of the good guys."

"Last warning: *Stand down!*"

"Agent Paquette, we have civilians on board. Trust me, you don't want to fire on us. I have my brother Joshua here."

A sigh of exasperation, then, "You were warned."

The connection died.

Roz said, "Keep going, Brandon. Take whatever evasive action you need. Suzanne—I know you can fly, and you're extremely strong and fast. Get out there and get them off our tail. If you can, disable one of the Jetmen and bring him inside. Paragon, you think you could fly one of their jetpacks?"

Cord nodded. "I'll give it a go."

"Everyone else, strap in and hold tight."

"You don't get to give me orders, Dalton," Suzanne said, getting out of her seat.

"Yes I do. You're our best hope of stopping them. Move!" She followed Suzanne to the hatchway and looked toward her brother. "It'll be OK."

Lance said, "What are *you* going to do?"

"I won't know until I'm out there."

Suzanne opened the hatch and the cold air instantly blasted through the Raptor. "Someone close this after us: The open door will slow us down. And be prepared to open it when we come back." She launched herself out.

Roz leaned out through the hatch and spotted a handrail to the left. She grabbed it and climbed, hand over hand, onto the top of the hull.

A moment later she saw them: a cluster of bright points directly behind the Raptor, coming in like oversized heat-seeking missiles. On her right Suzanne was streaking toward them.

Gripping the handrail as tightly as she could, she reached out with her telekinesis toward the Skimmers. The distance was much farther than she'd ever attempted, but that wouldn't be for long.

First one that gets in range . . . , Roz thought.

She saw Suzanne crash straight into the lead Skimmer, and the others scattered, spreading out in all directions before resuming their approach.

Roz felt a slight resistance against her telekinetic probe. "Gotcha!" She focused on the closest Skimmer, pushed against its thrust. The craft wavered for a moment, but kept coming. *Not close enough yet.*

Suzanne zoomed back toward the Raptor and caught up with a second Skimmer. She landed on its fuselage, smashed open the canopy, and tore off the pilot's helmet. A quick punch to the back of his head and the man was unconscious. As Roz watched, Suzanne leaped from the craft and it began to drift off to the right.

Roz focused again on the closest Skimmer, and this time she was able to grab hold of it. She flipped it onto its back and let go. Upside down, the pilot suddenly found himself hurtling in the wrong direction. His Skimmer crashed head-on into one of his colleagues, and the two craft tumbled slowly toward the ground, a tangled mess of ruined armor plating and sputtering engines.

Slaughter got two, I got two . . . Should be twelve left.

On the right, two of the Skimmers broke away from the pack, then two Jetmen peeled off to the left.

That leaves eight, Roz thought. *We might just . . . There's only seven! Where's—*

She sensed something behind her and whirled about: A

Jetman was zooming toward her from the front of the Raptor. *Sneaky—came up from beneath.*

She threw a telekinetic shield in front of her, a curve passing from the front of the craft over her head. The Jetman smashed into the invisible shield and bounced away in a shower of metal and plastic debris. One of his colleagues zoomed after him.

Roz sagged, almost lost her grip. Using her telekinesis so much always weakened her for a moment, but on the ground that was much less of a problem.

Another Skimmer zoomed up over the side of the hull. Roz struck at it, knocked it away. The craft tumbled for a moment, then righted itself and fell back.

It was then that the two Jetmen who had peeled off to the left chose to come back, shooting. A bullet sparked off the hull inches away from Roz's hand.

Roz lashed out at them. She struck one, but the other arced up, passed over the hull, and disappeared beneath it. *He's going full circle!*

The Raptor juddered again as the Jetman came back around for another attack. Roz lashed out with her shield but missed: He had abruptly altered his course and zoomed straight for the side of the Raptor.

The hatch—it's open!

The armored man slowed a little, reached the hatch—and was suddenly knocked back.

Roz had a brief glimpse of the Jetman tumbling away from the Raptor. He wasn't alone—Solomon Cord had leaped out and was tackling him in midair. They dropped out of view. *Please let him survive that!*

Then she spotted a dark shape approaching from the left, much bigger than a Skimmer. Another Raptor was bearing down on them.

To Roz's left a line of small pits suddenly appeared in the hull. *They're firing at us!*

Roz felt her weight shift suddenly and tightened her grip on the rail: The Raptor had tilted back and was now climbing almost vertically, spinning as it did so. She realized that Brandon was trying to shield her from the second Raptor's attack.

Three more Skimmers came at them from below, angling their ascent to bring them onto the top of the hull.

Then the Raptor stopped almost instantly and the Skimmers shot past. But the Praetorians' Raptor fired again, a powerful volley that sparked off the hull and tore through the far end of the handrail.

No!

The rail came away from the hull and Roz was suddenly falling.

She didn't know how high up she was, but the fall seemed to take forever. She had plenty of time to watch Slaughter attack the other Skimmers, and to see the Praetorians' Raptor slamming into the side of her own craft.

Then strong arms were around her, slowing her fall, lifting her up. Dazed, Roz saw Solomon Cord's face only inches from hers.

"Easy now," Cord said. "You're OK. I've got you."

CHAPTER 28

ABBY KEPT CLOSE to Brawn as they waded knee-deep through the swamp. Not only did his massive size provide good protection from the sun but she'd noticed earlier that something about him kept the mosquitoes away.

They were approaching Krodin's complex from the north. By listening to the voices and footsteps of the workers, James had figured out that the northern part of the structure was the least visited.

James, taking the lead, stopped and briskly shook his head. "Sound's fading. We're on the edge of the power-damper's range." He took a few steps backward, and Abby and Brawn stepped aside to let him pass. "Yeah, we're not going to get any closer and still be able to use our powers."

"We need to get Max out of that place," Abby said. "*Without* killing anyone," she added, glaring at James.

Brawn said, "Krodin's not going to let him out of his sight now."

"So what do we do?"

"Hold on," James said. "I can hear Krodin talking to one of the Praetorian commanders. . . . Listen."

Then Abby could hear it too: "We're not sure exactly who's on board," the commander was saying. "They've got at least one unknown superhuman with them. Female, strong, fast, flight capability. Rosalyn Dalton and Solomon Cord are present. Cord managed to get the jetpack and armor from one of the Jetmen."

"How many people have you lost?"

"Eight Skimmers, four Jetmen, one Raptor—it attempted to ram the stolen craft, but it looks like Dalton shielded it with her telekinesis. Our Raptor was forced to make an emergency landing. No hands lost."

"Take them down, Agent Paquette," Krodin ordered. "Whatever it takes. Destroy their Raptor if you have to."

Abby gasped. "No!"

James said, "Quiet, Abby. . . . I've got it."

Then they heard Krodin's voice say, "No, forget that. Pull back. There's nothing they can do to stop me."

"Sir?"

"You heard me. Return to base. Refuel and reload. Dalton and her people are a distraction, that's all. If they reach Louisiana, I'll deal with them personally; otherwise your resources are better employed elsewhere. We don't know what Unity are planning and we need to be on full alert, understood?"

"Sir, I—"

"I'll remind you of the penalties for contradiction, Agent Paquette."

"Yes, sir. Paquette out."

James opened his eyes and grinned. "That'll do it."

"*You* did that?" Brawn said. He slapped James on the shoulder and almost knocked him over. "That was way cool! But what did Krodin hear?"

"He heard her saying that they're forcing the Raptor to land and she'd contact him when she knew more. Should buy Roz and the others some time."

Abby stood up. "Good work. Can you contact Roz from here?"

"No, they're way too far."

"Then fly up and see if you can see the base yet."

James silently rose until he'd cleared the treetops, and then his voice appeared next to Abby. "Yeah, I see it. It's smaller than I thought it'd be. It's about the size of your school, Abby. Two floors, walls slope in a little. Looks like there's a garden covering the entire roof."

"Camouflage, probably," Brawn said. "From overhead it'll blend in with the rest of the swamp. Makes it very hard to spot."

James descended. "Maybe, but having the Carrier right next to it is a bit of a giveaway. There's no easy path between here and there." He pointed to the right. "So we'll go this way. We can't get within eight hundred yards of the base, but as long as Max isn't in the very center, we should be able to get closer than this."

A few minutes later they found themselves on the far

side of the shallow lake, crouched among the reeds, facing the northern side of the building. Krodin's massive Carrier was between them and the base, providing them with some additional cover. On top of both the Carrier and the base, armored Praetorian guards stood watch.

"Yeah, the whole exterior is alarmed," James said. "Motion sensors—they have a very distinctive hum."

Brawn was too tall to crouch down with the others: He was lying almost flat, half submerged in the muck. "So if we can figure out a way to get in and still have our powers, then what? Krodin's just gonna come after us. We split up?"

"No other way, really," Abby said. "You and James, me on my own. Whichever team finds Krodin first keeps him busy—the other one destroys the teleporter."

Brawn nodded. "All right. Except you two stick together. I'll do it alone—come in from the roof. James, they don't know we're here, do they?"

"If they do, they're not talking about us," James said. "I'm thinking there might be another way to do this. Instead of breaking in and all that . . . Why don't I just destroy the whole building from here? I'm pretty sure I can do it. The fact that I can hear them inside the base means the power-damper only affects us directly; it doesn't cancel out the effects of our powers, if you know what I mean. One massive shock wave right in the heart of the foundations and the whole thing will collapse and sink into the swamp."

"You can't. There are civilians in there," Abby said.

"So we warn them. Give them five minutes to get out."

"Won't work," Brawn said. "Think about it: Nothing we do will hurt Krodin."

"That's not the purpose of the mission."

"Oh, we're on a mission now, are we? But that's not what I'm saying. The point is that Krodin won't *let* the civilians leave. Not even if we ask him nicely. He knows we wouldn't hurt innocent people. So we stick to the original plan. . . . Which brings us back to how we get inside the building with our powers still working and without the alarm going off."

"I can muffle the sirens, no problem there," James said, "but that won't be much use if they have flashing lights or doors that seal automatically."

Abby sighed. "Wish I still had my bow. I could—"

Brawn interrupted her. "Heck with all this talking! *This* is how we get in!" He grabbed hold of the nearest tree and wrapped his massive arms around it, ripped it free from the ground.

The others dodged a shower of dirt, leaves, and flakes of bark as Brawn hoisted the tree over his head.

With a yell of exertion, Brawn threw the tree as easily as an ordinary man would throw a football. It arced through the air, sailed over the base, and crashed into the swamp on the south side.

"You missed," Abby said.

"Depends on what I was aiming at. Thunder?"

"I can hear Max. He's moving with most of the others to see what the noise was. . . . They're going outside. . . ." James's voice shifted in tone. "Max, this is Thunder. I'm aiming this sound directly at you. If you've still got the power-damping thing with you, get out of the base now! Head south, fast as you can."

"Did he hear you?" Abby asked.

"I think so. . . . Yes! He's left the building!" James grinned. "Keep going, Max." He looked at the others. "Get ready. A few more seconds and he'll have taken the power-damper out of range of the building. . . . Now!"

Abby raced forward, wading through the lake, but had barely gone ten steps before she felt herself rising out of the water.

"Better to fly than run," James said, appearing beside her. He put his arm around her waist and pulled her close. "Don't read anything into this. It's just easier."

She heard Brawn splashing through the water behind them. "Finally! Time for some needless property damage and wanton destruction!"

They were halfway across the lake when the building's alarms sounded and then instantly cut out.

Abby said, "James—the wall!"

"Got it. Cover your eyes."

She felt his muscles tense for a moment, heard what sounded like rapid gunfire, and when she opened her eyes again, a four-foot-wide ring of three-inch holes had appeared in the wall. "Brawn?"

A growl rose from the giant. He raced past Abby and James and threw himself shoulder-first at the wall. The weakened circle of foot-thick reinforced concrete was smashed through into the building.

"Go for it!" Brawn yelled. He stepped back, jumped, and landed on the roof.

James let go of Abby as they reached the opening. She hit the floor, rolled, and came up on her feet. They were in the complex's sleeping quarters, a large dormitory containing thirty lockers and the same number of bunks, many of which had been crushed by flying lumps of concrete.

"Where's the machine?" Abby asked.

"The largest room. Straight down the corridor."

Abby tore the steel leg from one of the ruined bunks as James destroyed the dormitory's doors with a sonic blast.

James whispered, "Four men outside. Armed."

"I can take four," Abby said.

"No need." James concentrated. "They're down."

Abby stepped into the corridor. The Praetorian soldiers were lying on the ground, their arms and legs waving and twitching.

"I messed with their sense of balance," James said. "They think they're falling. They're screaming too, but I'm blocking that."

From somewhere above came the sounds of gunfire, then shouts of panic.

"Krodin?" Abby asked.

"No, just Brawn beating up the Praetorians with other Praetorians. Krodin's . . . He's in the teleporter room. Looks like you're the one facing him. Just keep him busy long enough for me to destroy the machine."

They took off down the corridor and found that the doors to the teleporter room were open. They skidded to a stop.

Krodin was standing, arms folded and with no sign of concern on his face, next to what she assumed was the teleportation device.

The machine was much smaller than Abby had expected. She'd imagined something the size of a bus, a complex piece of machinery covered in lights and wires. Instead, it wasn't much bigger than a refrigerator.

A group of twenty men and women were standing behind Krodin. Some were soldiers; most looked to be technicians. One of the soldiers spun around, aimed his rifle at Abby.

Krodin reached out and gently pushed the gun aside. "That's not necessary, Remington." He smiled at Abby and patted the top of the machine. "Here it is. But to get to it, you have to get past me."

Abby muttered to James, "Now!"

"I've already tried a dozen times," James whispered back. "It's not working."

Krodin put his hands into his pockets and casually walked back and forth in front of the machine. "I'm waiting. Go on. Do something spectacular. Something heroic. I know—James, use your sound-manipulation ability to blast the teleporter into atoms." Krodin smiled. "You can't, can you? Abigail, why don't you make a run at it? Smash it to pieces with that lump of steel in your hands." He stepped aside. "I'll give you one free shot. Go on."

He strode toward them.

"It won't work," Krodin said. "You might scratch the paintwork, but that's OK. This thing doesn't have much of a resale value anyway." He laughed. "And now you're wondering whether I have another power-damping device, yes? No, there's only one, and it's still chained to Max's wrist. And Max is on the run, right? Desperately splashing through the bayou, keeping the power-damper out of range of this building. Even without his powers, he's a resourceful man, more than capable of outrunning my men long enough for you to destroy the teleporter. Even if they've already found him, they wouldn't have been able to bring him back so quickly."

Abby felt a knot tighten in her stomach. "No . . ."

"Yes. I'm not an idiot, Abigail. The power-damper has a transmitter that allows us to know its exact location at all times."

She heard dragging footsteps in the corridor behind them, and turned to see Max—soaking and splattered with mud from the waist down—standing between two Praetorian soldiers.

Krodin said, "Why would I send my men out to bring in Dalton when I have a perfectly good teleporter right here beside me?"

Max was dragged into the room and thrown to the floor at Krodin's feet.

Krodin crouched down and held up the power-damper, which was still attached to Max's wrist. "We have our late friend Casey to thank for this. Tell them how it works, Remington."

Remington cleared his throat and said, "It, uh, it strips away the energy that makes you superhuman. It's just temporary, though. When it's switched off, you get your powers back."

Krodin let go of the device and hauled Max to his feet. "And who took Casey's design and made it work?"

"Cord."

"Solomon Cord," Krodin said, smiling. "My favorite

human." He leaned close to Abby and in a fake whisper said, "You're my *second* favorite, but don't tell anyone."

Remington said, "Casey was hoping that he could come up with a way to harness—"

"Shut up, Remington," Krodin said. "Your bit's over. So, James and Abigail. Your cerulean companion is at this moment on the roof wondering why he's not so bulletproof anymore. Or he's dead and not wondering anything. Remington, organize a squadron comprising whatever men are still standing and able to pull a trigger and get Brawn down from the roof. You'll probably need ropes and hooks. I want him on the landing pad. If he tries to escape, your men are to immediately open fire."

Krodin resumed his pacing back and forth. "It's traditional, at times like these, to ask the prisoners a question. Which of you should I kill first?"

At the same time, both James and Abby said, "Max."

Krodin suddenly laughed, the deep, honest belly laugh of a man genuinely amused. "I like that. That's great. But I can't kill Max—he's useful to me. For the moment. No, it has to be one of you two, or Brawn if he's not already dead."

Abby took a deep breath and let it out slowly. "Can I ask you something? Something personal?"

"Fire away."

"It's not really a question so much, more an observation. You're the loneliest man in the universe, aren't you? Everyone you ever meet is going to die before you do. Back on the Carrier you told me to think of you as a force of nature. If that's so, then Mother Nature really has it in for you. And you told me to take the long view—that what you're planning will be better for the human race, in the end. But if you are *really* taking the long view, then nothing you do here matters. Nothing. You could sit on a rock for a billion years and get the same result. The human race won't last forever. Nothing does. No matter what happens, no matter what you do, in the end you'll be alone."

"Housten's coming back," Brandon called. "Someone get the hatch."

Lance moved to the hatch and hit the control to open it. Suzanne Housten was floating outside, keeping pace with the craft. The sleeves of her black jacket and sweater had been shredded to ragged, flapping strips, revealing the mass of deep cuts and dark bruises on her arms. "Give me a hand, kid."

Lance avoided catching her gaze as he reached out to grab Suzanne's arm. He hadn't wanted to see this woman again but had to admit that he was glad she'd made it.

Housten glared at Cord. "Raptor hit me point-blank. I was stunned, falling. But I saw you—you didn't come after me."

"I couldn't save both you and Roz. I chose the one who hadn't been planning to kill me."

"And *you*," Housten said to Brandon, "when the Praetorians dropped back, you kept going. You should have waited for us!"

"Why don't you complain more?" Lance asked. "It's fun listening to you."

"Enough!" Roz said. "Brandon, what's our ETA?"

"Forty-four minutes."

"All right. You've been there?"

"Many times." He looked up from the cockpit's screens. "They know we're coming."

Housten said, "They'll shoot us down before we get anywhere near it."

"I know a few tricks. I can get us pretty close. Certainly within walking distance."

Cord sat down in the co-pilot's seat. "You sure about that?"

Brandon grinned. "Trust me."

Then Lance asked, "Who are you?"

Everyone turned to look at him.

Ten-year-old Joshua answered: "He's Brandon. Max's pilot. You know that. Brandon Santamaría."

Lance nodded briskly. "Yeah, yeah. But who are you *really*, Brandon?"

Roz began, "We don't have time for—" but Lance cut her off.

"This is important, Roz. When Max left the Shrike, he ordered Brandon to take me to the Citadel and stay with me at all times. I've seen Max doing that thing where he controls people's minds, and I'm pretty sure he was doing it then. But Brandon *didn't* stay with me. Which means he's able to resist Max's control."

Brandon shrugged. "I think you're mistaken, Lance."

"I'm not. You can resist him. And not only that, you can do it in such a way that he can't tell. He can read your mind and you're able to fool him. So you're not just a pilot, are you? You're one of them. A superhuman."

"All right." Brandon smiled and turned back to the controls. "You can do better than *that*, Lance. You've been touched by it too, you know. You *and* Cord. There are no truly normal humans on this craft."

Lance felt the hairs on his arms start to rise, and he had to suppress a shudder.

"Suzanne, Roz, and I are pure superhumans. Joshua will get his powers in a couple of years. Lance, you and Cord are humans, but you've been changed. It doesn't happen often. Most people are completely immune to the energy that makes us superhuman. A few of us absorb that energy and can use it in a number of ways. Fewer still are altered by the energy but otherwise human." He tapped a command sequence into the keyboard. "Cord, you must have wondered why you were different. A natural talent with machinery and electronics? Please. In school you were average at best, showed little aptitude for anything other than football. Yet somehow you can build a powerful motorized suit of armor, a jetpack, advanced weapons. Equipment that even the best military minds are struggling to understand." Brandon turned back to face Cord. "You never wondered about that?"

"Of course I did," Cord said.

"And your conclusions?"

"I never drew any."

"Right." Brandon looked at Lance. "You I don't know quite so well. Not yet. But I can see it in you, Lance. You have a gift for understanding people, for making them believe whatever you want them to believe. You're a natural con artist." He smiled. "I've been working alongside Max for half a year and he never even suspected me. You had me figured out in a couple of hours."

Lance noticed a slight movement to his left; Roz was

clenching her fists, shifting her weight. She was getting ready to attack. On the other side of Roz, Suzanne Housten was doing the same.

"Wait," Lance said. "He's on our side, I think." To Brandon, he added, "Otherwise you'd have turned us in ages ago. So what's your game?"

Brandon stretched his arm out behind him and—without looking—entered another command sequence into the keyboard. "Why don't *you* tell them?"

Lance shrugged. "I don't know."

"Use that gift of yours. Figure it out."

"If you're on our side, then it stands to reason you're against Krodin. But you've obviously met him a few times, so why didn't you . . . ? Ah. He's too powerful for you. You know you can't defeat him."

"Go on."

"Not on your own, anyway. But I can't imagine that you've been sitting around doing nothing. If you're really against him, you'll have been doing *something* to stop him. Or at least slow him down. But it'd have to be something that he'd never be able to trace to you. . . . And that's why you're working for Max, right? Krodin trusts Max, and Max thinks he can control you. You could get away with almost anything and Max would never have any reason to suspect you."

Brandon spread his arms. "Bravo! And for an encore . . . ? Anyone?"

Solomon Cord pushed his way between Lance and Roz. "It's you. You're the one who's been the constant thorn in Krodin's side. . . . You're Daedalus."

CHAPTER 29

"YOU APPEAR TO BE the intelligent one—comparatively, at least. Tell me about this other reality," Krodin asked James. "Why do you seem to believe that it is so much better than this one?"

"Our time line doesn't have *you* in it."

"You don't understand the nature of time, James." He sighed. "I know you consider me some sort of barbarian, a man four-and-a-half millennia beyond his sell-by date, but it should be clear to you that's an inaccurate view. I have a perfect memory, and an unmatched ability to acquire knowledge. Cast your mind back to the battle at Windfield—a little over three weeks ago for you, but it has been almost six years for me—and you will recall that I mastered your language in a matter of hours. When I reappeared in that same location six years earlier—an empty field at the time—I did not, of course, understand exactly what had happened. All I knew then was what I perceived: that Pyrokine attacked me, then you and your friends disappeared, along with the power plant and all signs of the battle."

James thought, *If Lance was here right now, he'd interrupt him with something clever.* But James couldn't think of anything appropriate to say. He knew Krodin wasn't going to allow any of them to live.

Krodin continued: "When I realized what had transpired, I understood that I was free. I didn't know how far back in time I had traveled, but then I read of a remarkable young man called Maxwell Dalton, and I knew that it had been only a few years. I sought out The Helotry—not an easy task even with my abilities—and then destroyed their entire organization. I appropriated their considerable wealth and made contact with Max. Together we formulated a plan to save the human race from its own greed and stupidity."

"Yeah? Who's going to save it from *you*?"

Krodin sighed again. He crossed his arms and leaned back against the teleportation device. "You just can't grasp it, can you? You're so close-minded that you cannot begin to comprehend that my way is the right way."

"You're taking away everyone's free will!"

Krodin looked at James as though he were stupid. "So what?"

"It's a basic human right."

"Says who?"

"I . . ." James faltered and looked away. "It's not that simple."

"Make it simple."

"We are self-aware. We are sentient beings. No, more than that, we are *sapient* beings."

"By your own standards, yes, but I'll allow that. Humans are sapient beings. Gifted with the ability to reason, judge, choose, understand, and create. Biologically we're all animals, but these traits set us apart from the other animals of Earth."

"Right."

"So . . . Back to my question. Who decided—or concluded—that free will is a basic human right?"

Abby said, "We did. We decided for ourselves."

Krodin turned to her. "Hmm . . . Perhaps I should direct my future arguments to you, Abigail. Yes, that's a very good answer. Worthy of some consideration." He glanced back at James. "But you . . . You're a disappointment. Max? Take him out to the landing pad, put him next to Brawn, and shoot them."

Max Dalton stepped forward. "What?"

"You want me to repeat myself? Shoot them, and *keep* shooting them until they are unquestionably dead. And go no farther than the landing pad. Can't risk one of them making an escape and getting out of range of Casey's power-stripping toy, can we?"

"Don't do this!" Abby said, stepping in front of James. "You've won. You don't need to kill them!"

"But I want to."

James realized that for the first time since he'd entered the room he wasn't afraid. *We did our best. There's nothing more we can do. If this is it . . .* "I have a few last requests."

"Of course you do. What is it?"

"My mother and my sister. Don't harm them. Let them live in peace."

Krodin nodded. "Request granted. You have my word on that. Your stepfather?"

James shrugged. "Him too, I suppose. But, y'know, maybe you can arrange to have him shipped off to the far side of the world or something?"

"I'll consider that."

"And Abby lives. Whatever happens, she lives."

"Now, that one I can't promise. It really is up to her. If you're fnished . . . ? Max, take him."

Max moved toward James and Abby threw herself at him, but Krodin was faster. He grabbed her arm and pulled her aside.

"It's all right, Abby," James said. "I always knew we weren't going to get out alive."

"Well, I didn't know that! I thought we had a chance! Don't accept this, James! Fight! Don't let them do it."

Then Max said, "I'm sorry. None of us really has a choice here." He and James looked at each other for a moment. "Let's go."

They walked side by side out of the room, neither of them looking back.

In the corridor, the four soldiers James had earlier disabled had now recovered. They fell into step behind Max.

"So what's the plan?" James whispered.

Max didn't respond.

"Max?"

"There is no plan. I'm sorry, but this is where it ends for you. In the long run—"

"Don't," James said. "Please. Don't embarrass yourself any further."

Nothing more was said until they passed through the complex's main doors.

James saw Brawn sitting on the center of the octagonal landing pad, surrounded by seven armed Praetorian soldiers. The giant was slumped forward, covered in bullet wounds, each one enough to put a normal human out of action.

Brawn slowly raised his head and smiled as James and Max approached. "So how are we doing?"

"Not good," James said. He left Max's side and walked over to stand by Brawn.

At the same time Max signaled to the soldiers guarding Brawn to fall back to the doorway.

"Oh man . . ." Brawn looked toward Max and the line of soldiers. "This better not be what it looks like."

"It is."

Max cleared his throat, and said, "James Percival Klaus, also known as Thunder. Brawn, real name unknown. On the direct order of Chancellor Krodin, you have been sentenced to immediate execution by—"

Brawn roared at him: "We get it! Shut *up*, Dalton! What, you think you have to say the words properly or we'll complain about wrongful execution?" He grunted as he pushed himself to his feet. "Now give us a minute, will you? I want to say good-bye to my friend here. Or have you completely lost all humanity?"

"You, uh, you have one minute."

Brawn swayed slightly as he looked down at James. "This is for real?"

"Yeah."

"Huh. I knew from the start that hanging around with you guys was going to be trouble. So what happened? They teleported Dalton back here?"

"Yeah." James nodded. "Should have seen that one coming." He glanced back at Max, at the machine strapped to his wrist. "And now we're right in the middle of the eight-hundred-yard radius of the power-damper."

"Eight hundred yards isn't that far. We could run."

"We'd never make it."

"We might. I'm still pretty strong. Way stronger than a human, even without my powers. Look at this: I've been shot, like, fifty times or something. Hurts like crazy but I'm still not dead. So we run and you stay in front of me."

James shook his head. "Brawn, you can barely stand. We wouldn't get more than ten yards."

"Time's up," Max called. "Men, take aim."

James winced at the sight of the Praetorian soldiers raising their guns to shoulder height.

"On my command," Max said. "Three."

Brawn put out his massive hand, and James shook it. "Percival, huh?"

"Wasn't my choice. What's your name?"

Max said, "Two."

"I don't think that matters anymore," Brawn said. "I'll never be him again." He reached down and put his hands on James's shoulders. "How far did you say? Eight hundred yards?"

Max said, "One."

"Yeah. Eight hundred. Far too late now, though."

"Not for you," Brawn said.

James felt Brawn's muscles tense.

Max shouted, "Fire!"

And moving faster than James could have thought possible, Brawn lifted him over his head, pulled back his arms, and threw him.

The landing pad erupted with gunfire.

CHAPTER 30

ABBY HEARD THE ROAR of gunfire and dropped to her knees. "No!" *This can't be happening—they can't be dead!*

Through her tears she saw Krodin approach. He crouched down in front of her. "If it's any consolation, you won't have to grieve for much longer. You and the rest of your friends will die too."

She lashed out, struck him across the face with her closed fist. "You're insane! You're a *monster*!"

"Abigail, what you consider to be a monster others will, in time, see as—"

"Shut *up*, you psychopathic, heartless . . . *boring* man!"

Krodin sat back, clearly surprised. "Boring?"

Abby jumped to her feet. "Yes! 'In the end, it's all for the greater good,' blah blah blah! With your gifts you could be the greatest hero ever. You think you were put on this Earth to rule. Well, I don't know if there *is* a reason for someone like you to be here, but if there is, you've got it wrong."

Still sitting on the ground, Krodin shook his head. "Abigail, you just cannot understand—"

"*You* don't understand. You're not here to rule the human race—you're here to *lead* it."

He looked away from her.

"If you're going to kill me, do it now. But don't put me through any more of your lectures."

Slowly, not looking her in the eye, Krodin stood up. "Somebody . . . Fire up the teleporter. Bring—"

Max Dalton's voice boomed out over the base's PA system: "Chancellor . . . we, uh, we have a problem."

Using only his hands James hauled himself through the foul-smelling, stagnant water, his limbs heavy with cloying mud. The wound in his forehead had reopened, and he had to fight against the automatic urge to wipe the blood from his eyes. *Hate to think what sort of bacteria live in this swamp.*

After Brawn had thrown him, he'd arced through the air, cleared the lake, and crashed through the trees. His right leg had collided with a thick branch and there had been a horrifying *snap*—but whether it was from the branch or his leg he couldn't tell. Either way, his leg had been in agony since he splashed down in the middle of the swamp.

He grabbed on to a clump of weeds and hauled himself another few inches. The water seemed a little shallower now, so he turned onto his side. Blinding pain flared through his leg once more, and he had to bite his hand to stifle his screams.

He almost didn't dare look, but knew that he had to. And when he did, his fear of infecting the wound on his forehead seemed almost laughable: His right tibia had broken, the jagged end of its lower half protruding through his mud-encrusted skin.

How far did he throw me?

James tried to focus his enhanced hearing, but still there was nothing.

Not far enough. Yet.

Doing his best to ignore the pain, James crawled on.

Krodin dragged Abby with him out to the landing pad, where Brawn's enormous body lay prone and unmoving. His deep blue skin was barely visible beneath the blood.

"So what's the problem?" Krodin asked.

Max said, "He's not dead. I know it looks bad, but the bullets penetrated only about a half inch. He passed out just after we ran out of ammunition."

"You want me to finish him off, is that it?"

"No, we can do it. It's just going to take longer than we expected. The real problem is—"

Krodin interrupted. "Klaus. Where is he?"

"Brawn threw him, just as the men opened fire. Out over the lake."

"So *he's* not dead either."

"We don't know. Without his powers there's no guarantee he'd survive the fall. We could use the teleporter to bring—"

Krodin locked his hand around Max's neck and lifted him off his feet, shook him violently. "I want him found!

Send your men out to scour the area. And you won't use the teleporter because I don't want all of him brought back. Only his head, understood?" He threw Max to the ground. "You useless, *pathetic* little man! Your men will come back with James Klaus's severed head or I will tear off your arms and legs and feed them to the alligators!"

He grabbed Abby's arm again and steered her back toward the doors. As she passed Max, she stamped down as hard as she could on his left hand. She wasn't sure, but she thought she felt the bones crunch beneath her heel.

Krodin saw this and said, "Everybody hates Max today, huh?"

"Not as much as they hate you."

"This isn't a popularity contest, Abigail."

"Yeah, losers always say stuff like that."

Holding on to her arm so tightly that her fingers were growing numb, Krodin dragged her along the corridors and into a large, dark, screen-filled control room.

"The others?"

One of the technicians looked up and nodded. "They're coming. They're—"

"You know what to do."

On board the Raptor, Roz looked around at the others. They were all staring at Brandon Santamaría, who had returned his attention to the craft's controls.

What do we do? she asked herself. *If he is Daedalus, then . . .*

It was Lance who asked the question. "What powers do you have?"

Brandon answered, "Somewhat enhanced strength and speed, greatly enhanced intelligence."

"That's all? You can't fly or shoot lasers from your eyes or anything like that?"

Suzanne said, "All those reports about the things you did . . . Destroying Krodin's supply lines, picking off his patrols, killing his resident genius Casey . . . Being smart is all well and good, but how'd you do all that if you don't have any powers?"

Brandon smiled. "Smart? You have no *idea* how smart I am. There's not a machine or a computer in the world that I can't master." He tapped the screen in front of him. "You see this?"

Roz peered past Lance and looked at the screen. "We're being followed!"

"Relax. It's not the Praetorians," Brandon said. "It's me. Or, rather, my battle suit. You thought Paragon's armor was powerful? Compared with mine, his suit might as well be a set of pajamas. So. Here's the plan, Roz. You, me, and Suzanne are going in. Our first priority—our *only* priority—is to destroy Krodin's teleporter. The forces of Unity are already in the Gulf, and they'll be here within hours. Once the teleporter is gone, we get out of there."

"What about our friends? And Max?"

"You can try to get them out if you can, but only *after* we destroy the teleporter."

Roz felt Joshua's hand slip into hers. "But Max—"

"Max is a liability," Brandon said. "He thinks his powers make him special, but he's little more than a conduit for other people's feelings and opinions." He hesitated for a moment. "I should warn you now that if Max gets in the way—or even just slows me down—I will kill him."

Cord said, "No. We're doing this without you. You've already murdered hundreds of Krodin's people."

Brandon pushed himself back from the Raptor's controls and stood up, turned to face Cord. "You don't understand. You're new here. But Suzanne understands. Ever since Krodin came to power, this country has been under martial law. There's not one American who hasn't felt Krodin's noose tightening around his neck. Krodin's invulnerable and immortal—we can't kill him. But we're going to keep destroying his resources, slowing him down whenever we can."

Roz said, "What's that going to achieve? If you know you can't win, then . . ."

Beside her, Joshua said, "Because it's war. That's what you're talking about, isn't it, Brandon? I thought you were my friend!"

Brandon raised his eyes. "You thought Krodin was your friend too, Josh. So what do you know?" He turned to Suzanne. "You with me?"

"All the way."

"And you, Roz? Are you willing to do what's necessary?"

Roz looked at Lance and Cord, then back to Brandon. "There has to be another way."

"Oh, there are lots of other ways. But none of them are effective. The biggest threat to world security right now is that teleporter. We have to destroy it before Unity swarms in. Krodin doesn't have the facility to create another teleporter. It'll set his plans back *years*."

"Years don't mean anything to Krodin," Lance said. "He's immortal."

Brandon ignored him. "In my battle suit I can carry you down to the base," he said to Roz. "Your telekinesis is considerably more powerful than your counterpart's was. You can manipulate objects with pinpoint accuracy, right?"

"Sometimes, but . . ."

"In many ways your telekinesis works like a remote force field. You can create it anywhere you like." He tapped a forefinger against his temple. "Inside someone's brain, for example. You can block an artery, sever the optic nerves, or—if you don't think you can be quite so accurate—you just expand the force field until it turns your target's brain to paste."

"I'm not a killer!"

"Then start learning." Brandon glanced back at the Raptor's screens. "They're on full alert at the base." He rapidly typed a series of commands into the keyboard. "Hmm. I can guess what they're planning. We don't have a lot of time. I'm calling in the battle suit. Cord, get into the jetpack. You take Lance and Josh and you get out of here as fast as you can. And I'll take Roz. We go in hard and fast, people."

"I'm not going with you!" Roz said.

"It's your only chance to save your other friends," Suzanne said.

Cord was already strapping on the stolen jetpack. "Lance, Josh . . . Grab hold of me and don't let go. I'll need my right hand free to control this thing."

He moved toward the hatch, but Roz stepped into his way. "Mr. Cord, please . . ."

"We don't have any choice right now, Roz. I'll set the boys down and then I'll come for you."

Roz grabbed her brother, hugged him close, kissed the top of his head. "Lance, you watch out for him. You keep him safe."

Lance nodded. "I will."

At the controls Brandon was furiously typing at the keyboard. "I'm putting the Raptor on remote. The Praetorians can usually override any commands, but not this one. I've reprogrammed the computer. From now on it'll go only where I tell it to go."

"So it's a decoy?" Roz asked.

"Something like that."

The Raptor was blasted with cold air as the hatch opened and Cord stepped right to the edge. "Boys?"

Lance said, "Roz, I'm thinking I should stick with you. Mr. Cord can take care of Josh—and he won't have to worry about me too."

Roz shook her head.

Lance pointed at Cord. "Come on! You know what this guy is like! He'll set me and Josh down and fly into the battle and probably get killed." To Cord, he added, "You don't have any armor, remember? You're not bulletproof anymore. If I'm not there to look after Josh, then you'll *have* to stick with him. So I'll go with Roz. I can be useful."

Cord said, "No way, Lance. You're coming with me."

"Well, since you put it like *that*. No."

Keeping his voice low, Cord said, "In this reality your family is still alive. That's as close to a miracle as any of us are ever likely to experience. Lance, this is a suicide mission. You know that. The best we can hope for is to destroy Krodin's teleporter—without this reality's version of me they won't be able to create another one. But whatever happens, the odds of us getting out alive are tiny. There's no need for you to die too. And Joshua is going to need someone to take care of him."

"I can help."

"How?"

"Back in Windfield, I—"

"This isn't the same." Cord put his hand on Lance's shoulder. "I told you before that you're the bravest person I've ever met. That's still true. The world needs people like you, but you're not going to be able to achieve much if you're dead."

Lance looked up at Cord. "All right."

Cord nodded, then moved back toward the hatch. "Josh?"

The boy shook his head. "No."

Brandon shouted, "We don't have time for this—they'll be locking on to us right now! Cord, get out and take the kids with you!"

Roz said, "It's going to be OK, Josh."

"No it's not. You all think you're going to die, don't you?"

Lance said, "They just don't want us getting in the way. We'd get captured or something and then they'd have to come and rescue us."

"You're just saying that! Roz!"

"He's right. Getting captured is Lance's specialty."

Lance sneered. "Hey!"

"It's true. He gets captured—" Roz stopped, and looked around.

They were no longer inside the Raptor. Instead they were in the center of a large, brightly lit empty room. To one side stood a group of people, her brother Max among them.

"—all the time," Roz finished.

A tall, muscular man stepped forward from the group, and Roz felt a knot twist in her stomach as she recognized his face.

"A good observation, Ms. Dalton," the man said, walking toward them. "For those who have never met me in person, I am Chancellor Krodin. I'll be your executioner today. Anyone who tries to run will be shot down. In this room none of you have superhuman abilities."

Krodin stepped up behind Solomon Cord, placed his hands on either side of the jetpack, and crushed it.

Krodin turned in a slow circle, his arms spread to take in the whole room. "This is our primary storeroom. We had to move everything out first, so my men are a little cranky: Those boxes of ammunition are very heavy. We're right in the heart of my base here in Louisiana, and there is only one door in or out. The walls are reinforced concrete, almost a meter thick. That's about three feet for those of you who never got the hang of the metric system. Get used to this place, because this is where you'll be spending the rest of your lives." He stopped turning and grinned at them. "Which will be about twenty minutes. Maybe thirty if I feel in the mood."

He looked at Suzanne Housten. "I remember you from Windfield." He began speaking to her in a language Roz was sure she'd never heard before.

Suzanne swallowed and began to back away from him. "I . . . I don't know what you're saying!"

Krodin said, "So it appears. When we first met, you spoke

to me in that tongue. Or your counterpart did. She called herself Slaughter. She was coldhearted, cruel, remarkably violent. Led always by her emotions."

"That wasn't me!"

"Pity. I liked her." He looked around at the others. "Solomon Cord, or a shadow of him. Rosalyn and Joshua Dalton—at least Joshua is the same one I've met before. And Max's pilot, Brandon Santamaría. A traitor." He stopped at Lance. "You I don't know."

From Lance's expression Roz could see that, despite the situation, he was a little offended.

"Well, we've had some fun, haven't we? But it's over now. You have thirty minutes to say your good-byes. Feel free to use that time to plot a few futile escape plans." He moved toward the door, and his team followed him.

Krodin put out his hand to stop Max. "Not you. You're with them."

"But I . . ."

"Turn around, Max. Go back to your brother and sister. Your journey ends here."

Max hesitated for a moment, then tried to dodge past him. Krodin grabbed his arm and threw him back into the room. "Remington? Seal the door. And wait here with the device running."

Max walked over to Roz, and the doors slammed shut behind him. "That guy Remington is the key," Max said. "That thing he has temporarily strips our powers. It's got an eight-hundred-yard radius. Krodin's immune, of course, because it was used on him before."

Then the doors opened again, and Krodin pushed Abby

into the room. He was also dragging something huge behind him, and it took Roz a moment to realize that it was Brawn. The giant was unconscious, covered in countless bullet wounds.

"Clock's still ticking," Krodin said. "Twenty-nine minutes." He used his foot to shove Brawn farther into the room, then left. The doors closed again.

While Cord and Brandon checked on Brawn, Abby walked over to Roz. "Hey. You guys made it."

Lance said, "Yeah. Just in time, eh? You're, uh, looking well."

Then Cord stepped up to Abby. "Wasn't sure I'd see you again."

"What happened to you in Midway?" she asked.

"The resistance found me. They wanted to use me as a hostage."

Abby started to respond, then Roz saw pure rage in her eyes.

"You!" Abby screamed, pushing between Roz and Cord. "Slaughter!"

Lance grabbed her, wrapped his arms tightly around her. "It's not her, Abby. This woman is . . . She's not Slaughter."

Abby looked up at him. "Lance . . . I'm so sorry about what happened to your family."

"In this world they're alive. I got them back, Abby. It was only for an hour, but . . . I got to see my folks again."

Then Max Dalton called out, "Enough! This isn't the time for sentiment. We have got to think of a way out of this! Cord, you were never a superhuman—you haven't lost anything. How do we get out?"

Still holding on to Lance, Abby turned to face Max. "If anyone here deserves to die, it's you, Dalton! You put Brawn and James in front of a firing squad!"

"I had no choice!" Max said.

"Who's James?" Lance asked.

"Thunder. His real name is James. Krodin ordered Max to take them out and shoot them, and he did it!"

"James escaped," Max said, "and Brawn's still alive."

Roz looked at her brother for a long moment, then turned her back on him.

"Listen, this is important!" Max said. "If we can . . . Roz? Oh, come on! I did what I *had* to do. If . . . Cord, I know *you'll* understand."

Cord walked away from him.

"Brandon?"

The pilot glowered down at Max. "You really are a despicable little man."

Then Josh walked up to his brother. "I thought you were one of the good guys." He stepped back, found Roz's hand, and clung to it.

The silence that filled the room was eventually broken by Lance: "How much time left?"

Suzanne said, "About twenty-five minutes."

James had hauled himself through the water by holding on to the drooping branches of a mangrove. He pulled himself hand over hand until he reached the bank, then clung to the mangrove's root.

Just a little farther, he told himself. *Come on! It'll be easier on solid ground. You can do it—you* have *to do it!*

319

The agony in his right leg had faded to a dull throb, and he knew that wasn't a good sign. "Going into shock, James."

Overhead, to the left, he spotted another Raptor, heading south. He'd already dodged one of the flying craft by submerging himself in the cloudy water and holding his breath for as long as he dared.

He tried to focus his hearing again, but there was still nothing. *Got to be close to eight hundred yards by now.*

James knew he couldn't walk, and crawling without the buoyancy of the water was going to be close to impossible.

Then he remembered how his little sister, Shiho, moved around before she learned to walk. *That's it. That's what I have to do.* He clawed his way onto the bank, rolled onto his back, then used the roots to pull himself into a sitting position. *Got to scoot backward on my butt!*

He couldn't manage more than a couple of inches at a time, even with his good leg providing traction.

And then he saw the Raptor pass directly overhead, slow to a stop, and come back. *Aw no!* He began to scoot faster, ignoring the pain that juddered through his entire body with every movement. *Keep going! Could take them a few more minutes—there's nowhere for them to land!*

A hatch opened in the Raptor and an armored figure dropped out. The Jetman activated his jetpack to slow his descent as he approached James.

The Jetman touched down next to him. "James Klaus."

"Nah, you got the wrong swamp. James lives three swamps over."

The armored man signaled the Raptor, and another flyer descended and landed on the other side of James.

"So what now? You're going to shoot me in cold blood?"

The Jetmen looked at each other for a moment. "We've been ordered to, uh . . ."

His colleague finished the sentence: "We've been ordered to decapitate you and return with your head." He reached into a compartment on the armor's chest-plate and withdrew a long-bladed hunting knife.

CHAPTER 31

LANCE WALKED UP to the room's massive steel door and pounded on it with his fist. "Hello?"

After a moment, a small screen next to the door flickered to life, and Remington's face appeared. "What?"

"So . . . You again," Lance said. "You've never met me before, but I've met your counterpart in my world. He was a sadistic, unimaginative lackey. You don't seem to be that much different from him."

"You're never going to win the Nobel Prize for flattery, kid. You've got"—the man checked his watch—"twenty-one minutes and ten seconds left to live."

"Yes, I wanted to know the time too. But more than that. How does your teleporter work?"

Remington smirked. "*Dying* to know, huh?"

Lance let out a very fake laugh. "Oh, that's just hilarious. Seriously, though, how does it work?"

"What do you care? You'll be dead soon enough."

"Insatiable curiosity." Then Lance held up his hand. "No, forget it. You're a henchman. You probably don't *know* how the teleporter works."

"Matter of fact, I do. I majored in theoretical physics. Graduated summa cum laude."

Lance wasn't about to admit that he was impressed. "Let me guess. . . . It converts matter to energy and transmits it as a signal, right?"

Remington raised his eyes. "No, that's impractical. It'd take decades to decode a human body in that way. And how are you supposed to reassemble it at the other end? Look, every particle in the universe has a number of different attributes that determine its character and its place. Our teleporter generates an energy field and allows us to instantly redefine the location attributes of any particles within the field."

"So . . . You tell something that it is where you want it to be, and it goes there?"

"No. Well, yes. In the most simplistic way."

"But the thing you're sending doesn't have to be *near* the teleporter, right? You took us out of the Raptor. You can generate the energy field anywhere you like."

Remington nodded. "We can. It takes a lot more power and it's harder to set up. Much simpler to send things from within the teleporter's room. Why do you want to know all this?"

"Aim your teleporter at the following address: number seventeen Hendricks Avenue, Fairview, South Dakota."

"What? Why?"

"We want six extra-large pepperoni pizzas, two vegetarian

specials—one without onions—and ten sodas." In a fake whisper he added, "Max wanted a *diet* soda but, hey, what's the point now?"

"Yeah, very funny," Remington sneered. "Maybe in your reality there are still pizza parlors, but not here."

"But there used to be, right? Before Krodin showed up and ruined everything, like the ultimate version of your friend's dad turning up at your party. So I'm thinking . . . these attributes you say are part of every particle . . . they must also say *when* a particle is, as well as where it is, right? So you could use your teleporter to move the pizzas through time. Just like Pyrokine took Krodin out of the past."

Remington nodded slowly. "Huh . . . You might be on to something there."

Abby appeared beside Lance. "What are you doing?"

"Do you mind? I'm having a conversation with the evil henchman here."

Remington said, "*What?* I'm not evil!"

"You are, you know," Abby said. "You're allowing us to die when you could do something about it. You could disable that device that's dampening our powers."

"What, this thing?" Remington smiled and held up the machine. "No way, José."

Lance said, "I think you've just blown your chance of Abby inviting you to her prom, Remington. Plus, y'know, you're ugly."

"At least I'll still be alive tomorrow." The screen went blank.

"Alive and ugly!" Lance shouted. "Jerk." He sat down with his back to the door and gave Abby a weak smile. "I was kinda hoping that we'd run into each other again, but not like this."

She sat next to him.

"So, does this count as our first date, or our second?"

"Neither." She took Lance's hand and held on to it. "Lance, you're very sweet, but—"

"You're *dumping* me? At a time like this? Man, that's cold."

"As I was saying. You're very sweet—in an infuriatingly talkative kind of way—but you're not my type."

"Is it because I'm white? It is, isn't it? Because I can change."

"If only it was that simple."

"Thunder, then. I remember the way he looked at you. Like you're a field of carrots and he's a rabbit." He sighed. "Why do the cute ones never go for me?"

"Do you ever talk to them?"

Lance laughed. "Trick question, right? If I say no, you'll say, 'That's your problem. How are they supposed to get to know you if you don't talk to them?' But if I say yes, you'll say, 'That's your problem. You talk too much.' Am I right?"

"Pretty close."

Roz came over and sat down cross-legged in front of them. "Brawn's actually healing. Even without his powers, he is one tough guy. So what are you two talking about?"

Lance said, "We're wondering why you're so cool and your big brother's such a complete dipstick."

Roz looked down at the floor. "He's . . . He's not so bad, usually."

"Well, he picked me up after I escaped from prison, I'll give him that."

Abby said, "You were in *prison*?"

Lance nodded. "Yep. But with the aid of a big truck I released myself on my own recognizance."

"On any other day, that might seem strange."

The two Jetmen stood on either side of James. They both had knives and were arguing over which of them should remove his head.

"*I'm* not doing it. No way!" the one on his left said.

"You hafta. You're the one who found him."

"Right. I found him, you cut. That's how it goes. That way we both did our part. Otherwise it's me doing everything."

"We need to kill him first. It'd be easier to, y'know . . ."

James looked from one to the other, and back. *There could be a way out of this. . . .* He dug his hands into the blood-soaked mud around his legs. "Help me up. Help me to stand. If I'm going to die, I want to do it on my feet."

The men put away their knives and carefully lifted James up until he was balanced on his left leg.

The second Jetman saw the bone protruding from James's right calf and stepped back. "Man, that's *nasty*."

"You should be on *this* side of it," James said. "Then you'd know what nasty really is." He looked up. "Yesterday I learned how to fly. Not like you guys, with your jetpacks. I could fly under my own power. It's . . . It's something else. The best feeling in the world." He looked down again, thinking, *What would Lance say?* "And now you're going to kill me. Everything I've done, everything I never got to do . . . It'll be gone. Forever." He turned to the man on his right. "I don't blame you for this. Everyone dies, eventually, right?"

"Yeah, I guess. Except Krodin."

"I just wish I could fly again. One last time. Can you do that for me? Take me up. Just above the trees—let me feel the sun on my face. Then you can do what you have to do."

The man nodded. "Yeah. I guess we can do that. Put your right arm around my shoulder, and hold tight. I need *my* right arm free—that's where the jetpack's controls are." He put his left arm around James's waist. "Ready?"

"I'm ready."

James looked down, saw the ground fall slowly away.

They passed between the branches of the mangrove trees and then hovered in place.

James smiled. "It really is a beautiful world. The trees, the lakes . . . Even the swamps have their own beauty. Even the mud."

The Jetman said, "The mud is beautiful?"

"It can be, if used in the right way." He lifted his left hand. He was holding a large ball of soft mud. "See?"

The Jetman tilted his head forward. "I don't get it."

And James slammed the ball of mud into the man's helmet, smeared it across his visor. "*Now* try flying, you sick maniac!"

He grabbed the Jetman's right hand and squeezed on the control pads on the palm of his glove.

The jetpack surged, rocketing them into the air.

And suddenly James could hear *everything*.

He let go of the Jetman, blasted him with a shock wave that sent him spinning and crashing down through the trees.

He directed another shock wave down at the second Jetman, the impact tearing a six-foot-deep crater in the mud.

A third shock wave knocked the hovering Raptor half a mile upward, tumbling over and over.

Then James focused his hearing, directed it toward Krodin's building, eight hundred yards away. He remembered the distinctive humming and buzzing of the power-damping device and pinpointed the sound almost instantly.

James grinned. "Zap."

Abby jumped to her feet. "Whoa . . . What was *that*?"

On the floor nearby, Brawn stirred and groaned.

Standing over with the adults, Suzanne Housten clutched her head and swayed for a moment.

Brandon Santamaría suddenly straightened up, shook his head briskly, looked around, and started to grin. "Power's back. All right, people. The mission's the same—we go after the teleporter. Abby, Suzanne—you take point. Max—"

Max Dalton strode over to Brandon. "I don't think you're exactly qualified to take control here, Brandon."

Moving faster than even Abby could see, Brandon spun, pivoting on his left foot, planting his right deep into Max's stomach. Max flew across the room and crashed against the wall.

Abby and Cord simultaneously moved toward Brandon, but he took a step back and raised his hand. "Don't."

Abby stopped. There was something in his tone that told her he was more than willing to attack her too.

Brandon pulled back the left sleeve of his Praetorian pilot's uniform; around his forearm, close to the elbow, was a thin black band holding a single button. He pressed the button.

"Ten seconds. Stay close to the walls and cover your eyes, because this is going to get messy."

For a moment, everyone stared at him. Then Abby grabbed Lance's arm and pulled him away from the center of the room.

Then everything went black, and for a moment the ground seemed to drop away. Abby had the sensation of being caught in the middle of a hurricane. She felt herself slamming down hard onto the ground, felt the walls crushing in. Over a deafening roar she heard a high-pitched shout—a scream—then the grinding crunch of reinforced concrete being pulverized.

The air was thick with gritty, choking dust. In the distance sirens wailed, panic-filled voices rushed back and forth. Somewhere to her left a thick power cable sparked against the floor, providing brief glimpses of the rest of the room.

Lying next to Abby, Lance McKendrick—covered in dust and fragments of rock—was slowly, painfully getting to his feet. Nearby, Roz and Josh Dalton were huddled in the corner, Roz's arms wrapped around her brother.

And in the center of the room, the flashing sparks— maybe one every second—revealed a slide show of Brandon Santamaría.

Flash: Brandon, seemingly unharmed and unfazed by the devastation, stood looking up at the buckled hull of the Raptor that had crashed through the ceiling.

Flash: A pair of metal hands tearing another hole in the ceiling next to the Raptor.

Flash: A gold-and-black man-shaped machine, oddly hollow like an unfinished suit of armor, ripping its way through and landing next to Brandon.

Flash: The armor disassembling and piece by piece, re-forming around Brandon.

Flash: The armor sealing Brandon inside, a black helmet folding over his head.

And the final flash, before the room faded into complete darkness: Brandon, wearing the heavy armor, striding toward the large double doors, and something large and silver unfolding from his back.

Abby suddenly knew, somehow, who he was and what he had become.

He had become Daedalus.

Then a table-sized section of the ceiling collapsed into the room, allowing the daylight to flood through.

Abby saw Daedalus's gold-and-black-armored arms stretched out toward the steel door, clawlike toes extended from his boots, anchoring him to the ground as he pushed. Metal screamed, inch-thick glass shattered, and the door began to buckle outward.

Another push and he was through, out into the corridor.

Abby felt a knot tighten in her throat, and almost against her will she found herself following him, felt her hands clench into fists.

The dark corridor erupted in light as six of Krodin's Praetorian guards opened fire on Daedalus.

He rushed at the nearest guard, locked one armored hand around the man's face, and slammed his head so hard against the wall that the plaster cracked. Before the guard even hit the floor, Daedalus had launched a vicious, bone-crunching kick at another, picked up the third, and used him as a battering ram to smash his way through the other men.

Abby caught a brief glimpse of the odd framework on Daedalus's back, then he was gone, vanished into the darkness.

Abby stared at the fallen guards and said a silent prayer. *He's a killer. He crashed the Raptor into this building without even caring who might be hurt in the process.*

More gunfire echoed through the building, more screams, then Abby heard weak voices coming from the room behind her.

She stepped back through the ruined doors. On the far side of the room, rubble shifted and Solomon Cord's voice called out: "Is anyone hurt? Abby?"

"I'm OK. Daedalus is gone. He's . . ."

"Lance?"

Lance was sitting on the ground, holding his head. "I'm OK, I think. Got a headache the size of a bus, though."

Roz said, "Me and Josh. We're fine. I used a telekinetic shield. I covered Max with it too, but I didn't have time to extend it to cover—"

Cord interrupted. "Save the apologies for later. You did good. Anyone else?"

A chunk of masonry the size of a manhole cover was pushed aside, and Suzanne Housten—her clothing now almost completely ragged—clawed her way out from under it. She coughed into the dust-packed floor. "I'll survive."

"Good. Brawn?" Cord asked.

The giant stirred, groaned loudly. "Nothing broken, I think."

"Then get over here and help me. I'm pinned under a

girder or something. Lance? You're staying here with Josh and Max. No arguments."

As Brawn crawled over to Cord, Abby looked around and spotted a two-inch-thick steel pole a little over six feet long.

She snatched it up, gave it an experimental swing. It wasn't going to be as useful as her sword, but it'd do. She moved back toward the wrecked doors.

"Where are you going?" Lance asked. He grabbed her hand and tried to pull her back.

She pulled her arm free. "Out there. I've got to stop him."

"Are you *nuts*? Krodin will tear your head off!"

"He's not the one I have to stop. It's Daedalus. . . . I think he might be *worse* than the Fifth King. Out in the corridor, he just . . . He just killed a bunch of men."

Roz stepped between Lance and Abby. "How do you know who he is? You've seen him before?"

"No, but I . . . I just know. He was masquerading as Max's pilot. . . . He could have gone up against Krodin anytime, but he knew he couldn't defeat him. You see what he's done? There are so few other superhumans left, but when we appeared in this world . . . He didn't bring you here to help him. We're not his allies; we're cannon fodder. He wants us to destroy the teleporter while he keeps Krodin busy."

Suzanne and Cord approached, followed by Brawn.

"You're not going alone," Suzanne said.

Brawn nodded. "All of us, together."

Roz looked back to the corner of the room. "But Max . . ."

Abby didn't want to answer. Even the thought of Max Dalton set her teeth on edge. She turned away, climbed over the ruined doors and out into the corridor.

Lance watched the others go, then turned back to Joshua Dalton, who was sitting on the ground next to his brother. "How is he?"

Josh shrugged. Without looking at Max, he said, "Still breathing."

Lance bit his lip. "We can't stay here, but we can't exactly bring him with us."

"We're not leaving him!"

"I know that." *Come on,* Lance said to himself, *think! Brandon said you've got a gift for understanding people, so you should be able to come up with a way out of this.* "Josh, you know Krodin better than I do. There has to be *something* we can use against him."

Josh stood up, brushed the dust from his clothes. "Can't think of anything. He's, like, way smarter than anyone else, and way stronger too. How did you defeat him last time?"

Lance began to pick through the rubble, searching for something he could use as a weapon. "That's just it. We *didn't* defeat him. We thought we did, but all we really did was get him out of the way. That's not something we can do now. Whatever we do to him will only work once, because he just adapts himself to compensate for it. We can't beat him up, or shoot him, or strangle him. . . ."

Josh nodded. "Right. Like Rasputin."

Lance carefully picked up a large, razor-sharp splinter of glass that had fallen from the Raptor's cockpit. "What?"

"Rasputin. That Russian guy. The Mad Monk, they called him. Max told me about him once. People believed he was psychic, and he had great influence over the tsar. But he was nuts, and they decided they had to kill him. They poisoned him, but that didn't work. Beat him up, stabbed him, shot him. In the end, they drowned him."

Lance used the glass splinter to cut the sleeve off his jacket, then wrapped the sleeve around the broad end. "And that helps us how, exactly?"

"I'm just saying. I always thought it would have been easier if they'd found someone Rasputin cared about and said they'd kill them if he didn't stop."

"Is there anyone Krodin cares about like that?"

Josh shook his head. "Not anymore. Before he was brought to our time, he was married and had kids, but they're all long dead by now. We need to think of a way to hurt him that's never been done before."

"And you never guessed that Brandon was Daedalus?"

"No. How would I?"

A deep, powerful, angry roar came from elsewhere in the base, and the floor shook once more.

Dust and small fragments of concrete rained down on Lance, and he automatically crouched forward to shield Josh from the debris.

Directly overhead, the crashed Raptor shifted down a couple of inches.

"Josh, help me! We've got to get Max out of here before that thing flattens all of us!"

"We can't move him—he could die!"

"He definitely *will* die if we leave him." Lance looked down at Max. *How can you lift a man without touching him?* "We need Roz," he said to Josh. "She can use her telekinesis."

Josh nodded, turned toward the doorway. "I'll see if I can—"

Lance ran after him, pulled him back. "You will *not*! You stay here, I'll find her." He quickly looked around. "Wait here in the doorway—it'll be safer if more of the roof collapses. But keep out of sight. Got that?"

Josh looked as though he was on the edge of tears. "But . . ."

Lance reached out and squeezed Josh's shoulder in what he hoped was a reassuring manner. "You'll be fine. Trust me."

He readjusted his grip on the glass splinter and kept low as he climbed over the ruined doors.

OK, follow the sounds of the battle, he told himself. *And don't get killed.*

The corridor was strewn with debris: fallen ceiling tiles, shattered bricks, looping lengths of glowing fiber-optic cable. Somewhere above a pipe had burst, flooding the corridor with tepid, rank water that lapped around the top of Lance's sneakers.

Far off to Lance's left was a rectangular patch of red light, and it took him a moment to realize exactly what it was: a blood-smeared window.

In the darkness his left foot stepped on something that yielded slightly, and when he looked down, he saw that it was the half-hidden arm of a Praetorian soldier. The man's hand twitched every couple of seconds.

At least that means he's not dead, Lance thought. Then added, *I hope.* He crouched down next to the man, probed the dark water. *Maybe he had a gun. . . .*

Then something was splashing toward him, crashing into him.

Lance felt a large fist slam into his jaw, a heavy boot catch him in the stomach. He tried to scramble away, put his hand down on the unconscious Praetorian guard's face—it slipped and he fell forward, tumbled over the guard, and landed on his back.

He looked up to see Remington standing over him, his eyes wide with rage.

"What have you *done*?" Remington screamed. He plunged his hands into the water at his feet, came up with a small handgun. "You've killed more than a dozen of my men, you sick little punk! You trying to finish this one too?"

"No!" Lance shook his head. "It wasn't me—I just found him like this!"

Remington was gripping the gun so tightly that his hand was quivering. "His blood is all over you!"

Lance looked at his hands, chest, and stomach where he'd slithered over the guard. He was soaked in blood.

And then he looked at the fallen guard's face. It had been pulped, was barely recognizable as human.

He turned back to Remington. The man was standing almost directly over him now—there was no way for Lance to escape. "I swear it wasn't me!"

"Liar!"

The gun boomed in Remington's hand.

CHAPTER 32

AS HE RACED THROUGH the dark, flickering corridors Solomon Cord was certain that they had no chance of living to see tomorrow.

Ahead of him, Suzanne Housten—he still couldn't help but think of her as Slaughter—and Abby crashed together through a thick wooden fire door and simultaneously rolled through the shower of splinters and landed on their feet. They launched themselves at a squadron of armed Praetorian guards, spinning, kicking, punching.

Roz was close behind them, scattering the men aside like human bowling pins without even touching them.

Brawn was somewhere farther ahead: Cord could tell from his rage-filled screams and what sounded like brick walls being torn apart.

A Praetorian soldier lunged at Cord from the side; Cord slammed his elbow into the man's chest, then immediately dropped and swept his left leg in a wide arc that collided with the back of the soldier's knees, sending him collapsing to the ground. In one move Cord grabbed hold of the soldier's rifle by the barrel, jerked it free from the man's grasp, and carried the movement through into a spin that ended with the rifle's butt crashing into the side of the soldier's head.

Ahead, he saw Abby reach a corner and skid to a stop, Suzanne almost colliding with her. They both looked back to Cord, their eyes wide.

Roz too stopped when she got to the corner.

"What is it?" Cord called.

"Daedalus," Roz said. "And Krodin."

Cord could hear the blows now; it sounded almost mechanical—it reminded him of the noise of an old tenement building being demolished by a wrecking ball.

When he came to the corner, he saw that there was a lone Praetorian guard standing in front of Abby, seemingly oblivious to everything but what he was watching.

Then Cord realized that this was one of the base's main corridors, and that they were standing at the entrance.

Outside, on a large octagonal landing pad, Krodin was locked in a struggle with Daedalus.

Each man had his hands locked around the other's throat, their muscles and tendons—both flesh and steel—straining. Around them the landing pad's now-fractured concrete base was strewn with bloodied and broken soldiers, many of them twitching or trying to crawl away, most unmoving.

The Praetorian guard suddenly noticed Cord peering over his shoulder. The man jumped, then collapsed as Cord slammed his fist into his face.

"This is not a spectator sport," Cord said. "Abby, you know where the teleporter is?"

"I can find it."

"Lead the way. Roz, Suzanne . . . you stay here, keep watch. If one of them gains the upper hand, you help the other one. The longer they're fighting each other, the better off the rest of us will be." He was about to turn away, then stopped. "Where's Brawn?"

As if the giant had heard his name mentioned, Brawn was suddenly sailing through the air from somewhere overhead, leaping toward Daedalus and Krodin.

Brawn crashed into Krodin shoulder-first, sent him sprawling, tumbling across the broken ground.

"Let's move, Abby," Cord said. He took one last look at the scene—Daedalus was dropping down toward Krodin with the razor-sharp claws on his boots extended—then followed Abby back along the corridor.

Lying on his back in three inches of water, Lance McKendrick stared up at Remington, who was looking back at him in shock.

Lance had felt the bullet clip the side of his jacket, just below his left armpit. *He missed. I don't believe it! He's standing right over me and he missed!*

Remington swallowed loudly, dropped the gun, and backed away. "What . . . what *are* you?"

Without taking his eyes off him, Lance pushed himself to his feet. *His hand was shaking too much, or maybe there was dirt in the barrel or something. He missed, and he doesn't realize that's what happened.*

Still walking backward, Remington stumbled, almost fell. "The reports said you're an ordinary human!"

"Reports can be faked," Lance said, trying to keep his voice steady. "Where's the teleporter?"

Remington jerked his thumb over his shoulder. "Back that way. But the room is sealed. Emergency protocol kicked in the second your Raptor crashed into the base."

"Can you control the teleporter from anywhere else?"

"I can set up a link to it from my office."

"Take me there."

Remington shook his head. "No. Krodin will kill me."

Oh man, Lance thought. *If this doesn't work, I'm toast.* He stepped close to Remington. "Now you listen to me, you pathetic little weed. You will do whatever I tell you to do or we're going to reach the point where the words 'excruciating agony' aren't nearly strong enough. Do you understand me?"

"Who *are* you?"

"You know what happened to Krodin in my world?"

"Yeah . . ."

"Does the name Pyrokine ring any bells?"

Remington's eyes widened. "Oh no."

"Oh yes. Now do we have an understanding? Or would you prefer to go through the rest of your life with no fingers? It's a simple trick for me, turning matter into energy. Like I did to that bullet." Lance raised his hand, pointed at Remington's face in what he hoped looked like a sinister way, and added, "It's all the same to me, Remington."

Lance forced his hand to twitch a little, and Remington took a step back.

"Well?"

"I'll show you."

"Good. Any tricks and I'll vaporize you. Very slowly, from your feet up. Walk ahead of me."

As they passed the wrecked door to the large storeroom, Lance saw Joshua Dalton peeking out, and gestured to him to follow. "How far can the teleporter send something?" he asked Remington as Josh came out to join them. Lance put his finger to his lips and shook his head.

Josh nodded.

"Distance is meaningless," Remington said, "when you're working on the subatomic level. Every particle in the universe—"

Lance interrupted. "So it can pick up something from anywhere, send it anywhere else?"

"Yes."

"Then we're going to use it to send Max to the emergency room of the nearest hospital."

In the next corridor Remington stopped at a small door, then fished around in his pocket for a moment before pulling out a small key. He unlocked the door, and as he opened it, Lance held out his hand and said, "Key?"

Remington dropped the key into Lance's hand.

Lance held up the key between the index finger and thumb of his left hand. "And just so you don't get the idea of locking us in again . . ." He faked grabbing the key in his right hand and thought, *Please, Josh, don't say anything!*

Lance concentrated on his closed right fist, then opened it. He raised his hand to his face and blew away imaginary particles. *That ought to keep him convinced I'm Pyrokine.*

He pushed his way past Remington into the office. It

was smaller than he'd expected: a single desk containing a keyboard and screen and a bank of computer equipment against one wall. "Show me how to work it."

A half mile from the base, James Klaus bit his lip and tried to psych himself up for the coming pain. After he'd focused his shock wave on the power-damping machine, he'd lowered himself to the ground next to the unconscious Jetman and found a long steel cable attached to the man's belt. With considerable difficulty he'd tied the cable to his right ankle, looped it around a tree trunk, and was now holding on to the free end.

He'd seen it done once before, on a TV show.

I can do this. It'll hurt like crazy for a bit, but it's only pain. Pain is just a signal telling the brain that something's wrong, and I already know *that something's wrong. . . . So, brain, no need to tell me. OK?*

He lowered himself to the ground, wound up the cable's slack, and made sure he had a firm grip. His good leg was pressed against the tree trunk.

He took a series of short, deep breaths. *OK. Do it.*

He pulled hard on the cable, and screamed as he felt the bones in his right leg grind together. Then his hand grew slick with sweat and the cable slipped through.

James opened his eyes and looked. The jagged edge of the lower half of his tibia had slipped back beneath the skin.

He sat there shivering and sweating and panting for a long time, trying to wait out the pain.

I did it. OK. Now what? He looked around, saw the still-unconscious Jetman. *The armor on his leg—that'd make a good splint.*

James rolled onto his side and dragged himself over to the flyer.

From the relative safety of the base's entrance, Roz Dalton and Suzanne Housten watched with open mouths as the battle between Krodin and Daedalus raged on in the shadow of the giant Carrier.

Daedalus was faster, stronger, and more agile. His armor—whatever it was made of—seemed to protect him from even the most vicious of Krodin's punches and kicks. The complex metal framework on Daedalus's back seemed to act almost as a second set of arms, its twin thick limbs lashing out at Krodin, knocking him aside, snaking out to trip him up.

Daedalus's attack was relentless, merciless, devastating.

A few moments ago Daedalus had angrily slammed his clasped fists into the side of Brawn's head, even though Brawn had been grappling with Krodin.

Roz knew then that Abby had been right: Daedalus was worse than Krodin. Anyone would have to be completely insane to attack an ally so that he could get to an enemy.

Again and again, Krodin was forced back, but each of Daedalus's blows seemed to injure the Fifth King less than the one before.

She knew that Krodin was going to win. He could keep fighting forever, but eventually Daedalus's armor was going to run out of power.

Working together Roz and Suzanne had already taken the

fallen guards to safety, Roz using her telekinesis and Suzanne swooping down and lifting them away. Now they could do nothing but watch, and wait for either Krodin or Daedalus to gain the upper hand.

Again, Brawn recovered and leaped into the fray. He pulled Krodin free of Daedalus's grasp and tossed him high into the air.

Krodin came down hard on the Carrier's landing deck, and Brawn whirled about to face Daedalus. "What do you keep hitting *me* for?" Brawn bellowed. "I'm on your side!"

Daedalus looked up at the giant's face for a moment, then took a step back.

Suzanne nudged Roz. "What's he doing . . . ?"

The metal framework on Daedalus's back extended once more. The twin arms spread straight out on either side at shoulder height and then quickly began to unfold, the arms splitting into a series of thin strips.

In seconds, the mechanism was complete: Giant metal wings sprouted from his back. They flapped once, and Daedalus soared into the air, arcing toward the Carrier.

Suzanne whispered, "Of course. Daedalus."

Roz looked at her. "What does that *mean*?"

"Greek mythology . . . Daedalus was an inventor, a genius. King Minos locked him in a tower so that his knowledge could never be used by anyone else. Daedalus used feathers and wax to create wings for himself and his son. But Icarus flew too high, and the heat of the sun melted the wax. He fell into the sea and drowned."

"And Daedalus?"

"Daedalus flew."

Brawn limped over to Roz and Suzanne, examining his bloodied knuckles. "Now what? I still don't know which one I'm supposed to be fighting! We should just leave them to it and then take on whichever one of them is left standing."

The idea was so tempting that Roz found herself leaning toward it. She shook her head briskly. "No. We fight *with* Daedalus against Krodin. Daedalus might be insane, but I'm guessing he's still mortal. If we win and he turns on us and enslaves the planet, at least he'll eventually die of old age."

Suzanne's shoulders sagged, as though all the fight had left her. "Roz . . . Even if there was a hundred of us, we still wouldn't be able to defeat Krodin. You know that, don't you? My people have been gathering data on him for years. He has no weaknesses."

Roz stared at the Carrier, where Krodin and Daedalus were pummeling each other with such ferocity that they could hear the blows even where they were. "Everyone has a weakness. We just have to find it."

Brawn straightened up, slowly turned to the south. "Something's coming."

Roz looked. Above the treetops a dark dot was approaching. A fighter jet: It streaked overhead and then banked to the west.

"Reconnaissance," Suzanne said softly.

Another jet appeared, then two more, each one coming from the south and then taking a different path.

"Unity," Suzanne said. "They're here."

Lance and Josh looked over Remington's shoulders at the computer screen.

"We, uh, input the source coordinates here, destination coordinates here," Remington said. "Here we tell the system when we want it to activate, so we can queue them up in advance. Right now it's gearing up to run through a set of emergency procedures."

Lance looked at the complex list of figures that was rapidly scrolling up on a second screen. "What's all this?"

"Aw no!" Remington slid his chair over to the second screen's keyboard and began typing. "Fighters—*hundreds* of them! MiGs, Tornados, Hornets . . . Looks like the whole world has turned up for the party. This is exactly what Krodin was expecting, except that none of us were supposed to be here."

"Forget them," Lance said. "Unseal the door to the teleporter room."

"I can't. Krodin and Max are the only ones who can do that."

Josh said, "Then disable it."

"Same problem."

"All right," Lance said. "OK, let's think. . . . Right. If Unity wants to destroy this base, we'll let them. Set up the teleporter to send us all away from here. And send Abby first. Uh, and Roz too."

Remington shook his head. "McKendrick, that'll take ages to set up if we can't get into the teleporter room. At the subatomic level there's no easy way to differentiate between a person and his surroundings. It took nearly an hour to get the teleporter to lock on to you guys in the Raptor. Anything inside the teleporter room we can send almost immediately, because we know the precise shape of the room and we set up the energy field to match. When we pulled Max out of the swamp, we had to do a best guess. We took a hundred gallons of water and half a tree with him."

"We have to do *something*!"

Remington shrugged. "What's the point? They're already here. The base will be overrun in minutes." The first computer beeped, and he returned to its screen. "See that? That was an order to transport someone *inside* the base."

Lance gritted his teeth. "Shut down the emergency protocols. Now!"

Remington looked up at him. "Chancellor Krodin will—"

"Do you remember the key? Imagine that was your thumb."

Remington pulled the keyboard closer and began entering instructions. One by one, the pending orders began to disappear.

Josh, standing next to Lance, said, "Teleport Krodin out of here. Send him to the middle of the Sahara desert or some place where there's no one for him to hurt."

"It doesn't *work* on Krodin," Remington said. "Not anymore. Anything you do to him will work only once before his powers adapt to resist it, and he's already been teleported."

"So you can't even send him back to his own time?" Josh asked.

Lance said, "Even if we could, that would be the biggest mistake in human history, Josh! He's immortal, remember? If we did that, he'd have a four-and-a-half-thousand-year head start on us. He'd already taken over the known world by that stage—I hate to think what things would be like now with him having been in charge all that time."

"So what do we do?"

"I'm thinking." *We can't send him away, can't send him through time. But we've got an incredibly powerful weapon here. . . . There has to be some way we can use it against him!* Then he smiled. "Got it."

"What are we going to do?" Josh asked.

Lance ignored him. "Remington, lock the teleporter onto Krodin. Track his position at all times. Wherever he goes, I want the thing targeting him. You can do that?"

"Yeah, but what's the point? I just told you, it won't work on him!"

"Just do it."

Abby let the steel pole clatter to the floor and flexed her hands into fists. Her knuckles cracked.

For the past few minutes she'd been trying to force open the massive steel doors that sealed the teleporter room from the rest of the base. "I'm sorry, Mr. Cord. It's just not working."

Cord angrily kicked at a lump of fallen masonry. "There *has* to be a way!"

"My strength works best on metal, so I should be able to open the doors, but there's something else holding them closed."

"We're running out of time," Cord said.

"I know," Abby said, then muttered, "What would Lance do?"

"What?"

"Just, you know, wondering how he'd get in there. He seems to be good at that sort of thing."

Cord laughed. "You're right. If you can't solve a problem,

just ignore it. We don't go through the door. We go *around* it. Through the wall."

"Or the ceiling," Abby said. "Daedalus crashed the Raptor into the roof—it's already weakened." She snatched up the steel pole once more. "This way!"

They ran back along the corridor toward the dormitory where she and James had broken through into the base.

As Cord rounded the last corner to the dormitory, Abby grabbed his shoulder and suddenly pulled him back—just as a series of small craters appeared in the wall next to where he'd been standing.

A woman's voice called out, "This is Agent Amandine Paquette, chief of the Manhattan Praetorian Division. The base is completely surrounded! Drop your weapons and get down on the floor!"

Cord and Abby exchanged a glance, then Cord whispered, "I'll let her take me. You stay out of sight. First chance you get, go to the roof and break through to the teleporter."

"She'll kill you!"

"She won't. She'll want to interrogate me first." He pushed Abby back and called out, "Don't shoot! I'm alone and unarmed!" He placed his hands on top of his head, took a deep breath, and stepped around the corner into the dormitory.

Abby fought the urge to go after him; she knew he was right. She quietly backed away from the corner. A large section of the ceiling had partially collapsed, hanging at an angle against one wall. Abby crouched behind the array of water-soaked tiles, steel pole at the ready.

Angry voices drifted back to her: the agent yelling, "On your knees, Cord! Now!"

A man: "You two, cuff him, search him."

Four of them at least, Abby thought. *He's not superhuman, but he should be able to deal with four.*

Then Paquette's voice again: "The rest of you, search the base. Two teams of four."

Another eight. It's not going to be easy to sneak past them.

She heard approaching footsteps splashing on the damp floor, tightened her grip on the pole.

Through a gap in the tiles she saw shadows stretching across the floor.

Agent Paquette said, "You don't know me, Cord, but I knew the other version of you. I'm the new acting vice-chancellor."

They might not look here, Abby said to herself. She held her breath as the first soldier passed, then the second.

Paquette said, "Solomon Cord. By attacking this base you have committed an act of treason against the state."

A black-gloved hand reached around the edge of Abby's makeshift shelter and began to pull it aside.

"During a time of war there is only one punishment for treason: immediate execution."

Abby threw herself forward, crashing through the ceiling tiles and into the startled Praetorian soldier. Still gripping the pole in both hands like a quarterstaff, she rolled over him, landed on her feet.

She jabbed one end of the pole into the stomach of the next man just as the two who had passed were turning around.

Abby slammed the other end of the pole into the floor, vaulted over the fallen guard, and crashed feetfirst into one of the remaining men.

The last one had enough time to raise his weapon. Abby ducked and rolled, spun the steel pole around so that it slammed against the side of the man's knee.

He screamed as he collapsed to the side, and his automatic rifle erupted into life.

In the close corridor the sound was almost deafening. Abby kept low until the shooting stopped, then rolled to her feet. The wounded men were still screaming, and it took her a moment to realize that there were more screams than there should be.

Just beyond the corridor another half dozen Praetorian soldiers lay on the ground, shot at close range by their colleague.

Amandine Paquette's voice called out, "Whoever you are—stand down! I've got Solomon Cord here. Drop your weapons, put your hands on your head, and walk backward toward me. You have ten seconds to respond, or I will snap his neck!"

"Just a minute!" Abby replied, in the same tone she used when her mother asked her to wash the dishes. She dropped the steel pole and quickly looked around for something else— anything—she might be able to use as a less obvious weapon.

"Now!"

Abby gave up the search and did as she was told, walking backward into the dormitory and carefully stepping over the wounded Praetorians. As she rounded the corner, she saw, at the edge of her vision, Solomon Cord kneeling on the ground with the woman standing behind him: Her hands were on his neck. There was a gun in the woman's holster.

Superhuman, Abby thought. *She has to be. Otherwise she'd be using the gun.* She lowered her hands as she slowly turned around, and forced a smile. "You got him, then. Good. I've been chasing him all over the base." She waved her hand back the way she had come. "Come on, we've got some of his friends holed up in the teleport room."

Amandine Paquette looked at Abby for a moment, then said, "Huh. How come you're not singing 'Happy Birthday'? After all, you must think I was born yesterday if you expect me to fall for a line like that."

"I figured it was worth a go."

"Keep your hands where I can see them." Her eyes narrowed. "You're not one of Unity's agents. You're her, aren't you? The one who took down the Raptors in Midway. You simpleminded fools—this country *needs* Krodin! Eight minutes ago more than a million Unity ground troops touched down on U.S. soil. All along the Gulf coast, across the borders from Mexico and Canada. We don't know how they amassed so many troops without our early-warning system alerting us, but they're here. They've got upward of two hundred fighters in the air, and they're locking cruise missiles on to everything we have. Their aircraft carriers are already engaged with ours." Paquette let go of Cord's neck, then kicked him between his shoulder blades, knocking him facedown to the floor. At the same time she pulled her sidearm from its holster. "If we hadn't been so busy chasing you morons, we might have seen it coming!"

Abby didn't recognize the woman's name or her face. *If she is a superhuman, then who was she back in our world? If I knew that, I might have some idea of her powers.*

On the ground beside her, Cord rolled onto his back, then

pushed himself up. "We came here to stop Krodin before Unity could strike. We didn't know how insane Daedalus is. We have to stop *both* of them."

Paquette looked at him with disgust. "You're weak. Pathetic. Our version of Solomon Cord was ten times the man you are."

Abby had kept constant watch on Paquette's gun. It hadn't wavered once.

A crazy thought struck her: *Bullets are metal, and my powers give me some control over metal. . . . Maybe I'm bulletproof.*

She felt her heart racing at the thought. *Even if I'm not, I'm certainly stronger than Cord. I could take a run at her. If she shoots me, he might get away.*

She shifted her weight onto her right foot, tensed her muscles for the jump.

"Go ahead, kid," Paquette said. "I'm going to execute you both anyway." Abby jumped, and the gun flared.

CHAPTER 33

SO FAR, THE UNITY JETS had been making only low-level passes, and for that Roz was grateful. But according to Brawn—who seemed to have incredibly sharp eyesight— the whole base was surrounded by a wide ring of copters, all hovering in place. She knew that at any moment they could be given the order to attack: When that happened, it was all over.

Roz let go of Suzanne's hand and dropped the remaining four yards to the hull of the enormous Carrier. She hit the deck hard, rolled, and came to a stop on her feet just in time to see Suzanne streaking toward Krodin.

Suzanne slammed into the small of Krodin's back, sent him sprawling across the deck, ripping up blackboard-sized steel panels in his path.

Even before he stopped moving, Krodin snatched up one of the panels and hurled it at her like an oversized Frisbee.

Roz lashed out at the spinning panel with a telekinetic blast, knocking it a little off course: It sailed over Suzanne's head, missing her by less than an inch.

Then Roz suddenly realized why the Unity forces hadn't launched their attack: They were watching the fight.

Daedalus struck next, his wings folded back as he swooped down toward Krodin at an almost vertical angle. He struck hard, snagged Krodin's head with the claws on his boots, and launched himself upward once more, dragging the Fifth King beneath him.

Krodin reached up, grabbed Daedalus's ankles, and started to pull himself up.

Brawn leaped at them, his massive arms grabbing Krodin around the waist from behind, and held on.

Roz could hear the motors in Daedalus's beating wings begin to whine with the strain of keeping them all aloft.

Krodin roared with anger and started slamming his right elbow back into Brawn's face over and over as he pulled at Daedalus's claws with his left hand.

They were almost a hundred yards above the deck when Krodin broke Daedalus's grip.

As Brawn and Krodin tumbled down, Suzanne rushed at Krodin again, moving so fast that she was a blur. She struck his jaw so hard that the sound echoed across the swamp.

Suzanne held on as they fell, hitting him again and again, not letting go even when they crashed heavily onto the deck.

Brawn had landed on his back, still with his arms around Krodin's waist.

Roz rushed toward them. *Come on! Hit him again! Brawn, squeeze the breath out of him! Don't give him a chance to—*

Krodin caught Suzanne's wrist in his right hand, lashed out at her face with his left fist.

He let go, and Suzanne collapsed backward.

Before she had hit the deck, Krodin had pulled himself free of Brawn's grip and pounded down on the giant's stomach with an equally powerful blow.

Brawn screamed, rolled onto his side, doubled up in pain.

Krodin was not even breathing hard as he turned away and began to stride toward Roz. "You're going to die for this, Rosalyn. You, your brothers, your friends. And your friends' families." He stopped three yards in front of her. "The mark of intelligence is the ability to learn and understand. You fought me before, and I beat you. How could you be so stupid as to think you might win this time? I cannot be beaten." His face took on a look of exasperation, and he spread his arms wide. "Seriously. What did you think was going to happen?"

"We can't let you do to the rest of the world what you've already done to America."

"Yes, you can. Because you don't have a choice. You can slow me down, but I'm immortal. You can't stop me." He looked toward the horizon, and slowly turned on the spot until he was facing her again. "We are completely surrounded." He tapped a small communicator that was looped over his ear. "And I'm told that our forces are engaged all over the country. My Raptors and Jetmen against their copters and jets, my ground troops against theirs. They outnumber my troops by about three to one. It'll be a massacre. They will win."

"You knew this was going to happen?"

"Knew? I *planned* it this way, Rosalyn. Unity invades America, they win, they take control, then, in time, I take control of them. Eventually I'll have the whole world in my hands." He tilted his head a little to the side as he stared at her. "But you won't be around to see that. You are all going to die, and it will happen today."

"There's nothing I can say that's going to make you change your ways, is there?" She shrugged. "Nobody likes you, you know. After we fought you at Windfield, I read up on you. I know all about your past. No one *ever* liked you. Not your wife or your children or anyone you ever met."

"Is that so?"

"Yes, it is. You're a jerk," Roz said.

Slowly, Brawn pushed himself into a sitting position. He wiped the back of his hand across his mouth, brushing away the flecks of vomit.

Krodin laughed. "You say that as if your opinion of me is relevant. Well, perhaps I'll let you live. I've read that often kings would keep a jester in their court, a fool who was brave enough to tell the truth when all the noblemen were too scared to contradict the king. Or perhaps your friend Abby would be a better choice. She *is* stronger than you are, after all. Or maybe I'll let the two of you fight it out. The winner gets to live. But as for your newest companion . . ." Krodin looked past Roz.

She didn't need to turn around: She could hear the flapping of approaching metal wings, and moments later Daedalus landed close to her.

"He will most certainly die," Krodin said. "Like your other friend has just died."

Roz froze. "What?"

Krodin gestured behind him. "The flying woman. Slaughter's counterpart in this reality. She too was strong, but not strong enough."

"He's telling the truth," Daedalus said. "Her heart stopped a few moments ago. My armor's sensors can detect—"

Roz glared at him. "When we're done with Krodin, you're next. So shut up, Brandon! Or whatever your name really is."

Daedalus's full-face helmet split down the middle and folded away. "No, I'm not Brandon Santamaría. I killed him ten months ago, took his place. That wasn't easy. He didn't look like me and was two inches taller. Took a lot of surgeries to get it right. Do you have any idea how painful it is to have the bones in your legs constantly broken, stretched, and reset?"

Krodin said, "And since then you've been a constant irritation to me. You've killed hundreds of my men, caused close to a trillion dollars' worth of damage. And you killed Casey, the only human I've ever met who fully understood our abilities. But everything you've done is pointless. I will live forever. You have another seventy years, at best."

Daedalus nodded. "Casey was the one who figured out how to turn Solomon Cord into a superhuman genius. Without his skills you wouldn't be where you are, Krodin. You wouldn't have your teleporter, your Raptors, your little power-stripping toy. And without him I wouldn't have this battle suit. It's completely self-repairing, self-sustaining."

For the first time, Krodin looked hurt. "Casey built that? He betrayed me?"

Daedalus extended his hand palm-down, tilted it from side to side in a "so-so" gesture. "Not exactly, boss. I *am* Casey." He smiled. "I might not be immortal, but I'm way smarter than you are. You could never find me because *I* programmed your systems to ignore me. Your plan to take control by uniting the world against you? That was my suggestion, remember? But you're just too dumb to see what's really happening. *You're* not going to take control of Unity. I mean, why would I bark when I have a perfectly good dog to bark for me?"

Brawn slowly walked over to Roz. "Oh, he is *so* gonna wish he hadn't said that."

Daedalus continued, "But smart as I am, I wasn't able to foresee that these people would be pulled over here from their own time line." He shrugged. "Still not sure exactly why that happened, but I'll figure it out soon enough. You can't beat me, Krodin. I know all the secrets of the superhuman abilities, much more than I ever told you. There are forces at work here you simply cannot understand. There is a . . . I suppose you could call it a chasm, from which—"

"Enough!" Krodin roared. From his belt he removed a small communicator, raised it to his mouth. "This is Krodin. Priority zero."

Inside the base's dormitory, Amandine Paquette was looking down at Abigail de Luyando's unmoving body when the communicator attached to her uniform's collar beeped twice. "Reading you, Chancellor. Go ahead."

"I don't care what else is going on in the rest of the country, Paquette: I want every single missile in our arsenal aimed at my position. Blanket the area. Everything within a five-mile radius. You understand me? Everything. Wipe it out."

"But your work . . . The teleporter . . ."

"Let it burn. That's an order."

"Acknowledged. Paquette out."

Solomon Cord straightened up, glared at her. "You didn't have to kill her."

"Of course I did." She activated the communicator again. "This is Acting Vice-Chancellor Paquette to the fleet. Colonel Stewart?"

"Here."

"You heard the Chancellor's order?"

"We did. Prepping the weapons now. What about our people at your location?"

"Forget them. But send a squad to pick *me* up."

"So you're just going to abandon your own people?" Cord asked, gesturing to the wounded men lying on the floor.

"Acceptable losses. It would cost more to patch them up than they're worth. Any survivors will be Unity's problem."

"You coldhearted . . ." Cord turned away to face the large hole in the wall. "Then go. Leave me here. At least do me that honor. Let me die with my friends."

"And give you a chance to escape? Please. I'm no amateur."

Then behind him he heard a sudden rush of movement, the distinctive sound of a small hard fist thumping against flesh, the clatter of Paquette's gun hitting the floor.

"But you're enough of an amateur not to check whether Abby is bulletproof," Cord said. He turned back to see Paquette lying facedown on the ground.

Abby had her arms around the woman's neck, her knee in the small of her back. "Call them off!" Abby said. "Call them off or I swear I'll tear out your throat!"

"You wouldn't!" Paquette croaked. "You don't have the guts to kill someone! But *I* do. Right now there's a platoon of my men in Midway. We've got your family, Abby. So you let me go right now or they're dead!"

Abby stopped and looked at Cord.

"All right," Cord said. "We can talk about this. Abby . . . ?"

Abby relaxed her grip, and looked up at him. "OK, but . . ." She took a deep breath, closed her eyes for a moment. "No. No way. They don't get to win like this. Not by threatening innocent people."

"You don't have a choice," Paquette said. "You—"

Abby grabbed the woman's hair and slammed her head facefirst into the floor. "Shut *up*!" Still gripping Paquette's hair, she pulled her arm back and slammed it down again.

And again.

Inside Remington's office, Lance and Josh frowned over the computer.

"That one," Joshua Dalton said, tapping his finger against the screen. "That's the one."

"You're sure?"

"Oh yeah. Trust me, this is the sort of thing I know about."

"So how do we . . . ? Ah, got it." Lance turned to Remington, and grinned. "This is going to really, *really* make him mad, isn't it?"

Remington swallowed. "Yeah." He paused for a moment. "Yeah, he's not going to like this at all." Another pause. "Do it."

"What's it going to be, Roz, Brawn?" Daedalus asked. "Who are you siding with? Him or me? He's about to try to wipe you all out. But I can promise you that if you side with me, I'll destroy him forever."

"He's immortal and indestructible," Roz said. "What can you do?"

"Oh, I've figured out a way. Trust me."

Brawn rumbled, "You're kidding. Trust *you*?"

Then Krodin said, "I have a better offer for you. Allow me to destroy Daedalus—without interfering—and I'll let you and all of your friends live."

"Jeez, man, make up your mind," Brawn muttered.

"You can't *take* me, old man!" Daedalus roared back at Krodin. His armor's helmet folded back into place. "I've spent years studying your powers, and I built this armor to match everything you can do. Everything." He thumped his fist against his chest. "You want to know how that's possible? Because it *is* you! This isn't metal. This is a bio-organic compound cloned from your own DNA, infused with the same energy you have. That's why you can't break it. It heals as quickly as you do. This armor is alive. So give it your best shot. And don't be surprised to find that I've been holding back."

"Then shut up and *fight* me, braggart!"

Daedalus launched himself at Krodin.

What happened next was too fast for Roz to see, but the result was clear: Daedalus hung limp in the air in front of Krodin, with something red protruding from his back.

Brawn slapped his hand over his mouth. "He didn't . . ."

It took Roz a moment to realize what that red thing was.

It was Krodin's fist.

"Poor, pathetic Casey. He wasn't the only one holding back." The Fifth King shook his arm to the side, knocking Daedalus's body loose. It slid across the deck, leaving a thick red trail in its wake.

Krodin looked at it for a moment, then glanced at Roz and Brawn. "Why aren't you running?"

"I need to find my brothers," Roz said. "Say good-bye to them."

Krodin turned away. "I won't stop you. But you should hurry. You have only a couple of minutes. The missiles are in the air."

Abby felt Solomon Cord's hand on her shoulder.

"That's enough. She's out cold."

Abby let go of Amandine Paquette's head and sat up straight. She had lost count somewhere around ten, when the metal floor of the dormitory began to buckle.

What have I done? I could have killed her!

Cord pulled at her arm. "Come on, Abby. Her people will be here for her soon. We need to find the others, figure a way out of this place before the missiles hit."

They left Paquette's unconscious and bleeding body behind, and made their way back through the dark corridors.

"You OK?" Cord asked.

"Ask me later, when I've stopped shaking." She looked back. "The teleporter—we were going to the roof to find a way in."

"Forget it. It'll be destroyed along with the rest of the base."

"How much time do we have?"

"I don't know. Not much."

Abby jumped when a voice boomed out all around them. "Hello, hello? Testing, testing . . ."

"That sounds like *Lance*," Cord said.

"Hello!" the voice called again. "This is Radio Lance. This next song is dedicated to all you surviving Praetorian lackeys.

You're all stupid, ugly morons, and you smell like week-old barf. Thank you, that is all."

Abby couldn't help laughing. "That guy . . ."

"Yeah, he's something else," Cord said.

Lance's voice came again. "Oh, and if any of my friends are still alive, we're having a little get-together in Mr. Remington's office. Me and Josh are already here. Nothing formal, just come as you are. And you might like to know that we have control of the teleporter and we have a really cool plan. Trust me, you're not going to want to miss this."

Outside the base, Brawn stopped in mid-run, turned back to Roz. "Did you hear something?"

"No. Keep going!"

"I just . . ." He stopped and looked up. "Aw, bats on a bike! Now the Unity guys are joining the party!"

Overhead, swarms of mismatched copters—troop carriers and gunships—were closing in, forming into what Roz was sure was an attack pattern.

Brawn sighed. "A last-minute rescue would be really useful right about now."

Then a voice right beside them said, "Well, I'll do what I can."

Brawn and Roz looked at each other.

"Thunder? Is that you?" Roz asked.

"The one and only. Keep watching the skies."

They looked.

To the north a cluster of eight Unity copters bucked and swayed as though they'd been struck by a sudden and powerful crosswind.

The same force struck the other squadrons approaching from the other directions: Slowly but steadily the aircraft were pushed back.

Roz could hear their engines whining as they struggled against the invisible force, but it was irresistible: The circle of copters steadily expanded.

"Would you look at that?" Thunder's voice said. "Didn't even scratch the paintwork. I've tried talking to them, but they're not listening. But that should buy us some time."

"Nice work, Jim!" Brawn said.

"It's James, not Jim. Just get inside. I heard Lance say that he has control of the teleporter. He can program it to send us somewhere safe."

"Where are *you*?"

"North side of the base. The way Abby and I came in earlier. There's a heck of a lot of wounded Praetorians here."

Roz and Brawn rushed through the main doors—Brawn had to crawl on his hands and knees to fit through—and soon spotted Abby and Solomon Cord running toward them.

"We've been following James's voice," Abby said. "Are you all right?"

"Where's Suzanne?" Cord asked. "Daedalus?"

"They're dead," Brawn said. "Krodin killed them. All that time we fought, he must have been just toying with us."

James's voice said, "He's heading right for you. Lance? You got that teleporter operating yet?"

They heard Lance's voice next: "Uh . . . Hello? That you, Thunder? Where have you been?"

"The teleporter, you idiot!" Brawn roared. "Get us out of here!"

"Bit of a change of plans, guys," Lance said. "Only . . . We kinda need Krodin to not be here. He needs to be . . . let's see . . . about two miles directly to the south. There's a nice big swampy area with none of the Unity guys in it. Can anyone think of a way to make that happen?"

"I'll do it," James said. He drifted back out through the hole he'd blasted in the dormitory wall earlier, taking care not to bash his broken leg.

The pain was still agonizing, and it was taking almost all of his strength to keep from passing out.

"I have to do *everything* around here," he muttered.

Then he heard Lance say, "You do know you're still broadcasting, right?"

To his right he could hear Krodin's running footsteps, the steady beating of his powerful heart. He could also hear Krodin shouting orders into his communicator, demanding to know where his missiles were.

James rose over the building, turned toward Krodin. He directed his voice so that it would appear right in front of the Fifth King. "I don't know what Lance has planned, but I'm guessing you're not going to like it much."

He lowered himself into a sitting position on the edge of the roof and took a moment to focus.

Then he let loose with the most powerful shock wave he could generate.

The blast threw Krodin a hundred feet into the air.

Before he could fall back, James hit him again, knocking the Fifth King on a high arc that carried him out of sight, on a southern trajectory.

James directed his voice back inside the building. "That's never going to work on him again, you know."

Lance replied: "We're never going to *need* it again. Keep watching. Josh? Hit it!"

Something appeared in the sky to the south, something so large that for a moment James couldn't fathom it: a roughly spherical rock, but bigger than any rock he'd ever seen before. *If it's two miles away . . . Good Lord, it's got to be half a mile across!*

The rock crashed down and it felt like the whole world was trembling.

The shock wave rippled out from the fallen rock, scattering the fleet of Unity copters, sending thousands of tons of dirt and water into the air.

"Splat!" Lance said, laughing.

James was still staring at it a minute later when he heard the voices of Roz, Abby, and Brawn at the base's main entrance. He slipped down from the roof and drifted in their direction.

He arrived just as a ten-year-old boy came running out through the entrance and skidded to a stop beside Roz. "Oh, that is the coolest thing *ever*!"

The enormous rock protruded above the treetops, the dense cloud of dust and water slowly settling around it.

Roz took the boy's hand. "Josh, what . . . What is that?"

But Josh was laughing too hard to speak.

James dropped down next to him. "What did you *do*?"

Josh contained his laughter long enough to say, "We used the teleporter. *That* . . ." Josh pointed to the enormous rock. "That's an asteroid."

CHAPTER 34

JAMES DRIFTED ALONG the corridor, floating a few inches off the ground so that he didn't have to put any weight on his broken leg.

He found the small office and saw Lance sitting back in the swivel chair with his hands laced behind his head. Remington was standing next to Lance, looking nervous.

"Saved the day again," Lance said.

James laughed. "You dropped an asteroid on him."

"Yep."

"An asteroid."

Lance grinned. "Sure did."

"But . . ." James shook his head. "Man, you're something else."

"Yep."

"He's not dead," Remington said. "He can't *be* killed."

"I know," Lance said. "But that'll keep him busy for a long

time. He's strong, but it'll take him years and years to pound his way out through a half-mile-wide asteroid." He straightened up and pointed to the screen. "Look, we picked a heavy one too. It has a nickel-iron core. Probably worth a few bucks." He turned away from the screen. "You look like you lost a fight with . . . well, everyone."

"It's been a crazy couple of days, that's for sure."

"I hear your real name is James."

James glanced at Remington. "Oh great. Tell everybody."

"And I notice that your legs no longer go all the way to the ground."

"Yeah. Broke my leg when Brawn threw me. But I can fly now, which is handy. So. Slaughter was here. That must have been weird for you."

Lance stood up. "She . . . What do you mean 'was'? Don't tell me she escaped!"

"She's dead, Lance. He killed her. In the end, one punch was all it took. Same for Daedalus. Krodin was toying with them the whole time."

"Oh man . . . She didn't deserve that. She wasn't Slaughter, you know. Not here. When I first saw her . . . You heard about my folks?"

"Yeah. But they're alive in this reality, right?"

"They are. And I'm probably grounded again."

"Who isn't?"

Lance beckoned to Remington. "Follow."

They left the office and soon found the others in the corridor.

They were all covered in dust and grime, scratches and bruises. Brawn was crouched next to Max Dalton, his massive blue hand holding Max upright. "He's broken a few ribs," Brawn said, "but, sadly, he's going to make it."

James turned to Remington. "I remember you. In our reality you were a soldier. You practically tortured me and Lance. Try anything and you'll spend the rest of your life believing that you're falling. Understand?"

He nodded. "Yeah. Look, I was only following orders! I had to—"

James threw a cocoon of silence around him. "I don't think we need to hear his excuses."

"Thunder, what about the fleet?" Roz asked.

"They're panicking," James said. "They're not sure what's going on. They've been called back. Unity's sending a bunch of bigwigs in to talk to whoever's in charge." He looked around. "Um . . . Which one of us *is* in charge?"

Lance raised his hand. "Oh! Oh! Me! I'd be *brilliant* at being in charge!"

"Not a chance," Max began. "I . . ." He stopped when he saw that everyone was glaring at him.

"Looks like it's you, Thunder," Cord said. "Because there's no way I'm doing it." He turned to Lance. "An asteroid." He raised his eyes. "Man, that's going to take some explaining."

"To whom?" James asked. "With Krodin gone the country's power structure has been completely wiped out. It'll be years before everything's back to normal."

His voice weak, Max Dalton said, "We need an interim government. We can't just dismantle everything at once—the country would fall into chaos. I hate to say it, but for now it might be best to leave the Praetorians in power. Just until we can reestablish the democratic process."

Lance said, "Tch! Politics is so boring!" and walked away.

Abby limped after him. "Wait up!"

James felt a slight twinge in his chest as he watched Abby put her arm around Lance's shoulders. *Doesn't mean anything,* he tried to reassure himself. *He's just holding her up.*

Cord said, "Krodin will get out from under that asteroid. And it won't take long. He'll dig. It might only be a matter of months. We need to set up something to monitor his progress. And we need a plan. A way to get rid of him once and for all. Anyone got any ideas?"

They looked around at each other.

After a long moment, James said, "So it's not over? We're going to be fighting Krodin again and again? I can't accept that. There has to be a solution."

Lance lowered Abby into the chair in the small office. "So *that's* it? That's your big secret?"

"Well, yeah."

"It's not a big deal. I'm cool with it." He leaned back against the desk. "Listen, I . . . I have an idea for getting rid of Krodin. It'll work—it *should* work—but . . . There's a price, and I'm not sure I'm willing to pay it."

"What is it?"

He shook his head. "No, I'm not going to tell you. You might try to talk me out of it. But you trust me, don't you?"

"Of course."

Lance felt tears welling up in his eyes and angrily brushed them away. "OK then. Go . . ." He sniffed. "Go back out into the corridor and wait with the others, OK? And send Remington in. I need him."

"Lance . . . What are you planning?"

"It really is better if you don't know." He helped her out of the seat and led her to the door.

Then he sat down again and started typing on the keyboard.

Remington came in a moment later. "You lied—you're not Pyrokine!"

"I know. Sit down. Help me with this. You know everything about Krodin, right?"

He told Remington what he wanted to do. It took them almost fifteen minutes to set it all up.

"It'll work. When you're ready, hit the Execute key," Remington said. He stood up, and clapped Lance on the shoulder. "If the situation was reversed . . . I don't know if I could do it. You're a braver man than me, McKendrick."

"Thanks. Close the door, huh?"

Remington pulled the door shut behind him, and Lance reached for the telephone. He dialed a number from memory, and the call was answered after three rings.

"Hello?"

"Hi, Mom."

"Lance?"

"Yeah, it's me. I'm sorry, Mom. It's my fault that you got killed. If I hadn't gotten involved . . . she never would have come for you."

"You're not making any sense, Lance! Where are you? The TV said the country's been invaded!"

His tears were spilling freely now, but he didn't care. "Mom, I . . . I love you, Mom. I'm going to miss you. All of you. I'll be thinking of you every day, forever."

"Lance, what are you talking about? You're not coming home?"

"No, Mom. I can never go home again." He reached his hand out to the keyboard, his index finger hovering over the Execute key. "Good-bye."

He hit the button.

Everything changed.

Roz was suddenly knee-deep in the swamp. "What . . . ?"

Abby and James were beside her. Cord, Max, and Brawn were nearby. They all looked as confused as she felt.

"What happened to the base?" Brawn asked. "And the Unity fleet?"

Lance's voice came from twenty yards away. "There *is* no base. There never was." He started to wade toward them. "And there's no Unity either."

"What did you *do*?" Cord asked.

"The teleporter. I used it on Krodin."

Roz whirled around. "Where's Josh? Can anyone see him?"

Lance said, "Roz, he's OK. He's probably wherever he's supposed to be. And I'm sure that Slaughter is wherever *she's* supposed to be. And still alive, unfortunately. Actually, I'm a bit surprised that *we're* still here, and aware of what happened."

Max said, "Lance, the teleporter doesn't *work* on Krodin. He's immune to it." He frowned. "Oh. I see. That . . . That was the right thing to do."

Cord said, "We can't all read minds, Lance."

"Krodin's people tested the teleporter out on him, which

meant that it'd never work on him again. I found a way past that." He looked around. "Anyone got any clue which way is home?"

James said, "I'll check." He rose into the air, and a moment later they heard his voice all around them. "I see what could be a road. A few miles to the north. Follow me."

Brawn grabbed Abby around the waist and lifted her onto his shoulder. "No sense in everyone having to walk, kiddo."

"Thanks."

As Brawn passed Max Dalton, he pushed him over into the swamp, facedown.

Max started to get up, but Brawn put his massive foot on his back. "Give me one good reason not to do it, Dalton. Come on. One good reason."

Roz rushed over. "What are you doing!? After he saved your life!"

"You nuts or something?" Brawn asked. "This guy put me and James in front of a firing squad! He sold us all out to Krodin!"

"*He* was controlling *me*!" Max said. "You weren't conscious, Brawn—but the others were there. They remember it!"

"It's true," Roz said. "Max didn't have any choice. Let him go, Brawn."

The giant reached down and pulled Max free of the mud. "Sorry, dude. No one told me."

Max wiped the mud out of his eyes. "It's OK. After what we've been through, getting wet and mucky doesn't seem such a big deal."

"By the way, thanks for the save back there," Lance said to Max.

Max smiled. "You're welcome."

Cord said, "Yeah, that goes for me too. If it hadn't been for you . . ." He slapped Max on the shoulder. "You always come through for us, Max."

As they trudged on through the swamp, Roz moved close to Lance. "What did you do, exactly?"

"The teleporter could take anything from anywhere and send it anywhere else. I sent Krodin away."

"But *how*, if he's immune?"

"He only became immune to its effects *after* the first time. But they got the idea of the teleporter from the way Pyrokine pulled Krodin out of the past, right? So I pointed it at somewhere I knew Krodin was before the teleporter was tested on him. Almost six years ago, in Windfield. Right after the battle with us when Pyrokine accidentally sent him back there. Remington knew the exact moment Krodin arrived in the past. I took him from there and sent him away." He looked back for a moment. "This is why the base and everyone on it disappeared—Krodin never came to power. We're back in our own reality. No Krodin, no Praetorians, no Citadel in Central Park. I don't know why *we're* all here, though. Maybe there's a connection with whatever it was that brought us to Krodin's reality in the first place."

"So everything's back to normal?" Roz asked.

Lance nodded. "Back to the way it was for us yesterday morning. Except that we're all in a swamp in Louisiana and we can remember a world that never existed for anyone else."

Softly, Roz said, "Then in this world Victoria and her family are still alive."

"Who's Victoria?"

Roz smiled. "Never mind. You did a good thing, Lance." Then her face fell. "But . . . your parents and your brother . . ."

"Yeah. That . . . That wasn't easy. But there was no other way. Krodin would have gotten free and we'd have had to fight him all over again."

Behind him, Solomon Cord said, "Lance . . . where did you send him?"

"Somewhere far away. Trust me. He won't be coming back."

SIX YEARS earlier . . .

Krodin had never been so cold, in so much pain. The darkness pressed around him, blacker than any night he had ever seen.

But he knew he would not die. Not here in this cold and dusty land, wherever it might be.

The burning boy had attacked him, seared his skin, and then died in a blinding flash. For a brief moment Krodin had found himself in an empty field, the damp grass cool on his scorched body. Then, just as suddenly, he was here.

Already the wounds from the burning boy's attack were healing—soon his skin would be as flawless as ever—but the pains in his chest and throat were taking longer to subside.

What did those children do to me? What arcane power have they used against me?

He looked around the vast desert landscape, and vowed that—somehow—he would find a way back, even if it took him a thousand years.

He would have revenge.

• • •

An excerpt from *Modern Science* magazine:

Analysis of the unusual energy flare has so far proved fruitless. Initial speculation that it was nothing more than a minor meteorite strike was almost immediately dismissed. According to Anita Cairnduff, spokesperson for the National Aeronautics and Space Administration, "A collision would have left detectable traces—residual heat, a dust cloud—but our instruments have not yet picked up anything of that nature."

The true cause of the energy flare seems likely to remain a mystery for some time. Ms. Cairnduff has denied the rumors that the planned course of the next probe will be diverted to pass within range of *Amazonis Planitia*: "The flare is not on our list of priorities. There are far more interesting and challenging sites for us to explore, other secrets to uncover."

So it seems that this particular secret is one that Mars will be holding on to for a long time to come.